Unblinking, J. B. met her gaze. Six feet tall in her stocking feet, today in her three inch heels she nearly matched his height of six-four. He thought she was absolutely perfect. He could just tip his head forward and their lips would meet. No crick in the neck. He wanted to. Oh, how he wanted to taste her. Such luscious, kissable lips should be attended on a regular basis.

Mesmerized by the twinkle in his blue eyes and unwillingly fascinated by his mouth, Michael watched as the corner turned up and J. B. shook his head. "Don't change the subject on me, Michael. I'm only askin' you to dinner. Dinner with a friend. You eat dinner, so why not with me? You might enjoy the company."

weaves a page-turning suspense that kept me guessing—wrongly—until the end. Michael: A Gift of Trust is a tale of letting go of the past—learning to trust again—and discovering love and fulfillment in commitment. I can't wait for the next Willow Glen Story."

—Bonnie Napoli
author of Shadows of the Eclipse.

"MICHAEL; A GIFT OF TRUST is a must read for romantic suspense fans. Margaret B< Lawrence knows how to write a story that will keep your attention till the very last page. Readers be on the look out for the next novel by Margaret B. Lawrence. This is one writer to watch as she rises to the top of her profession." 3 stars***

—Jewel Dartt:
Midnight Scribe Reviews

"Margaret Lawrence's gripping, fast-paced story full of unexpected twists and turns, and the growing romance between a relentless homicide detective and a woman in peril who must learn to give him her gift of trust—and love, will keep you rooting for Michael and J. B. to the stunning end."

—Barbara Clark, author:
TEARS OF THE HAWK
A BREATH OF HEATHER
A TOUCH OF FIRE

"A suspenseful, beautifully written, heart-grabbing tale of how love and perseverance overcome fear and trauma to join two hearts as one."

Ann Bachman,
TOGETHER AGAIN and BROKEN DREAMS

Wings

Michael; A Gift Of Trust

by

Margaret B. Lawrence

A Wings ePress, Inc.

Romantic Suspense Novel

Wings ePress, Inc.

Edited by: Marilyn Kapp
Copy Edited by: Robbin Major
Senior Editor: Lorraine Stephens
Executive Editor: Lorraine Stephens
Cover Artist: Pam Ripling

Wings ePress Books
http://www.wings-press.com

Copyright © 2002 by Lorraine Stephens
ISBN 1-59088-960-6

Published In the United States Of America

August 2002

Previously published: ISBN 1-58697-981-7

Wings ePress Inc.
403 Wallace Court
Richmond, KY 40475

Dedication

For my editor, Marilyn Kapp.
"Thank you" seems very inadequate.

For Robbin Major, dedicated copy editor
for her expert touch in rooting out any typos.

For Pam Ripling, artist extraordinaire.
Thank you for the gorgeous covers

But most of all
For Gene;
Husband, lover, best friend, my hero,
And always
The wind beneath my wings.
William E. Stephens
1928-1993
I miss you

One

"No! Absolutely not, J.B." Driven beyond her endurance Michael Mainwaring would take no more. Good manners hadn't worked. Rudeness might.

She watched the look of determination settle more firmly on J.B. Anderson's face. All things considered, it wasn't such a bad face.

Every time she looked at him he brought to mind the old western movies on late night television. Tall and lean, his muscular body gave evidence of a regular workout. His western style suits, Roper boots and Stetson hat made him look like he'd just stepped off the silver screen from the late Forties or early Fifties. His demeanor only added to the picture. Always polite with ladies, firm and straightforward with men, he exuded strength of character she didn't often see. His reputation around town was of an honest man who worked hard at his chosen profession and was very good at it.

For nearly a year she'd watched him watching her. In court she'd turn and he'd be there, leaning against the back wall. He'd nod and smile. Every time she dropped in at The Whistle Stop he'd be on a stool, his finger hooked through the handle of a coffee mug. He'd smile, touch the brim of his Stetson and nod. At the courthouse she'd turn a corner and run straight into him. He'd apologize, grab her arms to steady her—and hold her just a beat too long.

She'd learned long ago not to trust any man, but lately the anonymous caller tormenting her and trying to drive her crazy made trusting J.B. impossible. Even though his behavior was nothing more than polite acknowledgement of her presence, his touch sent the panic rocketing to the surface. And there was nothing in his behavior she could complain about without sounding totally paranoid.

For the past two months he'd stepped up his campaign. Every time she turned around he was in her face: invitations to dinner, to lunch, or to go dancing. Some she ignored. Others she politely turned down, using one excuse after another. Most of her excuses were legitimate. She had a busy law practice and, by her own choice, she devoted many extra hours each day to working for her clients.

A sigh and a mental shrug brought her back to the problem at hand. J.B. hadn't become a homicide detective by giving up before reaching his goal. Apparently, this was no exception.

She wished she could trust him. Who better than a cop to help her out of the situation in which she found herself? She'd changed her unlisted phone number twice and the calls continued, almost uninterrupted. As if getting the new number caused only a minor hiccup in the stalker's campaign. How could he get the number again? And so quickly? Just as it occurred to her that J.B. might be able to find out who was harassing her, the next thought skittering into her mind stopped her mentioning it, and her stomach knotted painfully.

Could it be J.B. who called in the dead of night, breathing heavily for long seconds before whispering "Mickie?" She didn't *dare* trust. Especially not a police detective. Police officers easily obtained unlisted telephone numbers through their work.

"J.B., I want you to leave me alone." As the knot in her stomach grew, she took a step back, putting more distance between them.

She'd lived with this terror for weeks now, the nightly telephone calls, sometimes more than one. And the roses, delivered to her in her office or at the courthouse, made her begin to hate the scent of them. And there were the nightmares filling all the dark corners with menacing shadows. Fearing to dream, she fought sleep, not shutting her eyes until exhaustion claimed her. When she could no longer prevent it she'd doze off, falling immediately into terror-filled visions of evil—and awaken shaking, sweat-soaked and feeling sick. Lately, though her appetite was gone, she had consumed coffee by the gallon, and all the while telling herself this much caffeine could not be good for her.

She jerked her mind back to the present confrontation, snapping, "Must you always be around every corner? It's enough to make me wonder when you work. I'm sure Chief Dengler has better ways for you to spend your time than following me around."

Unblinking, J.B. met her gaze.

Six feet tall in her stocking feet, today in her three inch heels she nearly matched his height of six-four. He thought she was absolutely perfect. He could just tip his head forward and their lips would meet. No crick in the neck. He wanted to. Oh, how he wanted to taste her. Such luscious, kissable lips should be attended on a regular basis.

Mesmerized by the twinkle in his blue eyes and unwillingly fascinated by his mouth, Michael watched as the corner turned up and J.B. shook his head. "Don't change the subject on me, Michael. I'm only askin' you to dinner. Dinner with a friend. You eat dinner, so why not with me? You might enjoy the company."

Still trying to make him back off, Michael gave him a scathing look and turned to walk away. She took three long strides down the corridor, her heels clicking on the marble floor. She heard his loping gait following her and stopped abruptly as J.B.'s right hand grasped her elbow. Her gaze met his and she glared. "Take your hand off me." Though said quietly, it was clear she expected him to comply immediately.

Stunned by her hostility J.B. stood there, frustrated, mystified and hurt by her continued refusal to go out with him. And he couldn't give up. Not yet. "Okay, if not dinner, what about lunch?" His right hand still held her arm, and he snapped the fingers of his left. "We could go on a picnic."

He felt a nearly imperceptible shudder course through her.

"I said no! Now take your hand off me or be faced with a sexual harassment suit."

"Okay." He stepped back and raised both hands to shoulder height, palms forward. "You don't need to pull out the big guns."

J.B. never lacked for female companionship and the last time he could remember being turned down so often was when he'd worn braces in junior high. He snapped out of his reverie and blinked. "I don't understand."

Working hard to maintain an air of disdain, Michael's lips turned up in a Mona Lisa smile. "You don't understand 'no'? It's the same in Spanish and Italian, but I can say it in several languages. *Non. Nein. Nyet. Nae.*" She enunciated each word distinctly. "It really is very simple." She ticked off the invitations on her fingers. "I do not wish to have dinner with you, go to the movies with you, or go dancing with you. I had hoped you'd get the message, but apparently not." Her voice more harsh, she snapped, "And forget picnics. I hate picnics. Don't ask me out again. The answer will always be no. If you don't understand 'no', I can find a judge who will be happy to help you comprehend."

J.B. shook his head. "I understand 'no', Michael. I just don't understand why. Why can't we be friends?"

"It isn't necessary for me to give you a reason, J.B. It isn't even necessary for me to *have* a reason. All you need to know is I do not wish to go out with you."

J.B. looked into her eyes. Seeing she was tired of the battle, he nodded and sighed. For her sake he would back off. "Okay, Michael. You win—but you also lose. I'm not such a bad guy, and I truly believe we'd have a good time."

He didn't enjoy feeling defeated and some of his pain showed in his voice as he muttered, "I must be seven kinds of fool believin' every excuse you gave me, which makes me more than a little dense, I suppose." Everything about this puzzled him. The side of him that made him a good detective continued to question her vehemence. "I was only askin' for a date, not a lifetime commitment."

J.B. slapped his hat against his leg. "I made excuses, tellin' myself you were a busy attorney. Well, Michael, you can relax. I won't call. I won't send you any more flowers. I give you my word you won't run into me around every corner. Have a nice life, Michael. Enjoy your solitude." He watched her shudder, as if freezing cold air surrounded her body, and wondered at her reaction to his words. Convinced she only needed a little time, for now, he decided to give her the space she seemed to want.

Michael, holding on to the last thread of her control, and relieved she'd gotten her message across at last, nodded. "Thank you. I'm glad to see we finally understand each other." Though necessary for her own sanity, she knew she'd hurt him and didn't like it. Fighting the urge to run, she turned and forced herself to walk slowly away. Her stomach quaked. Her nerves made her feel as if thousands of tiny insects crawled over her skin. She trembled and fought to maintain a semblance of calm, telling herself she'd be fine in just a few more steps.

He'd mentioned phone calls—flowers. *Could it be J.B.? Oh, God. Could it*? Rounding the corner, she collapsed against the wall, finally allowing the shakes to affect her entire body. She wrapped her arms protectively around herself and trembled like an aspen leaf in a mountain gale.

She felt ill and clamped her fingers over her mouth, closed her eyes and, shuddering, took several slow, deep breaths. The litany in her head repeated. He'd mentioned phone calls and flowers. *Oh, dear God.*

J.B. watched her walk away. Six feet of willowy, lithe grace, she walked with the supple movement of a runway model. He'd hungered to taste her mouth the moment he set eyes on her. Her upper lip, fuller and slightly wider, curved up naturally at the corners. She was the most beautiful woman he'd ever seen and he wondered what had turned her into the ice maiden of Willow Glen.

He ambled toward the exit, the fingers of his hand jammed into his pocket. He could still feel the warmth of her skin on his fingertips. He brought them up to his nose and smelled strawberries. He smiled. She always smelled like strawberries.

He rounded the corner and stopped mid-stride. His breath left his body in a whoosh when he saw her. Trembling, tears coursing down her face, her fingers clamped her mouth so tightly they would leave a bruise. Dear God! Had he done this to her? "Michael?"

Her fear-filled eyes snapped open. She whirled and bolted like a frightened doe. J.B. darted after her. He intended to learn what terrified her so much she'd run from a cop.

She sped out the door, her briefcase banging her legs in her headlong flight. Looking over her shoulder, she saw J.B. in pursuit and gaining. Her heart raced, pounding in her chest. The roaring in her ears crescendoed as nausea churned in her stomach. Her vision narrowed to a pinpoint and extinguished.

Michael crumpled to the sidewalk in a faint as J.B. reached her. She moaned and stirred as he scooped her up and headed toward his car. "Shhh, be quiet, Michael."

"Put me down." Her speech was thick, her words slurred.

"In a minute." He slid her into the passenger seat and fastened the seat belt. The scent of his musk cologne enveloped her like a blanket. She couldn't breathe.

Michael's terror choked her and she fumbled at the buckle of the seat belt. She couldn't go with him. If he was the one stalking her she wasn't safe. Looking around for an escape route she noted they were in front of the courthouse on the Square. It was broad daylight. Surely someone would see. Someone would notice and come to stop him. The driver's door opened and J.B. entered the car. Too late.

"You'll be fine, Michael. I'll take you to the hospital. Try to relax." Worried sick about her, J.B. backed out of the parking space and slipped the flasher on top of his unmarked car. Terrified, Michael couldn't speak. Her throat nearly closed by panic, her breath rasped into her lungs in minute amounts. Her heart pounded painfully in her chest and seemed to grow in size, choking her. The thump-thump beat grew in volume, sounding like a kettledrum in her ears. She continued to fumble with the belt confining her as a scream built in her throat and was halted by the constriction there.

J.B. clasped her wrist, halting her attempts to escape.

Don't. Don't touch me. Let me go. Oh, God, please let me go. Her terror all consuming, she could take no more and the touch of his hand on her wrist pushed her once more into oblivion.

J.B. picked up his car phone and called ahead. The ER crew met them at the emergency entrance, lifted Michael from the car, put her onto a gurney and rolled her inside. J.B. parked the car and ran through the double doors looking around to see where they took her. A nurse told him to "have a seat". He paced the corridor, worry and fear roiling in his stomach like a hive of angry bees, as he waited for news.

~ * ~

J.B. thought back to when he met Michael the first time, more than a year ago. She had defended Lincoln Maitland at his murder trial. It was the first trial in years to make headlines in Willow Glen's newspaper. Around the courthouse they had taken bets she would go down in flames because she practiced corporate law. Handling the case brilliantly while ignoring the snickers from courthouse oldsters, Michael fought hard, throwing herself entirely into the case to save her best friend. In retrospect, he believed she'd have won even if Maitland's sister hadn't come out of the coma and told what happened.

The Maitland case would always make him sad and remind him of three-year-old Aimee Bradley. Her world had blown apart on a warm summer day when her father, Blake, had nearly beaten her mother, Lyssa, to death. Not satisfied to use his fists on his wife, Blake had hit his child as well. To protect her little girl Lyssa finally struck back, hitting Blake in the head with a cast iron skillet and fracturing his skull. He'd staggered into the back yard and fallen into the creek where he drowned.

And as evidence mounted, J.B. and his partner, Shag Dexter, charged Lyssa's twin brother Lincoln Maitland with the crime. They believed they were right.

When she walked into the interrogation room to represent her client, because of her name J.B. expected a man. The minute he looked into her eyes he felt as if he'd been hit right in the heart with a mallet. He'd never believed in love at first sight—until then.

When J.B. allowed himself to reflect, the memory of the closeness between attorney and client still bothered him. He'd never expected to feel jealousy and didn't like when it reared its ugly head.

Thinking back to her demeanor around him during that trial, her body language told him to back off. So he waited. He'd thought she was so involved in the case she just didn't have time for socializing. After the trial was over, he believed if she frequently saw him around town, she'd get to know him and go out with him. Toward that end he'd found a way to be wherever she was, and then for the past two months he had tried to get a date. But she always had a good reason why she couldn't accept.

~ * ~

Unable to wait longer for news of Michael's well being, J.B. slipped through the curtain into the examination room.

As Doc Carstairs listened to her laboring heart and lungs, Michael saw J.B. slip through the curtain and lost her battle for control. Struggling to sit up, she fainted as panic rose like an express elevator and crashed through the roof of her mind. The doctor caught her before she fell.

Crusty old Doc Carstairs, a family friend, turned and glared as if responsibility for Michael's problems rested squarely on J.B.'s shoulders. "What happened here, J.B.? I've never seen such abject terror in nearly forty years of medicine."

"Why, I don't…" J.B. ran his hand through his hair, feeling completely confused. And guilt that he might be the cause of her fear began to creep in.

Doc took J.B.'s arm, pulled him to the side of the cubicle and snarled, "Tell me, J.B. I need to know so I can treat her. What happened to her?" He swiped a hand down his face and voiced the first thought that had come into his mind. "She's terrified and I can only guess... has she been raped?" he asked softly.

Raped? J.B. stared at the doctor. Just hearing the word horrified him and he turned away. "Raped?"

Out of patience, the doctor snarled. "J.B., if she's been raped there are certain tests I need to run. And, though it's the most important, her safety isn't the only thing at issue. I'm required to collect evidence in case she decides to prosecute. It's the law. Oh, hell, you know that as well as I do. Now tell me, dammit. Has she been raped?"

He whirled to face the doctor. "No. I mean…Oh, God, Doc, I don't know," J.B. said in an anguished whisper. "She fainted at the courthouse. I was talkin' to her, askin'... Never mind." His hand slashed through the air. "It's not important." He took deep calming breaths. "Raped! I never... But, that'd explain why she..."

"Okay, J.B. Suppose you tell me what's going on here so I can treat my patient."

"I honestly don't know, Doc. But I intend to find out." He walked to the examination table, took her hand, and stared into space for several long minutes.

J.B. looked at her. Her head, set regally on a swan-like neck, was crowned by dark brown hair worn in a tight chignon. Her eyes fluttered open. She looked up at him and immediately closed them again. He looked at her skin, like alabaster, a perfect backdrop for large grey eyes slightly tip-tilted at the outer corners.

Her beauty took his breath away and he wanted her with an intensity he'd never before felt. But, if she'd been raped? Dear God. No wonder she ran from any contact with men. And no wonder he frightened her to death. If she'd been raped... his approach had been much too aggressive.

Michael opened her eyes, looking straight up into J.B.'s. Unwilling to maintain eye contact she turned her head away. He held her hand, clasping it gently in his own, but when she tried to pull it free, his grip tightened. Why was he here? For what possible reason would he remain here—unless he *was* the one...

Michael struggled to sit up and J.B. helped her. "I need to go home." She tried to pull her hand from his but he refused to let it go. She hated scenes so didn't struggle with him in front of the doctor.

"Doctor Carstairs, would you please ask one of the nurses to call a cab for me?"

"Certainly, Michael. Just as soon as I—"

"Never mind the cab, Doc. I'll take her home when you're through with her."

"No, J.B. I'll get a cab back to the courthouse. My car's there. I'll need it in the morning."

"You have no business drivin' right now."

She glared at him. "Why not? I've been driving for years, and with an accident-free record."

J.B. raised an eyebrow and shook his head slightly. "So now you want to break your record? You like higher insurance premiums?"

"I've been taking care of myself for all of my adult life. I don't need a keeper. I need my car to get back and forth to work and to see my clients."

"I'll pick you up tomorrow and take you to the Square to get your car." His voice dropped to a husky, deep bass. "For tonight it'll be fine. You've had a rough couple of hours and shouldn't be drivin'." He brushed his knuckles across her cheek. "Let me do this. Allow me to take care of you. Just for now. Okay?"

Feeling she had to be constantly alert to danger, she was weary to the bone and unsure of her ability to make a decision. But J.B. had done nothing to harm her. In fact, he'd brought her to the hospital when he thought she was ill. If he was going to hurt her, why did he bring her here? He could just as easily have taken her to his apartment, or someplace isolated.

Could her fears be coloring her perception of him, be making her unfairly question his motives? He seemed determined to help her whether or not she wanted his help. In spite of the fact he drove her crazy with his persistence and in spite of the questions she still had about him, she was beginning to trust him a little. His handling of her problem today was a mark in his favor on the ledger. And he *was* a police officer with a good reputation.

Uncomfortable with her protracted quiet J.B. put his hand on her shoulder. "Michael."

Michael took a deep breath. "Okay. I don't need anyone to 'take care' of me, but I'll let you drive me home. You have a point about my ability to drive right now. I don't think I'd be a safe driver."

Doctor Carstairs stepped over to them. "Michael, you had an anxiety attack." He picked up his prescription pad and began writing. He tore the sheet off and held it out to her. "This is for a mild tranquilizer. I don't recommend using them for the long term but they might get you through the next few days."

Michael shook her head. "No, thank you. I won't take a tranquilizer. I'd rather be in complete control of my senses." She turned to J.B. "Are you ready to go?"

J.B. helped her from the table and escorted Michael out of the hospital. She walked with her head high and J.B. marveled at her control.

When they arrived at J.B.'s car she squashed her momentary bout of panic. For a little while she'd pretend she was safe. She stepped into J.B.'s car and this time she fastened the seat belt for herself. She watched J.B., his long body moving fluidly as he walked around the car and got in. Leaning her head back on the headrest, Michael closed her eyes.

She recalled the first time she drove through Willow Glen. It was the place her heart had longed for when she was not even aware she'd been searching. She'd had a busy practice in Oklahoma City, in a firm where she'd been offered a junior partnership. She had intended to accept. Then a case, involving a client from Willow Glen, was put on her desk. She came to visit and fell in love with the town.

Within a week she'd found a Realtor, gotten lucky and found her house the first day looking. She turned in her resignation, and moved her life to Willow Glen—all in the space of two months. Everyone told her she was crazy, that she was risking everything on a whim. She'd never been more sure of, or less sorry for, anything in her life. She'd never looked back.

Even considering her present dilemma she hadn't changed her mind about Willow Glen. She loved this town where lofty old trees on both sides of the streets formed a canopy overhead. She loved the town square where the courthouse sat majestically at the center, and she liked being able to walk from her office to the courthouse by simply crossing the street.

As he pulled out of the parking lot J.B. looked at her and started to speak. Seeing her with her eyes closed, he changed his mind. He sighed deeply and glanced at her again. She was watching him.

"What were you planning to say, J.B.?"

"It was nothin'." He stopped for a red light and looked at her. "Oh, hell. Michael, it's supper time. We both have to eat and I'm starvin'. We're together in my car. Would you at least consider hittin' one of the drive-ins?"

With a sigh of resignation, she asked, "What did you have in mind?" It looked as if, in spite of her best efforts, she'd have dinner with this persistent man after all.

Worried about her appearance, she pulled down the visor and glanced quickly to see if she needed to comb her hair. In spite of everything, she was uncomfortable with the idea of going to dinner looking less than her best. She was grateful to cosmetic companies for developing the cover stick that helped her disguise the dark circles under her eyes. Now if she could continue to find the strength to keep up the facade she would feel she'd won part of the battle. She wished there was a 'cover stick' that would hide her inner turmoil as easily as the cosmetic hid the outward signs.

She'd put more effort into hiding her problem than into anything she'd ever worked on in her life. But she refused to allow the maniac to win. She wouldn't bow under his assaults. She would have more staying power than he and he would give up. Eventually. She hoped.

J.B. glanced over at her. Would she finally have dinner with him? He couldn't believe it. He also couldn't believe how nervous he was—afraid he'd say the wrong thing. "Well, there are several choices. We could have hamburgers, chicken, or pizza and there's always the submarine sandwich place." He glanced at her, wondering how far he could go with his suggestions. "Or, if none of those sound good, we could go to Oklahoma City to one of the steak houses or seafood restaurants. Your choice."

"No. Not Oklahoma City. By the time we got there, ordered, ate our meal and drove back to Willow Glen it would be dark. I'd rather be home before dark."

"Okay. Anywhere you want." A knot of apprehension formed in J.B.'s stomach. He'd waited for such a long time for her to go to dinner with him. He didn't like the fact she had to become ill before he had the chance. Would she go through with it—or would she back out at the last second?

Michael glanced at him. "I'll confess. I'll never get tired of hamburgers. Let's go to Hamburger Heaven on Southwest Sixteenth."

He'd eaten there before. Their hamburgers were good, but no better than a couple of other places he'd tried. He thought of himself as the gourmet of fast food establishments. "What's different about their burgers?"

"I like their bacon cheeseburger with nothing on it except barbecue sauce."

He grinned. "That does sound good." He thought about it, imagining the blend of flavors. "I've tried every other kind known to mankind—including a really awful concoction called a tofu burger." He shuddered.

She tried picturing J.B. eating a tofu burger... She was surprised when laughter bubbled up. She was amazed she'd gotten comfortable enough with him to carry on a normal conversation, and proud of being able to control her emotions. Thank goodness, she was again in control of her life. For the moment. Imagining his bachelor existence, she asked, "Do you eat out a lot?"

"Every night. Cooking for one means I also have to clean up the mess. I only eat breakfast at home, and that rarely. I usually go to the Whistle Stop. What about you?"

"For the past several weeks I've skipped breakfast or have only a slice of toast with my coffee." She thought about the reason. The late night phone calls had her stomach so tied up in knots, the thought of food made her physically ill. Unwilling to dwell on it right now, she immediately slammed the door on that thought.

"Too busy?" He glanced over at her and wondered what had caused that momentary expression of fear to flit across her face.

"Yes. I like to stay busy." She glanced up the street. "There it is, on your left."

"Yes. I've been here before. Do you want to eat in the car or go inside?"

"Inside, please."

~ * ~

Taking a last sip of coffee, Michael thought about feeling relaxed for the first time in weeks and sighed heavily. Her heart slammed into her ribs when J.B. placed his hand over hers.

"Do you want to talk about it?" He wanted her to talk to him about what bothered her. He leaned toward her, almost willing her to confide in him.

"No. Not really." She looked down at the tabletop, making designs with the wet circles created by condensation from the water glass.

Watching her, J.B. recalled that at one point he'd nearly stopped breathing, mesmerized by a Michael who willingly reached across the table and touched her napkin to the corner of his mouth. As soon as she'd noticed his frozen posture she had ducked her head and flushed with embarrassment.

"You ready to leave?"

"Yes, but I want to go wash up first."

"Okay." He stood and waited until she arose from the booth and then walked beside her.

"Where are you going?"

He grinned. "Did you forget? We're goin' to wash up."

She didn't bother to answer and pushed through the swinging door into the ladies room.

Emerging at the same time a few minutes later, they headed for the exit, walking past the booth they had vacated minutes earlier.

A couple of feet from the table she spotted the dead rose lying there. She staggered, fighting to remain upright as her stomach rebelled and she raced back to the ladies room, getting there in the nick of time.

J.B. spotted the dead flower just microseconds after Michael and saw her reaction. She ran before he had a chance to react. He walked to the ladies room door and knocked. "Michael?" When she didn't respond he motioned for one of the waitresses to come over. "Will you please check to make sure there's only one person in there, and if anyone is in there besides the lady who sat with me, please clear them out 'cause I'm goin' in."

"Sir, I can't allow you in there. This is the ladies room."

J.B. flashed his badge. "I *know* it's the ladies room, but I'm goin' in and you either clear everyone out of there except *my* lady—or I will."

"Yessir." She ran into the room and exited a few seconds later. "It's just your lady, sir. She's being sick, sir."

J.B. pushed open the bathroom door, "Stand here and don't allow anyone else in here until we come out." He walked inside and allowed the door to shut. "Michael?"

"Go away. Just go away, J.B. Haven't you done enough?"

He was stunned. "What are you talkin' about?"

"Why did you do it? We were having such a good time. Why would you do that? I don't understand."

"Michael, I'm the one who doesn't understand. Now suppose you tell me exactly what has you so spooked and more importantly, tell me why you put that dead flower on our table."

As pale as a ghost, Michael leaned her elbows on the sink running cold water over her wrists. She raised her head, looked in the mirror and saw his face. It convinced her he really didn't know what was going on. "I didn't put the flower there. I thought you did."

"Why in hell would you think I'd give you a dead flower?"

She sighed, closed her eyes and a shudder rippled its way over her body. "That's only a part of it. Someone has been giving me a lot of them recently."

Two

"Let's get out of here, Michael. I don't feel comfortable standin' around chattin' in the ladies room. We're going to one of three places. Your place, my place, or the station. Your choice. But before this night gets too much older you're goin' to tell me what's goin' on." When Michael nodded, J.B. took her elbow and escorted her out as if there was not a thing at all unusual about a man being in the ladies room.

J.B. walked with his hand at Michael's elbow and with every step, he struggled to withdraw emotionally. The moment his fingers touched her skin he knew objectivity to be a lost cause.

Tremors rippled over her skin and he watched her face as she struggled to remain calm. He'd never seen such control. One look at her eyes and he had a hard time maintaining the detachment he'd need to help her. He should turn it over to his partner.

He shook his head. *No! I'm a detective. This is a "case." I'm trained to be objective. If some nut case is threatenin' her, I* will *protect her and take him down.*

"Just a little farther, darlin'. Can you make it?" J.B. watched her nod and slipped his hand to the small of her back. He could think better if he didn't touch her soft skin.

Darling? Michael was startled by the endearment. He'd called her darling. It sounded so natural. A slip of the tongue? Or a word he used with every female he knew?

Michael walked beside J.B. pondering the situation about which she had ambivalent feelings. She liked his touch too much for her own peace of mind. She felt safer than she'd felt in months. And it gave rise to fears with which she'd lived for a decade.

She thought about her battle with fear. It would overwhelm her if she let it. Most days she won, functioning with no crack in the facade with which she faced the world. Other days she struggled minute by minute, and occasionally second by second, to keep the walls shored up. On those days, nearly sick with dread, she feared a small fissure would become a chasm. She would allow no breach. And she'd find out who was harassing her and file charges, putting an end to this. She'd missed too many hours of sleep recently and it was beginning to affect her work.

She concentrated on the present and the sensations caused by the touch of his hand as it came back to her elbow. It would be easy to get used to his caring concern. The calloused skin of his fingers, the tips slightly rough, was warm and soothing. A buzzing sensation swished up her arm, like an electric shock without the pain. Her breathing changed as the muscles in her abdomen tightened. Her reaction puzzled her and she tried to analyze it. The feeling was new and in no way resembled the fear usually engulfing her when a man got too close.

A sudden breeze whipped around the corner of the building molding her blouse to her body. Michael felt her nipples pebble against the silk fabric and tugged her jacket closed. She told herself it was because of the chill in the air and not J.B.'s hand on her elbow. The heat of embarrassment seared her face and she hoped J.B. wouldn't notice.

Fear still gnawed at her. Would there be a time in her life when she could spend an entire day feeling safe? A day when she could receive flowers or candy without thinking them a threat?

Michael took a deep breath and decided to tell J.B. why she was afraid. *Everything*? No. Not everything. Some things she could not talk about. To anyone.

When she recalled that night, shame still washed over her in waves. Shame that she'd put herself in that place at that time. Shame she hadn't fought harder. But most painful was the shame that she didn't have the courage to report it. Now it was too late. She'd lived with it for ten years. She could live with it the rest of her life. It happened so long ago, it couldn't possibly have anything to do with events currently driving her crazy.

Perhaps she could tell him about the phone calls, the notes, and the flowers. But what if J.B., or some other police officer, was the caller? Did she dare trust him? She still needed to figure out how her caller managed to get each new phone number.

Why on earth was this man stalking her? She couldn't imagine why she was his target. Always at the back of her mind was the worry—did he have murder in mind?

J.B. unlocked the car and held the door for Michael. Seeing her climb into his vehicle looked, and felt, *right*. She belonged with him. Forever.

He could visualize this happening daily. Every morning, after waking in each other's arms, they'd go to work in the same car. Maybe even have lunch together each day. *Whoa, J.B., old son. You're gettin' way ahead of yourself.* He shut her door, walked around the car and climbed behind the wheel.

"Okay, darlin', what's it goin' to be? Your place, my place or the station ..." He chuckled. "...which is also my place, but if you'll feel more comfortable there, if you can talk easier..."

She shook her head and took a deep, calming breath. "My house is fine. I'll make coffee." The minute the words were out she felt tension take over. *Oh, God. Is this a mistake?*

"Okay, your place it is. Coffee and talk. We *are* goin' to talk, aren't we, Michael?"

Michael looked out the side window. *What on earth am I going to do?* She took a deep breath. "Of course. We'll talk."

She closed her eyes and worked to relax. In her mind's eye she imagined a blue cloud, "calm", swirling, working its way up from her feet chasing the red cloud, "tension", away. She visualized watching "tension" whoosh out through the top of her head, while the "calm" remained. When stress held her in such rigid control she suffered actual pain, this was the only method that worked.

J.B. looked at her face and saw the closed eyes, the obvious anxiety, and knew he had a long road ahead. A surge of relief washed over him because she trusted him enough to allow him into her house. That was progress.

He felt good about the chance to develop a friendship. His mama always said, "Marry your best friend if you want to have a strong marriage." He would work hard to be her best friend and hope to progress from there. She didn't trust him yet. But, before many more days passed, she would. He'd make sure of it.

They drove in silence for a while before Michael raised her head and pointed to his left. "There it is. It's the two story white clapboard with the green shutters." She looked at it longingly, wanting to get inside where she felt a modicum of safety. She still had the intrusive nighttime phone calls to contend with, but at least she hadn't received any flowers or other "gifts" here. She hoped the man didn't know where she lived. She prayed her harasser had only the phone number.

J.B. thought it imprudent to reveal he knew where she lived. He pulled into the drive, stopped by the front porch and gently touched her left wrist. "Hold on, darlin', I'll be right there."

He exited the car and hurriedly scanned the neighborhood before walking around and opening her door. Escorting her up the steps, he was so busy watching her he didn't see it until her shocked expression alerted him. A split second later he spotted the florist's box by the door. Michael's posture rigid, she seemed unable to move, and he feared she might be in danger here. He simply must get her inside.

"Michael, where's your house key?" She didn't respond as she stared, mesmerized by the box. He grabbed her purse, opened it, and took her keys. "Which one fits the door?" No response. He fumbled them. Each second brought him more concern. It was taking too long to get her to safety.

He always maintained command of his emotions. They were out of control now. Every instinct told him to throw her to the porch and cover her with his body. *And traumatize her more?* She didn't need that. Her emotions, already batted about like a Ping-Pong ball in a hot game of table tennis, were on the ragged edge.

Staying between her and any danger, he tried three keys before he found the right one. He pushed on the door and pressed his hand to her back, guiding her gently toward the inside of the house—and safety. She watched the box, skirting the perimeter as though expecting it to explode.

"Come on, Michael, let's get inside. That'll wait." She gave no indication she heard. He led her through the foyer into the living room. At the sofa he coaxed her to sit. Like a zombie, she stared toward the front door.

J.B. tossed his Stetson on the back of the sofa, squatted in front of her, took her face in his hands, and forced her to look at him. "Michael?" Her eyes glistened with unshed tears and she looked back toward the door much as she would have at a hissing adder. He rubbed her arms and spoke gently but firmly. "Look at me. Come on, darlin', listen to me. You're all right." He took her chin in his fingers and gently turned her face back toward him. "Michael."

When she made eye contact with him he nodded. "That's it. Look at me." It nearly broke his heart to see the fear in her eyes. Her fists, white knuckled, clutched her skirt. A drop of blood beaded on her lower lip.

"I'm here, Michael, and I won't let *anyone* hurt you. Do you understand?" At her nod he stood. She grabbed his hands and held on as if to a lifeline. He squatted back down to her eye level. "I'm goin' to check it out. We'll see what's in the box." She held his hands, obviously unwilling to let go just yet.

He wanted to comfort her, to hold her safe. He sat beside her and put his arm around her, trying to pull her close. She jerked away and J.B. derided himself for putting his need to comfort her ahead of her need to have a zone of safety. He offered his hand, palm up. She looked at it, then wrenched her gaze to his eyes, a wary look on her face.

"It's all right, darlin'. Take my hand like you did a minute ago. Hold on to me, Michael."

Her plea came out half sob and half whisper. "Oh, God, why won't he leave me alone?" She tentatively reached out, her gaze on his eyes as if trying to probe his soul. He watched her as she fought the battle for control of her emotions. With a sigh she grabbed his hand and held it with both of hers.

A half-hour later she relaxed enough to scoot into the corner of the sofa.

"I'll be right back, darlin'. Wait here." J.B. walked to the front door. The distorted view looking through the oval, beveled glass window told him nothing. He opened the door, stepped out and saw no one outside.

Inside the box were eleven dead roses tied with a red ribbon. Were they mates to the one at the restaurant? He walked in and put them on the table by the front door.

"Where's your phone, Michael?"

"It's there," she whispered and pointed toward the corner of the room to an antique cherry wood writing desk. A European style rotary telephone rested on the corner. He walked over and dialed a familiar number.

"Shag? I need a favor." He closed his eyes and shook his head. "C'mon, Shag. No jokin'. It's important." He explained the events of the evening to his partner. "Interview the restaurant employees. I don't hold much hope anyone saw who put the dead flower on the table, but we have to ask." He rubbed his face. "Thanks, pal. I'll owe you."

He felt ashamed he hadn't asked questions while he was there. How could he forget to do something that should be second nature? He'd been too concerned about Michael to think about doing his job.

He rang off and walked to her. "Do you feel comfortable talkin' about this now?"

She looked around her living room, fear obvious on her face, and whispered, "I hoped he didn't know where I live." She choked back a sob and, looking down at her fists clenched in her lap, she whispered, "Nothing is going to stop him, is it? He's going to get me, no matter what I do."

"Not if I can help it. And you can take that to the bank."

She pressed her fingers to her lips to stop their trembling and looked up, her lower lids brimming with tears. A shuddering sigh escaped. "Thank you for being here, J.B."

He sat and attempted to put his arms around her, his only intention to comfort. Again, she jerked away.

"Darlin', suppose you tell me what this is all about."

She wanted to trust. Always self-contained, she'd never shared her private thoughts. And, though she'd intended to tell him about the phone calls, this invasion of her home made her want to draw back into her shell. She'd been reared to keep her mouth shut about personal business. "What is *what* all about?"

"Oh, c'mon, Michael, I'm a cop. Are you questionin' my intelligence?" He glared for a moment. "I wasn't born yesterday and I'm smart enough to figure out a lot just from seein' the dead flowers."

She shrugged. "So, do you think it's a practical joke?"

"Is *that* what you're callin' it?" He snorted and shook his head. "Darlin', as the kids say, 'get real.'"

"The flowers *are* dead. Doesn't that sound like a joke?"

"It might, darlin'. Except I watched you bein' sick when you saw only one dead rose at the restaurant."

"Well, I got a little upset at the time. But maybe that flower wasn't meant for me. What if it was meant for you?"

"Now, why would anyone send me a flower—dead or alive?"

"What if the delivery man put it on the wrong table?"

"Then why did eleven dead roses—the rest of the dozen—show up here on your front porch and—"

"But..."

J.B. held up his hand to halt her interruption, " ...if it's a 'practical joke' why are you so upset?"

"Well, I...it could be I just hate to see flowers die."

"That's a good one, Michael. You do think fast on your feet, don't you?" He shook his head. "Come on now, I think it's obvious. That's not the first bunch you've received, is it? I'd guess someone's been causin' you a lot of problems. Sendin' flowers. Makin' late night phone calls?" Her swift intake of breath said he was on the right track.

He raised his eyebrow and looked at her, his head tipped slightly, speculating, "That's why you got so upset and fainted. It's why you had what the doc called an 'anxiety attack'."

Michael leaned forward and attempted a glare. "Wait a minute. What makes you think the dead flowers have anything to do with me becoming upset today? Did it ever cross your mind that I became upset because you were harassing me?"

J.B. shot to his feet. "Harassin' you? I was *not* harassin' you." When she opened her mouth to speak he shook his head. "No!" He looked her squarely in the eye. "I know that's what you said, but we both know all I wanted was a date."

"Most men would take 'no' for an answer. They wouldn't ask over and over again."

He sat down beside her and grinned. "All right, so I'm hard headed and tenacious." It suddenly occurred to J.B. they were way off the subject at hand and he shook his head. "Damn! You're good, darlin'. You're really good."

"What does that mean?"

"I guess that's why you're such a good attorney. We weren't talkin' about me askin' you for a date. We were talkin' about you receivin' dead flowers. Let's get back to *that* subject."

"I thought my getting upset *was* the subject." Michael stood. "I promised you coffee." She glided through the dining room to the kitchen, leaving a determined J.B. to watch her retreating back.

"I'm not givin' up, Michael. Coffee or no coffee, you're goin' to answer my questions."

He stretched his long legs out and crossed his ankles. Leaning his head back, he closed his eyes and speculated on the possible causes for terror at seeing the dead roses. Being a cop, he didn't have to think too hard.

As Michael watched the coffee drip through the automatic coffee maker, she thought about confiding in J.B. Could she trust him? Enough to tell him everything?

"I wish I knew what to do." The fact she spoke aloud, even in a whisper, startled her.

"Michael? Stallin' won't work. I can always come in there."

J.B. wouldn't give up. Just as he'd said...hard headed and tenacious. "I knew that," she whispered.

Michael put the coffee, mugs and other necessities on a tray and added a plate of cookies. She hoped chewing cookies might keep his mouth occupied for a while and give her time to think.

When she carried the tray into the living room J.B. stood, took it and placed it on the coffee table. "Now, let's get back to what we were discussin' before you left the room."

"J.B., we're going to have coffee."

"I distinctly remember you also agreein' to talk."

"Well, haven't we been talking?"

"Okay, Michael, you just ran out of time." He turned his gaze more fully on her face to gauge her reaction. "You were smart enough to graduate high school at sixteen. You graduated law school *summa cum laude* and were snatched up immediately by one of the top law firms in Oklahoma City. You passed the bar on the first try and were offered all kinds of perks, includin' the possibility of a future partnership with the firm."

Michael stared at him. How could he know that?

With a raised eyebrow, J.B. continued. "How'm I doin' so far?" Her shocked expression didn't stop him. "You stayed there for a couple of years and decided you wanted your own practice. I'd give a lot to know why you left that cushy job."

Had he investigated her? Why? Unless he—

He leaned toward her. "Practically from day one, your practice was successful and you gained great publicity with the

Maitland murder trial last year." He looked at her for several seconds, then growled, "So don't pretend you're stupid. And don't treat me as if I am."

Her eyes rounded in shock and she drew back from him. Who did he think he was? Always laid back and easy going, she never thought to see the day he'd actually raise his voice. "J.B.? How..."

He interrupted before she could voice her concerns. "Yes, Michael. It's good ol' J.B. I can become angry as easily as the next guy. Just because I don't yell all the time doesn't mean I don't get mad. It's just that I'm adult enough to control my temper—most of the time.

"Now, I'm tired of this game you've been playin' and I want answers. If you won't talk to me as a friend, then you talk to me as a police officer—at the station." He pulled a notebook out of his pocket and grabbed his pen. "Start at the beginnin'."

"The beginning?"

"Michael!" He pounded his fist on his knee, scooted forward to the edge of the couch and turned to her, his notebook on his knee. "Are these the first flowers you've received?"

"No." Michael's eyes looked everywhere but at J.B.

"How many times have you received flowers?"

"I don't remember." At his outraged expletive she looked directly at him. "I don't know for sure. Maybe ten or twelve."

"Were they always dead?"

She nervously picked at her nail polish. "No. Not always."

"So, some were fresh flowers, just like you'd get from any florist?"

"Yes. There were a couple of really beautiful bouquets."

"Michael, I sent you a bouquet of flowers a couple of months ago." He watched her eyes widen and fill with fear. "No. Not roses. I sent daisies because they reminded me of you.

The florist called them Marguerites." He couldn't prevent the pain in his voice. "I never heard if you got them."

"J.B., I never received any daisies. They're one of my favorites. I'd remember." He opened his mouth, but she spoke first. "I would have sent a thank you note."

A wave of relief washed over him. He thought she'd ignored the gesture. "Okay, back to the subject. Is that all he's done? Send flowers?" J.B. looked up and glared when she didn't immediately respond.

"No." Michael's voice was barely above a whisper as she picked more frantically at her nail polish.

"Phone calls? From a man?"

"How did you...never mind. I suppose it's usual."

"Tell me about the phone calls, Michael."

"They always come in the middle of the night."

"What does he say?"

Michael smoothed her already smooth hair, poking and prodding at the chignon at the nape of her neck. She closed her eyes and the muscles in her jaw clenched and relaxed before she finally responded. "At first there's a lot of heavy breathing. That goes on for a few minutes." She came to a dead stop and looked away, clearly uncomfortable with going on.

He wouldn't let up. "And then?"

"Then he says..." She didn't want to tell him. It would lead to a place she didn't want to go.

"What does he say?" When she sat there picking at one of her cuticles he stood up and walked around the room, raking his fingers through his hair. "Michael, you're drivin' me crazy."

A momentary panic flitted across her face and she blurted out, "I don't believe this has anything to do with my...there's no connection between this and..."

"What are you talkin' about?"

"Nothing. It's just..."

"Talk to me. What does he say?" Shag had accurately accused J.B. of being implacable when on the hunt for information in a case.

"In the beginning he'd whisper 'Mickie' before he hung up."

"Mickie?" At her nod he asked, "Is that significant?"

"Not so far as I know." She stopped and took a deep breath, blew it out slowly, and shook her head. "No, I don't think so."

J.B. waited quietly for a moment. Okay, she was holding back. "Go on. You said they consist of heavy breathing and then he says 'Mickie'?" At her nod, he asked, "Did that change at any time?"

"Yes. After I got my first unlisted phone number."

"How did it change?"

"The first call that came to the new number, he snarled at me. He—"

"Snarled? I thought you said he whispered when he called."

"A snarl is the only way I can describe it. He sounded so vicious. I thought by getting an unlisted number I had solved the problem. When the phone rang I was sound asleep and resting for a change. I grabbed it and as soon as I said 'hello' he snarled at me."

"What did he say? Can you remember exactly?"

"Oh yes. I'll never forget. In this hissing, savage voice he said, 'You shouldn't have done that, Mickie. You made me angry. You aren't going to like me when I'm angry.'"

She pressed her hand to her upper lip and took a deep shuddering breath. "I'll never forget my first thought when I heard what he said." She glanced at him, then to her clasped hands. "I thought he sounded like some character out of those grade-B movies. I convinced myself it was a teenage boy, who watched dumb movies with hokey dialogue. I barely stopped myself telling him I didn't like him much when he *wasn't* angry."

"If it is a teenager, how could he get your number? It wouldn't be easy. Directory assistance wouldn't give it out."

Did she dare suggest it could be a cop? She glanced at him. "Maybe he's a computer hacker. I don't know. I didn't think about the whys and hows at that particular moment. When he called, I barely prevented myself laughing because he *did* sound so much like a juvenile pretending to be tough.

"However, I also remembered the reports on TV about gangs who do serious bodily injury to each other. Even if it is a teenager harassing me, he could still be dangerous."

"That's a fact. There are times when I wonder if we make a difference and ask myself why we bother."

"But you do always go back into the fray, don't you?" She smiled at him, then nearly jumped out of her skin when the phone rang. "Oh, God."

"Don't panic. It's broad daylight. Has he ever called during the day?" The phone rang a second time.

"No. He's only delivered flowers during the day."

"Then go ahead and answer. Remember, I'm here."

Her thready voice indicated her fear as she picked it up and said, "Hello?"

A look crossed her face that J.B. couldn't classify. For a moment he thought it was fear.

Turning her back she curled into her shoulder. Keeping her voice low, she snapped, "That's impossible."

He watched her stiffen, her knuckles whiten on the phone.

She softly moaned, "What have you done?"

Immediately after that J.B. recognized outrage.

Michael glanced at him over her shoulder and then in a harsh whisper she asked, "You never change do you? This is just another of your games. Another way to manipulate me."

She closed her eyes as the muscles in her jaw knotted, and gritted through her teeth in a low vibrant voice, "No! I've told you repeatedly—I have no intention of ever coming back. Our connection was permanently severed ten years ago."

J.B. watched her face, wondering who could be on the other end of the line. Blessed with extraordinarily good hearing, he was shocked by what he heard next.

Just above a whisper, Michael's voice displayed her determination. "Do not call me. I don't wish to speak with you ever again, Father." She replaced the receiver.

Within seconds the phone rang again. "Oh, please, leave me alone." She picked it up on the second ring, her gaze on J.B.'s face. She listened, breathed a sigh of pure relief and handed the phone to him. "It's for you."

He took the receiver. "Anderson." He listened briefly. "Yeah, I was afraid of that. With a crowd that size no one would notice when he dropped it." J.B. hunched his shoulders. "That's what I thought. Thanks, Shag." For several minutes they discussed the case. J.B. spoke more forcefully. "I don't *intend* to leave her unprotected. This guy is gettin' more darin' all the time." He wiped his hand down his face. "He also left roses here." J.B. glanced at Michael. "Yeah, I thought it was *real* cute." He looked at Michael and smiled. "I'll see you in the mornin', Shag." He disconnected and walked to the sofa.

Michael looked up, resignation on her face. "He didn't find out a thing, did he?"

"No, but I wasn't expectin' him to. It was a long shot."

"So what do we do now?" She looked unbelievably fragile, as if the slightest puff of wind would blow her away.

"We get back to what we were doin' before he called. Finish tellin' me about the phone calls. And to be honest, I'd really like to know about the one you just got."

"From your partner?"

"Michael, don't play dumb. The other call."

"I won't talk about that. It's my business."

He sighed in resignation. "All right, get back to the calls you receive in the middle of the night."

She sighed and ducked her head. "After changing my number made him angry, his calls were more frequent. More savage in content. He sounded as if he hated me, but didn't make any outright threats at that time."

"You should have brought this to the department."

"By this time I didn't trust *anybody*. He learned my second unlisted number." At his look of surprise she nodded. "Yes, I had it changed again. This time he had the new number within three days. What I kept remembering was that cops can get telephone numbers, whether or not they are unlisted."

"You suspected me." It wasn't a question. Her behavior toward him suddenly became crystal clear.

"J.B., every time I turned around, there you were. I couldn't sneeze without you saying 'bless you.' You dogged my footsteps day in and day out. You even watched me in court. I'm a corporate attorney, not a criminal lawyer. You, taking an interest in cases that didn't involve the police, made no sense."

"Yeah. That wasn't the brightest move I ever made."

"I couldn't go to The Whistle Stop because you'd be there drinking coffee. I ran into you in the hall at the courthouse."

"I wanted you to get to know me. I thought if I hung around a lot, that'd do the trick."

"Did you have to be so relentless?"

He grinned sheepishly. "Guess it didn't work out the way I planned."

"No. It didn't."

"Sorry, darlin'. I had no idea why you were so standoffish. I'd heard you didn't date, but I thought for sure you'd go out with me. As Shag has told me on more than one occasion, I can be an arrogant son-of-a-bitch at times."

"You certainly can."

He chuckled. "You don't have to be so quick to agree." He raised an eyebrow. "What set you off today?"

"I had a really nasty phone call last night. I don't remember a decent night's sleep. You were asking me for a date and mentioned a picnic..." She quickly glanced away from him. "Let's just say picnics bring back bad memories. That's why I had the panic attack. It had been building for weeks and..."

A loud crash resounded in the room, followed by the sound of falling glass.

Michael screamed, curled into a ball on the sofa cushions, and covered her head with the pillow.

J.B. whirled toward the window, staring at the gaping hole and the shattered glass that lay scattered all over the floor.

Three

Oh, God! A bomb? J.B. leaped to his feet and scooped Michael from the couch, pillow and all. He held her clasped to his chest as he ducked behind the sofa. Unwilling to let go of his precious cargo, he knelt, embracing her as gently as a mother cradling a child.

Glancing down, he saw her body quivering like a bowl of gelatin and soothed her with strokes on her back. He'd never known anyone could shake that hard. Cuddling her closer he put his cheek near hers.

"Shh, darlin'. Don't be afraid. I'm here." She didn't respond, nor open her eyes. "Are you hurt?" She continued to shiver. He looked for blood on her clothing and found none.

"No." The agonized whisper barely passed her trembling lips. "Why? Why is he doing this?"

"I don't know, darlin', but..."

"If I knew why it might be easier to take." She cuddled closer to J.B.

"I know, darlin'. The senseless violence always gets to me, too." He set her gently on the floor. "Michael, I need to find out what it is...see if it's a bomb."

"A bomb? Oh, God, be careful. J.B...?"

"Stay here and I'll go see." She clung to him as if he were her lifeline and he gently pried her fingers from his shirt. "I'll come back as quick as I can."

J.B. put her on the floor and looked down at her, stroking his hand over her hair. She curled into a tight ball and lay there with her eyes tightly closed. J.B. left her there, knowing he need not be concerned she would stand up.

Crouching, he ran to the paper wrapped object. *Be careful. It's evidence.* But, if it contained a bomb the couch wouldn't protect them. He surveyed the scene, filing all the details in his mind. Careful to preserve any fingerprints, he picked up the object, touching only the corners, and gingerly removed the rubber band. A note was wrapped around the half-brick. He laid it back on the floor and with the help of his pen, unfolded it.

You'RE a trAMP. sEnd HIM aWAY.

Slowly, so slowly, Michael's fear began to dissipate and anger began to creep in. She could hear J.B. creeping over the floor in front of the couch. She was angry with herself that she'd allowed fear to nearly paralyze her again. She intended to take control of her life...beginning now.

Where is J.B.? "J.B.?" she whispered. Michael took a deep breath and made a conscious effort to relax. Trying to overcome the fear took all her strength. She called again, this time slightly louder than a whisper. "J.B.?"

His name, only a breath of sound, didn't go much beyond the space surrounding her. But J.B. heard. Fearful other bricks might follow, he remained in a crouch and scurried back to Michael. "I'm here, darlin'." He noted her eyes were dilated, her skin pale and sweat dampened, and her breathing ragged. But he was no longer concerned whether she could comprehend what he said. "It's okay. It's not a bomb. You can relax."

"Not a bomb?" She stared at him for a moment and then closed her eyes, "Thank God."

J.B. stroked his hand over her head and leaning down, kissed her brow. "I'm goin' to check around outside. Okay?" He gently rubbed his hand across her shoulders. "Stay here till I get back."

Though he didn't hold out much hope of seeing who threw the brick, he ran to the window and peeked from behind the edge of the drapes. No one ran down the street. No one stirred.

He returned to Michael, picked her up and walked around the couch. As he sat she started to skitter off his lap. "Let me hold you. Okay?" She gazed into his eyes for long moments, unmoving. J.B. took a deep breath. "I need to hold you for just a minute." When she still didn't respond, he put his cheek briefly against hers. "It's okay, darlin'. It wasn't a bomb."

Staring into his eyes, she gave him an abrupt nod. He sat and held her on his lap, pulling her head to his shoulder; he kept his hold loose. Earlier she had been unwilling to be held. He wanted her to know—she had a choice. It felt wonderful to hold her in his arms and not have her jerk away.

After a few minutes, without conscious thought or intent, he caressed her upper arm, his hand stroking from shoulder to elbow. He was so enraptured by the scent of her, the feel of her in his arms, he fantasized it could go on forever. He placed small kisses at her temple, the corner of her eye. Without planning, he nuzzled his way down her cheek to the corner of her mouth. He was so lost in his dream world, he didn't know his hold became more confining with each passing minute.

At first she didn't notice, thinking only of how good it felt to be cradled in his arms. But gradually, as the stroking and nuzzling continued, the fear began to invade her senses. Pushing the fear back she tried to hang on to the feelings of safety, of warmth, of tenderness. There were too many years—

years of living with the fear of being touched, the fear of being held against her will. Unable to fight these feelings, and with her heart pounding, her breath coming in gasps, Michael scrambled from his lap.

J.B. sat stunned by the abruptness of her departure from his arms. Then he realized what he'd done. He leaned forward placing his elbows on his knees and his face in his hands. He scrubbed his hands down over his face, then looked up at her. "I'm sorry. I got a little carried away. I only wanted to comfort you."

"Comfort me? Is that what you call it?"

"Yes, that's what I intended. But I also wanted to comfort *me*. I was afraid you'd been hurt. It scared the hell out of me."

"I know the feeling." She pressed her fingers against her lips for a moment as tears brimmed. "He's trying to kill me, isn't he?"

"Maybe, but he'll have to go through me to do it."

"That's just it, J.B. This guy is a nut. He could kill you, too."

"Well, he can try, but you're forgettin' one thing. This is what I do for a livin'. I 'protect and serve'." He grinned. "It says so on every blessed one of the police cruisers in this city."

"This is no joke, J.B."

"I know, darlin', I know. But laughin' sometimes helps." J.B. stood up, walked to the phone, and called Shag. After filling in his partner, on the latest episode, he turned to Michael. "You aren't stayin' here tonight. I'm takin' you to my place or a hotel. Your choice."

She looked at him as if he'd lost his mind. "Your place?"

"I have plenty of room. Two bedrooms. They each have their own bathroom. You can have your pick and sleep in whichever bedroom you want." He wanted her to stay with him, wanted to see her sitting in his living room, sitting across from him at the breakfast table. Just imagining it, picturing it in his mind, his body reacted. He couldn't hide the fact he wanted her. He feared he'd alarm her, and quickly sat down. He leaned forward, bracing his elbows on his knees and concentrated on counting the flowers on the drapes.

Michael was tempted to go with him to his place. But the ever-present fear rode her soul like a banshee. She'd never sleep at his place—never rest knowing he was so near. "I can't go to your place, J.B."

He stood and nodded. "Okay. A hotel it is."

Michael arose from the sofa, walked out to the foyer and into her room. J.B. walked over beside the window and looked out from behind the sides of the drapes. Nothing moved in the neighborhood except an old black and tan coonhound trotting down the street. Three houses down and across the street a marmalade cat lay on the porch railing, basking in the evening sun and licking its outstretched leg.

Willow Glen just being Willow Glen. Quiet neighborhoods. Pets roaming off leash. Everyone inside getting ready for their supper. Everything *appeared* normal. Quiet. J.B. turned back to the room. He couldn't leave Michael's house with a hole in the window. He'd have to board it up before they left.

A short time later Michael came out of her bedroom carrying a tote bag and make-up case. "Okay, I'm ready."

"Do you have anything in your basement or in the garage that we can use to close up this hole? I don't think it'd be a good idea to leave the house vulnerable."

Michael stopped. "I didn't think about that." She bent over, set down the luggage, put her fingers to her temples and pressed, massaging as she straightened up. "I can't think."

"Do you have a headache, darlin'?" J.B. walked to her and touched her shoulder. "Let me see if I can get rid of some of that tension."

"No. Let's just get out of here. I don't want to be here after dark." Turning around, she looked around the room. "Will I ever feel safe here again?" she whispered.

She looked back at J.B. "I don't have any idea what's in the basement. I haven't been down there since right after I moved in." She shuddered. "I haven't had reason to." She refused to admit it gave her the shivers.

"I'll go see what's down there."

Michael nodded. "Okay. But hurry."

"Quick as a wink." He started toward kitchen and stopped. Turning back, he chuckled. "I guess I should ask...where's the door to the basement?"

"Through the kitchen, and then through the pantry."

At the bottom of the steps J.B. stopped to get his bearings. From the corner of his eye he saw a shadow move. Pulling his gun, he whirled around and snapped, "Freeze!" A cat jumped up onto the sill and leaped outside...through the *open* window. *The wide-open window.*

"Michael!" J.B.'s roar could be heard across the street. No response. He started up the stairs shouting again. "Michael!" Halfway up he muttered, "Hasn't she got better sense than to leave her basement window open?"

Michael appeared in the doorway, a perplexed look on her face. "What, J.B.? Why are you shouting?"

He peered up at her. "Why is the window open down—"

"Why is... Open?"

"Yes, open. It's like—"

"I don't kn—"

"—an invitation. You might as well plant a sign on your front lawn...." He brought his hand up, moving it from left to right through the air, his thumb and index finger three inches apart as if measuring the size of the type. "...saying..."

"A sign? Are you crazy? I don't know how—"

"Hey, burglars. It's open. Help yourself!" J.B. finally heard her and stopped his diatribe. Looking up sheepishly, he grinned. "I got a little carried away, didn't I?"

"You certainly did. Do you honestly believe I'd have stayed in this house day after day—or night after night for that matter—if I'd *known* the window was open down there? I told you I haven't been down these stairs since right after I moved in. I can assure you that window was *not* open when I was down there last."

"Sorry I flew off the handle. It scared me to think of you living here with a window open. All he'd have to do is slide through to have access to your entire house. Is there a possibility someone *has* been in here?"

"I don't think so. Nothing's missing."

Michael stood, hugging her waist, as pale as he'd ever seen her.

"Don't worry about it, darlin', we'll take care of the problem right now." He walked down, closed and locked the window. He checked the window and the lock, thinking it wouldn't hurt to have someone look at it. It hadn't opened by itself.

Over in a dark corner, he spotted a piece of plywood. It was too large but he decided to use it anyway. Upstairs he asked Michael, "Do you have a hammer and nails?"

Michael smiled. "Yes. I had to hang every picture and painting in the house." From a kitchen drawer, she took a tack hammer and a sack of nails. All three-quarters of an inch long.

J.B. looked at the tack hammer, glanced in the sack and shook his head. "Michael, my grandmother had darning needles bigger than these things you're callin' nails. They might keep the kid next door out of here...if he isn't more than three or four years old. A determined man would walk through anything

42

nailed up with these as if the barrier was paper. I need a *real* hammer and nails."

Michael turned away. "I'm sorry. I didn't think..."

"No, *I'm* sorry. I keep puttin' my foot in my mouth...hell, try both feet." He looked down at his boots. "Believe me when I tell you, it's a tight fit with boots this size."

Michael, looking at his boots, laughed. "Try the garage. There are some tools and things left there by the previous owner."

"I'll be right back. If anyone comes to the door, don't answer." J.B. went out to the garage.

A short time later he returned with the tools to find her staring at the note. "Don't let it bother you, Michael. We're goin' to catch him."

Michael watched him work. "I am truly sorry, and feel so guilty that I dragged you into all this, J.B. I wish I could have handled it on my own."

J.B. looked at her and put his hand on her shoulder. "Michael, guilt get's heavier with each step you take.

"Now, don't worry about the window or any of this. We'll get a glazier to come to the house and we'll get it fixed."

"I have to be in court at nine a.m. How am I going to be available when he needs access to the window? I still have to call to find a glazier and experience tells me no one will be available right away. I'll be lucky if I can get somebody here before a week is up."

"Will you trust me to take care of it?"

"What do you mean—take care of it?"

"I mean, give me your keys. In the morning I'll come over and call someone. I'll guarantee to have it fixed by the time you get home tomorrow night. How's that for a deal?"

"It sounds too good to pass up." She smiled. "What have you got in mind for tonight and in the morning?" Michael blushed when she realized how her question could be misinterpreted. "I mean...well, my car..."

"Yes, your car is still downtown." J.B. pretended not to notice her discomfort. "I'll take you to the hotel tonight. In the mornin' I'll take you to the courthouse. After I check in at the office, I'll get the window fixed. Tomorrow evenin' I'll follow you home."

"You don't have to do that. I can—"

"Sure I do, Michael. Until we catch this nut, you're my main priority. One of the things I'll do tomorrow, while I'm waitin' on the glazier, is fill out the paperwork on this case."

"This *case?*"

"It became a case the minute I discovered someone is stalkin' you. Now, let me check out the rest of the house to make sure it's secure and then let's get out of here."

Michael nodded and watched J.B. walk to the door across the foyer from the living room.

When he got there he stopped and asked, "Do you mind if I walk through your bedroom?"

"No. Go ahead."

Michael watched him walk through the door and for a brief moment the feelings that engulfed her were warmth and tenderness. It looked *right* to see J.B. going into her room. *Normal.* She daydreamed, for a split second, that he walked through that door on a regular basis—then the fear took over again.

A few minutes later J.B. walked over and picking up her luggage, took her elbow. "Are you ready?"

As they walked out the door, Michael looked over her shoulder and said, "J.B., I don't want to go to the hotel. It's too big. I wouldn't feel comfortable there."

"Okay." J.B. helped Michael into his car and stowed her luggage. "As I said, you're welcome to stay at my place. I still have that extra bedroom. My sister uses it when she visits. I think you'd get a good night's sleep." He walked around the car and got in.

"No. I'm sorry."

"Well, what *do* you want to do?"

"What about going to the bed and breakfast? It's small and cozy. I'd feel safe there with Mrs. Hall and the other guests. Besides, she's a client of mine. I handled all the legal work when she turned that old house into a business establishment."

"Okay. The Come On Inn it is. I think it's a good idea. You'll be safe there. And Mrs. Hall is a sweetheart-and-a-half." J.B. backed out of her driveway and headed down the street.

Michael smiled as she looked at him, and her eyebrow raised. "So, a 'sweetheart-and-a-half', is she? You flirt with ladies of all ages, I see."

He couldn't believe she was joking with him. "Of course I do. I have to spread myself pretty thin at times, but I manage to get around to all the beautiful women I can find." He chuckled. "All jokin' aside, darlin', Mrs. Hall has been a friend since right after I transferred to this police force."

"How did you meet her? I hope it was not as a cop."

"No..." He chuckled. "...well, not exactly." When Michael didn't say anything, J.B. went on to explain. "One day I was drivin' down the street and saw her strugglin' with a large carton almost as big as she is. She was tryin' to drag it up the steps and into the house. I stopped and helped her. That's all there was to it, except she invited me to stop by for coffee anytime I was in the neighborhood. So I did.

"We have coffee two or three times a month, but not always at her place. Sometimes I'll buy her a cup at The Whistle Stop." J.B. pulled into the driveway of the huge Victorian house and got out to help Michael with her luggage.

He hadn't thought to call ahead so worried whether or not there would be a room. He was ambivalent about the situation. Part of him hoped there would be no room and Michael would agree to stay at his place. While another part of him knew if she stayed at his place he wouldn't sleep a wink thinking about her being so close...and yet not nearly close enough.

His knock on the door brought Mrs. Hall. "J.B., you scoundrel, I haven't seen you in a coon's age. Did you finally come by for a cup of coffee?"

J.B. grinned, leaned over and kissed her on the cheek. "Not today, gorgeous. I brought a guest. Have you got room?" Mrs. Hall smiled up at Michael, took her by the arm and pulled her through the doorway. "Well, of course. I'll always have room for Michael."

She looked out on the porch where J.B. still stood with the screen door at his back. "Come in this house, you handsome man, you." When J.B. walked through the door, she grabbed him and pulled him down for a hug.

Turning to Michael, she winked. "I have to take advantage of every available opportunity to get some good looking man to put his arms around me. If I was thirty years younger I'd give you a run for your money, honey. And you can bet your bippy on that." Her jolly laugh echoed through the house.

Michael blushed. "Oh, but, I'm not...we're not...J.B. is a friend. That's all. He's just a friend."

"Aw, go on with you, Michael. Who are you trying to kid?" She leaned over and, in a stage whisper said, "You'd be crazy not to be after J.B. He's what my granddaughters call 'a real hunk'."

"That's what I've been tryin' to tell her." J.B. chuckled.

"No, really. I mean..." Michael turned to J.B. who grinned, apparently enjoying the teasing from Mrs. Hall. "J.B., will you tell her..."

"Tell her what, darlin'? That I've been tryin' to get a date with you for months? Should I tell her you won't give me the time of day?" He laughed. "She'd never believe that." He turned to Mrs. Hall, "Would you, beautiful?"

"No, I certainly would not." Mrs. Hall turned toward the stairs. "Come on upstairs and let's get you settled. Dinner will be ready in about a half-hour. J.B., are you going to grace us with your presence?"

"No, ma'am. I have a couple of things I need to do before callin' it a night." At the top of the first flight of stairs he put his arm around her shoulders and walked down the hall with her tucked under his arm. "But I'll take a rain check."

Michael walked into the room and looked around, her eyes shining. "Oh, Mrs. Hall, this is beautiful." Peacock colors of teal, purple and lavendar shimmered. A quilted bedspread matched drapes on either side of the windows. The fabric, a riot of lilacs, in purple, lavendar and pink with deep green leaves, looked so real Michael expected the room to be filled with their fragrance. Sheers in the softest lavendar nestled between the drapes. The wallpaper displayed tiny clusters of deep purple lilacs scattered over the lavendar background. The bed took Michael's breath and she looked at it in awe. A box bed, the huge antique needed the step provided to climb up to the high mattress, and it fit beautifully under the high ceiling. Michael turned to Mrs. Hall. "I may never want to go home."

Mrs. Hall smiled with obvious pride. "I'd forgotten you never saw the house, Michael." Then she frowned and her voice displayed her obviously hurt feelings. "I did send you an invitation to come to the grand opening."

"Oh, I'm sorry. I don't know what to say. I never received an invitation. I'm so sorry I missed it."

"You never got it?" When Michael shook her head, Mrs. Hall looked perplexed and muttered. "I knew I should have followed up with a phone call." She walked over and smoothed the already smooth spread and turned to J.B. "You can put the suitcases down on the luggage rack." She bustled to the door. "I'd better get back to the kitchen and get our dinner on the table. Are you sure you can't stay?"

"Yes, ma'am. I wish I could. Somethin' really smells good, even all the way up here."

Mrs. Hall laughed. "That's roast chicken with mushrooms and wild rice. If you change your mind, I'll set a place."

J.B. set Michael's luggage down. "Well, darlin', I guess I'd better go and let you get settled in. I'll come by in the morning, whenever you say, and take you anywhere you want to go. Seven-forty-five okay?"

"That's too early for court. But you can take me to my car. I'll have time to go to the office before my client and I have to appear."

"Seven-forty-five then." J.B. put his hand in the middle of her back and quickly bending toward her, he kissed her on the lips. He heard Michael's gasp as he walked toward the door. Now he'd done it. He wondered if she'd wait around for him to pick her up in the morning. He ran down the stairs and out the front door, whistling *The Most Beautiful Girl in the World.*

Michael stood, stunned, her fingers pressed to her lips and a bemused smile on her face. She couldn't believe the feelings of warmth, of being loved and cherished, that so brief a contact with his lips could engender. She stood for long minutes slowly stroking her lips and remembering how his mouth felt on hers. For the first time, the brief contact had left her unafraid.

She'd unpack later. After washing, she went to see if she could help Mrs. Hall. When she arrived the other guests were in the living room and Mrs. Hall had announced dinner.

There were three families at the Inn. Mrs. Hall made introductions around the table. "Mr. and Mrs. Armstrong and their children are from Nebraska." Six-year-old Teddy chattered on and on about visiting The Cowboy Hall of Fame. Jessica, age five, complained she'd wanted to go to the zoo.

"The Bakers and their daughter, Judy, are from Florida."

Judy looked to be suffering from a terminal case of ennui. Huge sighs, and poorly disguised gaping yawns characterized the teenager's time at the table. She ate little, pointedly sneering at the food on her plate, and would have left the table if not for the repeated glares from her mother.

"Mr. Roundtree is here from the panhandle on business. Mrs. Roundtree and the children came along to see the sights." Three children, all under the age of five, were fighting to remain well behaved, but were tired and unable to sit still. Finally their mother took them upstairs to bed.

Mrs. Hall chatted with all of them. Anyone looking in a window would have imagined the group to be a large family gathered for a holiday meal.

~ * ~

J.B. met Champ at the door and helped him carry in his tools and the replacement glass. He grinned at his sibling, "I appreciate you comin' over so quick."

"No problem, *big* brother."

"Watch it. You may be taller, but I'll always be older and I can still whip your butt."

Champ laughed. "Well, what've you got yourself into this time?"

"I'm workin' on a case." J.B. paced the living room briefly before sitting in the recliner.

"Since when do you take such a personal interest in a case?"

"Since I'm goin' to marry the woman who lives here."

"What?" Startled, Champ nearly dropped the pane of glass he held. "How well do you know her?"

49

"Well enough. I decided—the first time I laid eyes on her last year—she was the woman for me. I've been tryin' to get a date with her for weeks."

"Why couldn't you date her?"

"She wouldn't go out with me."

"Right. Tell me another one, brother. I know you. You date anyone you want. Always have."

"Not this time. She refused repeatedly." J.B. sighed. "I have to protect her. I want to catch this guy, more than I've wanted any perp before. I can't allow him to harm..."

"Whoa. What do you mean? Is some guy after her?"

"Yeah. She's bein' stalked." J.B. stood and paced. "On top of that, I think she's been raped. Just like Keely. I don't know when but..."

"My God. Are you out of your mind? You can't go back and change the past, J.B. You've carried that around for years now. Don't you think it's time to let it go?"

"I should have been there for her, Champ. One of us should have been there for Keely."

"Dammit, the reason you weren't there for Keely was because you were away at college. Even if you'd been here you couldn't have protected her."

"But if I'd been here we might have been able to help her. She needed me and I wasn't there."

"Do you think rescuin' this woman is goin' to make up for you believin' you let Keely down? You can't change what was."

Slow to anger, J.B.'s temper when unleashed was a force to behold. "Damn you, Champ, you don't know what you're *talkin'* about. Get your nose out of my business."

"Why would you want to take on somebody with that much excess baggage? How could you hope to have a normal life?"

"I'd take Michael, any way she'll allow, excess baggage and all."

"That's insane. If she's like Keely she's not going to be able to give you a normal relationship."

You have your definition of 'normal' and I have mine. Now fix the damned window before I decide I don't want to let you live."

~ * ~

Michael didn't remember ever feeling so relaxed and at peace. She watched these families and realized she wanted one of her own. She'd never have that. She fought to stem the tears that threatened. She looked down as Jessica tugged her sleeve.

"Hey, lady, didja ever thee the heffelumps at the thzoo?"

"Yes, I have. They're lovely. Elephants are one of my favorites. Do you have other animals you like to visit?"

"Oh, yeth, I love bears. I like to frow peanuts at 'em."

The doorbell pealed and Mrs. Hall answered. She returned to the dining room carrying a florist's box.

"Michael, that rascal's putting his heart and soul into courting you. You'd better latch on to him before someone grabs him out from under your nose."

Michael laughed. "Mrs. Hall, J.B. and I are just friends. He was pulling your leg earlier. Well, that's not exactly true. He *has* asked me for a date, but I told him...well, I don't have time for dates. My practice keeps me too busy."

"Child, there is nothing in this life more important than finding your life's mate, the keeper of your heart. If you've found him, don't let him slip through your fingers." She handed Michael the box and stood back, waiting to see what kind of flowers J.B. might have sent. "I'll bet he sent you roses."

Michael shuddered at the word 'roses' then untied the ribbon to remove the lid. With a huge smile on her face she folded back the tissue paper, and gasped as she convulsively pushed the box to the floor.

~ * ~

J.B. drove down the gravel road, dust boiling in a spiral behind his car. He turned beneath arched uprights proclaiming this Anderson land. Only coming 'home' ever evoked this feeling of peace. Under the cottonwood he got out and surveyed land that had nurtured his family since the Land Run of 1889.

"J.B., you rascal, get in this house."

"Hey, gorgeous. What have you been up to?" He loped over, scooped her up, and whirled her in a circle.

"Put me down, you fool. I'm too old for your games."

He set her down and stepped back to look at her. "Mom, you're still more beautiful than almost anyone I know."

She smiled. "Come in and tell me about her." In the house they headed for the kitchen, the family's gathering place.

J. B grinned. "Her? What her?"

"J.B., you were five when you told me, 'You're the beautifullest mama in the whole world.' Later, it was 'Beautiful Lady, can I have the car?' Now, suddenly, I'm 'more beautiful than *almost* anyone you know'." She grinned. "And it's about time. I was beginning to think you'd never make me a grandmother."

"Well, it hasn't gotten that far yet, but I'm workin' on it as hard as I can."

She chuckled. "On the grandbabies?"

His face turned red. "Uh, well, no. It's a bit soon."

"What's her name, J.B.?"

"Michael Mainwaring. She's an..."

"Ah, the attorney who defended Lincoln Maitland last year."

"Yes. If I have my way, Mom, she'll be your new daughter." He reached for the coffeepot. "Changing the subject, I haven't heard from Keely in quite a while."

She sighed. "She's not doing well. A couple of weeks ago, the husband of one of her patients trotted up to her in the parking lot of the hospital. He only wanted to say thank you. It was after dark. She went into hysterics."

He winced. "Is she ever goin' to have a normal life?"

"Not the way she's living it. It isn't normal to exclude the entire male population from one's life."

"Mom, I still feel so guilty about Keely." When she started to protest, he shook his head. "I know I couldn't have prevented it. I was too far away. But I always protected my Sunshine Girl and I failed her this time."

"No, J.B., that boy failed her. He was responsible for protecting her. He did the opposite."

"I know." He glanced away for a moment. "Mom, I'm not sure, but I think the same thing happened to Michael."

"Oh, dear God." She shuddered. "How is she handling it?"

"Not well, but if I'm right, it happened a long time ago."

The phone in J.B.'s inside coat pocket jingled.

Four

Startled and shocked, Mrs. Hall ran to Michael. She looked at the box that lay on the floor, the contents scattered under the table. Anger clouded her features as she saw the dead roses splayed over the carpet. "That's not funny," she hissed. She glanced at Michael, who sat and stared at the mess on the floor.

"Michael? Sweetie." She knelt and grabbed Michael's hand, alternately stroking and patting. When that brought no response she gently caressed Michael's cheek. "Come on, love. You're all right now."

Some of the guests stood watching, unsure whether or not to become involved. One of the men, after fidgeting for a short time, walked over beside Mrs. Hall and squatted down. "Is there anything I can do to help?"

"Yes, please. Would you moisten a wash cloth in cold water and bring it to me?" She looked at her friend, and smoothed the hair back from her temple. "Such a sweet girl to have so much trouble."

Michael's body jerked and she shook her head, as if to negate what her eyes told her.

He's found me. He's found me here, too.

She was breathing much too fast. Mrs. Hall feared Michael would hyperventilate. "Shhh. You're okay, Michael."

Michael raised her head and looked around. "Oh, God. Why is he doing this to me? Why?"

"Shhh, Michael, you're all right. Calm down." When Michael struggled to stand Mrs. Hall pushed on her shoulders, "No, no. Stay where you are for a few minutes."

"Here you go, Mrs. Hall." The guest extended the moist washcloth. "Is there anything else I can do?"

"No, thanks. This'll be fine."

"Maybe I could help her to the couch for you. That way you won't have to kneel on the floor."

Amanda Hall smiled up at him, thinking she was very lucky with the guests who chose to stay at her home. "You're very kind but I think we'll wait a few minutes for Ms. Mainwaring to get her feet back under her. Figuratively speaking, of course."

"I'm fine, and I think I can stand without difficulty."

Amanda shook her head. "No, you rest for bit more. You're still pale as a ghost and we're not in any hurry here."

Several minutes passed as Mrs. Hall gently wiped Michael's face with the cloth. Michael became more and more agitated wanting to get away from being the center of attention. She was not at all comfortable in the situation. "Please, Mrs. Hall. I'm really okay."

At last Mrs. Hall allowed her to get on her feet, and insisted on walking beside her to the sofa. Holding Michael's elbow, she watched every step as if Michael was a frail eighty year old woman. "Mrs. Hall, please don't be concerned about me." She didn't want to seem ungrateful. This dear lady only wanted to help, but Michael had reached a decision as she sat there attempting to control her fear. And she wanted to begin now.

At the sofa she had no choice but to sit down unless she wanted to do bodily injury to Amanda Hall. With a sigh, she collapsed onto the soft cushions. "Thank you, Mrs. Hall."

"Call me Amanda. Now, you sit down here and stay put." Not wanting to cause Mrs. Hall any more trouble, Michael complied. She could think just as easily here as anywhere.

Mrs. Hall bustled over to the telephone, dialed a familiar number and waited for it to be answered. The moment she heard J.B.'s voice, she took a deep breath and launched her attack. "James Buchanan Anderson, I'm ashamed of you. I know you like your little practical jokes, but this isn't funny." Amanda Hall shook her index finger as though J.B. stood in front of her. "I don't see how you could possibly consider this a joke. You frightened this child nearly out of her wits. And me, too." From her pocket she produced a handkerchief and wiped her forehead. "What? I'm sorry. What did you say?" Using the handkerchief in her hand, Amanda swiped at the nonexistent dust on the table where the telephone sat. "But, I thought...I mean, she..." Mrs. Hall, for one of the first times in her life, was at a loss for words. "Well...uh."

After taking a moment in which she pulled herself together, she squared her shoulders and with a brief abrupt nod, spoke into the phone. "J.B., I'm sorry. I thought you sent her this box of dead roses." Amanda tucked the handkerchief back in her pocket and put her hand to her mouth as she listened. "Yes, all right. I'll lock up and we'll see you in a few minutes." She hung up, looking more than a little chagrined.

She turned from the phone and saw one of her guests start to pick up the flowers. "No. Don't touch them. They're evidence in a police investigation. I think it would be a good idea if we all just sat here and waited for Detective Anderson to arrive. He'll be here shortly."

Michael sat on the couch in the parlor. From where she sat she could still see the roses. A sudden shaft of rage shot through her as swiftly as an arrow to the target. *How dare he invade this house with his sickness? How dare he involve Mrs.*

Hall and her guests? She didn't need this kind of thing in her house. This is going to stop. I won't ever again let him scare me. And I won't allow him to disrupt my life anymore.

Michael stood up from the couch and walked to the window to look out at the street. She didn't expect to see the man standing out there. He wasn't an idiot, she'd give him that. But he was a fool if he thought she'd take any more of this without fighting back. She would take no more of his abuse. She would no longer sit around like a shooting gallery duck, just waiting on the bastard to come after her.

What are my options? I could get a gun. No, that's not my style. I don't think I could actually shoot someone. So, what else is available? I'm not a tiny woman. That should count for something. Maybe I can learn to protect myself with Karate, or Judo. That might work. Could I take a martial arts course? Are there such things readily available?

"Mrs. Hall, may I..."

"Amanda. You're to call me Amanda."

Michael's face flushed, and she looked up and smiled. "Amanda. I'll remember from now on."

"May I help you with something, dear?"

"Where is your copy of the yellow pages?"

Amanda walked over and opened the drawer in the table and pulled out the thick volume. "Here you go."

"Thanks." She'd talk to J.B. about self-defense classes. She didn't have a clue which of the martial arts would be the best for self protection, but she'd find out. And she'd learn what she needed to know to protect herself. From this point on she would go on the offense. Having reached a decision she felt the tension drain from her body. For the first time since this mess began, she felt in control again.

She opened the book and looked for the Martial Arts listings. She saw listings for Judo, Ju-Jitsu, Karate, and Tai

Kwan Do, among others. She had a lot of choices, now all she had to do was research it and see which was best suited for her needs.

She stepped over to the window and looked out. She told herself she wasn't watching for J.B. *Where is he?* She thought she'd made her decision about what she needed to do to protect herself, so she didn't need him. *He should be here by now.* She almost convinced herself it didn't matter how long it took him to get there. *What's taking him so long?*

As she watched the street and thought about implementing her plan, J.B.'s car pulled into the driveway. *It's about time he got here.*

She smiled seeing him unfold his lanky frame from the car. A person could make book on the fact J.B. would clap that Stetson on his head before he had his body completely upright. She nearly laughed aloud when her thought became reality. Appearing to have only a casual interest, in case he was being observed, J.B. turned and looked around the neighborhood as he slipped into his jacket. He turned back toward the house, his long strides eating up the distance in record time.

When the doorbell rang Mrs. Hall was already on her way before Michael could move. J.B. walked in the door and as he bent to kiss Mrs. Hall's cheek, his eyes were busy searching for Michael. As soon as he located her and noted she was standing and appeared to be in good health, he looked toward the dining room. His eyes narrowed as he spied the roses spread over the carpet. He gave Mrs. Hall one final hug and headed in Michael's direction.

"Hello, J.B. I'm sorry Mrs. Hall dragged you back here." *Liar.* "It frightened me for a moment when the flowers arrived because I felt completely safe here. It wasn't the brightest I've ever been, feeling so confident he wouldn't know where I am. It's obvious, of course. He followed me here."

"No, darlin', he followed *us* and I apologize because I didn't pick up on the fact we had a tail. I'm gettin' real sloppy here lately, but that's goin' to change startin' right now." He put his hand at her waist and pulled her into his arms for a gentle hug. He didn't prolong it, and stepped back in almost the next second. "Are you all right now?"

"Yes." When she saw his raised eyebrow, she smiled. "I really am. Mrs. Hall wouldn't let me get out of the chair until *she* felt better. I think it scared her nearly to death."

He glanced over at their friend. "She does look a little peaked. You go tend to her and I'll take a look at these roses to see if he left us a clue this time." He turned toward the dining room and took only one long stride before she stopped him.

"First, J.B., I have a question." When he stopped and turned back toward her, the expression on her face startled him. He saw strength, determination, and courage. All emotions he'd never seen there before. Oh, he'd seen her attempts to display those emotions before, but—for the first time—this was the real thing.

It was obvious she still fought the fear. She pushed it back as if her fear was as substantial as concrete. But now it was obvious to anyone who cared to look—she, herself, was ready to do something about her situation. She looked hell-bent on solving her own problems, fighting her own demons, and ready to take no prisoners. He didn't remember ever being so proud of anyone before in his life.

He turned back, facing her straight on. "You've made a decision of some kind haven't you?"

"Yes. I want to know where I can take classes in one of the martial arts. I don't care which one. I want the one best suited for protecting myself."

J.B. smiled and nodded. *She really is ready to start fighting back. Finally.* "Good idea, sweetheart. I'll see what I can arrange."

He walked over to the dining room table and bent down to take a look at the florist's box and the flowers. There were no clues of any kind on the box, not even the name of a florist. Someone had access to blanks—boxes not yet printed with the florist's logo, name and address. *Another piece to the puzzle.*

J.B. looked over the contents of the box, hoping there'd be a note, some clue to point him in the right direction. Plain green tissue paper, plain white box. Roses could be purchased at any flower shop...or even grown in one's own garden. Could the perp be a gardener? But then there was the question again. Why would he be stalking Michael? None of this made any sense.

Anger began to boil and build, making him want to put his fist through the wall. Through anything. He wanted to punch someone's lights out. Particularly he wanted to knock the perp's teeth down his throat. Then he'd like to keep the momentum going, shove his fist on down until he could grab the son of a bitch by his... ankles and turn him wrong side out.

In frustration he ground his teeth. Why was this perp always one step ahead of him?

He felt the skin of his face tighten and the hair on his head stand on end. He had to ask the question. If he didn't, he could be spinning his wheels and getting nowhere for a long time. Unless they were being followed every minute of the day, only one person could keep up with where they were at all times. *Could Michael be sending the flowers to herself?*

He glanced at her, speculating on the possibilities. She looked so vulnerable. He could see the fear in her eyes. Could she be this good an actress?

He thought about it. Nah. She had to "act" when in the courtroom. It was all part of her profession. But that didn't make her a liar. It was all a part of her job.

Just as it was a part of his job to sometimes act as if he had more evidence than he actually did just to see if the suspect might confess. It was a part of the game played every day on the playing field of that sport they called "Justice".

No, he didn't think she was doing this herself. He recalled how frightened she had been at the courthouse and later at the hospital. She couldn't have faked that. The terror was too real.

He stood up and walked over to her as she stood where he'd left her, watching out the windows. He felt ashamed that he'd doubted her, even momentarily. He put his hand at her waist and turned her around to face him and spoke in muted tones. "There isn't any point in hiding out here. He knows where you are. I'd rather not put Mrs. Hall in danger."

Michael closed her eyes, took a deep breath and nodded. She looked at him, understanding clear in her eyes. She kept her tone low. "I hadn't thought about that." Then she turned away and asked in a voice so soft and low it was obvious she'd meant the question for her ears only. "Have I always been so self absorbed that I didn't see the forest for the trees?"

He pulled her against him, her back nestled to his chest, his arm around her waist. He put his mouth near her ear and spoke just above a whisper. "I don't think you're self absorbed at all, darlin'. What I think is you've been driven to the end of your wits by this bastard and I intend to put a stop to his little game A.S.A.P."

"What should I do? I can't go home because of the broken window."

She felt J.B.'s smile against her neck, then he muttered, "Actually, you can. The window is fixed."

She pulled out of his arms and whirled around. "How in the name of common sense did you get it fixed so fast?"

J.B. grinned, looking pleased with himself. "My brother owns a construction company. I called and told him I wanted it fixed yesterday. I'm his big brother, and having a little bit of good sense, he high tailed it over to your house and had the window fixed in short order." He chuckled. "He always did what I told him to do."

She grinned. "Always?"

"Oh, yeah. He likes his head exactly where it is."

She feigned a look of shock. "Are you telling me you beat up on your baby brother?"

His grin widened for a moment as memories flashed through his mind. "Sure I did. On all of them. Mom told us we had to settle all our differences among ourselves." He grinned unrepentantly. "The last time she settled any of our fights we were all small enough that, out of the dog pile of swinging arms and flailing fists, she could wade in, pick us up by the waistband of our jeans and toss us in five different directions."

He chuckled, and his eyes became unfocused as he remembered. "She told us then that it was the last time she'd referee. She said if we broke any bones we'd lose our allowances until the medical bills were paid. That slowed us down a tad, but it didn't stop us. Hell, there were times when any one of us would have given up our allowance for life just to beat up on a brother.

"Some day remind me to tell you what I did when Benjie tricked Keely into climbing the big cottonwood tree in the back yard, then climbed down and left her there."

Her voice displaying her envy, Michael said wistfully, "It must have been fun growing up in a house full of siblings."

"Uh huh, it was, for the most part. We always had someone to play with." He was startled by the suddenness of the change when he heard her next remark.

"I guess I'd better go pack my things so we can head home." She thought about being alone in that big house and momentarily her stomach quaked. *No! I'm going to be fine.* She headed for the stairs, her long legs making short work of the trip.

Within five minutes she was back down the stairs, and calling for Amanda.

Mrs. Hall scurried in from the kitchen, the overhead light sparkling in her silver hair. "Yes, Michael? Oh, you're leaving? But you don't have to do that. Don't you think it would be better to stay here?" She looked at J.B. "J.B., she'd be a lot safer here."

"Well, you could be right, but then we don't want to put any of your other guests at risk, now do we?"

Amanda's mouth gaped open and her eyes widened. "Oh, dear me. I hadn't thought about that." She turned to Michael and took her hand. "But will you be all right?"

"Yes. I'm going to be in my own home. I can lock my house and be as snug as a bug in a rug. Thanks to J.B.'s brother, my window is repaired faster than I ever thought possible. Don't worry about me, Amanda." She bent, put her arm around Amanda's shoulders and hugged her friend and client. Placing her cheek atop the silver pouffe of hair worn in the Gibson Girl style, she murmured, "Don't fret, dear friend, everything will work out. You'll see."

She turned to J.B. and smiled, looking more like she was heading for an amusement park than going home. "Okay, cowboy, let's hit the trail."

J.B. looked at her, surprised that she seemed so self assured. *Either something happened between when she went upstairs and when she came down, or she's acting for Mrs. Hall's benefit. Yeah, that's probably it.* He convinced himself that's what she was doing, so he was surprised when her demeanor didn't change once they were in the car. He drove down the street mulling it over in his mind, trying to figure out what was going on with her.

Michael wondered why he was silent. He drove with an above-average skill and competence while taking note of oncoming vehicles as well as watching those behind them. She figured it out and asked, "J.B., are you watching to see if someone is following us?"

He glanced at her before turning his gaze back to the front. "Um hmm. I'm keeping my eyes open. I want to know if a car makes the same turns we do. It's too dark now to do more than watch headlights."

"I wondered why you were taking such a circuitous route. We could have been to my house twice in the time it's taking us."

"Well, darlin', it could be I'm just enjoyin' your company, you know."

She watched his face illuminated in the glare of headlights from oncoming cars. A strong face, clear eyed, honest. Rather a 'what you see is what you get' kind of man.

He looked over at her and smiled.

"Nah. I believe you're perfectly capable of prolonging the trip to spend more time with me, but somehow I don't think that's what's going on here."

"Yes it is... It just isn't the only thing that's going on."

A few minutes later they pulled into her driveway and J.B. turned to her. "Wait a second until I come around." He quickly got out of the car and paused a moment to take a look around.

Michael snorted and muttered, "Not that again." She gave a fatalistic shrug and again spoke aloud. "If he's going to shoot me, he's going to shoot me, even if he has to go through you to do it, big guy." She opened the door and was out of the car before he could make it around the back. She stood up and looked around for a moment.

"Dammit, Michael. I told you to wait a minute."

She smiled. "I heard you—darlin'." She sauntered up to her front door, leaving him standing there with his mouth open and his eyes agape. She dawdled along as if she didn't have a care in the world, and all the time she needed to get inside the house. Having arrived at the front door, she leisurely searched her purse for her key.

J.B. looked around, and growled, "You need a keeper." His long strides rapidly brought him to the steps and he took them two at a time.

"Really? I thought that's what you were doing."

Her grin put him over the edge of whatever control he had. He glared at her, stuffed his hand in his pocket, pulled out the key she'd given him, unlocked the door and, not too gently, pushed her through the door.

Inside the house he grabbed her by her shoulders forcing her toward him. "Now, sweetheart, I want an explanation. What's changed?"

"What do you mean, 'what's changed?'"

"I think you know exactly what I'm talkin' about. You were a basket case earlier today, then shortly before leaving Mrs. Hall's you began to behave as if you haven't a care in the world."

Michael glared down at his hands on her shoulders, then a determined look settled on her face and she snapped. "I've decided to go on the offensive, that's all. I'm tired of him turning my life upside down."

J.B. looked at her, his gaze going over her features as if reading every pore for information. Then he looked into her eyes and smiled at what he saw reflected there. "That's good. Oh, yes, I like that." He looked as proud as a father whose child just brought home something precious she'd made at kindergarten.

Unaccustomed to receiving praise, Michael basked in it. "Can you tell me what methods of self protection are available for someone in a hurry to learn?"

"There are several methods, but unfortunately they all take time to learn."

"I don't have a lot of time. I want to feel secure when I walk through the halls of the court house, and I especially want to feel safe in my own home."

"I know, sweetheart, but we're talking years here, to become an expert."

"I don't need to be a black belt, or whatever it's called. If this guy comes up and grabs me from behind I want to be trained well enough to throw him over my shoulder and then, if necessary, break something important—though I'd settle for an arm or a leg. I will no longer be his victim. It is as simple—and as complicated as that."

"Okay. The first thing you need to know is what to do the next time he calls."

"What do you mean?"

"There are a lot of experts in the field who believe the best thing you can do when you get an obscene or harassing phone call is to quietly hang up the phone the moment you realize who is on the other end. Try not to gasp or say anything at all, and above all don't shout at the caller, scream or slam the phone down."

"I think I can do that. I never answer the phone on the first ring anymore anyway. It takes until the second or third ring for me to get up my nerve. Now about the martial arts. Which method do you think is the best?"

"For throws, probably Judo. If you're interested in learning how to strike and kick, then Karate would most likely be the better choice, but if you want to go whole hog, take a course in Ju Jitsu. It covers all the bases."

"How long would that take?"

"That's the drawback. At least a couple of years."

"We have already discussed the fact that I don't have a couple of years."

"But there are courses of a few weeks that might give you enough to do what you want to do. Let me check into it to be sure, because, to be honest with you, I'm no expert. I got a little of it while in training at the academy. They teach a forty hour course. There is so much more to know on the subject, that, by comparison, what I know about it you could write on the head of a pin and still have room for the Gettysburg Address." He arched an eyebrow. "How's that for honesty?"

"Admirable. Most men I've met consider themselves experts on every subject that comes up in a conversation."

"Hey, darlin', that's a little rough, don't you think?"

"Maybe a little. But I can only speak from my own experience."

"I'll check into this tomorrow and have the information for you by the time you get ready to come home."

"All right, then I guess we'd better call it a night. It's getting late." Michael started toward the foyer, intending to escort him to the front door. She stopped cold when J.B.'s question registered on her consciousness.

"Where do you want me to sleep, darlin'?"

She whirled around. "What? Sleep? You're planning on sleeping here?"

"Of course I'm sleepin' here. Where did you think I was goin' to sleep?"

"Why, at your own home, of course."

"No, no, sugar. I guess we're still not clear on the subject. I'm stickin' to you like a cockle burr to a collie dog. You might as well get used to this ugly mug, because it's goin' to be your shadow for the foreseeable future. At the very least, until we nail this guy..." His voice dropped to a barely audible mutter. "...and if I have anything to say about it, for the rest of your life."

"What was that?"

"What was what?" He turned around and took off his coat, draped it over the back of a chair, then walked over to the couch. "If you have a pillow and a blanket I can sleep right here on your couch."

Fear raced through her body as quickly as a car running a lap at the Indy. "No." She backed up a step. "No, J.B." Another backward step toward the front door. "That's not a good idea."

"Yes, it is. If I'm here when he calls then I can help you get through the rest of the night." He looked at her, his eyebrow cocked. "That's why you have circles under your eyes, isn't it? He calls and wakes you and then you're afraid to go back to sleep."

"Yes."

The whisper was so soft he didn't really hear it, only saw the movement of her mouth. Her tongue darted out nervously, moistening the velvet softness and his gaze followed the movement of her tongue. He wanted to kiss her, to feel the yielding of her lips against his. Most of all, he wanted her to kiss him, put her arms around his neck, and let him hold her. Her body would fit his exactly like a key fit a lock.

"J.B.? Why are you staring at me like that?"

"Oh." He ducked his head, his cheeks reddened slightly and he raked his hand through his hair. "Sorry, darlin', I guess I drifted off for a minute there. It's been a long day. What say we hit the hay?"

"But... Where will... How can you.... J.B., that sofa isn't long enough for you to stretch out on."

"I'll be fine. Just bring me a pillow and a blanket. I can hang my feet off over the arms. It won't kill me."

"I'm not going to be comfortable with a mmm... mma... with someone else in the house."

"Well, sugar, lock your door if you're afraid, but it's insultin' as hell to think you still don't trust me."

"I'm sorry." She looked ready to burst into tears. "I'm sorry, J.B., I don't mean to insult you, but you see, I... uh... I..." She stood wringing her hands, her distress obvious on her face and in her body language.

"Don't worry about it, Michael. Just go to your room, lock your door and then if you still don't feel secure, put a chair against it."

She ran through the foyer, into her room and he heard the click of the lock. Seconds later he also heard the sound of a chair being scooted against the door. He closed his eyes, tipped his head back and sucked air in through his clenched teeth. Would he *ever* get her to trust him?

He looked at his watch. Nearly midnight. "Don't they say 'Time flies when you're havin' fun?' I hope someone lets me know when the fun begins. I sure wouldn't want to miss it." He snorted. "Anderson, they've got a net waitin' for you."

He sat down, pulled off his boots, grabbed his jacket off the back of the chair and putting his head on a sofa cushion, covered his shoulders with the jacket. A few minutes later he heard the unmistakable sound of the chair being scooted away from Michael's door. He didn't move, waiting to see what she might do next. Within seconds her door opened and she scurried over and dropped a blanket and pillow on top of him, muttered a hurried 'good night' and practically flew back to her room.

J.B. sat up and put the pillow behind his head and flipped the blanket out and allowed it to flutter down over him. After a while he relaxed and entered a dreamlike state, envisioning a time when he would sleep every night holding Michael in his arms. The fantasy led him into deeper and deeper sleep.

~ * ~

Michael lay in her bed and, as her grandmother was fond of saying, she was as nervous as a long tailed cat in a room full of rocking chairs. She fidgeted. She tossed. And turned. She punched her pillows. She got out of bed and smoothed the sheets and blankets, crawled back into bed—and began the process all over again.

J.B. Anderson lying on her sofa led her mind in a direction she didn't want to go. She recalled his kiss... and how it felt. Every nuance came back as if it happened only moments ago.

She thought about his caring concern for her safety. Of how he always tried to put himself between her and any perceived threat. And the way he came running the moment he thought she was in trouble.

He was kind, and considerate. He had a dry wit, and she loved his sense of fun. And yes, he was tenacious. He refused to go away just because she asked him to leave her alone. He was so determined she didn't think she'd ever get rid of him. She smiled. "I could count on him to always be there." Her whisper startled her and she jumped, surprised she'd spoken her thoughts aloud.

She raised her head and looked at the bedside clock. Half past one. She'd better get a little sleep or she wouldn't be able to function in court in the morning. She turned on her left side facing the window and drifted to sleep watching the shadows of the leaves cast by the bright light of the moon.

Michael slept soundly, dreaming of warm arms holding her safe. Of soft lips smiling before swooping down for a quick kiss. And of laughter.

A sound intruded. She fought to drift up from the dregs of slumber. While her mind lay muffled in the cotton wool of sleep, the sound invaded again. She struggled to identify it. A ripping sound. Fabric tearing?

Suddenly she was mentally alert before her eyes opened. She wondered, did the alarm buzz? Her eyes fluttered open. Like a living thing, darkness as black as pitch hovered in the corners, ready to suck her into its inky desolation. She raised her head and peered at the bedside clock. After blinking a moment, her eyes focused on the digital readout. Two-thirty.

Something moved in her peripheral vision. A shadow materialized at the window. Like a doe trapped in the beams of oncoming headlights and frozen by fear, Michael couldn't move a muscle to protect herself. Her breath came in short, sharp pants. Gasped in through her open mouth, it whistled into her lungs.

She watched his arms raise high above his head. In his hands he clasped a knife. Riveted by the sight, her heart pounded—pounded, too fast. She couldn't think. Her breath rushed out leaving her lungs empty. She fought to pull it back through her wide open mouth.

She shook her head in negation. She wanted to deny the evidence before her eyes. Her hands gripped the comforter. Rhythmically wadding and releasing the fabric. She heard a scream, unaware it issued from her throat. Nor, in her terror, did she realize for whom she called. "Jaaaa Beeee!"

Five

J.B. raced silently. Thoughts, as rapid as laser blasts, flashed through his mind. He paused and listened at the door. His heart froze at her cries of terror. *Is he in there? Think! Dammit, think! Do what you know.*

He pushed the door. It didn't budge. He remembered. She'd locked it. Had blocked it with a chair.

"Michael. Open the door." The screaming stopped. She continued to whimper.

Terror roared through him. He kicked the door above the knob. Wood splintered. The chair shuddered, then crashed on its side. Gliding through the narrow opening, he slid into the room. Crouched against the wall, arms thrust out, his hands grasped the gun, an extension of himself. He swung his body in a half circle, checking out the room. Bright moonlight, dimmed only slightly by sheer curtains, poured in through the windows. It shone like a spotlight on Michael's bed.

No intruder here. Only Michael. A wave of relief momentarily turned his bones to jelly. Huddled against the headboard, her body clearly defined by the luminescence, her hands clutched the comforter to her throat. The bright radiance sparkled off the tears gliding down her face.

J.B. spoke gently. "Michael, shhh. It's all right, darlin'." The whimpers stopped. He jammed the gun into the waistband at the back of his jeans and stepped to the side of the bed. Speaking in a soft, reassuring voice he crooned, "You're fine. I'm here. I won't let anything hurt you." He wanted to take her in his arms, hold her, comfort her. Now was not the time.

He flipped on the lamp, tipped her face up and spoke louder. "Michael? Listen to me. No one is here. It was only a bad dream." Cupping her face between his hands, his thumbs gently massaged her temples. "Sweetheart, can you hear me?"

"Yes." The sibilant whisper hissed out between staccato inhalations. She shuddered. "J.B.? Is he gone?"

"Michael, you had a bad dream. That's all. Only a bad dream. You're okay, and I'm here. No one is here except us." He sat on the side of her bed, watching her face for any sign his close proximity exacerbated her fear.

When she showed no aversion to his nearness he scooted a little nearer and took her hands. Her grip was so hard that, within seconds, his fingers tingled from lack of circulation.

"J.B., he was trying to come in my window. I saw him."

J.B.'s gaze swung to the window. "I'll go see." He walked to the window and looked out. He saw no sign anybody had been there. Nothing moved except the tree limbs. As they swayed gently in the breeze, their shadows danced across the grass in the yard.

"Sweetheart, it was a bad dream. Nobody is out there." He walked back and sat down on the side of the bed, and took her hands. Looking into her eyes he spoke softly. "You screamed and I ran in here. It took only a minute or two. You were alone."

"J.B., it wasn't a dream. A man was here. He had a knife." She gripped his hands tighter and shook them. "I saw him, J.B." Her voice rose on a note of hysteria. "I saw him."

Unchecked tears continued to flow down her face and drip off her chin. J.B. freed his hand from her grip and pulled a tissue from the box on the night table. Trying to bring a sense of normalcy back for her, he said, "Here. Blow your nose, darlin'." He grabbed another tissue and, taking her chin in the palm of one hand, he gently patted her cheeks dry. "Now, listen to me. You only had a bad dream. There's no one out there."

He could see the fear receding from her eyes. Taking its place were determination, and a little anger. "J.B., listen to me! I'm not crazy and it *wasn't* a dream. A noise woke me. I thought it was..." She paused, her brow wrinkling in thought. "...it sounded like fabric tearing."

Trying reason he asked, "Could you have dreamed the noise?"

More insistent, she said, "No." She leaned toward him, arguing her case. "I was dreaming, but it was a *good* dream. The sound is what woke me." Her voice rising higher, she pleaded, "Why won't you believe me?"

"It's not that I don't believe you, darlin'. But, think about it... We'll rule out all possibilities. *Could* it have been somethin' else?" He glanced at the window trying to find an explanation that would give her peace of mind. "Maybe a tree branch brushing against the window screen?"

Anger, barely repressed, hoarsened her voice. "J.B., I'm not an idiot. I know what I heard. And what I saw." She sighed. "At first, before I was completely awake, I'll admit I was confused. I wondered if it—if what I heard could be the alarm clock buzzing. I glanced at it. I read two-thirty. Out of the corner of my eye I saw something move at the window."

"Look at the window now, Michael. You can see the shadow of the tree limb. Could that be what you saw and heard?"

Her temper broke free. "Dammit, J.B., why are you insisting it was the tree limb? When I looked toward the window I saw a man." Her voice grew louder. "I repeat. I. Am. Not. An. Idiot. I can tell the difference between the shadow of a tree limb and the shadow of a man. There was a man standing there. He had a knife." She clenched her teeth, closed her eyes and took a deep breath, ending on a shudder. She opened her eyes, leaned forward and stared intently into his eyes. Her voice softened, lowered to just above a whisper. "I saw the knife, J.B. He raised it over his head, like this." She demonstrated what she'd seen. "Now, does that look like a tree limb?"

"All right, darlin', I'll go outside and check it out."

She shuddered again, and grabbed his wrist. "No. Please, don't go out there, J.B."

"How can I check it out if I don't go out there?"

She grabbed him, throwing her arms around his neck. Just as quickly, she realized he was shirtless and released him. Her eyes widened as she took in his appearance. A thick mat of golden brown hair covered his chest—and arrowed down to disappear into the waistband of the navy briefs peeking out of his—his *unsnapped* jeans. Shoeless, shirtless, hair uncombed. A five-o'clock shadow decorating his jaw, he looked even more like he'd stepped off the silver screen out of a western. She leaned back and pulled the comforter up to her shoulders. She liked what she saw but he made her nervous.

"He has a knife. What if he stabs you?" In her concern for him she forgot her own fears. Dropping the comforter, she grabbed his shoulders and looked into his eyes. Her gaze intense, she attempted to convey her fears. "I don't want you hurt." She briefly rested her forehead against his shoulder. "I couldn't stand it if he hurt you. Please don't go out there."

"I'm a cop, darlin'. I'm trained to take care of myself."

"But don't you need a back up, or is that only on TV?"

The warmth of her concern washed over him like a gentle wave on the shore. Even if she was using it as an excuse to keep him near her, he couldn't bring himself to leave her alone.

He wanted to hold her, fit her to him like a second skin and keep her safe. And have her touch him, hold him. He ached to run his hands over her silk and satin skin and pull her so close he couldn't tell where he ended and she began. He wanted to breathe in her essence, taste the warm honey of her mouth. And he didn't dare. It would scare the living daylights out of her.

"Okay, darlin'. I'll stay here with you. But let me make a quick phone call, okay?"

When she nodded, J.B. picked up the phone from her night table and walked away as far as the cord would reach. He dialed the number and after only one ring, his buddy responded. Speaking softly, he rumbled, "Shag? I need another favor." He glanced over his shoulder and saw Michael listening to every word. "Michael saw someone at her window tonight. He had a knife." He listened quietly for a moment, then spoke even more softly. "She's afraid to be left alone long enough for me to go check it out." He pushed his hand into his pocket, pulled out a quarter and walked it over his fingers. "Can you come over and bring a kit, just in case he left footprints in the flower bed?" He nodded his head watching the quarter traverse his fingers in the opposite direction. "Thanks, Shag." He was quiet a moment, pocketed the quarter, then nodded. "Yeah. When you get here, ring the doorbell."

He walked back to the bedside, replaced the telephone on the table and sat down beside her. Trying to calm her, he talked quietly. "Shag Dexter is comin' over. He can check out the flower bed. If there are footprints out there he'll make a plaster cast. When we catch the bastard it'll be one more nail in his coffin. And I promise you, darlin', we *are* going to catch him. You have my word on that."

He wanted to ease her mind but didn't know how. He stroked the backs of her hands with his thumbs as he talked. Her grip didn't relax one iota.

She needed to occupy her mind with something mundane, something that didn't remind her of the terror that filled her life. "Tell me about Benjie leaving Keely in the tree." Her voice, though whisper thin, sounded stronger.

J.B. chuckled. "Benjie loved to climb trees. He'd pretend he was Robin Hood in Sherwood Forrest. At other times he was a king in hiding from an evil sorcerer."

"Was it fun to grow up with so many brothers?"

"Yeah. It was. Anyway, to get on with the story, when he was nine he climbed up the big cottonwood in the back yard. Keely wanted to climb up with him and she was only five."

"Five? She wanted to climb a big tree when she was five?"

"Uh huh. She had a lot of courage back then." He smiled in remembrance of the young Keely. "She couldn't get up to the lowest limb, even from the short ladder Benjie had used. So he climbed down and gave her a boost."

Michael's grip on J.B.'s hands relaxed. He turned and leaned against the headboard beside her. He watched out of the corner of his eyes as he continued to relate the incident.

"Keely was excited and climbed higher than Benjie. She was smaller and more easily supported by smaller limbs. She told us she felt like she could see all the way to Oklahoma City. It was being able to see so far that beckoned her to the very top of the tree. Benjie tried to talk her into comin' down, but by then she'd looked down."

"Dear God. What happened?" Michael stealthily moved, in small increments, away from J.B.

"I'd been out ridin' fence earlier and happened to see the R.E.C. truck down the road. They had a cherry-picker on their truck. I rode down and asked them if they'd help. Thank God they did. They were a lot closer than the fire department."

Michael was now sitting on the very far edge of the mattress. "You said to remind you what you did to Benjie."

"Aw, I didn't really do anything. I just threatened to hang him by his overall straps from that same tree." He could see her struggling with her discomfort at having a man sitting on her bed. She really made every effort to relax and take part in the conversation.

"J.B., who gave Champ his nickname? Does he box?"

He laughed. "No, he doesn't box. He really hated both his names, Chester Arthur." J.B.'s grin spread, nearly from ear to ear. "Mom called him Champ when he continually started fights in school. Actually she gave each of us our nicknames."

"So she called you J.B.," she attempted a smile, "which is short for James Buchanan, and..."

His head swivelled sharply in her direction as his eyes widened. "How'd you find out about that?"

"Amanda. When she called and yelled at you on the phone."

"Oh, yeah. I'd forgotten." He ducked his head. "I don't like bein' called James Buchanan. Mom knew it after the first day of school. So I became 'J.B.'"

"Then why did she name you James Buchanan?"

"She didn't. It was Dad. Every one of us is named after a U. S. president. Dad thought if he named us after important men, we might aspire to greatness someday."

"What about your sister? She's not named after a president."

He grinned. "No. Mom and Dad had a deal. He'd name the boys. She'd name the girls." He chuckled. "I remember one time at the dinner table, Mom said she didn't think she was ever goin' to get the chance to give one of her babies a name 'cause she just kept shellin' out ornery boys."

Michael laughed. It was a small one and followed by a shuddering breath, but still a laugh. He felt he'd made progress with that tiny bit of mirth.

"What are all your brothers named..." She smiled. "...and what are they called?"

He grinned at her. "Well, I'm the oldest then John Tyler is next in line. Ty is a doctor in Oklahoma City. After Ty is Franklin Pierce. Cowboy works on the ranch and raises the prettiest Santa Gertrudis cattle you'll ever see. You already know Champ owns a construction company. Benjamin Harrison, the infamous Benjie, is a veterinarian."

"And your sister?"

A wave of sadness rippled over him and he glanced away for a moment. "Keely Anne is an RN in Tulsa. I'm very proud of her. She struggled hard to get her nursing degree. She fought an uphill battle emotionally and still graduated in the top five percent of her class."

She looked at him and smiled tenderly. "You love her very much, don't you?"

"Yeah. I do." He stood and smiled down at her. "Now, do you think you can go back to sleep?" He thought if she went back to sleep he'd go out and look for tracks himself rather than wait on Shag. He needed to know if she'd dreamed the whole incident.

"I don't feel sleepy right now."

He wracked his brain to think of something to quiet her enough she'd be able to sleep. He smiled when he remembered. He had something perfect for the job. "Michael, will you go into the living room with me?"

She looked at him warily. "Why?"

"You need to rest or you'll have dark circles under your eyes." He winked. "I don't think you want to go into court tomorrow lookin' like a raccoon." He'd hoped to get a smile but she continued to stare at him, her eyes as big as saucers.

"Yes. I'll go in the living room. Did you want to talk some more?" She threw back the covers and stood beside the bed, unaware of the picture she made in the white sheer batiste nightgown. Even though it covered her from neck to ankles her body was clearly outlined by the lamp behind her.

"No, not talk. I have somethin' else in mind." He was aware, after seeing her in that gown, he'd have a tough battle with himself for the rest of the night. The reaction of his body to the sight would scare her to death. He wanted her to feel comfortable with him, to want his arms around her as much as he wanted to hold her.

She'd learn. It would take time, but he had plenty of that. He could wait. He grabbed the robe from the foot of the bed and dropped it around her shoulders, then taking her hand he led her into the living room and settled her on the couch.

He walked to the stereo. When he'd come over with Champ to fix the window, he brought a stack of CDs. He sorted through them, then turned and smiled at her. "I have something here I think you'll enjoy. It's from my collection." He slid the CD into the slot. As the music poured into the room, he took a chance and picked her up. She stiffened. Walking over to the recliner, he settled into it, holding her on his lap.

He felt tension still controlling her body. "Just sit back and try to relax." He pulled her against him, placing the back of her head on his right shoulder. "Close your eyes, darlin', and allow the music to ease you. Imagine this beautiful music carryin' your fear into the darkness outside this room."

Michael's eyes closed and she listened for a short time. He could feel her muscles relaxing slightly as the music worked its magic. Minutes later she looked up, her gaze meeting his. "Did you say this was from your collection?"

"Uh huh. It's one of my favorites." He smiled before closing his eyes and letting his head fall back on the chair.

Her voice full of wonder, she murmured, "What is it, J.B.? It sounds familiar but I can't place it."

"That's Julian Lloyd Webber on the cello, playing his brother Andrew's *Music of the Night.* You've probably heard it sung more often than played."

Michael smiled. "I'm not sure *Phantom of the Opera* is a good choice right now but this is one of the loveliest versions I've ever heard." She turned and curled into his arms, her right arm going up to his left shoulder, her head more firmly on his right and her face nestled into his neck. "It soothes the soul."

"Yes. Exactly." J.B. loved that she cuddled with him. He began to soothe her gently with his hands, rubbing up and down her back. He tried to ignore the tension building in his own body as her breast pressed against his chest and her scent invaded his nostrils.

"I would have pegged you for a country music fan," she mumbled, and yawned.

"Mmm hmm, I like that, too," he rumbled softly. Very gradually he felt her tension lessen. Her breathing eased into a gentle rhythm. She slept at last. He'd hold her the rest of this night—and the rest of her life—if she'd allow it.

And he'd find out who was trying to drive her insane.

Headlights flashed over the windows. He hoped they indicated Shag's arrival. J.B. didn't want to disturb Michael but he wanted to talk to his buddy as well as go out and look under her bedroom window for tracks. He pulled the lever, folding down the leg support and sat up. Holding Michael in his arms he stood, walked to the couch and placed her there as tenderly as he would an infant. She never made a sound. He placed a soft kiss on her forehead and went to the front door.

When he opened it, Shag stood with his hand outstretched, his finger extended toward the doorbell. J.B. snaked his hand out and caught Shag's wrist just short of his target. "Shhh. Don't wake Michael."

"You act like a father who's worried about me waking the baby." Shag grinned.

J.B. reddened slightly. "Well, she's only been asleep for a few minutes and it wasn't a pleasant experience we're talkin' about here."

Shag shrugged. "No, I don't suppose it was. Let's go look for those tracks." Shag started down the steps and turned back to J.B. "Aren't you coming?"

"Yeah. Hold on while I pull on my boots." He pulled them on, looked back over his shoulder toward the living room, heaved a sigh and turned to Shag. "Okay. Let's go." He hoped she didn't wake up while he was out of the house.

The two men walked around to the side of the house, J.B. leading the way. When they were within five feet of Michael's bedroom window they stopped. Shag turned on the large, powerful flashlight he carried and directed the beam around the area.

Shag muttered, "No tracks."

"Not surprisin'. We haven't had any rain in a few weeks."

Shag arched an eyebrow. "Yeah, but doesn't she water her lawn like everybody else?"

J.B. sounded disgusted. "I don't know." He looked at his partner. "She was terrified. I thought she was havin' a bad dream. She convinced me she saw someone. Holdin' a knife."

"Okay, let's take a look at the flowerbed." At the side of the house Shag flashed the beam of the flashlight. They peered intently at the ground, shining the flashlight from various angles hoping to pick up some indication of an intruder. "Nothing. So what now?"

J.B. glanced at his partner then back toward the flowerbed. What he saw sent a chill up his spine. "Well, would you look at that?" The words were a hushed whisper.

"What?" Shag looked to J.B. to see what he was peering at so resolutely. Leaning against the house, directly under Michael's window, was a two-foot long piece of one-by-twelve. If placed on the edge of the foundation that jutted above the ground, and then laid over the flowerbed to reach the row of bricks that bordered it, it would make an effective bridge on which to stand *without leaving tracks*. "What we've got here, J.B., is one smart cookie. In fact, it scares the hell out of me that he's smart enough to know not to leave tracks."

"That's one of the things that's been botherin' me."

Shag squatted down and took a closer look. "But why was he dumb enough to leave the board here?"

"Maybe Michael screaming and the noise of me kicking in her door scared him off. It gives us a break. The fact he left no prints in the flowerbed is just one more piece to the puzzle. He's always one jump ahead, almost as if he knows the law. Michael was convinced it could be a cop because he keeps gettin' his hands on her unlisted number."

Shag stiffened. "Are you saying you think we have a rogue cop on our hands?"

"No. I'm not sayin' anything right now, just speculatin'." He knelt down and touched the board on the edge. He glanced up at the screen. "Shag, shine the light up here."

'What've you got?" He turned the light toward the screen.

"The screen's been cut right next to the frame. That's what she heard that sounded like fabric tearin'." His breath hissed in through clenched teeth. "Sonofabitch. At least now we're sure she wasn't dreamin'. I can fight the real thing but it's damned hard to fight imaginary bad guys, no matter how real they are in someone's head." His mind flashed back to Keely's battle to

83

get over nightmares and he shuddered. "Let's get back in the house to my lady."

"*Your* lady?" Shag looked at J.B., incredulity all over his face.

"Yeah. Mine." J.B. grinned. "She just doesn't know it yet." He started toward the front of the house. "But she will. I guarantee."

In the house Michael slept on—until the phone rang. She raised her head, leaped from the couch before coming fully awake and ran to the telephone. She held her breath for a second before picking it up on the third ring. Trying to sound businesslike she said, "Hello." As soon as the word came out of her mouth she knew she'd failed. She sounded terrified.

She gasped. "Mother?" She looked over her shoulder, checking to make sure she was alone. "Mother, where are you?"

Her mother's breathless, whispery voice came through loud and clear. "I'm at The Pines. He had me committed, Michael. Can you do anything? I sneaked down to the nurse's station to make this call."

"What's he doing now? Why did he do this?" Michael shuddered as a chill raced up her spine.

"I don't know what he's doing, or why. Can you get me out of here, hide me out for a while until he calms down?"

"I'll see what I can do when I get in to my office this morning. I can't do anything at the moment. I'll come and get you later today, after I get out of court. I have a case on the docket for nine a.m. and I should be through by midafternoon. Stay calm and wait for me." She hung up the phone and walked back to the couch.

Before she sat down the phone rang again. "What does she want me to do? I can't do anything about this until tonight." She picked it up on the second ring.

The moment he started his evil litany she quietly hung up the receiver as J.B. had instructed. Within seconds it rang again. She again picked up the phone and said, "Hello." Again he started his tirade. She quietly replaced the receiver. This time she walked to the couch and sat down, took a deep breath and fought the fear. She refused to allow him this victory. The phone on the desk rang and rang and rang.

J.B. and Shag entered and heard the phone. J.B. hurried in and saw her on the couch. "Is this the first call, darlin'?"

"No. The third."

"Okay, go answer it and then hand it to me."

She walked to the phone, and went through the same routine as before except after saying "Hello" she immediately handed the receiver to J.B. She wouldn't allow one word of his poison to touch her again. Walking like a zombie she returned to the couch.

J.B. listened for a few minutes and then, as if talking to Michael, said, "You know, sweetheart, this is one sick son-of-a-bitch." He gently replaced the receiver and joined her on the couch. "Don't let him get to you, darlin'."

"No, I won't." She looked and sounded emphatic as she gritted out, "Not any more." She sighed and put her head down on her folded arms resting on her knees. "I'm getting used to getting by with two or three hours sleep. I keep telling myself he's getting by with the same. That, at least, is some comfort."

Shag stepped over in front of the couch, squatted down and forced himself to ignore looking at the thin nightgown she wore. "You know, Ms. Mainwaring, you might be wise to get an answering machine. In fact, I'm really surprised that you don't have one."

She raised her head and looked at Shag. "I do have one at the office but I hate those infernal machines and their beeps so I didn't want one in my home."

"You know, it's too bad our local phone company doesn't have Caller ID available yet, but with the right type of answering machine you could not only screen your calls, you could also record your conversations and get him on tape."

Her eyes widened and she sat staring, stunned. "Why on earth didn't I think of that? I'm a lawyer. I should have thought of getting his voice on tape to use for evidence."

J.B. put his hand on her shoulder. "I'll pick one up tomorrow while you're in court and it'll be installed by the time you come home. I'll make sure it has the capability to record conversation. From now on you can record his calls."

He was always there for her. Without fail. Michael smiled at J.B. "Thanks, big guy." She patted his chest and turned away. "But save the receipt so I can reimburse you. Right now I'd better take a shower and get ready for work. Maybe I can get a couple of hours work done before I have to be in court."

Shag mouthed the words, "Big guy?" He laughed silently as J.B. glared.

~ * ~

J.B. pulled up at the front entry of Michael's office building. "I'll pick you up when you get off work. Where and when?"

"J.B., that isn't necessary. I can take a cab home and then drive my own car from now on. Since you'll have the answering machine installed by the time I get home, I can make a tape when he calls. I'll be fine."

"When are you goin' to get it through your head? Pretend I'm stuck to you with super glue."

Michael shook her head and exited the car. "Okay. Meet me here at five o'clock."

"You got it, darlin'."

Michael walked through her office door, crossed the room and stopped in front of her secretary's desk. "Lyndi, I need you to make a call for me."

"Sure, boss. That's what I'm here for."

"I want you to call The Pines and see if you can get Dr. Ralph Maynard on the line. When you reach him, put the call through to me if I'm still here. If you can't reach him before I have to leave for court I want you to find out exactly what condition my mother is in, and why she has been committed to The Pines."

"Your mother...." Lyndi looked shocked and ducked her head. "Sure, boss. Anything else?"

"No, that's it for now." Michael walked into her office and closed the door.

Thirty minutes later her intercom buzzed. "Yes, Lyndi."

"Um, Michael, Dr. Maynard is not available at the moment but I left a message for him to return the call."

"Okay. Thanks."

~ * ~

Michael stopped at the bank of elevators at the courthouse, a stack of file folders pressed to her chest with her left arm. In her left hand she clutched a cup of coffee. Her purse hung from her left shoulder. In her right she gripped her brief case. She prayed no one jostled her elbow and spilled the hot beverage down the front of her suit. When the elevator doors opened she stepped into the car.

A larger-than-usual crowd was present today and all apparently needed to ride this car. As they pushed her farther and farther to the back, panic rose. Claustrophobia. The only curse she admitted to—until the man began harassing her. "Excuse me? Excuse me, please. Let me through. I need to get off." She inched her way forward.

People separated to make a pathway. A man in the front held the doors while she worked her way through the crowd trying not to baptize someone with her hot coffee.

A hand reached out as quickly as a rattler making a strike and snagged her keys. They were out of her purse and into his pocket without anyone on the elevator being the wiser.

Including Michael.

Six

Outside the elevator Michael leaned against the wall and looked to see if anyone had noticed her loss of composure. Straightening, she pulled her shoulders back, held her head high, and walked to the stairs.

The elevator. After years of pushing herself, she could manage it for short trips if the car wasn't crowded. One day— one minute—at a time. The walls of a stairwell never closed in on her. She pushed open the door to the stairs and climbed three flights to Judge Archerd's court.

Five hours later Michael sat at the defense table listening to her client rehash the case. She had personal business to attend to and wanted him to shut up and go away, then felt guilty. Ecstatic over the win, he was exuberant in his praise. She stood, shook hands with him, then turned to gather the papers scattered over the table. Masters walked away giving her more credit than she felt she deserved. She was grateful her guardian angel had worked overtime today.

On autopilot throughout most of the trial, she wondered how she'd managed. She massaged her temples, trying to ease an aching head that felt as if a man using a jackhammer had taken up residence. Her eyes were scratchy, burning. Every muscle in her body yearned for a moment of relaxation.

She had to get some sleep. If she didn't she'd collapse. Where could she go to guarantee getting the sleep she needed? *He* located her everywhere she went.

"Ms. Mainwaring?" The bailiff walked up to the table, his hand outstretched. At first she thought he was offering his congratulations on winning the case.

"Hello, Charlie." Though she did it regularly because of her work, she hated shaking hands. Unwilling to offend him, she stretched her hand forward.

"Believe these are yours." He dangled keys from his thumb and index finger.

Startled, she looked at the keys, then picked up her purse and searched frantically through it. "Why, yes. They are. Did I drop them?"

"Don't know, ma'am. 'spect so. One of the deputies found 'em on the elevator."

She recalled her headlong flight earlier. She'd bumped into several people in her hasty retreat. Her purse might have tipped enough to dump the keys. "The elevator?"

Charlie nodded. "A deputy from the jail found them when he went down for coffee. The ID tag identified them. He knew you were in here, so he brought 'em to me. I was going to give 'em to ya at the recess but I forgot 'til now."

"I'm glad you remembered."

He laughed. "Yeah, me too."

"Thanks, Charlie." Michael finished packing her briefcase and grabbed her purse. Leaving the courtroom she turned automatically toward the elevators and stopped. The memory of her earlier experience still had her stomach cramped into knots. She turned to the stairs. She'd tackle the fear of the elevator another day, when not so tired. When she felt stronger.

On the north steps of the courthouse she checked her watch and realized she was a couple of hours early. J.B. wouldn't have arrived yet. She spotted her car and headed toward it knowing she'd have time to take care of the problem with her mother. Inside the car, she picked up her car phone and called Lyndi.

"Lyndi, did you reach Dr. Maynard?" She listened a moment, her fist clenching in frustration. "Did they tell you when he *would* be available?" She put her head down on her forearm resting on the steering wheel. "I see. Sounds to me like they gave you the royal runaround. I'm going out there to check in to this. If J.B. calls, unless he asks you specifically, don't let him know I've left the courthouse. He'd have a fit." She snorted. "Yes, I know I should listen to him, but I think I'll be all right for a little while. If *I* wasn't expecting to get out of court this early, then surely this maniac will be as taken by surprise as I am. I'll try to be back in the office by the time J.B. is looking for me. Thanks, Lyndi."

Michael drove out to The Pines and began to relax a bit on the drive. When she arrived at the gates of the facility she pulled up to the intercom and buzzed. The tinny sounding voice asked for identification and the name of the patient whom she wished to visit. She gave her name and her mother's name. The crackling response came back saying her mother was not allowed visitors at present until she'd completed orientation. Michael asked how long that would be and the disembodied sounding utterance was: "*Check with her doctor.*"

The electronically controlled wrought iron gate and the high stone wall surrounding the complex would have kept out the most daring escape artist. It was certainly daunting for one attempting to get inside. She drove away feeling frustrated, angry, and so tense she thought her head would burst. The drive back to town didn't relax her as the drive out had done.

Arriving back at her office building she looked at her watch. "Oops. J.B. will be looking for me." She jumped out of the car and raced into the building. At her office door she smiled tiredly at her secretary. "Hi, Lyndi. Any messages?"

Lyndi stood and tsk-tsked as she shook her head. "Nothing that can't wait until you sit down, have a cup of coffee and relax. You look like something the cat dragged in and the dog wouldn't have."

Michael closed her eyes and tipped her head forward, massaging the back of her neck. She looked up and raised an eyebrow. "Thanks, pal. I really needed to hear that."

"How'd the case go? Was it a rough day?" Lyndi's face clearly displayed her concern, and, from Michael's experience with her, she knew her secretary and friend wouldn't ask questions of more than a general nature.

Michael alternately rotated her shoulders and rolled her head around from side to side. "Yeah, but we won."

Lyndi clenched her hand, raised it and bending her arm, jerked her elbow back toward her body. "All right!" She winked at her boss. "I never doubted for a minute that you would."

Michael looked at the other desk in the room, currently unoccupied. "Where's Winslow? I thought he'd be working on the Taylor brief."

"He said he needed to run to his father's law library."

Puzzled, Michael's forehead wrinkled in a frown. "Why?"

"I asked the same thing. He remembered a case in one of the law books at Rauthuell, Deavers and Myers that might help."

"It's true they have a more extensive library, but I wish he'd discussed it with me. Did he say when he'd be back?"

Lyndi shrugged. "Nope. Just said 'see you later' as he walked out the door."

"Okay. I'll talk to him when he gets back and see how far he's gotten with it." She rotated her head from shoulder to shoulder. "In the meantime I could use that cup of coffee you mentioned and I don't even care if it's fresh. I'd drink muddy water right now if it was hot and would give me a well needed pick-me-up."

Lyndi laughed. "Would you keep me around if I made muddy water?" She walked to the counter, not expecting an answer. "Fresh coffee coming right up. It won't take more than a couple of minutes." She glanced at her boss and friend. "In the meantime, why don't you go sit in your office and try to relax? Your messages are on the desk."

Michael frowned. "Anything important?" She paused in the entrance to her private office. "Did J.B. call?"

"Nothing important on any of the cases. Detective Anderson called three times just before you arrived, more irate with each call. He said..."

The door burst open. "Michael, what the hell do you think you're doin'?" J.B. stood glowering.

Startled by his abrupt entry, Michael stood silently looking at him for several seconds. J.B. continued to glower at her, his arms akimbo.

With a sigh Michael raised an eyebrow. "Hello, J.B." She turned to her secretary. "Lyndi, this is the 'Detective Anderson' who drove you crazy a while ago." She turned to their visitor. "J.B., be nice to Lyndi Hilliard. I'd really hate to lose her. She's the best secretary south of the Kansas border."

Lyndi grinned. "North of it, too."

J.B. looked at the young woman sitting behind the desk in Michael's front office. About five feet six, with ash blonde hair, he'd guess her to be around twenty-five years old. Permanent grin lines bracketed her wide, full lipped mouth. Her nose was a little too large for her face but most people would never notice. They'd never get past the most arresting pair of charcoal grey eyes he'd ever seen. She was lovely and it reinforced his belief that Michael was a remarkable woman. Most women he knew would not have such an attractive secretary sitting in their front office. Of course Michael didn't have any worries in the looks department, either.

Michael watched J.B. smile, his eyes sparkling, totally unaware he oozed sex appeal from every pore. It came as natural to him as breathing and he paid it about as much notice.

His deep voice rumbled, "Hello, Lyndi. I'm pleased to meet such a modest young woman."

Lyndi laughed. "My dad always told us we had to ring our own bell. Nobody else would pull the rope and flap the clapper for us."

J.B. laughed, his eyes twinkling. "I think I'd have liked your dad, Lyndi."

She grinned and winked. "No doubt." Flipping her hair over her shoulder, she walked across the room toward the coffee maker. She looked back at J.B. "I'm making fresh coffee for Michael. Would you like me to bring you a cup, too?"

"That'd be nice. Thank you."

Michael watched the interchange. She fought the urge to drag J.B. out of the front office. He was flirting with her secretary. Most hurtful of all, Lyndi flirted right back. Michael didn't like it. Not one bit. And she definitely didn't like that it bothered her. She tried telling herself she didn't care. Her temper rose. *That's just like a man.*

Michael strolled into her office, attempting nonchalance. Sitting at her desk she concentrated on the messages arrayed there but couldn't get her mind off the lighthearted conversation in the other room.

The phone rang. Her private line. She punched the button and picked up the receiver. "Michael Mainwaring." Closing her eyes, she leaned back, calling up the strength she'd need. "Hello, Father." She took a breath. "What have you done with Mother?" Unconsciously she picked at the pale pink polish on her thumbnail as she cradled the phone with her shoulder. "No. I told you the last time you called. I won't move back home. Now tell me why you put her in The Pines." She raised her hand to her eyes, gripping her temples with thumb and index finger. "If you want someone to run the house and hostess your business dinners, go and get Mother released from the psychiatric hospital." She gritted her teeth. "Yes, I tried to see her, but they wouldn't let me in." She leaned forward and ground out, "I'm going to get her out of there, even if it takes a court order." His shout made her pull the phone away from her ear. "You moved her?" Without giving him time to answer she snapped, "Where?" An exasperated sigh hissed out, "All right Father, you don't have to tell me. I'll find her and bring her home with me. And I won't be returning to your home. Ever. I don't intend to have this conversation again. To use a phrase I've heard you use so often with me— 'Your problems are your own. Solve them. Don't come snivelling to me.'" She quietly replaced the receiver.

Within moments the phone rang again. She closed her eyes, took a deep breath and picked up the receiver. "Yes?" Her eyes widened in surprise and delight. "Hello, Linc. No, I'm not mad at the world. I just thought it was my father again." She rotated her head on her shoulders. "Enough about that. How are you and Cari?" She threw her head back and laughed. "But that's wonderful. Twins. I'm delighted. Boys, girls, or one of each?" She grinned. "How are mother and children doing?" She reached across and grabbed a pad of notepaper. "What's the room number? Of course I have to come see her and the babies." She smiled. "Yes, Linc. I'll see you tonight." Michael sat and contemplated the news. Her friend Lincoln Maitland and his beloved Cari had twin boys. Would *she* ever have children? With her background would she be a good mother?

A few moments later J.B. sauntered in and settled in the chair in front of her desk. "What's the matter, darlin'? You look like you just lost your best friend."

She looked up, staring him straight in the eye. "Have I?"

"Have you what?" He appeared to be genuinely perplexed.

"Lost my best friend." Her emotions were in turmoil. Depression caused by having to deal with her father had boomeranged to elation at the news of Linc and Cari's twins. The final straw was the fact she recognized her jealousy and questioned her sanity. She had pushed J.B. away, insisting they be only friends. She looked at the startled expression on his face. "Never mind. I'm just tired."

Lyndi carried in two mugs of coffee on a tray with sugar and creamer. "I forgot to ask what you take in your coffee, J.B."

"Just black." He took the mug off the tray and smiled up at Lyndi. "Thanks." He breathed in the aroma. "I needed this."

Lyndi set the tray on Michael's desk, and put the other mug in front of Michael. "Need anything else, boss?"

Michael shook her head. "No, thanks." She put her hand to her temple. "On second thought, I'll take a couple of aspirin."

"Coming right up." Lyndi exited the office and closed the door. A few moments later she stepped back in after a brief rap on the panel. "Sorry, Michael, but the aspirin bottle is empty. It's odd because it shouldn't be. I just bought it a couple of weeks ago, and it contained a hundred tablets."

"Would you see if you could borrow a couple from your friend down the hall?" Michael bent her head forward and massaged her temples again. "My headache is causing vision problems."

"Sure thing. I'll be right back." Lyndi left Michael's office and shut the door behind her.

J.B. got out of his chair and walked around behind Michael. "Lean back, darlin', and let me see if I can help."

"There's nothing you can do, J.B." She felt a great deal of guilt for her inability to help her mother and angry over the confrontation with her father. Add her ambivalent feelings for J.B. to the mix, and her emotions churned like a whirlpool.

J.B. put his hands on her shoulders and pulled her back in the chair. "Michael, don't give me a hard time. Lean back here and let me help. Sometimes you can be the most stubborn and exasperatin' woman."

She sighed and leaned back in the chair. As he massaged her shoulders and the back of her neck, his thumbs worked magic on the tense muscles he found there. A sound escaped her throat before she could repress it—not quite a moan, heavier than a sigh. "That feels so good. I can feel the tension easing already. How do you do that?"

"Keely taught me." He massaged for a few more minutes then unexpectedly stepped to the side of her chair and scooped her up in his arms. He gave her a brief hug before relaxing his grip.

"What are you doing?" He'd startled her. Her gaze flew to his face trying to identify his intent.

"You'll see." He settled her on the desk, scooting her back until the bend of her knees touched the smooth wood. Stepping directly in front of her he pulled her forehead down to his shoulder. Putting his arms around her, his fingers worked their sorcery on her spine.

Wonderful, she thought, the ache easing with each stroke of his magic fingers. Within moments the massage turned more sensual. Almost of their own volition, her arms slid up and wrapped around his neck as she pressed her ear to his chest. She listened to the beat of his heart accelerate. Feeling completely safe for the first time in a long while, she drifted into a dreamlike state. His voice rumbling under her ear didn't disturb her reverie.

"That's nice, darlin'. I like that." His fingers curled under her chin, and tipped her head back. With nibbling little kisses, his lips gently brushed back and forth across hers. It was the briefest of contacts giving her no time to panic. He kissed her eyelids and nose, each temple and cheek, working his way back for another butterfly kiss.

Enthralled, Michael never opened her eyes, enjoying the feeling of being cherished, of being treasured. "Mmmm, nice," Michael whispered. A barely audible soft moan emanated from deep in her throat. Surprised, her eyes flew open. She looked up at him, thinking how odd it was that she wasn't frightened. "You're wonderful, J.B.," she murmured, then her eyes widened when she realized how much she revealed.

J.B. realized how far she'd come since they'd first met. He didn't want to push her back to being the woman with a wall around her. He grinned. "Well, darlin', haven't I been tellin' you that for months now?"

Michael smiled. "Mmmm. You're as modest as Lyndi."

He chuckled and leaned down for another kiss, thinking this was the nicest moment of his life. Just as his lips made contact the office door burst open. His head jerked up to see who intruded while he pulled Michael off the desk and put her behind him.

A man stood in the doorway, left hand gripping the knob. At a glance, J.B. catalogued the man's description. Eyes round and magnified by thick lenses, his gaze darted from Michael to J.B. and back again. Sweat-dampened oily hair looked as if he'd styled it with an eggbeater. Perspiration dotted a high forehead above a slightly too-wide nose. He breathed through his open mouth indicating a sinus problem. His chocolate brown pin striped suit looked rumpled, as if he'd slept in it.

"Uh. I'm..." The man backed toward the outer office, pulling the door closed as he departed. "I'll just..."

Michael stepped around J.B. Her voice gentle, she spoke to the intruder. "Winslow, wait a minute."

He froze in the half open door, his eyes blinking, his breath gasping in through a partially open mouth. "Yes, ma'am?"

"I'd like to introduce a friend of mine. J.B., this is Winslow Rauthwell. Winslow, this is J.B. Anderson."

"Pleased to meet you, Winslow." J.B. stepped around the desk, his hand outstretched. Winslow stared at him as if mesmerized by a snake. Finally he stuck out a sweaty palm. His handshake was brief, the grip released almost immediately. He glanced at his palm as if expecting to see some stain or mark.

Michael looked at Winslow and asked kindly, "Did you finish the Taylor brief?"

"Uh, no, ma'am, but it's, uh..." He poked at his glasses with his middle finger. "Well, I should be through in..." He wiped the palm of his right hand down the front of his thigh. "I can finish it by..."

Michael smiled at him and asked softly, "Do you think you'll be able to finish it by tonight, Winslow?"

He became even more flustered, his gaze darting all over the room. "Uh, well..." He wiped both hands on his slacks and pushed his glasses up again. He stood gaping, his mouth opening and closing like a fish out of water.

"Winslow?" She started toward him.

His body jerked as if jabbed with a pin. "Tonight. Yes, ma'am. Tonight before I go home."

Her voice gentled even more. "Winslow, if you're having problems with it, maybe I can help."

"Uh..." He looked over his shoulder as if looking for a place to hide. "No, thank you, ma'am. I can...well, I..." He took a deep breath and nodded his head. "Before I go home tonight." He went out and shut the door.

J.B. looked toward the door, his head shaking as if unable to believe his eyes. "Who was that?"

"I just introduced you. That's Winslow Rauthwell." Michael turned back to J.B. and chuckled at the expression on his face.

He looked at her and raised an eyebrow. "Related to W. Clayton Rauthwell III?"

"Uh huh. This one is the fourth to bear that name, and he's Clayton's one and only son."

"What's he doin' here?"

"He's interning with me until he passes the bar."

"No, I mean, why here instead of his father's office. It seems to me a father would want his son to work with him."

"You saw him. He's a sweet young man but his father scares him to death. Clayton and I argued frequently during the time I was in his office, so he thinks I can give his son some backbone."

"Darlin', the only way you could give that boy some backbone is to implant it surgically."

"Don't be unkind, J.B." Her censoring gaze met his.

"I don't mean to be unkind but that kid is a walkin' bowl of jello. His father must think you're a miracle worker." He rubbed the back of his neck and looked at her speculatively for a moment. "Tell me about these arguments between you and the senior Rauthwell. How bad was it?"

"Oh, not the kind you're thinking about. We argued cases endlessly. He told me one time that the arguments with me helped him prepare for trials."

"No personal animosity?"

"No. I'm not aware of any." She walked to the window and looked out for a moment. "Understanding his problems with his father, I feel sorry for Winslow. I didn't want to take him on but I felt I owed Clayton. I worked at his law firm when I got out of law school and he was a big help getting my career started. I learned a lot working with him."

"Yes, darlin', I know." He looked at her, his eyebrow raised, reminding her he'd given her a blow by blow account of her career.

"That's right. You do know. And you've never told me how you learned so much about me."

J.B. laughed. "It was during the Maitland trial. Kopecky was expounding on how you had this great reputation but no experience in criminal law and he was going to whip your butt."

"He gave you all that information about my life?"

"Uh, well, he only knew about your academic life. He had his investigator check up on you so he'd know who he was up against." J.B. frowned. "I still don't know all that much about your personal life."

Lyndi knocked on the door and at Michael's invitation she entered with a bottle of aspirin. "I'm sorry to take so long, Michael, but I had to run to the pharmacy. Eveline didn't have any aspirin either.

Michael looked up, startled. She'd been unaware her head no longer ached until Lyndi returned with the aspirin. "I'm sorry you went to the trouble, Lyndi. I don't need them now. My headache seems to have magically disappeared." She glanced at J.B. "I think I have J.B. to thank for that."

"Are you ready to go home, darlin'?" J.B. walked up behind her and put his hands on her shoulders, his thumbs automatically beginning their soothing massage.

Lyndi stood in the doorway, smiling. "I can hold the fort here, Michael. Why don't you go home and get some rest?"

"I think I'll do that. Maybe a long soak in the tub will help me get a good night's sleep." She reached for her briefcase but J.B.'s hand was seconds ahead of hers.

"Grab your purse, darlin', and let's go get some supper. What sounds good to you?" Before she had a chance to answer he said, "I think I'd like to have fish tonight. How does that sound to you?"

She turned and looked up at him, grinning. "Aren't you taking a lot for granted? What if I don't want fish? What if I want chicken? I have my car now. I could get what I want."

"Nope." He grinned right back. "I'm a cockle burr. Remember?" He took her by the arm and escorted her out of the office.

When they arrived at Michael's car she stepped to the driver's door and inserted her key.

"What do you think you're doin'?" J.B. stood on the sidewalk, exasperation clear on his face.

"I'm getting in my car." She chuckled, "And to think they call you a detective."

"All right, you make all the jokes you want, but I don't think it's a good idea for you to drive your car. We can leave yours here and take mine."

"No, J.B., I'm taking my car home." She got in, shut the door, locked it, fastened her seat belt and started the engine.

"Well, hell." J.B. sprinted for his car. By the time he'd backed his car out of the space, Michael was a block away. He smacked his fist on the steering wheel. "Dammit, you're not pullin' this on me." He reached over, grabbed the flasher off the dash, and put it on top of the car. Cars cleared out of his way as he picked up speed. "You forgot I'm a cop, didn't you, darlin'?"

Michael pulled in to her driveway. By the time J.B. arrived she stood leaning against the side of her car, laughing. Walking back to J.B.'s car, she slid into the passenger seat and grinned. "Isn't using that flasher for personal business called an abuse of power?" When he snorted she chuckled. "Now, let's go get that fish."

J.B. looked into her eyes for a full minute before saying a word. When he did speak, it was a mere whisper. "Fish isn't the only thing I'm hungry for, darlin'." He reached over, put his hand on the back of her neck, pulled her toward him, and his lips settled on her mouth as if coming home. This wasn't the butterfly touch of his previous kisses. It was deeper. His tongue outlined her mouth as his lips moved gently over hers. The merest instant before panic could rise in her chest he broke the contact and looked into her eyes.

"Don't ever scare me like that again, darlin'. I don't handle it well. Where you're concerned, I tend to become a little crazy. Especially when you may be in danger."

"Listen, big guy, I was in court today without your company. Why is driving my car home any different? Especially when I knew you were right behind me."

"Right behind you? I had to use the flasher to catch you. This maniac could have separated us in a heartbeat. You drove off, leaving me standing on the street as if you didn't have a care in the world. All it takes is a moment's inattention, Michael. And as for today in court? You were surrounded by the sheriff's deputies and the bailiff. I told them if anything happened to you they'd answer to me."

"You had me watched?" She was outraged he'd had guards on her without her knowledge. "How do you expect me to ever walk on my own two feet if you don't give me the chance?"

"Darlin', after we catch this sonofabitch, you can have all the freedom you want. In the meantime, I won't put your life in jeopardy. I'm not givin' that bastard a free crack at you just so you can prove somethin'—to yourself or anyone else." J.B. pulled her across the seat, twisting her around to face him, and tightened his arms around her.

She wrapped her arms around his neck and held on. "All right, point taken." She leaned back against the steering wheel and looked up into his eyes. "I'll try to follow the rules from now on. I just didn't think driving my car home, with you following me, would be dangerous." She leaned forward and placed a quick kiss on his chin, then scooted back across the seat and fastened her seat belt. "Now, could we go eat?"

J.B., holding onto the thrill of her quick kiss, backed the car out and drove to a popular seafood restaurant in town.

During dinner he watched Michael pick at her food. "Darlin', are you fearing a repeat of the dead rose?"

"It crossed my mind." She glanced around nervously. "Do you think he's here?"

"Relax. Enjoy your meal. It's safe to leave the table to dance or go to the restrooms. The table is under surveillance."

She stared into his eyes, her own wide with surprise. She looked around the restaurant, fear tightening her gut. "Who's watching?"

"Darlin', I said relax. My partner, Shag, is on duty. Take a look over there." He nodded his head slightly toward his right. When he saw her look, he spoke softly again. "If anyone leaves anything on this table he'll see and follow him. Then we'll have him. Of course, chances are Shag's wastin' his time. I don't think the guy is stupid enough to pull the same stunt twice, but we thought it was worth the effort."

Michael breathed a sigh of relief and, appetite now back, finished as much of her meal as she could, given the fact it was now stone cold.

"Would you like to dance?"

She shook her head. "No. Thanks, anyway." Too afraid of coming back from the dance floor and finding a dead rose on the table, Michael couldn't face it. Even knowing J.B.'s partner was there to help catch this man didn't ease her nerves. The whole idea of creating a scene terrified her. She fought this battle one minute, one hour at a time. For this minute and this hour she was too tired and had gone too long without sleep. She'd face the dragon tomorrow and hoped to get enough sleep tonight to have the strength she'd need to slay it.

"Well, I guess it's time to head home then." After paying the bill, J.B. escorted her out the door knowing their chance to catch this guy tonight was gone.

Arriving at Michael's house J.B. exited the car and took a look up and down the street before walking around to her door.

She sat staring at the house. When J.B. opened the door she looked up. "You know, for the first time since buying this house, I wonder if I'll ever feel safe again." With a sigh she got out of the car.

They walked up on to the front porch, his arm around her waist. She tipped her head over and rested it on his shoulder for an instant. Lifting it again as they arrived at the front door, she yawned. "I'm so tired. It's several hours yet until bedtime. I'd love to get a solid eight hours of uninterrupted sleep."

"We installed your answering machine today. We can turn the ringer off on the telephone so you won't even hear it. That should take care of the problem."

"Don't you remember? My phones are the European style dial phones. No volume control. They can't be turned off completely. My previous experience with this man ensures that the quietest ring will wake me. If he calls me I'll know it. Whether or not I answer the phone."

"Okay, we'll come up with something else. Maybe bury the phone under pillows or something. Give me your house key."

He unlocked the door, pushing it open. When she gasped he grabbed her, pulling her behind him.

He looked inside and couldn't breathe for a moment. A bolt from a crossbow protruded from one of the risers half way up the stairs. Pinned there by the bolt was an envelope on which Michael's name had been glued, from letters cut out of magazines and newspapers.

Seven

Her first glance told her it was lethal. J.B. grabbed her. Pulling her inside, he placed her back to the wall. Fear thrummed in her stomach. Choking fear. Eating like acid on newly formed determination.

Her gaze riveted on his face, she watched. He checked out the foyer and living room. His hand on her shoulder, he spoke softly. "Stay there." Walking to the bolt he inspected it carefully. She concentrated on J.B.

She ignored the obscenity protruding from her stairs. J.B. dropped to his knees and sighted down the arrow toward the door. She closed her eyes.

"Looks like the bastard shot it through the mail slot."

"The mail slot?" She turned her head and stared at the innocuous little flap. It had provided this maniac with a point of entry. "I'm beginning to understand how a normally nonviolent person could be driven to commit murder," she murmured.

J.B. crossed to her. He put his hands on her shoulders and looked into her eyes. "He'll never get his hands on you." He pulled her into his arms. "This is a threat, but since you weren't home at the time it's not a direct threat."

"What do you mean it's not a direct threat? He invaded my home with that obscenity." Outrage bubbled and churned in her gut as she stood leaning against the wall with her hands clenched in to fists.

In spite of his own fury, J.B. attempted to soothe her, stroking up and down her arms. "Yes, but he meant to intimidate you, not do bodily harm."

Furious that she'd been upset again, J.B. left the foyer. In the living room he dialed Shag. "How quick can you get over here?" He made a growling sound in the back of his throat. "To Michael's, of course. I have some evidence for the lab." He raked his fingers through his hair. "Sorry, I didn't mean to snarl."

"This time the bastard shot a crossbow bolt through the mail slot—with a note attached." His fingers raked through his hair again. "Okay, we'll get pictures before we pull it out and take it to the lab." He listened a moment and sighed. "Shag, you always lose the coin toss. I never carry a kit and I don't have one with me now. No latex gloves."

After hanging up the phone, he returned to Michael. She turned her head and finally took a good look at the bolt. Her eyes glistened with unshed tears.

J.B. closed his eyes and sighed when he saw her face. "Come on, darlin', think about this. He made sure you weren't home. He knows your schedule." He glanced at the missile and murmured, "He seems to know every move you make." At her quick inhalation of breath his gaze darted back to her. "All I'm sayin' is—he *wants* to scare the livin' hell out of you. Don't let him win."

Michael's gaze jerked around to J.B. "No. I won't." She glanced at the arrow again before turning back to him. "We're going to catch him."

J.B. growled, "You bet we are. Workin' together, we're goin' to make sure we put him away." He put his hand on her shoulder. "He doesn't know it yet, but his ass is grass and I'm a lawn mower."

Michael stared at him, feeling for the first time that she could stand up to this maniac. So long as she had J.B. at her side.

J.B. looked at her face and smiled. "You're not goin' to let this guy intimidate you any more, are you?"

"No. I'm not." Michael looked toward the bolt. Fascinated by the sight of it, she took a few steps toward the stairs. Her legs trembled at the thought of what that fearsome projectile could do to human flesh. She feared for a moment her knees would buckle but she gritted her teeth and went closer.

"Don't touch it, darlin'."

Her hands came up shoulder high. "I wouldn't dream of it." She stepped to the balustrade and leaned against it peering closely at the missile. It had every appearance of being razor sharp. "That really looks dangerous. Is it as lethal as it looks?"

"Yeah. The sonofabitch used a crossbow."

"A crossbow." It wasn't a question. Her tone of voice indicated disbelief in the choice of weapons. Her eyes wide, she turned to J.B. "How is Karate—or Judo—or any of the martial arts, going to stop something like that?"

"None of the martial arts would protect you from something fired from a distance. We're just goin' to have to make sure he doesn't get a crack at usin' it. Or any other weapon. I'll do my best to stay between you and any danger, but you're goin' to have to help by not takin' any unnecessary chances."

She trembled at what he said. She couldn't stop imagination painting vivid pictures. "It's working, J.B. Oh, God, just thinking about what that thing could do to you..." She threw herself at him, clasping her arms tightly around his neck.

He wrapped his arms around her waist and pulled her close, not realizing her major concern was for *his* safety. He pressed her head to his shoulder. "Shh, darlin'. I'm here for you. Always." He slipped his thumb under her chin and tipped her head back. "Always, Michael. Do you hear me?" When she nodded, he placed a quick kiss on her lips and pulled her head back down to his shoulder. "Just hang in a little longer. All right?"

"Yes, but hold me for a minute. Okay? Just for a minute, please?"

"It'd be my pleasure. I'll hold you anytime you want, for as long as you want." He wrapped her more tightly in his arms and savored the feel of her, the scent of her. As his hands caressed her back, his eyes closed and imagination took over. In his mind he pictured making love to her. His hands moved unerringly down to cup her buttocks. He pulled her body in closer alignment to his own. His mouth slid around, raining nibbling kisses on her cheek, her chin, working his way to her lips.

The kiss began as a brief encounter but when she opened to him he was lost. She had never responded to him before now. Euphoria shot through him like a lightning bolt, igniting long suppressed desire.

Want. Need. Hunger. Like balls of flame from a Roman candle, they shot through him. His mouth moved to her throat and he felt the thundering beat of her heart.

The second he felt her struggling, pushing on his shoulders, he turned her loose and backed away. His breath came through his open mouth, his lungs pumping like a bellows. He bent, placing his hands on his knees. "I didn't mean for that to..." His voice trailed off and he slowly straightened. He looked squarely into her eyes.

She stared back at him, pupils dilated, lips slightly parted. "J.B.?"

He took a deep breath and ran his hand around the back of his neck, massaging. "No, that's not true. To be honest, I wanted it to happen. I just didn't plan on it happenin' right now or right here. In case you haven't figured it out, I want you. I've wanted you from the first moment I laid eyes on you." He paced in front of her. "Sometimes I want you so bad I ache all over. That's not goin' to change. I'm goin' to be wantin' you the day I draw my last breath."

Michael appeared mesmerized. "I see."

He'd hoped for more of a response. When she said nothing more his temper frayed. "Do you have a problem with that?"

Her lips trembled and she nodded her head. "Uh, well... Yes, I do."

Shocked, he gaped at her. His hand went to his hair, raking his fingers through the already disarrayed strands. A thought occurred to him. He whirled back and looked at her from under his brows. "You do like men, don't you?"

He saw the light of understanding dawn in her eyes. "Oh! No. I mean, yes I... uh... I..."

"Michael, you know I've wanted to date you. You can't be unaware of how much I care about you and how much I want you. That's something I've been unable to hide. So what's the problem? Is it me?"

"J.B., I..."

"Talk to me, Michael. Do I have a prayer with you?"

"If I... I don't..." She stared at him, unable to explain.

"Can't you just give me a straight answer?" Rising anger was evident in his voice. Nearly out of patience with her, he clamped his teeth together before he said more than he intended.

"I want to, I'm trying, but I..." If she allowed any man into her life it would be J.B. A part of her wanted him there.

"Michael, you have to make a decision."

She reminded him of some half-tamed wild animal. Darting forward to snatch a bit of food from the proffering hand, then racing out of reach to savor the morsel. They couldn't continue as they had been. It wasn't good for either of them.

Tears shimmered on her lower lids as she looked through the windows. "I wish..." Her gaze came back to him. "Why can't we be just friends?"

"Because I want more, Michael. I want a life with you. I want to build something together, a life span with all the peaks and valleys. One in which we have children and someday grandchildren. I'm your friend now. But it isn't enough.

"Mom always told us to marry our best friend if we wanted a good and lasting marriage. I want to be your *best* friend, Michael. I want to be your husband. Your lover."

She'd already figured out that much. "J.B., no matter how I feel about you, that's not going to happen. I can't be..."

The doorbell rang. Engrossed in the conversation and not ready to end it, he'd been unaware of Shag's arrival. He grabbed the door, jerked it open and snarled, "What'd you do, get over here code three?"

Shag raised his brows and stepped back. "Whoa, buddy. What's with you?"

J.B. turned his back and stepped farther into the house. "Come in, Shag."

Shag walked in and glanced from Michael to J.B. He shrugged his shoulders and sauntered to the stairs. "A bolt. For someone experienced, it's an easy shot." He took photos from all angles. After crouching at the door for his final shot, he rose to his feet. "I guess we'd better dust it for prints."

J.B. growled, "You're wastin' your time. This bastard's too slick to leave his prints."

Shag nodded and calmly proceeded with the job.

J.B. escorted Michael out of the foyer to the living room where he seated her on the couch.

His voice a soft rumble, he leaned toward her. "I'm sorry I pushed so hard, Michael. I told myself I'd give you all the time you needed. I guess I don't have as much patience as I thought I did. I won't press you again. I'll back off."

"But that's not..."

At her startled look he shook his head. He'd concentrate on remembering his job. "I said I'd be here for you. That hasn't changed. From now on I'm here only as Detective Anderson. In fact, if you prefer I can return to the formality of callin' you Ms. Mainwaring." He rose from the couch before she had time to say anything else.

Shag, wearing latex gloves, carefully pulled the bolt from the riser. He'd already dusted it for prints. As they'd surmised, he found none. However, he still wanted to keep it as pristine as he found it. He hoped the lab might be able to come up with something they couldn't find in the field.

Shag freed the envelope from the bolt and handed it to J.B. Using tweezers from Shag's kit, J.B. carried it to the table. "The bastard didn't even seal it so we don't have a snowball's chance in hell of gettin' any DNA." Bending over the table he carefully extracted the letter from the envelope and lifted the top fold.

Unaware Michael stood looking over his shoulder, her sharp intake of breath alerted him to her presence. He whirled around and glared at her. "What are you doin'?"

She glared right back. "It was meant for me. I intend to see what he says." She moved closer. Repeating his earlier words back to him, she asked, "Do you have a problem with that?"

"No." He bent over the letter again and turned down the final fold. "Damn!"

Cut out of magazines and newspapers, the content of the letter was terse and to the point.

> GEt tHAT baSTaRD OuT OF youR HOuse.
> nICE GIRLS don't hAVE MEN in THEir BEDroomS. I WON't WARn You aGAIN.
> heED ME or I kILL Him. YOU ARE MINE!

Michael gasped. "Oh, my God. He means you, J.B. He's going to do something to *you*. You have to stay away from me." She whirled to face Shag. "You have to take over..." Her eyes widened and she shook her head. "No. Not you, either. He'll harm you—or anyone else who tries to help me." She backed toward the living room. "Won't he?" Her voice rose. "I can't be responsible for someone else being harmed. I can't."

"Michael." J.B. walked toward her, his hands outstretched. "Michael, listen to me for a minute." When he saw her eyes focused on his, he took her hands. "Is there a friend you can stay with until we catch this bastard?"

"What friend?" The poignant question told a great deal.

"Michael, there must be someplace you can go. Some friend or family member with whom you can stay. Just for a short period of time." He watched her shake her head. "I can't believe there is nobody."

"Nobody." Quietly spoken but emphatic, she was resolute.

"Michael, what about your father and mother? You could stay with them." The expression on her face told him he'd just insulted her.

"Not an option. Ever." Determinedly she stared at him.

J.B.'s temper flared. "Dammit, Michael, we're talkin' about your life here. Have you forgotten that?"

"I haven't forgotten a thing, J.B." She bent toward him, glaring back. "I was living with this before you came along."

"I know. I also know you have problems with your father, but surely, with your life at stake you could..."

She had never been so angry. "J.B., you listen to me because I won't repeat myself. I will not *ever* go home again. There is nothing that would induce me to set foot in that house."

Unable to believe it, his shout rang out. "Are you tellin' me you'd rather die?"

"Yes." Her voice, raised in anger, had become hoarse.

Shag stepped between them. "Hey, you two. Quit shouting at each other. Do you think we could all get back on the same team here?"

Michael ducked her head, a sheepish expression on her face. She brought her hands up to cover her eyes. "I'm sorry. I apologize. To both of you." Her face turned fiery red. "I can't believe I was shouting." She dropped her hands and a look of disbelief crossed her face. "I *never* shout."

J.B., a feeling of relief coursing through him, looked at Shag. "It isn't the first time you've heard me shout, buddy. It probably won't be the last."

J.B. turned to Michael. "It looks like you're stuck with me for protection."

"That's fine. Or you can go back to your life and allow me to handle this problem." She shrugged.

"To quote you—'not an option'."

"Okay, so what are we going to do about this jerk?"

"I like the sound of that 'we' you used." He smiled at her. "The first thing we're goin' to do is get you out of here."

"What good will that do? He always knows where I am."

"True, but I'm takin' you to someplace I *know* will be safe—even if he finds you."

"And where in the world would I be safe?"

"My place."

"Your place? I don't think so."

Shag joined the conversation. "Ms. Mainwaring?" When her gaze moved to his face, he put his hand on her arm. "It's a good idea."

She looked at him reflectively, her eyebrow raised. "Why?"

"It's a secure building. People living there have to use keys. Anyone else has to be buzzed in by one of the tenants."

"Don't you think it will only make this man more angry if I go to J.B.'s? He's already making death threats against him."

J.B. nodded. "Yeah, it probably will." He unconsciously rubbed his hand up and down her back. "You have to realize, it isn't goin' to make a bit of difference what you do or where you go. He's goin' to keep on harassin' you until we catch him. As for his threats against me—well, I think I'm on his... uh... list just because I'm helpin' you. At this point he'd probably come after me even if I stayed away from you."

"That's a pleasant thought." She rubbed her hands up and down her arms trying to get rid of the chill bumps.

"I wish you could think of somebody who might have a grudge against you. Then we'd have a stab at catching the bastard." He sighed. "Well, what's it going to be?"

"Okay. I'll pack my bag." She walked toward her bedroom door. Without turning around, she said, "You know he'll find me there, too, don't you?"

"Yeah. But maybe we'll catch him this time." They watched her enter her bedroom. "Shag, we have to hope this bastard slips up. Soon. We have to get him. Before he drives her completely crazy—or worse."

Shag nodded. "We're working on it. Doing the best we can."

Raking his hands through his hair, J.B. snapped, "Well, dammit, that's not good enough."

Shag put his hand on his partner's shoulder. "That's all we *can* do."

J.B. walked over to the letter on the table and scanned it again. "We have to do better." He looked his partner squarely in the eyes. "I can't lose her, buddy."

Shag's voice was filled with compassion. "We'll stay on it and make sure you don't."

Michael walked out of her bedroom carrying her tote bag and picked up her briefcase and purse. She walked to the door and turned toward the men. "I'm ready to go, J.B. I hope you're going to feed me."

"How can you be hungry, darlin'? We just ate."

"You ate. I was too concerned about this jerk being in that restaurant watching us." She grinned. "It's way past my usual dinner time. You won't like me when I'm so hungry I could chew on the furniture."

J.B. laughed, surprised to see her making jokes so soon after their disagreement. Maybe tonight she wouldn't pick at her food.

Shag picked up the letter and the crossbow bolt from the table, put them in evidence bags and stripped off the latex gloves. Exiting the house with J.B. and Michael, he got in his car and waved as he drove away, headed for the lab.

In the car J.B. watched her for a few moments to see if her facade would slip. "Do you like Chinese?" J.B. scanned the cars behind him, then looked back at her.

"Sure. Chinese is fine. Are you going to get carry-out or would you prefer to eat at the restaurant?"

"Let's get carry-out and eat at my place."

"I'd like that better, I think, but first I'd like to run by the hospital."

"Hospital? What's the matter? Are you sick? Do you hurt somewhere?" When she didn't immediatley respond, he snapped, "Michael...answer me."

"I would if you'd give me a chance. I want to visit Cari Maitland. She had twins."

"Oh." J.B. looked at her, a sheepish expression on his face. "Um, guess I panicked, huh?"

At the hospital they exited the elevator on the maternity floor and saw Lyssa Bradley and Graeham Rutherford just going into a room down the hall. They followed and walked in right behind them.

"Hi Cari. How are you feeling?" Michael walked to the hospital bed and leaned down to kiss the pretty blonde who sat up against the raised head of the bed holding two blanket-wrapped bundles.

"I'm fine but I'm not sure how 'daddy' is doing. He drove the doctors and nurses crazy."

Michael laughed. "Yeah. I can picture that." She looked over her shoulder and turned just in time to be engulfed in a rib-cracking hug by a very tall dark man whose hair very nearly rivaled her own in length. She tugged on his ponytail and pulled his head back. "Don't hug so hard. I need to breathe."

J.B. stood back watching the interchange and had a very primitive urge to slug the big jerk who was hugging *his* girl. He knew their history, and was aware they were best friends and had been since grade school, but he couldn't stop the feeling that he wanted to protect his woman. He walked over with his hand outstretched and the thought crossed his mind that at least while shaking hands Maitland would have to take *one* of his arms from around Michael.

Michael turned out of Linc's embrace and back to Cari. "Are you going to let me hold at least one of them?"

Cari grinned and then looked up at her husband. "Sure, which one would you like to hold?"

"Well, I'm going to want to hold both of them, but only one at a time, please. I'm afraid I'd drop one of them if I tried to hold them at the same time." Michael stretched her arms out reaching for the baby in Cari's right arm.

She was startled when Linc stepped forward and lifted the baby out of Cari's left arm. He turned and held the baby toward Michael. "Wouldn't you like to hold Michael first?"

"Michael?" Her gaze swiveled to Cari and then back to Linc. "You named one of the babies Michael?"

Linc grinned. "Yeah, and the other one is named Graeham."

Michael swiped at the tears rolling down her face. "Oh, Linc. Cari, I don't know what to say."

Cari grinned. "Just say yes to being their godmother."

"Oh, yes. Absolutely." Michael turned to J.B. and held the baby up for him to see. "Isn't he beautiful? Look at all that dark hair."

She turned back to Cari. "He looks exactly like his daddy."

Cari smiled. "They both do. They're identical. There was only a half-ounce difference in their weight. They're probably going to be as big as their daddy, too."

"Lord save us." Lyssa, who had been standing back from the crowd, laughed. "Am I going to get to hold them as well? I have to be able to go home and report to Aimee, giving her all the details on the new babies."

A short time later J.B. and Michael left the hospital and headed for the Chinese restaurant. At the restaurant they ran in together. He seated Michael in a booth and got her a cup of tea while he placed the order.

Back at the car he stowed their dinner in the back seat.

Michael looked over her shoulder at the large sack. "How many people are you planning to feed?"

"Just us. You said you were hungry. I don't want to see you nibblin' on my furniture." He got the response he hoped for.

Michael laughed. "It looks to me like you're going to be eating Chinese food for a very long time, Detective Anderson."

"It'll freeze."

At his apartment he put plates and chopsticks on the table while Michael put the food out.

She looked at the chopsticks, glanced at him and back to the chopsticks. "Do you really use those things?"

"Uh huh, but if you don't, I have a fork you can use—or you could let me feed you." He looked at her, a hopeful expression on his face.

"That's okay," she said dryly, "I know how to use them."

"Aw shucks." His mischievous grin earned him a gentle shot on the arm. He decided he loved her playfulness. It was a side to Michael he hadn't seen before now.

After they finished eating Michael loaded the dishwasher while he stowed away the left over food. He watched her work beside him in the kitchen and fantasized it could be this way every day—if she'd only give him the chance. He wanted that chance more than anything else he'd ever wanted in his life.

When the kitchen was clean he took her by the hand and led her to the living room. Going to the stereo cabinet, he asked, "What do you want to hear? I have classical—Bach to Wagner. I even have C and W if you'd prefer it."

"Something soft and soothing. I'd like to relax so I can sleep tonight uninterrupted by...him."

After putting a CD on the stereo, he grabbed her hand and walked to the couch. He stretched out on it and held out his arms, inviting her to stretch out in front of him. "Come on, sweetheart, get comfortable."

"What are you doing?"

"Well, darlin', I think that'd be obvious. I'm going to cuddle with you."

"Cuddle?"

"Cuddle. You know what 'cuddle' means, don't you? That's where I hold you in my arms. All you have to do is—enjoy being held. I guarantee *I'm* goin' to enjoy it."

She stood, a tiny smile turning up the corners of her mouth.

"You'll be layin' in front of me. You can face away from me, if it'll make you feel more at ease. You'll be free to get up anytime you feel the least bit uncomfortable. I give you my word I'll never do anything you don't want me to do."

She ducked her head like a shy little girl. "I know, J.B."

When she settled on the couch facing him and curled into his arms he thought she could not possibly give him a greater gift than her trust. For a moment he thought his heart would burst with joy.

Michael put her head on his left shoulder and her hand on his right and snuggled to him. She breathed in his scent. So uniquely J.B., it brought to mind the great outdoors. Pine woods, that was it. She tucked her nose into the crook of his neck and took another deep whiff, and curled more tightly into him. His arms around her gave her a feeling of safety she'd been long denied by the recent events of her life. Her hand slid from his shoulder, down across his chest and, through his shirt, she felt the crisp, curling mat of hair on his chest. She got a sudden mental image of running her hands through it and could almost feel it on her fingertips.

After a while, as the music washed over them like a gentle wave on the shore, surrounding them with peace, she closed her eyes and relaxed more than she had in the past several weeks. She could hear the steady rhythm of his breathing and she drifted to sleep feeling cherished.

J.B. relaxed into that dreamlike state halfway between asleep and fully alert. He couldn't believe the change in her attitude. After this afternoon's argument he'd thought he no longer had hope. Now he did. He thought of his hopes for the future. A future in which Michael was in his arms every day—and every night. A time when, for her, there would be no fear of loving and being loved.

As J.B. settled deeper into sleep, a beeper sounded bringing him fully awake.

At first he thought it was his, but within seconds he realized it was coming from her purse on the lamp table.

Michael sat up and looked around bleary eyed. "What?"

"It's your beeper, darlin'." She stood up, staggered, and looked around as if unsure of where she was. He stood up and settled her on the couch, then grabbed her purse and handed it to her. Already alert to the implications, he asked, "Do you often get emergency calls in the middle of the night?"

Now becoming more alert, she shook her head. "No. Only rarely."

"Okay. Let's check this out." He grabbed his cellular phone. "Let's see what number you're supposed to call."

She reached in and pulled out the beeper, looked at the read-out and held it up for his perusal.

"Do you recognize it?"

"No. But I haven't memorized all my clients' numbers, either." Not yet seeing the implications, she grinned. "That's why I have a Rolodex at the office."

"Let's check it out, darlin', then we'll see."

"Check it out? Why?"

"Because this bastard has managed to get his hands on your phone numbers, so who says he can't have your pager number?"

"Oh." She felt her heart skip a beat. "I see."

J.B. called the station and gave instructions. "Check out the address that corresponds with the phone number. Dispatch a car to that location. Bring in for questioning any and all males residing or visiting at the address."

Twenty minutes later the pager sounded again. The readout displayed the same number. Michael became nervous. "J.B., what if one of my clients really needs me? What if it's a legitimate call?"

"What if it isn't? Wait just a few more minutes, darlin'. Give the boys in blue time to do their jobs. It isn't like you're a doctor or something and have to race off to save somebody's life. Whatever the emergency might be for a legitimate client, it can wait for a few minutes. Okay?"

"Okay." She sat on the edge of the couch, visibly nervous and what J.B. thought of as 'twitchy'.

Fifteen minutes passed and the pager sounded again. The same number displayed on the screen.

"I'm going to call it, J.B."

"Okay, darlin'. They've had about enough time to get there."

Michael dialed, and counted the rings in a whisper. "One. Two. Three. Four. Five. On the sixth ring, she heard a click. She stared up into the sky blue of J.B.'s eyes—and nodded.

Eight

"Michael?" J.B. stepped over and put his arm around her. He softly asked her, "Who is it, sweetheart?"

"It's him." Her harsh whisper sounded painful. She replaced the receiver. "He has my pager number." She sat on the couch, her elbows on her knees, her chin on the palms of her hands. "I'm tired of this. Just so tired."

Speaking calmly he said, "As near as you can remember, tell me exactly what he said."

Her voice raspy, she answered, "He said, 'Hello, Mickie. Did you really think you could get away from me?'" She took a deep breath. "I didn't want to believe it could be him."

J.B. pulled her into his arms. "We'll wait a few minutes for the station to call. I hope they got him." He held her close and kissed her temple as his hands soothed, stroking up and down her back. His body remembered the feel of her in his arms earlier. His mind told him to get down to business. "Was that all he said?"

"I didn't listen for anything else." She shivered, burying her face in the curve of his neck. "I heard his voice and replaced the receiver before he had a chance to say more."

Her soft voice vibrated against his throat setting off explosions of desire in his blood. He tipped her face up and took her mouth under his for a brief kiss. He felt her response and gloried in the fact she didn't struggle to break free.

In spite of the circumstances, his body reacted to the kiss. To her nearness. He wanted to savor these moments. He clamped down on his need. He told himself—*Deal with the phone call*. "Darlin', we knew he'd find a way to contact you here. He isn't surprising us anymore."

She shuddered. "No."

The breathy sound fluttered against his throat. The rein on his control threadbare, J.B. gritted his teeth and held on. Because of the threat to her he found himself thinking more often as a man than as a detective. He wanted to protect her. Cavemen probably felt this way when something threatened their mates and the need to protect was a part of the genetic code for most men, even in today's society. In his mind, if not in hers, she was already his other half. He could convince her. Couldn't he? Of course he could. A piece of cake. All he needed was time.

He hugged her and smiled. "Don't let him get to you."

"I won't." She clung, gripping his shirt, burying her face as if trying to dissolve into him. "I'm so glad you're here."

That admission was progress—and it sent a thrill through him like none he'd ever before felt. "So am I, darlin'. So am I." He couldn't imagine being anywhere else.

He grew tired of waiting on the call so grabbed up the phone and called the police station. Tucking the receiver between his shoulder and ear, he maintained the gentle contact with Michael. His hands continued to soothe as he talked. The major break-through, that she felt comfortable in his arms, did not go unnoticed. He reveled in it.

"This is Anderson. Any luck on that phone number?"

Her arms crept around his waist, pressing her breasts against him. He gritted his teeth, wanting to pull her closer, make her a part of him He wanted her here, with no barriers. Skin to skin—and he had to stop thinking about it. This wasn't the time.

He tried to concentrate on the report from the desk sergeant. All he could think about was the feel of her warmth through the silken smoothness of her dress. Silk on satin. And the scent of her. Strawberries and cream.

"Mmm. I see." He lost his train of thought and tried to remember what the sergeant said. "They patrolled a four block radius around it?" Michael pulled back and looked at him. Unable to stand the loss of contact, he gently pulled her head back to his shoulder. "Okay, thanks. Tell them thanks for tryin'."

She stepped back. "J.B.? They didn't catch him?"

He wanted her back in his arms. "No, darlin'. It was a pay phone. He was gone when they got there. The uniforms reported they think they just missed him."

"What made them think that?"

"When they arrived at the location, they found the phone danglin' by the cord. They figured he dropped it and ran. My guess is he had a car nearby. Once he was in his car they'd have no way of knowin' which vehicle our perp was drivin'."

"So he got away again." She stepped back into his arms, put her head down on his shoulder and her arms around his waist.

J.B. took a deep breath and hugged, wanting to absorb her into his body. She fit him perfectly, her breasts nestling against his chest, her hips mating exactly with his. No other woman had ever felt this right in his arms. "We'll catch him, darlin'. It's just takin' longer than it should." He chuckled, tipped her head and looked into her eyes. "Besides, we have somethin' he didn't count on when he started his little game."

"Oh really?" Her puzzled expression made him chuckle again. "And what's that?"

He raised an eyebrow and grinned. "We have *me* on our team."

Michael smiled and brought her hand up to cup his cheek. "Well, there's that famous Anderson modesty again."

"Ah, but darlin', we've already established that I'm bull headed, smart, and I never give up. Right?"

"Right." Now, it was her turn to raise an eyebrow and smile. "And what's more, you're stubborn, bright and tenacious."

He loved the fact she felt enough at ease with him to joke. He grinned. "I thought that's what I just said."

"Well, my goodness." She grinned. "That must be where I heard it." Unable to suppress the small laugh, she stepped back, slid her hand to his and gave a little tug before dropping it and heading for the hallway.

"Where are you goin', darlin'?"

"To bed, of course."

"Bed?" J.B. croaked. "Er... uh... sweetheart, what did you have in mind?" Part of him hoped she meant his bed. His saner self knew better.

"Which bedroom is mine?" She looked at him silently for a moment and asked, "You did mean what you said, didn't you?"

"Yes, darlin', I always mean what I say, but you can't blame a guy for hopin'." He sauntered over beside her and pointed down the hall. "It's the second door on the right. You'll have your own bathroom."

"Thanks. Where's my tote?"

"It's in there."

"Thanks." She leaned forward and kissed him, taking him totally by surprise. "Good night, J.B. Sweet dreams."

"Good night, darlin', and the same for you, too." He watched her walk down the hall, unable to breathe. *She* had kissed *him*.

J.B. checked the locks on the doors and windows. He flicked off the stereo, turned out the lights, and headed for what he foresaw as a sleepless night.

Two hours later her screams of pain awakened J.B. and he slipped into his jeans and raced to the guest room door. "Michael?" He knocked but, lost in her private hell, she didn't hear him. His guess had been accurate. He heard and finally understood why, like a yoyo, she was in his arms one second and spinning away the next.

Quietly opening the door, he entered the room.

She thrashed on the bed, pleading. "Rand, please stop. Don't! You're hurting me."

His feelings of rage and helplessness over Keely's rape came roaring back, redoubled. Pain stabbed his heart. She'd carried the pain alone, for years.

"Darlin'?" He feared sitting on the bed, or touching her. "Wake up." He raised his voice. "Michael?"

Her eyes flew open and she skittered back against the headboard on the far side of the bed. Obviously disoriented, her gaze darted around the room. She pulled her feet under her like a cornered animal looking for a way out of the trap.

His voice soothed. "Michael. Wake up, darlin'. It's J.B. I won't hurt you."

Her gaze flew to his face. "J.B.?" She looked around the room again. "Where am I?"

"You're at my place."

"Oh." She slumped down, going as limp as a wet rag. Her eyes closed and her head dropped forward. Then the shaking began. She shivered as if frigid air surrounded her.

J.B. wanted to do something to help her. He wanted to take her in his arms and hold her, make her feel safe again. "Do you want to talk about it?"

Her head jerked up, her eyes filled with fear. "No." She pulled herself back into a tight little ball and looked around frantically. Lips trembling, she whispered, "Talk about what?"

"Michael, I heard. I know what that bastard did to you." He reassured, "You don't *have* to talk about it, but I think you should. If you don't want to talk to me I can get you a phone number. You can talk to someone tonight."

Michael shook her head. "No." She wrapped her arms around her knees. "I couldn't."

"You need help, darlin'. You don't have to deal with this alone. I learned that when my sister, Keely, was raped."

"Raped?" She slid off the bed, backed into the corner of the room and crouched on the floor. She said it as if the word was razor sharp and slicing her soul. "Raped?"

He walked around the bed and squatted in front of her. "Yes, raped. On a date... when she was in high school."

"High school? Oh, God. That poor baby."

"What made it worse was that we knew the entire family. His parents were friends of our parents. Keely had known him her whole life. She trusted him. *We* trusted him."

Michael stared into his eyes. "W-w-was he.... um...... was he p-prosecuted?" Her chattering teeth made it difficult to talk.

"Keely didn't tell anyone when it happened. Later she broke under the pressure." He ran his fingers through his hair. "No one knew what happened until she tried to commit suicide."

With trembling hands she reached out. "Dear God."

He grasped her hands and held on to the contact. "She's workin' as a nurse in Tulsa. She still doesn't date. Doesn't trust men. She chose obstetrics and gynecology so she doesn't have to deal with male patients."

She looked into his eyes as if trying to read his soul. "Did your father think it was all her fault?" The telling little question, asked in a strangled voice, revealed a great deal.

Horrified, J.B. exploded, "No!" When he saw her wince his voice gentled. "Darlin', why would you think that?"

She resembled a cornered doe searching for an escape. "Oh, no reason."

"My God, is that how your family dealt with it?" Now was not the time to get into it. She needed to deal with the rape first. Then he'd help her deal with her family's reaction.

He stood, took her hands and gently pulled her up and put his arm around her shoulders. "Let's go into the living room and get comfortable. If you feel like talkin', you can, but you don't have to, okay? It's your choice."

"Okay." She stepped away from him and walked toward the living room, her mind so involved with what he'd told her she was oblivious to the fact she'd forgotten her robe.

J.B. grabbed the extra blanket off the foot of the bed and followed her.

In the living room he left the lights off. The only source of illumination came from the hall. Settling in the recliner, he pulled her into his lap. When she looked uncomfortable for a moment because he wore no shirt, he wrapped the blanket around her shoulders.

"It's all right. You have nothing to fear from me. I wouldn't hurt you for anything in the world."

"I know. I feel safe with you, safer than I've ever felt in my life." She settled more comfortably into his lap. "I'm sorry I keep jerking away from you all the time. I don't mean to. I guess it's just habit."

"It's all right, darlin'." He held her close, his hand making soothing circles on her back. "Do you think you can talk about it?"

"I've never told a soul… except…"

"I know, but don't you think it's time you did? You'll be surprised how much better you'll feel."

Sounding hopeful, she asked, "Really?"

"Yes, really. Mom always says, 'A burden shared is lighter'."

Michael took a deep breath. "I don't know where to begin."

"The beginnin' is always good. And darlin', anything you tell me will be confidential. I won't repeat it without your permission."

She looked into his eyes and nodded. "Thank you." Her hands covered her eyes briefly. "I never dated in high school."

"Never?" Though surprised by the disclosure he tried to keep the amazement out of his voice.

"Never. All the boys were shorter. None of them asked me out."

"Sometimes boys are stupid, especially when they're teenagers."

Her head jerked around. She smiled when she saw the grin on his face. "I was shy. I doubt I'd have accepted even if they'd asked." She took a deep breath and plunged into her story. "The uh..." She swallowed, stretching her chin up, and swallowed again, then cleared her throat. "The incident happened in college."

He noted her breathing pattern change. Faster, more shallow. "Did you get over your shyness in college?"

"No. Everytime Rand asked me out, my roommate pushed for me to accept. I didn't understand why he wanted to see me. I was a beanpole—tall, skinny, and ugly."

"Darlin', if there's one thing I'm sure about it's that you weren't ugly. Not ever."

"Yes, I was." She blushed.

"What about Rand?"

"He kept asking me out and I kept telling him 'no'." And Bonnie kept insisting I was crazy for not accepting his invitations. She pushed and pushed for me to go out with him, saying he was a big man on campus. A football star. That I was crazy not to go out with him." Her hand wiped the single tear trickling down her cheek. "I never understood why she did that. Why she pushed so hard."

"So you went." His voice displayed no censure.

"Yes." Her face turned red and she looked away, unable to meet his eye. "I just wanted her to shut up about it, to get off my back. I thought if I went, he'd find out how boring I was and he'd stop asking me out."

"But that's not what happened, is it?" J.B. dreaded hearing what was coming next, but she needed to say it.

"I learned later, the only reason he wanted to take me out was to win a bet."

That wasn't what he'd expected to hear. Rage, hot as sizzling lava, shot through him. He reined it in, fearing she'd think him angry with her, and asked quietly, "What bet?"

She looked away, humiliated. "They had a name for me." Her voice sounded strangled, "They called me 'Princess Ice'."

He felt her pain as she told him and tried to comfort her, holding her closer. "People can be very cruel. I can only imagine how much it hurt you to hear that."

"Yes. Especially after what happened on that date."

"Can you tell me about it?"

She sat silently, staring into space.

"Take it slow and easy. Put your head back here on my shoulder, close your eyes and try to remember it the way it happened."

A shuddering inhalation, then a sigh. "That won't be hard. I relive it in my nightmares all the time. I can remember every vivid and nasty detail as if it happened yesterday." She shivered and turned toward him, curling in on her shoulder.

He kissed her temple. "Remember it now, when you're awake. All you have to do is say it out loud."

She nodded, turned, drew her knees up, and placed her ear on his shoulder. Surprised, she realized she was more comfortable in this position and buried her nose in the curve of his neck.

Allowing her mind to drift back, she shivered. J.B. pulled the afghan off the back of the recliner and placed it on top of the blanket. She didn't notice. The memory hit her senses in vivid detail. She moaned in remembered pain. Her words came haltingly at first. As the tale unfolded, her pain was as real as the day it happened.

J.B. held her, murmuring soft words of comfort and love as he listened.

~ * ~

"I thought we were going to a movie." Though nervous, she tried to keep her voice steady.

He smiled. "I'd rather picnic in the moonlight. You know, 'A loaf of bread, a jug of wine and thou'. Especially thou."

"Please, Rand. I want to go back to the dorm."

Rand Halstead spread a blanket on the ground beside his silver Porsche 911. "C'mon, Mickie, don't be such a baby."

The knot in her stomach rivaled the Rock of Gibraltar. "Take me home."

He kicked off his shoes and knelt on the blanket. Before she realized what he planned, he pulled her from the car, and snickered. "Hey, babe, it's just a little loving between friends."

Within moments she was on her back, pressed to the ground. "Please, take me home." She cringed as the odor of sweat and musk assailed her. "Why are you doing this?"

Grinning down at her, he grabbed her wrists. "Don't be a prude, Mickie. Everybody does it. We'll have fun. I promise." His fingers bruising, he pulled her wrists up, using her arms like a vise to hold her head immobile.

"Don't." She scissored her legs to break free. His legs clamped around hers, holding her still and vulnerable to his violations. Her breath rasped in her ears. Nausea roiled in her stomach. "You're hurting me." Her teeth clamped down on her lip and she tasted the coppery tang of blood on her tongue.

Pulling her blouse free, his hand snaked under it, and pushed up her bra. His fingers pinched her breasts painfully.

"Don't, Rand. Don't do this." Tears filled her eyes. Wracking sobs tore from her throat. His hand slid under her skirt and tore her panties away.

"Relax. You'll like it, I promise." His voice raspy, his breathing hoarse and panting, he whispered, "It only hurts the first time, but I'll make it good for you."

More terrified than ever before, she pleaded, "Please, Rand. I don't want you to... Don't!"

Her clothing disappeared shred by shred. "Stop it, Rand. Please stop." She fought, but terror took over when she heard the rasp of his zipper. She screamed, "Let me go!"

His strength made him the victor.

~ * ~

Afterward, she lay, a huddled mass of pain and humiliation as he stood over her zipping his slacks. "It won't hurt next time." He slipped on his loafers and knelt on the grass, his hand stretched toward her hair.

She scuttled away, dragging the blanket with her, trying to cover her nakedness. Her voice hoarse and unrecognizable, she rasped, "Don't touch me."

"C'mon, Mickie, no sense crying. The worst is over. I promise, it won't ever hurt again. You'll see. You'll feel better about it tomorrow."

Refusing to look at him, she slipped on her shoes, and trembling, rose to her feet. Wrapping the blanket around her shoulders, she walked toward the university.

"Hey, Mickie, where are you going? I'll take you back."

Ignoring him, she continued on her path.

"Get in the car. I'll take you home." He followed a short distance behind her for a while. "Mickie? Don't be this way."

She trudged on, shivering, unable to stop the tears that continued to pour down her face. His voice sounded farther away. When his words penetrated her pain, she stopped and turned around. "What? What did you say?"

"I said I had a good time and asked if you want to go out again tomorrow night."

Shuddering, she turned and plodded down the road.

~ * ~

Exhausted, Michael shuddered, curling in to J.B.'s body seeking refuge from her thoughts. "I shouldn't have gone." Her tear washed face turned up to him. "If I hadn't..."

"Darlin', it wasn't your fault. Do you hear me? None of it was your fault. You trusted him to behave like a gentleman."

Tears coursed down her cheeks like a river on a rampage. So many tears. Her hoarse whisper broke his heart. "It *was* my fault. If I'd stayed home he could never..."

"No, Michael. You had the right to say 'no'. I *heard* you tellin' him 'no' over and over again. He didn't listen."

She pressed the tips of her fingers to her upper lip, and nodded.

"You told him to stop. But he didn't stop, did he?"

"No." She turned her face back in to his shoulder, wrapping her arms around his neck. Sobs shook her. "He wouldn't stop."

J.B. spoke gently. "It was *his* fault, sweetheart. It was *all* his fault. He didn't have the right to do what he did. Nobody has the right to do what he did."

For the first time in her life, someone said what she needed to hear, what she'd needed so desperately to hear more than ten years ago.

It wasn't her fault.

He held her, cuddled her like an infant, soothing her with soft murmurs and caresses while she cried for the girl who had lost the battle on that night so long ago.

When the sobbing slowed to an occasional shudder he lifted her head and looked directly into her eyes. "I love you, Michael."

"What?"

"I love you. Don't worry. I don't expect you to say it back. I love you—even if you don't love me."

"How could you?"

"It's real easy, darlin'. I never believed in love at first sight 'til you. I fell like a Douglas Fir under a chain saw."

"I... uh... J.B.?" He had lifted the burden she'd carried for over ten years and now he'd given her the words she'd never heard in her life. She didn't know how to respond.

"It's okay, sweetheart. Don't worry about it." He pulled the lever lowering the leg rest. "Do you want me to make you some warm milk?"

"No." Her tear damp face broke into a smile as she shuddered. "I hate warm milk."

"What about a cup of tea? I think one of Keely's herbal blends might be just the thing."

She put her hand on his cheek. "Do you spend a lot of time rescuing women from their nightmares?"

"Nah. Just those I love." He loved her and planned to tell her often. He figured she hadn't heard those words nearly enough.

A deep, shuddering breath, ending on a sigh, followed by a yawn, indicated her exhaustion. She snuggled closer and put her left arm around his neck, nuzzling her face against his throat. "Mmmm. You smell good."

The instant reaction of J.B.'s body had to be squelched. Now was definitely not the time. She was only beginning to trust him. Not as just a police detective who could keep her safe, but really trust him—as a man. If he wanted this trust to grow into something stronger, and more lasting, he had to make sure he ignored the warm skin glowing through the satin nightgown. And the strawberry scent surrounding her.

He stood up with her in his arms. Allowing her legs to slide to the floor, he turned her loose. Striding toward the couch to put a little distance between them, he turned on the lamp.

She walked over and hugged him around the waist and stepped away. "Let's make some of that herbal tea you mentioned. How does chamomile sound to you?"

J.B.'s breath stopped in his throat as she moved away. Her body was clearly outlined by the lamp he'd turned on moments ago. Mesmerized by the sight, he couldn't breathe. Above a waist that looked much too small for a woman as tall as she, the gentle swell of her breast was crowned by beaded nipples.

The picture, engraved in his mind, set his blood racing, pounding, building a driving need. His heart hammered like a tom-tom, choking him. Before he remembered to breathe his lungs burned like a hopper filled with the living fire of molten steel.

She had no idea—couldn't possibly know what it did to him. Abruptly he sat back down. "Uh, you go ahead, darlin'. I've... uh... There's somethin' I need to take care of in here."

He'd lifted such a burden from her soul by listening, by not judging her guilty, she wanted to do something for him. "Is it anything I can help you with?"

He forced himself to give the answer she needed at this moment. "No," he croaked. "You make the tea."

"Could it wait 'til after we have our tea?"

"Oh—no—I don't think so."

"Okay. When the water boils, I'll bring it here."

"Oh, yeah, sure. That'd be nice." J.B. thought he just might die from the exquisite pleasure-pain caused by the picture his mind continued to replay.

She went to the kitchen and J.B. leaned his elbows on his knees, mumbling, "Chamomile tea. That ought to do it, all right. If it solves my problem, I'm goin' to get rich bottlin' the stuff. I might even get to likin' it."

Michael called from the kitchen, "J.B.? Did you say something?"

In a strangled whisper his answer rasped out, "No." He rubbed a hand down his face, and spoke louder. "No."

She appeared in the doorway. "What?"

"Never mind, darlin', it wasn't important. I was just thinkin' out loud. You go ahead and make that tea."

"Oh. Okay." She turned back to the kitchen, chattering away, sounding almost light-hearted. And totally unaware of his discomfort. "Tea coming right up. It should be ready in about three minutes."

A few minutes later she returned to the living room to find him exactly as she'd left him. She carried a tray, two mugs, cream, sugar, and the teapot covered with a knitted tea cozy. "The tea's ready."

"Okay." Having gotten his raging libido under control he opted to keep his eyes closed until she no longer stood in front of the lamp.

Michael noticed his posture. "Do you have a headache?"

"No, love. I'm a little tired, I guess. Don't worry. Go ahead and pour the tea." He scooted back on the couch and mumbled, "I sure hope this stuff works."

"What stuff works?"

"Oh, I... uh… Keely swears by chamomile tea to relax you and put you to sleep. I think that's what you need."

"Tea?"

"No. A good night's sleep. Have you ever had chamomile tea before?"

"No, but I like to try new things sometimes."

A few minutes later he sipped at the tea as he watched her face when she took the first taste from her cup. He laughed when she wrinkled her nose and quipped, "I guess it's an acquired taste."

Michael looked down at her cup for a moment. She took another taste. After setting the cup back on the tray she asked dryly, "How long does it take one to acquire this taste?"

J.B.'s laughter rolled. "I guess Keely's supply of chamomile is safe from future invasion."

"Uh huh. At least from me. I think I'd rather take my chances on getting to sleep without it."

J.B. carried the tray to the kitchen. When he returned he pulled Michael to her feet. "Do you think you can sleep now?"

"Yes. I feel more at peace than I've felt in years." She put her arms around his neck and kissed him on the cheek. "Thank you. What would I do without you?"

"Darlin', I intend to make myself so indispensable you won't be able to think of drawin' your next breath without me. Things have changed a lot in only a few days. A short time ago you didn't want me near you." He put his arms around her waist and pulled her close. "Now, how about a real good night kiss? That little peck on the cheek just isn't goin' to do it for me."

His deep husky voice sent a thrill down her spine. Without hesitation Michael leaned in to him, lifting her mouth to meet his. Her arms went unerringly around his neck. Surprised there was no fear, she fitted her body to his.

She found breathing difficult. Her skin tingled as the musky aftershave drenched her senses. The silky hair at his nape curled through her fingers. She was drowning in new sensations. Her heart pounded like a caged bird—but she wasn't afraid.

The kiss ended before she was ready. She rested her head on his chest, listening to his heart race. She was surprised to find she didn't want to leave his arms—wanted to put off separating from him for the night. She smiled and backed away. These feelings were too new. She didn't have a clue how to deal with them.

J.B. had intended to keep it brief—for his sake as well as hers, but as always when near her, he lost all control of his emotions. Finally he stepped back and fought to pull air into his starving lungs. "I'd better let you get to bed. You need to rest." J.B. walked her to her room, kissed her one last time then went down the hall to his own bedroom.

Michael crawled into bed and slept like a baby until the alarm went off two hours later, and she awoke more rested than she had in years.

~ * ~

J.B. pulled up in front of the courthouse. "I'll pick you up at noon for lunch." He leaned over and gave her a quick kiss. "I love you, Michael."

She ducked her head shyly, "Yes. I..."

"It's okay, darlin'. Say it when you feel it."

"But I think I do."

"No, darlin'. If it was there, you'd be wanting to shout it from the rooftops—just like I do."

Michael got out of the car, grabbed her briefcase and trotted up the sidewalk to the building. She turned at the door, smiled and waved. J.B.'s smile would carry her through to lunch. As she hurried along she rehearsed the details of her case on the docket in Judge Jeffers' court. This one would not be a cakewalk. She had to get her act together, concentrate, if she hoped to win.

She glanced up and saw the elevator doors start to close. "Hold the elevator, please." She jogged toward the waiting car. Arriving at the open doors, she looked up into the face of her nightmare. Rand Halstead.

Choking. Can't breathe.

Heart pounding too hard. Roaring. Pain.

Nine

Her nightmare. Rand. Here in broad daylight, smirking at her. She'd hoped, prayed, never to see him again. He stood watching, waiting, reaching toward her. *Don't touch. Don't.*

"Hello, Mickie. Long time no see."

His voice grated like a fingernail on a blackboard. Her nerves frayed. She raced away, looking over her shoulder as she sprinted through the door. Running, fleeing to find safety. No safety. Anywhere.

A wall stopped her flight and she bounced back a step.

"Sweetheart?"

The deep rumbling voice broke through her panic instantly. Refuge. Her safe haven.

"J.B." A ripple of relief feathered over her skin. Launching herself into his arms, she remembered how to breathe. Even clinging like a limpet she wasn't close enough. "J.B."

His voice a welcome rumble, she heard him. "Darlin'?"

Down to her soul she knew. Nothing—and no one—could hurt her.

"What's the matter?"

Standing in the bright sunshine he held her. In his arms the darkness slowly receded.

J.B. instantly responded to protect her and engulfed her in his embrace. He didn't know which way to turn to put himself between her and danger. Her arms clasped his neck so tight he feared it would snap. As he soothed her, his gaze checked out every man on the street. He absorbed the shock wave of her tremors.

"Michael?" He slid his arm under her knees, picked her up and walked to his car. He let her legs slide down, and unlocking the door, he sat on the passenger seat, his legs extended out of the car, and held her. She curled into him, her face buried in his neck like a frightened child. "Talk to me, sweetheart."

"Rand's here. I saw Rand." Her voice quavered.

"Halstead? Here?"

"Yes." A shuddering breath. "In the court house."

J.B. looked toward the building. He couldn't help wondering. Had she actually seen Halstead, or had she imagined him because of her nightmare last night? Her terror seemed real. Her arms nearly choked him to death. But he had to ask. "Sweetheart, could you be mistaken? Maybe it was someone who resembles him and you thought it was him because of the memories that you dredged up last night."

"I will never forget his face, and I'd never get it mixed up with anyone else's face. It was him."

He picked up the radio and asked dispatch to send Shag to his location.

J.B.'s voice penetrated her terror and Michael glanced up, confusion and self-doubt evident on her face. "I didn't imagine him, did I?" She now questioned her sanity wondering if the incident occurred or if, as he suggested, she'd made a mistake. Another thought occurred. What if she'd conjured up an apparition? She closed her eyes and memory returned. "He spoke to me." She eased away and confirmed what she believed. "I saw him. He was there. He spoke. He called me 'Mickie'."

"We'll check it out. Exactly where did you see him?"

"The elevator." Her heart no longer pounded—no longer felt like it would burst through her chest. Her breathing nearly normal, cold sweat still beaded her brow.

"Are you okay now, darlin'?"

"Yes. Better. It was a shock. So sudden. For him to be here now. I mean—after last night." She took a deep breath and covered her face with her hands. "I thought I was more in control the last few days. The nightmare coming back was..." She looked off across the square. "Seeing him threw me for a loop."

"You're doin' real well, darlin'." J.B. smiled at her. "I'm proud of how you've handled everything he's thrown at you the last couple of days."

She looked into his eyes and saw admiration. He was proud of her. Never before in her life had anyone been proud of her. Her self-esteem rose another tiny degree. Then something he said registered. "*He's* thrown at me? What do you mean?"

"Think about it, darlin'. You're bein' harassed. He shows up at the courthouse. Coincidence? I don't think so."

"So you think it's Rand who is calling me?"

"We're goin' to find out."

"I looked through those elevator doors and saw his face, and I don't know what happened." She looked as if she saw something at a great distance. "I thought it was ten years ago."

"That's understandable. You relived the experience only last night. Your reaction is perfectly normal. Seeing that face so soon afterwards was bound to make you have a flashback." He frowned slightly. "Did he touch you?"

"No." She shuddered at the thought. "No, he didn't."

"Good." J.B. rubbed his neck.

Watching him, Michael looked embarrassed. "I nearly knocked you over when I came flying out of the court house."

"Nah. I can take it." He grinned, a teasing quality entering his voice. "You can throw yourself at me anytime you want, darlin'."

Her startled gaze came up to meet his eyes. Seeing them twinkle, she giggled. She sounded nearly hysterical. Realizing her emotions were still too near the ragged edge, she feared tears would flow and clamped her teeth together.

It suddenly occurred to her he should be at work. "Why did you come back?"

"You forgot your purse. I noticed it on the car seat after I left here."

"I never forget my purse." She looked around her, genuinely perplexed. Plaintively she mumbled, "Why would I forget it this time?"

"Don't know, darlin'. Maybe because you only got about three hours sleep last night? And that wasn't in one stretch."

Shag pulled into a nearby parking space, climbed out of his car and loped over to where they sat. "What's the problem, buddy?"

"Well, we may have gotten lucky."

"Oh really? That'd be a switch."

"Yeah. There's a possibility our perp is in the court house."

"How do we know it's him?"

"We don't. Not until we take him in for questioning."

Shag grinned. "So we're guessing here?"

J.B. glowered. "Shag, take my word for it. We have reason to suspect this bastard."

"Okay. Does he have a name?"

"Name's Rand Halstead." J.B. turned to Michael. "Can you give us a description, sweetheart?"

Michael's voice barely above a whisper, she responded, "Yes. About six-three. Blond hair. Icy blue eyes."

Shag busily took notes. "About how much does he weigh?"

Michael looked at him, surprised. "I don't know. How would I know that?"

"Just a guess will do."

She stood up and walked a few steps away and turned. "He was a football player."

Shag muttered, "That's a big help." He asked, "Bigger than J.B.?" He gestured for J.B. to rise. "Stand up, buddy."

She looked at J.B. standing. "Yes."

"How much bigger?"

"For heaven's sake, I don't know. I guess maybe twenty or thirty pounds heavier."

"So, about two-thirty to two-forty."

"Whatever." She didn't have a clue how to guess someone's weight.

"Where did you see him?"

"At the elevator." She glanced at her watch and her heart plummeted. She had to hurry. "J.B., I'm going to be late for court. I don't want to be cited for contempt."

"Whose court?"

"Judge Jeffers."

He grinned. "Darlin', this is your lucky day."

"I don't think so."

"Yeah, it is." J.B. picked up his car phone, and dialed a number. "Hi, Sheila. Let me talk to the man." He winked at Michael. "Hello, Uncle Judge. It's J.B."

Michael's eyes widened. She turned to Shag and mouthed, "Uncle Judge?"

Shag grinned and murmured, "His mother's brother."

J.B. continued his conversation. "Uncle Steve, I need a favor." He grinned. "How can you turn down your favorite nephew?" He laughed. "Okay, okay. Ms. Mainwaring is due in your courtroom. She's going to be a couple minutes late." J.B. cleared his throat. "She spotted a suspect we've been looking for. He was in the elevator here in the courthouse. She took time to report it. We're checkin' it out." He winked at Michael. "Yes, sir. Thank you. She's on her way."

Dismayed, Michael croaked out, "J.B., what did you do?"

"Got you a few minutes delay. Now come on. Let's get you to court while Shag starts lookin' for Halstead."

"You're going with me?"

"Sweetheart, with Halstead runnin' loose in the courthouse, do you really think I'd let you go in there by yourself?"

"But, I can... J.B., I'm an attorney. I'm representing a client. I mean... I have to present a certain image. How is it going to look if I have a police escort into court?"

"Oh, not into the courtroom. Only to the door." He sprinted toward the steps of the building, dragging Michael along behind him.

Keeping up with his long legs wasn't easy. In fact, nearly impossible. Even when one's own legs were considered long. Into the stairwell, two steps at a time. *Can't keep up this pace. Have to have breath to speak.* "J.B., you look—ridiculous carrying—my purse," she panted out between gasps for breath.

He chuckled. "It doesn't bother me if it doesn't bother you, darlin'."

Where did he get the breath to laugh? "No." She'd never make it. "Of course..." She tried to catch up. "...not." Her arm would come out of the socket in another moment. "J.B., slow down," she gasped.

"You don't need—to take the stairs—two at a time," she admonished, panting like a steam engine.

He grabbed her briefcase, put his arm around her waist and took the steps at a near-normal rate. Only one at a time. "That better, darlin'?"

"Much." When she caught her breath she'd tell him. She could have done without the stair exercise. She'd never had a weight problem. Racing through the halls of justice like this wasn't civilized. And besides, no one needed to reach the third floor in a minute-and-a-half. "Uncle Judge, huh?"

J.B. chuckled. "Yeah. Uncle Steve is one of the good guys. He used to let us steal his apples. After we ate as many as we wanted he'd make us pick the rest on the trees. He left baskets of fruit on the porches of people goin' through hard times. He always knew where there was a need."

"What a remarkable—childhood—you had, J.B." She could breathe normally in another minute or two. She hoped.

"Was it so different from yours, darlin'?"

"Oh, yes. Remind me to—tell you about it sometime."

He looked down and met her gaze. "I'll do that."

They arrived at the doors of the courtroom. J.B. gave her a brief kiss, glanced through the doors—and stopped dead still. "Well, darlin', would you look at that?"

Michael looked. And gasped. "Rand."

"What I thought, too." He pulled his phone out of his pocket and called Shag. "We've got him on three. Uncle Steve's court." He kept his arm around Michael, pulling her close. "Okay. I'll wait." He disconnected and stepped away from the door before handing Michael her purse and briefcase. Within a few minutes Shag came loping down the hallway.

"What've we got?" He stepped to the court room door and looked inside. "Oh yeah. I love it when someone falls into our laps." He turned to J.B. "Maybe it's too easy."

"That'll be the day." J.B. placed Michael against the wall. "Wait here, darlin'." He turned to his partner. "Okay, let's go get him."

The two men walked side by side down the aisle and stopped just back of the first row. Shag stepped behind Halstead while J.B. moved beside him and flashed his badge.

Halstead remained seated and glanced at the badge. "What can I do for you..." He looked more closely at the badge. "...Detective...?" He looked questioningly at J.B.

"Anderson. J.B. Anderson." J.B. put the badge away and gestured to Shag. "This is my partner, Detective Dexter."

Looking over his shoulder, Halstead asked, "Is there a problem?"

Shag nodded. "Might be. May I see some I. D.?"

Rand rose and reached into his inside pocket.

J.B.'s body tensed. "Uh uh. Take the hand out slow and easy. And empty."

The ex-football star looked around the courtroom. Noting the little scene was the center of everyone's attention he flushed slightly. "What the hell is going on here? You asked for I. D. I need to get my wallet."

"Okay. Hold the coat open and reach in with two fingers."

The man followed instructions and removed the wallet from his inside coat pocket. "Okay? It's just a wallet. For crying out loud, what do you think I'm carrying in there?"

Michael halted in the doorway, watching. Rand looking over Shag's shoulder, made eye contact with her. His smile of recognition sent shivers down her back.

"Hello, Mickie. You going to run away again? You could tell these detectives that I'm not a terrorist."

J.B.'s low growl was barely discernible. "Maybe only with women." He glared and snapped, "Now let's see that I. D."

Halstead, looking puzzled, handed over his driver's license. "Will that do?"

"For now." J.B. checked out the license and handed it to Shag. "Call for wants and warrants."

Rand paled. "Wait a minute here. What do you mean, 'wants and warrants'? Am I being arrested?"

"Not yet." Thinking about what this sonofabitch had done to Michael all those years ago, J.B. wanted to beat him to a pulp. And if Halstead was the one harassing her now, he might go ahead and do it—even if it meant his job. It'd feel real good to knock those shiny white teeth down the bastard's throat.

"Detective Anderson, do you mind telling me exactly what's going on here?"

Shag walked back to J.B. "No wants, no warrants. You want to check him out with NCIC?"

Rand Halstead spat out, "What the hell is NCIC?"

Shag glanced at him, answering mechanically. "National Crime Information Center." He turned back to J.B. "Well?"

"Maybe. Later. Depends on his answers." J.B. turned to Halstead who listened intently to their conversation. "Will you voluntarily come down to the station to answer some questions?"

"I can't do that. I've..."

J.B. grinned. Maybe he'd get to cuff this bastard, and lead him out of the courthouse under arrest. "Did you hear that, Shag? He doesn't want to answer our questions."

"Wait a minute." Visibly shaken, Halstead's gaze darted from Shag to J.B. and back again. "Just a minute. I didn't say I didn't want to. I said I can't. I was ordered to appear here today under subpoena."

J.B. shrugged. "Okay. We'll wait."

"For what? What the hell is going on here?"

"All rise." The bailiff's voice resounded through the courtroom and stopped conversation.

Judge Jeffers entered the courtroom and took his seat. He looked toward the knot of people standing there and crooked his finger at J.B.

J.B. sauntered to the bench. "Hi, Uncle Steve."

"Don't you 'Hi' me, you young rascal. What have you gotten yourself into now?"

"I need to take that man in for questionin'. He's been subpoenaed to testify here today. So I'll wait until you're through with him."

"What are you questioning him about?"

"Uncle Steve, you see that beautiful woman standin' there by the door?"

The judge looked to the entryway. "Ms. Mainwaring?"

"Yeah." He looked at the judge and grinned. "That's my future bride."

"You're engaged?" The judge looked offended. "Your mother didn't tell me you were engaged."

"I'm not. Yet." J.B. looked at Michael and smiled. "I haven't told her yet."

"J.B., you don't *tell* a woman she's going to marry you. You *ask* her."

"Umm hmm. I know. I'll ask her." His grin spread even wider. "And then I'm going to tell her she has to say yes because she can't possibly get along without me."

The judge raised an eyebrow and smiled. "You always were such a timid soul."

J.B. laughed. "But you like me the way I am, don't you, Uncle Steve?"

The judge sighed. "J.B., what does any of this have to do with the witness we were discussing?"

"Oh. Well, someone has been stalking Michael and we have reason to believe it's him."

"I see. So, what you need to question him about has nothing to do with the case on this morning's docket?"

"No, sir."

The judge gestured with his gavel. "Then sit down over there and wait your turn."

"Yes, sir."

J.B. walked back to Michael. "Sweetheart, Halstead has been called to testify in this case."

"His name wasn't on the witness list I was given. I wonder why?"

"Let Uncle Steve handle that question. But this means you're goin' to have to question him. Can you handle it?"

"I have no choice. My client is depending on me."

"I'll be here. Right behind Halstead. If you feel things closin' in on you, just look back here and see me sittin' here—lovin' you. Imagine me holdin' you in my arms when we get home tonight."

"I..." She put her arms around his waist and felt comforted at the speed with which he responded. She looked into his eyes and murmured, "Why are you so good to me?"

"That's easy, darlin'." The deep bass rumble of J.B.'s voice vibrated against her ear. "Because you deserve it—and much, much more. Remember, I love you." He turned her loose and stepped back. "Go get 'em, darlin'. You slay this dragon and the next one will be easier."

She walked down the aisle deliberately making eye contact with Rand Halstead. When he grinned at her she stared straight into his eyes pretending she was looking at something loathsome. It worked. She watched his grin shrivel—and die.

Three hours later, the case won, she returned to J.B.

"Darlin', I'm proud of you. You were brilliant the way you handled Halstead."

Unused to praise, Michael blushed. "I didn't do any more than any other lawyer would have done."

"Oh, come on, sweetheart. You should be clicking your heels. You had a shock this morning. A lot of people would've folded."

"It was what I'm paid to do." Her face flamed even brighter. "I guess I'm pleased with the outcome."

"Michael, don't act like a stiff necked snob. It's okay to feel pride in your accomplishments."

Shag walked over, escorting Halstead. "Ready to go, buddy?"

"So, Mickie, you got something going with the detective here?"

J.B. leaned in, his nose an inch from Halstead's. "You want to walk out of here with those shiny white teeth in one piece—and still attached to your mouth?"

Shag stepped in. "Back off. Maybe I'd better take him in my car to make sure he gets there. By the book, J.B."

"Yeah," J.B. growled. "By the book."

Michael grabbed J.B.'s hand. "I'll go to my office."

"What about lunch, darlin'?"

"I'll have something sent in. Don't worry. I'll be fine."

"I'll walk you to your car and follow you around the square."

~ * ~

Three hours later Shag and J.B. stepped out of the interrogation room. J.B. stretched and yawned. "It looks like he's goin' to walk—for now."

"J.B., I think it's time you clued me in on why you're being so hard on this guy. I would've let him go two hours ago."

J.B. glowered. What steamed him was, unless they could get enough on this bastard to file charges, they'd *have* to let him go. "You mean, in spite of the fact the bastard owns a sporting goods store—with easy access to crossbows?"

"Yeah. In spite of that fact. He doesn't have a record of any kind. It's possible our perp purchased the crossbow from the man's store but that doesn't make Halstead guilty of anything except owning a store. I've watched you, buddy. This is personal. You've never gone after a suspect with the same vigor as you have Halstead. Now, tell me what's going on—what haven't you told me?"

J.B. walked away a couple of steps, rubbing the back of his neck. He turned and walked back. He couldn't tell Michael's story. Not without her permission. He'd given her his word anything she told him would be confidential.

"Let me make a phone call. Maybe I can answer you."

He stepped to his desk and called Michael. "Hey, Lyndi, let me speak to the boss." He laughed. "Listen, all the beautiful ladies remember my voice, so why should you be an exception?"

J.B.'s heart rate increased at the sound of delight in her voice when Michael said his name. "Hello, sweetheart." He'd give anything not to bring her pain. "I hate to do this at all and I'm really sorry to discuss it over the telephone, but it's important." He listened as wariness crept into her voice. Stalling, he cleared his throat, knowing he couldn't put off asking the question.

Taking a deep breath, he leaped in with both feet. "Shag asked why I'm leaning so hard on this jerk. Darlin', he needs to know it isn't just because I don't like the bastard's looks." J.B. closed his eyes and clenched his teeth as he heard the little moan she tried to suppress. "Shag's my partner, darlin'. He knows me and knows I'm holdin' out on him." Her trust in him became crystal clear in her tone, even more than in what she said. "He'll keep your confidence, darlin'. I trust him completely." He sighed with relief. "Thanks. I know this isn't easy. I love you, Michael."

J.B. returned to where Shag stood outside the interrogation room. "Shag, what I'm goin' to tell you is strictly confidential for right now. No charges were ever filed, hell it wasn't even reported to anybody so far as I know."

"What the hell are you talking about, J.B.?"

"Halstead raped Michael when they were in college."

"Damn." Shag's breath whooshed out of his lungs along with the expletive. He remembered J.B.'s sister, Keely. "That sonofabitch."

"Yeah, my sentiments exactly. And then some."

"J.B., he's a bastard, or at least he was in college. We haven't got a thing that says he's continued the same pattern to the present. We can't prove he's the stalker. We've got zip. Zero. Nada. We have to let him go."

J.B. sighed. "I know. I hoped he'd crack if we kept up the pressure. Cut him loose." He grabbed his jacket and headed toward the door. "Catch you in the mornin'. I'm takin' my lady to dinner."

When J.B. arrived at Michael's office she wasn't there. He was furious and snarled at the hapless secretary sitting behind her desk. "Where the hell is she, Lyndi?"

"I don't know. She didn't say. She made a few phone calls and then she left."

"Didn't you think it strange that she didn't leave you a number where she could be reached?"

"To be honest, no, I didn't. She has her pager with her."

"Oh. Well, page her. I want to know where she is and I want to know now." He paced a circle in front of Lyndi's desk.

"Sit down, Detective Anderson. That's fairly new carpet. We'd like the loft to remain the same over the entire floor."

J.B. grinned sheepishly and settled into a chair. He attempted to read a magazine. He flipped through it too fast to do more than spend a microsecond of attention on each page. When the phone on Lyndi's desk rang he jumped. He leaned forward ready to spring from the chair if it were Michael.

Lyndi grinned. "Hey, boss, there's an insane man here looking for you."

That's all she got out of her mouth before J.B. grabbed the phone. "Michael, where the hell are you?" His eyebrows raised. "You're doin' what?" He grinned. "Well, I'll be damned. Okay, darlin', I'll wait here for you, but not for long. Okay?" He handed the phone back to Lyndi and, still grinning, sat in the chair again. This time he actually looked at the magazine.

~ * ~

Michael hurried through the door an hour later. Strands of hair had slipped from her usually neat chignon. Her flushed face and sparkling eyes radiated an air of excitement. She hurried to J.B. and pulled him out of the chair for a rib-cracking hug. Smiling she gazed into his eyes, rose on her toes and planted a kiss on his mouth.

She glanced over her shoulder, a grin on her face. "Hi, Lyndi. Anything important come up while I was gone?"

"No, not anything that can't wait. Winslow finished the Taylor brief and put it on your desk."

"I'll look at it in the morning." She turned back to J.B. "Come on, big guy, let's go home to my house. We can shower and change. Then I want some dinner. I've worked up an appetite."

J.B., mesmerized by the changes he noted, couldn't take his gaze off her and allowed her to pull him along toward the door. Outside the door he pulled her into his arms and kissed her.

Michael thought she might float away. She wanted the kiss to go on forever. J.B.'s soft lips moving over hers sent a wave of euphoria flowing over her body. She was aware of every nerve ending, every hair on her body. She put her arms around his neck, wanting to be closer. The incident of long ago never entered her mind. J.B.'s kiss washed it away. She wanted to touch his skin and ran her fingers under the collar of his shirt.

"Oh, God, darlin', we've got to stop this. I may turn to ashes if we don't." J.B.'s gasps for breath sounded only slightly harsher than her own.

He grabbed her hand and hurried to the street. "Let's get home so we can take showers. I think I'll opt for a cold one. Does your water temperature control have a setting called 'North Pole'? Or maybe it'd be better if you had a setting called 'Antarctica'."

Michael laughed. "Are you sure you'd want it that cold?"

"Right now? Oh, yeah."

Arriving home, Michael hurried into her room and stripped off her clothes as she went. Her hairpins came next and she dumped the lot of them on the vanity before stepping into the shower.

Only minutes into J.B.'s shower, his fantasy about taking a shower *with* Michael had him turning the hot water off completely.

A while later, Michael stepped out of her bedroom wearing dark wine slacks with a pale pink blouse. A wine and pink paisley scarf looped around her neck, held in place with a vivid pink butterfly pin. She looked at him and smiled. "Do I look okay?"

"Oh, darlin', you're so beautiful you take my breath away."

"You look handsome, J.B." A momentary spasm of fear flitted over her features. "There's something I want to do, and I'd like you to hear me out, okay?"

"Sure, sweetheart. What do you want to do?"

"I want to go back to The Hamburger Place. It's not just that I'm hungry for my favorite hamburger. To use your words, I need to 'slay the dragon'."

"We can order burgers and pick them up to bring back here." He wanted to protect her, even from her own fears.

"No. That's not the same. It's important, J.B. If I can't go back there, then I won't be able to enjoy one of my favorite meals. I can't allow him to take any more of my freedom." She smiled. "One of the things I learned in the Ju Jitsu class this afternoon is, take control of my own life."

"All right. The Hamburger Place, it is."

Walking in the door was hard, but she did it. J.B. was wonderful, distracting her with nonsense. She didn't remember ever laughing so much.

Back home J.B. pulled her into his arms. *Pagliacci* with Luciano Pavarotti seemed a perfect ending to the day.

"I love you, darlin'," He pulled her across his lap, her legs stretched along the couch, and pulled pins from her hair. The ebony silk cascaded over his arm. His fingers stroked through it. "Your hair is beautiful. I thought it would be."

"You saw it that night when *he* came to my window."

"Yes, but I didn't get to run my fingers through it." He kissed her, his fingers tangled in her hair. Her mouth opened tentatively giving him access to her honeyed sweetness. He groaned, pulling her closer. With her arms around his neck, her breasts pressed against his chest, he might lose his mind.

"J.B., I..."

The doorbell rang. J.B., thinking it could be Shag, got up to answer. A large manilla envelope lay pinned to the porch with a hunting knife. The name and address had been cut out of magazines.

Ten

J.B. looked around the neighborhood. Nothing moved. He pulled the handkerchief from his pocket, removed the knife and slipped it in his belt loop under his coat. After another quick look around the area he grasped the envelope by the corner, using his handkerchief.

He hated this. When could he give her some good news? He returned to the living room. "I'm sorry, darlin'. He's left another letter. Maybe, if we're lucky, he left his fingerprints on the paper. Then we'll have him."

She sighed. "One can always hope. Let's see what it says." Was this becoming so commonplace it no longer terrified her? Maybe. But she suddenly realized that J.B.'s presence in her life was the biggest part of the equation. She no longer felt alone and with him beside her she could face anything. Without him she'd have been terrified. The note left at her door along with all the other intrusions into her home would have sent her over the edge.

J.B. put the mailer down on the coffee table. With his pen he carefully lifted the flap and held it open. Pulling the pencil from his pocket, he used the eraser to cautiously slide the paper from the envelope.

Michael noted the care with which he removed the evidence. "Unsealed. As you pointed out the last time, no DNA. He knows how to protect himself. That's why I've always thought it could be a cop."

"Yeah, darlin', I can see how you might. But with all the junk on TV, and all those how-to books proliferating the shelves, not to mention what one can find on the internet, anybody can learn anything now days. It'd be easy to find out DNA can be lifted from saliva left on the flap of an envelope."

"I suppose." The paper looked blank as it slid out of the envelope. She watched J.B. flip it over, using the pen set.

Michael leaned forward—to see her past come back to haunt her. She stared in dismay at a copy of a page from her college yearbook. Her face paled when she saw her photo.

J.B. looked at the picture of a younger Michael. The knife dripped blood. Drawn diagonally across her face, it made a graphically vivid picture. Her youthful beauty was still apparent in spite of the defaced photograph. He glanced at her. The look of vulnerability on her face was painful to see.

"I hope he doesn't have to earn his living in the art world." Michael noted J.B.'s startled glance. "Sorry, just a little *stab* at humor. Pun intended."

"You're good, darlin'." He chuckled. "It has to be Halstead. Who else is also connected with your college days?"

He stormed to the phone and dialed Shag. "Pardner, I think we have him." He ran his fingers through his hair. "Maybe." He listened, then responded. "He sent her a photocopy of a page from her college year book. It has a little additional art work." He pulled the ever-present quarter from his pocket and watched it traverse his knuckles. "Yeah. A knife. Dripping blood. The juvenile bastard has watched too many movies." He slipped the quarter back in his pocket. "Yeah. That's fine. It isn't goin' anywhere. Okay. See you tomorrow."

Michael stood and walked over to J.B. "Is Shag coming to pick it up?"

"Yeah. He wants to nail this bastard as much as I do." He put his arms around her. "Especially if it *is* Halstead."

In her stocking feet, Michael stretched up on her toes and kissed J.B. Taken by surprise, he quickly recovered to take over and deepen the kiss. As long as she was willing, and unafraid, he'd kiss her until his lips fell off.

The ring of the telephone startled them and they jumped apart. Michael stared at the phone. "I dread answering every time the phone rings."

"I know." J.B.'s heart had soared with her response to him. It plummeted with the intrusion of the device that had become an instrument of torture for Michael. "Go ahead and answer it darlin', and remember, I'm here."

Michael picked up the phone and took a deep breath, prepared to hear the harasser's voice. "Hello."

She stood straighter, more rigid and her tone of voice sounded dead. "Father." She hunched her shoulders but quickly straightened them again. "No." She turned her back on J.B. and tucked the phone between her shoulder and her left ear. "No." She spoke more emphatically. "No! We've already had this conversation."

J.B. refused to allow her to shut him out, and stepping behind her, wrapped his arms around her waist. He pulled her back against him, put his face next to her right ear, and kissed her cheek.

His eyes widened as he heard her say, "I've told you repeatedly I will not return home. Ever. You can solve your problem by bringing Mother home, or at least tell me where you put her so I can get her out." She shook her head. "Hire someone. I'm not available." She looked up toward the ceiling, closing her eyes. "The problem is of your own making, and the solution must be yours as well. Mother will, more than likely, take care of it for you, though why she would is beyond my comprehension."

She put her arm over J.B.'s, where it clasped her waist, as she listened for long moments. "No, you lost any right to my loyalty ten years ago when *you* displayed no loyalty to me."

She moved away from J.B. and walked the few steps to the window. As she listened, the phone cradled by her shoulder, she nervously picked at the polish on her thumbnail. "Yes, I do feel sorry for Mother, but not for the reasons you've mentioned." She took a deep breath. "I feel sorry for Mother because she has allowed you to take over her life. *She* no longer exists. If you brought her home from the psychiatric hospital tomorrow, she'd kiss the bottoms of your feet, scurry off to hide and nothing will have changed." She listened for a moment. "What she *should* do is kick you in the behind as she shoves you out the door. The smartest move she could make would be to divorce you and take you for everything you own. I've told her if she ever needs an attorney for that purpose I'll be happy to serve *pro bono*. Don't call me again." She stepped over to the desk and quietly hung up the phone.

J.B. turned her around and, his gaze never leaving hers, grasped her hands. His thumbs caressed them from knuckles to wrist, as his fingers curled into her palms. He watched her face, gauging her readiness to talk with him after the confrontation. He leaned forward and kissed her gently on the forehead.

His voice, the soft husky rumble of a contented cat's purr, washed over her and encouraged her to trust completely. "Don't you think it's time you told me what's goin' on here, Michael? That was not a typical 'father-daughter' conversation."

"I wouldn't know. I've never had a 'typical father-daughter conversation'."

"Do you want to talk about it?"

From force of habit, his gentle question pushed her to withdraw into herself and pull the mantle of secrecy more tightly around her. "Not really."

"All right. It's your decision. Always."

But this was J.B. "I don't know if I can." Michael pulled her hands from his and looked at this man who, in a relatively short time, had become so important to her. Her eyes brimmed over with tears as she tried to relax and accept the comfort he wanted to give her. She could see the love shining from his eyes.

"You already know I won't break your confidence."

"Yes. I know I can trust you with anything, but this is so difficult to talk about. So... humiliating."

What had her father done to earn her mistrust and animosity? "Sweetheart, did talkin' to me about the rape help you at all?"

She nodded, then looked up with haunted eyes. "Yes."

J.B. walked over and sat on the couch. "I'm here if you want to talk. It's your decision, sweetheart, just like before."

She paced the floor as thoughts flew back and forth in her mind, careening like tennis balls volleyed at Wimbledon. He already knew about the rape. Somehow it had been easier to reveal that outrage. Revealing her father's reaction to the incident was much more painful. One's father was supposed to be supportive. Pain, as fresh as if the conversation took place only yesterday, flowed over her.

Doubts overflowed like a river in a spring flood. If her father didn't believe her, why should J.B.? If J.B. learned of her father's reaction, would he judge her and find her wanting? Would he walk away? He said he loved her, but how could he? Her father didn't. Had never loved her. Her mother, too busy hiding from her father and attempting to protect herself, paid no attention to her daughter. If she was so unworthy that her own parents couldn't love her, how could J.B.?

She sat down and rocked back and forth, her arms clasped around her waist. Losing him would overwhelm her. Acute appendicitis had not been this painful. At that moment, like a flash out of the blue, she realized she loved him. She didn't know when it crept up on her, but love him she did and if he walked from her life it would destroy her.

She thought about not telling him. But she'd always believed if you loved someone you trusted them completely. No secrets.

J.B.'s voice intruded on the quagmire of her thoughts. "Sweetheart? Try to talk about it. If you get started and can't go on, that's all right. But there is nothing you can't tell me and there is nothing on this earth worth the anguish you're goin' through right now."

"Okay." Her quavering voice displayed her anxiety but she agreed because she trusted him. She'd never been so frightened in her life, nor had the stakes been higher. "You know about the rape."

"Yes." J.B. switched off the lamp. The yard light cast a soft glow through the front windows. "Is this about your father's response to the news of your rape?"

Her startled gaze met his, and moisture gathered on her lower lids.

"I know there's something that keeps you from sleepin' well. From eating as you should." He reached over and took her hand. "I only want to help you."

"Yes. It *is* about my father's reaction to the rape."

J.B. knew he wasn't going to like this. The look on her face told him he might want to add her father's name to the list of people he wanted to beat to a pulp for hurting her.

"Come here into my arms and tell it exactly as you remember it. I'll hold you safe. I love you, Michael."

She went into his arms like a homing pigeon reaching its nest at the end of a long journey. Closing her eyes she allowed her thoughts free rein.

Her mind slammed back ten years.

~ * ~

She was seated in her father's study. He stood in front of his desk, glaring down at her. The memory was still so vivid she remembered the colors in brilliant detail. The soft green of the wall paper with the border in forest green and burgundy. The beige, forest green and burgundy plaid drapes over pale green sheers. The dark walnut of the woodwork and the heavy, massive furniture constructed especially for her six foot five inch father. Every feature of the room was etched in her memory, right down to the mallard ducks in the prints on the walls.

Her hands could still feel the grain of the wood in the arms of the chair. She remembered the sun slanting through the curtains directly into her eyes as she faced him.

His tone of voice, as always, implied he was speaking to a lesser being. One far beneath his dignity to acknowledge, and it angered him that he was forced to recognize her existence.

He glared at her and barked, "What's the matter with you, Mickie? Tell me. Now!"

As always, her father's voice sent a shiver of fear over her skin. She didn't remember a time when she hadn't been afraid of him. She wanted to love him, to be able to be in the same room without fear turning her stomach to a boiling vat of acid.

She'd dreamed some day he would love her. She'd hoped an accomplishment, some achievement, would make him care for her. But he was as cold as an ice floe in the Arctic Ocean.

As she got older she occasionally wondered how he'd managed to generate enough heat to sire her. Perhaps her mother had known some trick that thawed him out for that one time. From the way Mama skittered around the house, scurrying to stay out of his sight, she doubted they'd ever had a loving relationship. She cringed when she recalled all the times he'd referred to her mother as worthless because she hadn't produced a son. She remembered, as a small child, how she'd wished she could find a magic potion that would turn her into a boy so her father would love her.

As she sat in front of him picking the pale pink nail polish from her thumbnail, her mind leaped from one thought, one memory, to another. She was aware the physical display of her anxiety annoyed him but was unable to stop the nervous habit. When he snarled, her head yanked up and her gaze snapped to his face.

Though he hadn't done it often, there were times when he used physical insult as a weapon. Anytime he felt she wasn't paying close attention, he slapped her. She closed her eyes and centered her mind. If she could convince him she attended his every word, he wouldn't hit her this time.

"Answer me, damn it! I expect a response from you when I ask you a question."

She looked at him, fear and apprehension quaking through her body, took a deep breath and blurted, "I want to drop out of college, Father." She knew what his response would be before she ever opened her mouth. That's why she'd put off this talk for two weeks while she pretended an illness she didn't have. She didn't know if she'd find the courage to go back to the university.

"Why?" One word, hurled at her like a spear. He never bent, he never gave up on what he wanted. And he didn't care how much it inconvenienced anyone else. Nor how much, or whom, it hurt. As the saying went, it was his way or the highway.

She struggled to keep her voice calm and reasonable. While her insides trembled, she fought for quiet composure. "Please. I would prefer to stay home. I don't think I'm cut out for university life."

"I want an answer, Mickie." His hand slapped down on the desk. "Now!" His voice, lower and more menacing, grated on her nerves. "No more stalling. Tell me." He bent forward, his nose inches from her own.

She stared up into his eyes, momentarily unable to utter a sound.

"If you don't tell me, I'll call Simmons. He'll find out." His roar convinced her he would have Simmons wade through every one of the students in her class at the university to get the answers to his questions. She'd have to tell him. With Simmons' help, he was perfectly capable of destroying her... and he wouldn't care one whit.

"I, uh... please, Father. Can't I just drop out?"

She watched him walk toward the telephone, pick it up and dial a number. He barked a command into the phone. "Simmons, get over here. I have an assignment for you. This will take top priority until you get the ans..."

"No-o-o." Her piercing wail interrupted the conversation. She leaned forward, hands clasped in desperate pleading, "Don't. I'm begging you."

"Hold on a minute, Simmons." He turned from the phone. "Are you ready to talk?"

She'd known she couldn't win. She nodded. She'd have done anything to avoid bringing someone else into this. She'd tell him. All of it. She wanted to run and hide in the farthest, darkest corner she could find, but she'd tell him... and his condemnation would pour over her with the force of Niagara Falls.

He spoke briefly into the phone, "Never mind for now, Simmons." Hanging it up, he walked back and stood in front of her. Waiting. Watching. After two or three minutes went by he snapped. "Mickie, this is your last chance."

She huddled into her chair, cowering away from what lay ahead of her. "I was..." In spite of her effort to hold it back, a sob tore through her throat. "I was raped."

He didn't even act surprised, only barked, "When?"

"Two weeks..." A shudder shook her. "Two week ago."

He took a deep breath, "By whom?"

She couldn't believe him. He asked his questions in as cold and analytical a voice as she'd ever heard him use. It mattered not one iota that his daughter, his only child had been violated. Her hands clenched into fists in her lap. Did he care about her at all?

"Do I go to the phone again, Mickie?" He straightened from where he rested his hips against his desk.

"No." She whispered, "It was Rand Halstead."

"Ahhh. The football player? Are you pregnant?"

"No!" The agonized whisper barely got past her lips.

"If you had to let somebody screw you, at least you had the good sense to pick a real man. A football star and not some wimp."

"What?" She couldn't believe even he would be this callous. "Father, I didn't 'let' him do anything. I was raped." She couldn't help raising her voice. She wanted to punch him in the mouth for what he'd said to her.

"Don't you raise your voice to me." He slapped her. "If you were a boy you'd *be* the football star. I'd have something to brag about to my friends and you'd be the one all the girls chased. But no, your mother couldn't give me the son I wanted.

Had to have the surgery that prevented her ever giving me my son. You're as worthless as she is."

She couldn't prevent the tears flowing unchecked down her face.

"What did you do, Mickie, chase after the kid, then change your mind after it was all over?"

"No! I told you, I was raped!"

"I don't want to hear that word again. Women cry rape every time things don't go their way, then some poor guy has to face a police investigation. Don't you put that kid through this kind of trouble. I'm sure he doesn't deserve it.

"Now, for what you *are* going to do. You'll go back to school. You'll study hard and finish at the top of your class.

"You cavort around with all the boys you want to as long as you keep your grades up. But don't you dare get yourself pregnant. Do you hear me? You'd better make sure you don't come home swelled up with a kid because if you do I'll withdraw my support. I won't have it. God, why couldn't you have been a boy? I wouldn't have these worries." He stormed out of his study slamming the door and leaving her shaking.

~ * ~

Michael glanced at J.B. "It was as if I'd been raped all over again. I felt dirty. I wanted to get in the shower and scrub until all the skin came off." She looked toward the moonlight coming in the side windows, but didn't really see what was in front of her.

J.B. pulled her closer into his arms and watching her glassy eyed stare, took her hands and rubbed them to bring her back from where her mind had taken her as she remembered her father's betrayal.

"Sweetheart, your father sounds like a heartless, unfeeling sonofabitch. I don't know how a man like that could have produced someone as sweet as you." He kissed her eyes, and her damp cheeks. "How did you keep from fallin' apart when he slammed out of the room like that?"

"I sat there for a long time. His reaction was the final straw. I was determined I would never again grovel at his feet hoping for a crumb of understanding."

"I don't think he's capable of it, darlin'."

"You're right. After that I no longer expected a miracle. I was amazed at how freeing it was. How strong I felt when that feeling, of a burden being lifted, washed over me. I vowed I'd quit hoping for that which was hopeless, stop dreaming of what would never be."

"What did you do then?"

"I reached several decisions. I made a mental list to guide me for the rest of my life. I'd finish college. That had been decided, by him, when he laid down his edicts. He allowed me no other choice."

"Why was he so adamant you'd finish college?"

"I suspect he feared it would reflect badly on him. Then, and now, appearances are everything. That's why I was ordered to graduate at the top of my class." She shrugged. "He accepted nothing less than perfection.

"Like a good soldier, I followed orders. I committed my every breath to graduating with honors. And, following my own agenda, I planned to get a job. I intended it to be a job that paid well enough I could support myself, without any help from him. I knew I would never again depend on him. And I'd leave home—and never look back.

"I reached these decisions and made another. I wouldn't do it for his sake, but for my own. He'd never wanted a daughter so I'd remove myself from his life. We wouldn't see each other and we'd both be happier."

"What about your mother. Do you ever see her?"

"Not any more but she called me the other day. He put her in a psychiatric hospital. I knew that before she called. He'd called and told me that much. *She* told me which one, The Pines, but when I went out there I wasn't allowed inside the gates.

"I wanted her to have a real life. A life away from him, and I offered to help more than a year ago. I made sure he was out of town on a business trip and I went to see her. When I offered to help her get a divorce she became terrified and raced back to her room."

"Didn't she protect you from him when you were growing up?"

"No." She took a deep breath. "My mother was too weak willed to be more than a ghost-like figure around our house, and too terrified of him to try to make any changes."

"So you never really had a close relationship with her?"

"Oh, I occasionally saw her scurrying through the house. I had little contact with her. He wouldn't allow it. He said he hadn't wanted a daughter but since he was stuck with one he wouldn't 'allow her to be a weak-kneed, lily livered nothing like her mother'. Nothing from my childhood brings me warm memories." She turned her head and looked directly into his eyes. "Do you know, I have no memory of ever having shared a meal with my mother?"

J.B. was shocked by this revelation. "Was she ill?"

"No. We didn't have family dinners. I was fed in the kitchen by the servants."

"Didn't you ever eat at the family dinner table?"

"As a teenager I was ordered to appear on the first Sunday of each month, to report on my progress at school. Plates of food were put in front of me. I never ate. I couldn't get the food past the lump in my throat."

"Did your mother ever come and share your meals with you?"

"No. My earliest memories are of a series of nannies. They never lasted long. Certainly never long enough to form any attachment to me, nor to allow me to learn to care for them."

J.B. noted her exhaustion. So tired her speech aped one who'd had far too much to drink. "Are you too tired to go on?"

She shook her head, then turned her face into his neck, embarrassed by what she had to admit. "J.B., no one in my life *ever* said 'I love you' to me, until you." She looked up at him and, her voice slightly higher than normal, asked, "Don't you think it's strange? A woman my age has *never* been told those words?"

Her tears flowed. He hoped they healed. "Oh, my love. Your father didn't deserve you. How did you survive that household?" He kissed her, a gentle kiss, only to comfort her.

He looked at her. She was nearly out on her feet from exhaustion. "Sweetheart, I think we need to get you to bed."

"Mmm hmmm."

He held her. Her eyes closed, her head lolled, supported by the proverbial 'wet noodle'. In this case it had been cooked to mush. He stood and carried her to her bedroom.

"Darlin', you need to get undressed. You're tired."

Her arms wrapped around him and she snuggled her face to his neck, breathed deeply and mumbled, "Mmmm, smell good."

J.B. had a brief talk with his libido, then laid her on the bed and unbuttoned her blouse. As he slipped each button through its buttonhole, he looked up at her face for a reaction. He'd back off if she showed any fear.

From the moment he'd placed her on the bed she'd drifted deeper and deeper into slumber. He got her skirt and blouse off, then her half-slip. He clenched his teeth, took a deep breath and stripped off her pantyhose. She lay before him, sound asleep. And looking more beautiful than he'd ever seen her, wearing a bra and pair of bikini briefs—fire engine red bikini briefs. Unable to stifle his moan he turned quickly away from the sight before him on the bed.

He walked to her bureau and hunted until he found a nightgown. Raising her upper body he slipped it over her head and allowed it to fall down around her waist. For his own peace of mind he needed to cover her. He lifted her slightly, unhooked her bra and removed it. After struggling for a few minutes trying to ensure her modesty remained inviolate, he got her arms through the sleeve openings. He breathed as if he'd run a five-mile race and had been out of condition from the starting blocks.

Her hair was so beautiful, he wondered why she wore it in the tight chignon. Out of its restraint, the long silken strands tumbled as if alive and breathing. Crackling, they slithered over his arm.

He picked her up and struggled to turn down the covers on the bed. In her sleep she wrapped her arms around his neck. He bent to lay her on the bed, but she refused to release her grasp.

"Darlin', let go so I can cover you and go to the livin' room."

"No." A barely audible mumble, but he heard. "Hold me."

"I'm sleepin' in the recliner, like every night."

"No." Her arms tightened. "Please. I want you to hold me." She still sounded drunk.

"Oh, my love, you don't know what you're sayin'. You're exhausted. Get some sleep and when you're awake and alert, if you want me to hold you, I'll jump at the chance."

"It's okay," she mumbled. "Don't blame you."

He was unsure she knew what she was saying. Or if she knew she was talking to him. She sounded so sad, so alone.

After hearing her story he wanted to hold her for the rest of her life—and keep her safe.

Michael rolled to her side and a tear trickled out of the corner of her eye and dripped from the bridge of her nose.

"That does it." J.B. kicked off his boots, stripped down to his shorts and crawled into the bed. He put his left arm under her and marveled at how well she fit. She was perfect. Her head on his shoulder, she snuggled her face into her favorite spot.

She buried her nose in his neck and mumbled, "Mmmm. Smell good." Within minutes her even breathing indicated deep sleep.

On the other hand, J.B. didn't expect to get much sleep.

The results of his talk with his libido had lasted only through undressing her. Lying next to her, holding her in his arms, breathing her strawberries and cream scent was driving him crazy. Her skin, like satin, seemed to call out to be touched. His fingers, almost with a mind of their own, caressed her upper arm as it lay across his chest. When she brought her leg up across his thighs he kissed goodbye any hope of sleeping a wink.

An hour later Michael slid on top of him, her long silken hair splayed over his chest. J.B. raised his head and looked at the clock. Two-thirty in the morning. Only five more hours and he could get up. Oops, wrong choice of words. He laughed silently. In five hours he'd get out of bed—and take another cold shower.

Later, he again looked at the clock. Four-thirty. Mentally he groaned. He'd 'go with the flow', as Shag frequently told him to do. At last, he drifted into sleep, his arms holding her.

~ * ~

The shadowy figure, dressed in black, moved stealthily up to the front door and opened the screen. He slipped the key into the lock and held his breath until he made certain the copy of her key worked. Silently he slipped through the door and stood in the foyer surveying the area. Listening for any sound to indicate the presence of another human being, he crept on silent feet to the doorway into the living room. Nothing moved. No sound disturbed the quiet.

The cop had to be in her bed. The bitch.

His furtive movements making no detectable sound, he moved to the living room and bumped something with his toe. Her high heels lay on the floor where she'd kicked them off, one upright and one on its side. He picked them up and dropped them into the bag he carried.

He glided over to her desk and switched on a penlight. He flashed it around over the papers scattered there. A file folder of one of her cases lay there. It was too irresistible. He opened it and removed two pages from the file and dropped them into the bag with her shoes.

Removing an envelope from his pocket he put it in the letter holder. It melded right in with those already there.

He looked around the room and spotted the black glass swan on the mantle. He added it to his bag.

He flashed the pen light around the room and spotted the envelope and sheet of paper he'd left for her. He grinned. The cop was collecting evidence, was he? Let him try to explain to his chief what happened to the evidence that got away. He chuckled silently, picked up the evidence and tucked it into his bag along with everything else.

After listening to make sure he was still safe, he crept out of the house as silently as he'd entered.

Eleven

Michael awakened gradually, feeling warm. Comfortable. And safe. A thick mat of curling hair lay under her cheek. She sighed. Pleasure coursed through her, and she rubbed her cheek against the velvety cushion. Under her ear, the steady beat of J.B.'s heart brought serenity to her soul.

Where are we? Too horizontal to be in the recliner. *The couch*? Trying not to disturb him, she carefully moved her hand to search for the back of the couch. No. Not the couch. Her bed. *How did I get here?*

She never thought she'd welcome a man into her bed, but with J.B., a sense of being loved and cherished surrounded her. *Loved and cherished*. Both emotions had been foreign to her before he entered her life. So many changes since J.B.—and she wouldn't trade *now* for *then* for all the gold in Fort Knox.

Her body lay sprawled on top of him. Her left knee rested on the mattress between his thighs. The contact with his bare skin sent a tingling sensation thrumming up her body—like receiving an electric shock. But not in the least unpleasant. Her right arm lay along his left, her hand resting in his palm. Unexpectedly his fingers curled, locking with hers. The tactile contact sent her heart—as well as J.B.'s—into a faster rhythm and her ear picked up the different cadence.

Her eyelids fluttered open, her eyelashes tangling in the silken mat under her cheek. She felt the stirring of his manhood against her thigh and moved sinuously without thought or fear. A swift inhalation and suppressed groan vibrated against her cheek as his fingers gripped hers more tightly. She stroked the fingers of her left hand back and forth through the curls, finding the coin-sized spot nestled within, and circled it with her finger.

J.B. lay quietly, afraid to move, enjoying every second of her exploration. He'd known the moment she awoke. Filled with trepidation, he'd lain there waiting for her reaction to his presence in her bed. Holding her, feeling her body molded to his, awakened parts of him better left sleeping. He could sleep like this—*wanted* to sleep like this—holding her exactly this way for the rest of his life. But he wanted more. Much more.

He felt her eyelashes flutter and tangle in the hair on his chest. Her head moved slightly and she tipped her face up and looked into his eyes. For a moment he was lost in that gaze, then he raised his head and smiled. "Good mornin', darlin'." He gave her a quick kiss, wanting to deepen it but afraid of losing control and frightening her. "Did you sleep well?"

She smiled. "Mmm hmm. Like a baby. I don't ever remember sleeping better." She put her hand against his cheek, pulling his face down for a brief and gentle kiss. "How about you?"

"Oh, yes, I got some sleep." He hugged her. "Darlin', we need to get out of this bed. It's gettin' late and we can't forget our jobs." He lifted her off him and deposited her on the bed beside him. "Besides, if we *don't* get out of here in the next couple of seconds, uh..."

"Oh." She scrambled to the foot of the bed, her face turning pink. "Did I hurt you?"

He stared for a moment at the picture she made, her hair tumbled about her shoulders, the areolas of her nipples shadowing through her nightgown. His gaze drifted down to a darker shadow lower on her body and he closed his eyes. "I'll live." He swung his legs off the bed to sit on the side, and mumbled, "At least that's what I keep tellin' myself."

Noting the direction of J.B.'s gaze, Michael looked down at herself. "How did I..." She scrambled off the bed and slipped into her robe. "I don't remember putting my nightgown on last night. I must have been more tired than I knew."

"You were exhausted, darlin'. Totally out of it. In fact you were practically unconscious."

"Then how did I..."

"I undressed you and put your gown on you."

"*You* did?" She turned beet red and hurried into the bathroom. He had undressed her. And nothing more. Her unconscious mind trusted him or she could not have slept through having him strip off her clothes. Trustworthy. Yes. J.B. was worthy of her trust.

A few moments later J.B., hearing the shower, gathered his clothes and boots and mumbled to himself. "I'm goin' to have to bring some of my clothes over here. Takin' a shower and then puttin' on dirty clothes is defeatin' the purpose." He walked down the hall to the other bathroom. Looking at himself in the mirror, he mumbled, "I need a razor here, too."

He completed his shower and arrived in the kitchen at the exact moment the coffee stopped dripping and Michael started popping bread into the toaster. He looked at the still-damp hair cascading down her back and curling slightly at the ends. At the way her eyes sparkled when she glanced at him. And the way her robe hugged every luscious curve of her body. A nearly inaudible moan rippled through his throat. "Could we try that good-mornin' kiss again?"

She smiled and walked eagerly to him. Stretching up on her toes, she wrapped her arms around his neck. "J.B., I...I..."

He clamped his mouth on hers before she could complete the sentence. If she said *the* words—when he heard them the first time—he wanted to be sure the feelings were real and not only gratitude. Gratitude for protecting her, for loving her, for helping her deal with the rape and her memories of her father's reaction.

His soft lips moved over hers, his tongue's gentle invasion sending shivers of delight over her skin. She never knew it could be like this, never dreamed the contact could be so wonderful. His lips moved to her neck, sending her blood rampaging through her veins like white water roaring through a gorge. She gasped and tightened her grip on his waist. "J.B., I..." His lips again captured hers.

Within seconds he broke the contact and backed away. "Darlin', it's gettin' harder and harder...uh..." He snorted. "...no pun intended..." He raked his hand through his hair. "We either have to move forward to wherever this is goin' or we have to back up—all the way to only shakin' hands."

"No more kisses?" She didn't want to cause him pain, but she tried to imagine not kissing him. The picture that thought put in to her mind was more barren than her life before he entered it. She then tried to envision going to the next step and knew it wouldn't happen today. "I'm sorry. I'm being selfish aren't I?" She turned away from him, her face pink with embarrassment.

"No, darlin', you're only bein' self protective and I can't blame you for that. Not after what you've been through. It's just that I can't take much more of this and stay sane. I want you. We've already established that fact. When you feel safe moving to the next step, I'm here."

She turned back to face him. "I slept with you last night." Her face reddened further but she didn't break eye contact. "I, uh, I liked it. I thought..."

"That's part of the problem, darlin'. Now I *know* how it feels to hold you in my arms all night. I want it to be an every night occurrence. I want to spend the rest of my life holdin' you, lovin' you," He leaned slightly forward and stared into her eyes. "...and makin' babies with you."

She wasn't ready to hear this. "I need to go get my shoes. Where did you leave them last night?"

Shoes? She was thinking about shoes? "In the livin' room."

"They aren't in there." She saw the beginning of protest. "I already looked. I have only one pair of red shoes. I wore them yesterday and planned to wear them again today."

He walked to the living room and stopped, pointing to where he'd last seen them. "They were here where you kicked them off last night."

"Where did they go?" They began a search. "Why don't you check in this part of the house and don't forget to look under the couch. I'll check out the bedroom, sitting room and closet."

Back in the living room, Michael scratched her head then turned toward the back of the house. "Not that I expect them to be there, but the only place we haven't looked is upstairs in the unfinished part of the house and since neither of us has been up there, it would be a waste of time to look." Michael got down and looked under the couch again. "It doesn't make sense. Where could they be?"

J.B. stood up. "I smell a rat." After checking for the third time, he rose from his knees in front of the couch. "Is anything else missing or out of place?"

She looked around the living room, turning at last to the fireplace. The bare spot on the mantle stopped her cold. "My swan."

In the doorway, looking toward the front entry, he faced away from her. "What about..." He turned and his gaze drifted along the mantle. "It's missing."

She responded as if he asked a question. "Yes." She turned to face him. "How?"

"Your shoes and the swan. Let's check to see what else is gone."

While they'd searched for her shoes it never crossed her mind to look for anything else missing. Michael now diligently searched the house.

"Since I haven't been here long enough to know if anything is missing, it'll be up to you, darlin'." They went through the house together, omitting the bedroom where they'd slept.

Finally back in the living room, Michael walked to her desk. She glanced over the papers and paraphernalia covering the top. Next she systematically searched through the drawer. When all appeared normal there, she returned to the top. Beginning on one side, she worked her way across, gasping in surprise as she noticed a small, pale blue, nearly square envelope. Slightly out of alignment with the others in her letter holder, it hadn't been there yesterday.

Instantly at her side J.B. asked, "What is it, darlin'?"

Her heart racing, she pointed. He grabbed his handkerchief, lifted it from the holder and dropped it on the desk. "It's from Amanda Hall." He used his handkerchief to hold the envelope while he slit it with Michael's letter opener. The contents proved to be the invitation Michael never received...to Amanda's open house.

"I've never seen that before." She glanced up at him. "I'd swear it wasn't there yesterday."

"I believe you, darlin'. I think we had a visitor last night." Suddenly a thought occurred and he whirled toward the table on which he'd left the photo of her and the envelope. "Damn!" He walked over and looked behind the table on the floor, but he *knew* it wouldn't be there. "The bastard stole the evidence that was layin' here." His rage barely leashed, he grabbed his phone. "That sonofabitch had the nerve to enter this house with us in it. He's toyin' with us. Thumbin' his nose. This makes it real personal. And I'm goin' to take him down."

Michael continued to look through the items on the desk, and almost as an afterthought, picked up the file holding the Taylor brief. Anger bubbled through her as she looked inside the folder. "J.B.?"

In the process of dialing, he glanced up. "What else?"

"The first two pages of the Taylor Brief are missing. It's sick—*he's* sick. The contents of this file are confidential. Whatever problem he has with me, he had no right to bring anyone else in as a focus of his mania." She slammed the file down on the desk. "No right. I won't allow him to harm my clients." She stormed across the room, turned and stomped her way back. "We have to get him."

"I know, darlin'. It's frustratin' as hell."

Her clenched fists pounded on the desk. "He was in this house. Going through my things. How dare he? He was here while we slept." She looked at J.B. "How could we sleep through that? How could *I* sleep through that? I hear every noise this creaking old house makes."

"Darlin', you were sleepin' in my arms last night. Maybe for the first time in a long time you felt safe enough to *really* sleep."

She stormed back across the room to the mantle and stared at the spot where her swan usually sat. Now vacant, the thought of the stalker invading her house offended her all over again. She felt almost as violated as she'd felt after the rape. But the difference was that this time she was angry.

Michael stopped raging as J.B. picked up the phone, dialed and turned away to speak with his partner. "Shag? He was inside the house durin' the night." His complexion turned ruddy. "Yeah, go ahead—have your laugh. In fact, have two of them. You remember the evidence you were goin' to pick up and take to the lab? He stole it." He held the phone out away from his ear and the sound of Shag's laughter could be heard across the room. "You're absolutely right. I slept through the whole thing."

Michael watched as the ever-present quarter appeared in his palm, made the trip across his knuckles, then dropped back into his pocket. She didn't believe him even conscious of the habit.

J. B sighed. "I've got a kit this time. Just come on over here and you can help me dust for prints." He listened a moment and groused, "Yeah. It *is* a waste of time, but we still have to go through the motions."

He raked his hand through his hair. "Okay, I understand. I know this isn't the only case we have. Yeah, tomorrow morning. We're leavin' here in a few minutes, so nothin' will be disturbed. Besides, our prints are already all over the place."

Michael edged toward him pointing to her wristwatch. He nodded at her and again spoke into the phone. "Before we leave here I'll check the doors and windows to see where he came in." He listened a moment. "Okay, what are you goin' to be doin' today?

"Anything I should know about?" He chuckled. "I know you're Super-Cop. I have every faith in you. You'll solve all the cases all by yourself and become chief." He laughed outright. "Okay. See you in a few minutes."

He replaced the receiver, set the phone back on the desk and turned to Michael. "Shag sends his regards."

"What's so funny?"

"Oh, he was just jokin' around, not anything I can repeat."

"Oh. Guy talk."

"Uh huh." He walked over and stopped in front of her, placing his hand on her cheek. "Are you doin' okay?"

"No. I'm shaking with anger. I want to do something about this."

"I know, darlin'. I've talked with a lot of people who've had intruders in their homes. One woman said it was almost like bein' ra...." His mouth opened and closed several times as he stared at her. "Oh, God, I'm sorry. I wasn't thinkin'."

"Don't worry about it. You can't start watching every word that falls out of your mouth. If you do we'll have some very uncomfortable conversations. For both of us."

His gaze never left hers. "You're right, but I don't want to hurt you, ever."

"I know. Besides, it had already occurred to me that this made me feel *almost* the same as I did the night I was violated by Rand Halstead. Not quite, but almost." Putting her hands on his chest, she toyed with one of his shirt buttons as she stared into his eyes. "Will you answer a question for me?"

"Sure, darlin'."

"I don't mean to sound accusatory, but—" She glanced away, then brought her gaze back to his. "—how long does it usually take on a case like this?"

"Well, it..."

"I'm really tired of just sitting here waiting for him to come to us. I'd like to know when we begin to call the shots. What I really want to do is go out and find him—be there when he's caught." Her fists clenched on his shirt, wadding it in both hands as she made her point. "I want to look him in the eye and tell him what I think of his sick mind." Unaware she did it, her fist thumped his chest. "I'm so tired of not doing anything but waiting on *his* next move."

"I understand what you're feelin', darlin', and I'd like nothing better than for you to have that chance. Hell, I'm frustrated, too. But where do we start?"

Taking his question literally, she responded in frustration. "I don't know. I'm not a cop." Her rage showed in the hoarse rasp of her voice. "I refuse to continue to sit and do nothing, just waiting on his next assault."

"There has to be a starting place. Give me a clue. An idea, somethin'—hell, anything to go on. Someplace to start—a beginnin' that sends us in the right direction. You're an attorney. You know we can't stand on the street investigatin' everyone we see. The law protects John Q. Citizen against that sort of thing."

She sighed. "I know." She turned and paced between J.B. and the window. "I want to *do* something, dammit. I want to...to...oh, God, J.B., I want to pound on him until my arms ache. I've never—do you hear me? I have *never* before in my life wanted to hit another human being." Her frustration raised her voice in pitch and volume.

"I'm glad you feel that way. But from bitter experience I can tell you, it won't make you feel one bit better."

"I'm not a violent person, but I'm having some very violent fantasies everytime he does something else." She shivered. "Maybe I need *my* head examined."

"Come here, darlin'." When she came to him, he took her in his arms and his lips settled on hers like a bee on a flower. He intended a gentle kiss. Only a brief brush of his lips on hers. The contact cut long-held restraints. Holding back, not an easy task at any time with her, reached *impossible* in a microsecond when she responded.

Both forgot the passage of time as she opened to his tender invasion and his tongue gently probed the sweet recesses of her mouth. Her tongue's counterpoint nearly sent him over the edge.

Her arms came up to enfold him and she arched her body more fully against his. Fitting together like two pieces of a puzzle, they each strained to get closer. He cupped his hands over the soft roundness of her bottom and lifted, bringing her up against his need. Of its own volition his body thrust forward and he nestled in the juncture of her thighs, beginning a rhythm he could no longer control.

Her soft moan nearly undid him. He groaned and moved his mouth down to the pulse point below her ear. She arched her neck in surrender and ran her fingers into his hair to pull him nearer.

They didn't hear the phone for several long moments.

When the ringing finally intruded J.B. wanted nothing more than to ignore it. "Mmm, darlin', ahh, the phone," he rasped. His lips worked their way across from one ear to the other.

"Mmmm hmmm. Let it ring." Michael turned her head to again find his mouth.

"Might be important." His mouth opened over hers and took possession. Heat permeated his entire body. His breath rasped into starving lungs. He burned. And ached to bury himself in her honeyed depths. He wanted to look into her eyes as she flew over the edge.

She turned and planted nibbling kissed along his jawline. She'd never felt like this before. She didn't want him to stop. She thought if they stopped they'd never get back to this place. She breathed in J.B.'s scent with each gasp for air. He filled her with a need, a hunger, she feared would never be filled.

"Darlin'?"

"Don't stop. They'll call back."

The answering machine switched on. Seconds later, groaning as they separated, they heard the message loud and clear. "Hey, boss, hope you haven't headed for the office. We've had a power failure in the building. The air conditioner is off. The lights are off. The computer is off. Since I can't type up the brief you're working on—I'm off. I'm going to my..."

Michael took a deep breath and grabbed the receiver. "Lyndi? What happened?" She listened. "Any other buildings shut down?" She smoothed her hand over her chignon, poking in a few stray hairs. "Sounds like you have everything under control. Cancel my appointments today and then lock it up." She turned around to face J.B. "I'm going to take the day off. Tell Winslow to go home as well. You do the same. Don't worry about the Wallingford brief. You can do it tomorrow." She rubbed her forehead. "Okay, thanks. Page me if you need me." She replaced the receiver and stared into space.

J.B. waited for her to tell him what she planned for her day. She tugged at her lower lip, and walked by him as if she didn't know he was there.

"Hey, darlin', what's goin' on?"

"Oh, sorry. I'm probably just worrying for the sake of worrying. I'm getting—what's the expression?"

"Gun shy?"

"That's the one. It seems odd that the building where my office is housed suffers a power failure and no other building down town is faced with the same problem."

"Did Lyndi check with the power company?"

"Yes. They have a crew on the way to find the problem."

"Then everything is handled. Right?"

"I suppose, but I'd still like to know why only my office building is affected."

"I don't see how our perp could do something like that. He'd have to be well versed in how the electrical system of the building works. I could have Shag check it out if you'd like."

She sighed. "No. That's okay. Maybe it's only my paranoia showing."

"No, you're careful. That's not such a bad thing." He sauntered to her and put his hands on her shoulders. "Since you have the day off, how'd you like to go meet my folks?"

Startled, her gaze flew to his then back down to his shirtfront. "Oh, I'd love to meet them. But do you think... I mean..." She touched her forehead briefly to his chest, then looked up at him, blushing charmingly. "I'm nervous."

"No need to be. They haven't eaten any attorneys in years. Decided to swear off when the last one gave 'em heartburn."

She laughed, placing her cheek against his chest, her arms around his waist and hugged him. He could feel the tension ease out of her body as the stiffness seemed to drain away and she relaxed against him. "J.B., you idiot." She looked up, vulnerability evident on her face. "But what if they don't like me?"

"Ah, darlin', they're goin' to love you."

"Should I change?"

"That depends. What are you changin' into?"

"I don't know.... I could..."

He grinned. "If you're goin' blonde, I'm partial to brunettes, and I'd really hate it if you changed into a man."

She laughed and banged her fist against his upper arm. "Not me. My clothes. Should I change my clothes?"

He laughed, lifted her off the floor for a rib-cracking hug and kissed the end of her nose. "Wear somethin' comfortable. We're goin' to a workin' ranch."

She sped to her bedroom and shut the door. In a short time she emerged wearing powder blue denims and a navy blouse with a powder blue and navy plaid scarf around her neck. She looked in the hall mirror, shook her head and fled back to the bedroom.

Next she wore a bright red blouse, navy skirt and white shoes. At the mirror again, she muttered, "No, not this either. I look like the American flag."

Her next choice was a purple and teal paisley shirtwaist dress with a butterfly pinned to her shoulder. Again she glanced at herself. "Not right. Why can't I find something to wear?" she whispered. She started back to the bedroom.

J.B. snagged her waist and pulled her to him. "Whoa, darlin'. You're only meeting my folks. Plain, ordinary, *nice* people. You're beautiful no matter what you wear."

"But I want them to like me."

"They will. And it'll have nothin' to do with what you're wearin'. Quit worryin' so much." He hugged her.

"I've never been this nervous before."

"Grab your purse, darlin', and let's get out of here. I need to stop by the cop shop on the way."

Thirty minutes later J.B. stood in Chief Dengler's office explaining the theft of the evidence.

"So, Anderson, ya let the evidence get away, didja?" Grossly overweight, Chief Dengler sat behind his desk, an open box of chocolates in front of him.

"As I said, Chief, the perp got into the house while we were sleepin'. He didn't make a sound or I'd have heard him."

"He have a key?"

"There was no sign of B and E, so I guess it's possible."

"Ya can't devote twenty-four hours a day ta one case, Anderson. Ya got other cases ta handle."

"Yes, sir. Dexter and I are workin' those assigned to us."

Dengler fastened a gimlet-eyed stare on J.B. "Yeah, but ya ain't sleepin' at the victim's home in any other case, are ya?"

"No sir." J.B. barely held his temper in check. "Where I spend my off time is my business."

"Only if it doesn't interfere with your job and in this instance the case *is* your job." The chief pulled a quarter out of the tray on his desk, looked up at J.B. with a look of disgust and dropped the coin back in the tray.

J.B., pretending not to notice, pulled a quarter out of his pocket and watched as it began its journey across his knuckles and back again. He noted, without looking up, that the chief had stopped talking and also watched the quarter. "Will there be anything else, Chief?"

"Nah, get on outta here, but don't let any other evidence slip through your fingers."

"Yes sir." J.B. walked out the door but stood watching through the crack...and grinned from ear to ear as the chief attempted to walk the quarter and failed. Finally he threw the quarter across the room and muttered, "Damn that Anderson, anyway."

Within minutes they were on their way as J.B. drove to the ranch, keeping up a running commentary on the ranching operation.

"For a cop, you know a lot about ranching."

"We all had to learn as we grew up. Cowboy is the only one of us that's really crazy about it though, so he'll probably inherit the ranch."

"Will that bother you?"

"Nope. He works hard on the spread and deserves it. He's earned it literally by the sweat of his brow. Introducin' the Santa Gertrudis was his idea. He's earned quite a reputation and put the Lazy A on the map with his breedin' program.

"Benjie's veterinary skills come in handy and we all work durin' the busy seasons. Tendin' to the new crop of calves, wormin', and castratin'..." He saw her face and burst into laughter. "Sorry, I didn't mean to shock you. There are certain parts of it that aren't meant for polite conversation I guess."

"That's all right. I enjoyed hearing you talk about it with such pride." She glanced out the side window. "I feel the same way about my house. I've worked so hard trying to restore it to what it was at one time."

"Was it in pretty bad shape when you bought it?"

"The roof leaked and did major damage to the second floor. It will have to be stripped down to the framing and I simply have not had the money to do more than repair the roof."

"What were you plannin' to do with a house that size?"

"Size never entered my mind."

"How come? Big houses usually mean plans for a big family and you said you never intend to get married. Besides, I'd think a house that size would've been expensive."

"No. Four heirs battled for five years over a very small estate. They finally agreed to sell it." She shook her head. "Attorney fees were eating their lunch. They each had one. I doubt much was left after the years-long battle. They advertised it as a 'fixer-upper' and it had a price I could afford."

"Were you the attorney for the estate?"

"No. That wouldn't have been ethical. I found it through a real estate agent when I decided to move to Willow Glen. I originally asked her to find a condo, an apartment or a small house."

He glanced at her, a questioning look on his face, "And she didn't know what the word 'small' meant?"

She laughed. "She talked about the house and how she wished she had the money to buy it and fix it up herself. I asked to see it and fell in love with it. My search was over at that point."

"It is a beautiful old house but from what I've seen of it, the cost of refurbishing it is going to take a major investment. Maybe more than it's worth."

"No. I'll live in it the rest of my life. And before I die, it will be brought back to its original glory."

"That determined, are you?"

"Yes, that determined." As J.B. turned on to the dusty road, Michael saw uprights supporting a sign declaring this Anderson

Ranch. At each end of the sign a circle enclosed the letter 'A' which lay on its side. "Why is the 'A' on its side?"

J.B. drove across the cattle guard and through the open gate. "That's our brand. It's called a "lazy" A when it's layin' on its side like that."

"Do you still brand cattle?"

"Yeah. Every spring."

Shocked, she blurted, "That seems so cruel."

"This may not be the old west, but there are still rustlers out there, darlin', only now they drive big rigs and haul them off by the truck load."

As they progressed down the road Michael nervously smoothed her hands down the front of her dress. "Uh, J.B., I don't think this is a good idea. You didn't even call your mother to tell her we were coming. That's uh...well, I guess it's not rude exactly, but..." She twisted the rear-view mirror toward her and checked her make-up and hair. "I think we should go back to Willow Glen and call before we come out next time."

J.B. cocked an eye her way, readjusted the mirror and pulled to the side of the road. "Darlin', you've got nothin' to worry about. I promise. My folks will love you."

"Don't you think they'll mind that we're arriving unannounced?"

"Nope. I never call before I come out. None of us do. We just show up."

"But that's so..."

"Informal? That's the way we do things here, darlin'."

"My father would never stand for that kind of thing."

"Your father is a prize pri...uh." He glanced at her. Even if her father *was* a prick, he was still her father. "It's your father's loss."

"I want to make a good impression on them and I feel like my stomach is tied in knots."

He pulled her into his arms and dropped nibbling kisses from her right ear around to her left. From there he worked his way to her forehead, the tip of her nose and at last settled on her mouth.

Michael forgot her nerves, she forgot they were sitting in his car. All her senses were focused on the way it felt to be in J.B.'s arms. "J.B.," she breathed, "I..."

"Shhh. Just give me another kiss and then we'll go on to the house." He settled his mouth briefly onto her full lips and nibbled before raising his head.

Michael's head lay in the crook of his neck, her eyes closed, she breathed deeply taking his scent into her lungs. Her hand stroked into his hair and tried to pull him back. "J.B.?"

Groaning, he had to get himself back in line or his condition would be obvious to his mother. Thinking of his mother helped him bring his libido under control. He glanced at the dashboard clock. "Oh, good. We're in time for lunch."

"Why is that good?"

"Because everybody will be here at the same time."

"Everybody?"

"Mom, Dad, Cowboy, and probably Benjie. Champ lives in Willow Glen and Ty lives in Oklahoma City."

"And Keely lives in Tulsa."

"Yeah. But everybody still livin at home will be here. It's possible Benjie might have had a call to another ranch."

"I think I know what they mean when they talk about the 'fight or flight syndrome'." She drew a shuddering breath.

"Which do you want to do?"

"Stop grinning at me. You know I'd like nothing better than to turn around and run as fast as I can."

He sobered. "But what are you *goin'* to do?"

"I'm going to stay here with you."

He smiled. "That's my girl."

He pulled up in front of the house, got out, loped around to her door and opened it. "Welcome to the Lazy A." Joy washed over him at seeing her here on the home place.

Michael stepped out of the car and grabbed J.B.'s hand. "Hold on to me, please, J.B."

"Always." He led her to the front porch and up the steps.

As they arrived at the door it flew open. Michael stared directly into the eyes of J.B.'s mother. Standing toe to toe with her, Michael realized she also stood nose to nose. "Oh-h-h-, you're six feet tall, too." *And beautiful.*

His mother's smile lit up her entire face. Dark, nearly black hair, frosted only slightly at the temples, glistened in the sunlight as wisps fluttered around her face in the breeze. Eyes as blue as the summer sky, surrounded by the longest, thickest lashes Michael had ever seen, flanked a patrician nose. Her skin glowed, giving her the look of a much younger woman. She could have passed for J.B.'s older sister.

And like J.B., charm oozed from every pore.

Twelve

"Hi, Mom." He put his arm around Michael and smiled. "Michael, this is my mom." He pulled her closer to his side and turning his gaze to his mother, he smiled. "Mom, this is Michael. You've heard me mention her name a time or two, haven't you?"

Elise Anderson brought her hand up to her eldest son's cheek. "Oh, yes. Once or twice." She winked, and turned to Michael. "How lovely to meet you at last, Michael. Welcome to the Lazy A." Smiling, she pulled Michael into her arms and gave her a hug. Feeling the momentary stiffening she quickly withdrew and stepped back, smiling as though unaware. "I'm so happy to meet you. I've heard wonderful things about you from my son."

"Have you?" Michael asked breathlessly, smiling at J.B. "I've heard wonderful things about you, as well."

"Well, he's prejudiced, you know." Elise smiled at her son and putting her arm around his waist, she hugged him to her side. She turned to Michael and winked. "About both of us."

Michael's face reddened. "J.B. has told me a little about his childhood. I envy his close relationship with his brothers and sister, and most especially with his father and you." Michael realized she was talking too much, displaying her nervousness, but couldn't stop the flow. "I can't imagine a lovelier place to grow up than here."

"Yes, our life here can be wonderful. However, we do have our moments of trouble like every other human being on the planet." She smiled at her guest. "If we're lucky your visit will be a peaceful one."

"Thank you, ma'am."

"Oh, please, that's too formal. Won't you call me Elise?"

"Thank you—Elise. What a lovely name." Michael concentrated on speaking in a less shaky voice.

Elise led them toward the back of the house and Michael's gaze wandered quickly over the lovely living room through which they walked. Autumn colors shimmered throughout the room. Dominated by a huge stone fireplace, the room exuded warmth. A grouping of easy chairs, and a sofa surrounded a coffee table made of a huge sheet of plate glass on top of a monstrous piece of driftwood. Scattered around on the hardwood floor, Navajo rugs echoed the same warm colors.

As her gaze drifted around the room she spied a painting. Michael stopped so abruptly J.B., who followed, crashed into her and had to catch her before she fell. Above the mantle, a landscape depicted a small lake surrounded by trees dressed in fall colors. The painting was so beautiful she could nearly hear the ripple of the gentle waves on the shore and the rustle of the leaves as they drifted from the trees.

"Oh, this room is lovely. So warm and welcoming. And that painting is exquisite. It takes my breath away."

"Thank you. I'm proud of the painting, too. Adam painted it while recuperating from his accident."

"Adam?"

"J.B.'s father."

"Oh, my goodness. He's very talented, isn't he?"

Elise Anderson seemed to swell with pride. "Yes. He is. He'll be pleased to hear someone else thinks so. He thinks I only give him compliments because I love him."

Michael turned to J.B. "Do you paint?"

"Only buildin's. Keely inherited Dad's gift. It bypassed all the boys."

Elise chuckled. "We gave all of the children paints and brushes when they were small hoping one of them would show a spark of talent."

J.B. put his arm around his mother's shoulders and kissed her cheek. "And they didn't give up until we were teenagers."

Elise patted J.B. on the shoulder and they continued toward the kitchen. "We were tenacious, yes."

Standing with a big grin on his face, J.B. waited for Michael to catch up.

She strolled over and stopped in front of him and murmured for his ears only, "So that's where you got it."

"Uh huh." He glanced toward the kitchen and turned an unrepentant grin toward her. "We learned at Mother's knee. And Dad's." He leaned slightly forward, his lips just a hair's breadth away from her mouth.

Michael's head snapped back and she quickly stepped away, whispering, "J.B.! Not in front of your mother! Behave yourself."

His mischievous smile mocked her shyness. "I love you, Michael."

"Hush." Red crept up to her hairline as she ducked her head.

Elise called to them, "Come on into the kitchen and we'll have lunch. I hope you won't mind eating at the kitchen table."

"Oh, no. Certainly not. I told J.B. we should have called first instead of just dropping in on you."

"My dear, J.B. is aware that we don't stand on ceremony here. All the children know this is still home and always will be. They come and go at will and not one of them ever calls first." She laughed. "If they did, with the size of this brood, I'd be tied up constantly answering the telephone."

The kitchen was alive with the aroma of hearty vegetable beef soup simmering on the stove. The pale lemon wallpaper gave sparkle and brightness to the room. The table, covered with a pristine white cloth, was set with soup plates and flatware as if company was expected.

"Oh, are we intruding?"

"Intruding? Of course not." Elise looked genuinely puzzled. "Why do you think you're intruding?"

"Your table is already set for company and I thought..."

"My dear, this is how the table looks for every meal. I never know which of my brood is going to show up so I just set the table as if they were all going to be here." She stopped to stir the soup. "J.B., would you call them in?"

"Sure." He stepped to the door but before he could open it a large man burst through knocking J.B. backward.

"Oh, sorry. J.B., I saw your car and came to get you. I need your help..." He stopped, glanced at Michael, then to J.B. and finally back to Michael. "My apologies, ma'am." Then turning back he grabbed J.B.'s upper arm. "I need your help, big brother." He turned to his mother. "Mom, I'm sorry to spoil your lunch but Dream Weaver is loose again. He's in with your Herefords."

"Cowboy, why can't you keep him locked up? That bull's sex drive is completely out of control." She sighed. "You'd better get him out of there before he totally destroys my breeding program."

J.B. laughed. "What's the matter, Mom, you don't like crossbreds?"

"I swear, J.B., if his semen wasn't so valuable I think I'd have you boys castrate him. It isn't so bad when he gets in with the Santa Gertrudis. Even if we have to make an adjustment in our planned breedings, at least he's in with the right breed, but that rascal wants my Herefords as well. He can't understand why Sonny Boy should have a harem."

J.B. looked at Michael's puzzled face. "Dream Weaver is Cowboy's Santa Gertrudis bull and Sonny Boy is Mom's Hereford bull." He chuckled. "He's also her big pet."

Elise, on a roll complaining about her son's troublesome bull, continued. "It would save us a bundle on vet bills alone if we cut off his..."

"Mom!" J.B.'s gaze shot from Michael to his mother and back again. "Take it easy. You're talkin' to a city girl."

Elise laughed. "I'm sorry, but I already owe Benjie your first born son and we're working on Ty's." She looked over and saw Michael's shocked face and laughed. "I was joking, dear. Benjie lives here and doesn't charge a fee. Take everything we say with a grain of salt and forgive my complaints. That bull has run through barbed wire fencing and been stitched up so many times he looks like a patchwork quilt. Not a pretty sight."

J.B. walked over and gave Michael a quick, hard kiss on the mouth, turning her face beet red. "I guess we'll see you when we get him back to the barn." As they went out the door he asked his brother, "How did he get out of the corral this time?"

"That new kid we hired forgot to lock the gate. That damned bull can get the gate open if the padlock isn't on it."

Michael's hands jittered down her sides as she glanced nervously at Elise. J.B. left her—with his mother—a woman she'd met only minutes ago. She wanted Elise Anderson to like her. More than anything she'd ever wanted before in her life, she wanted this woman's approval. She took a deep breath, straightened her shoulders and stepped forward. "Is there anything I can do to help?"

"No, dear. The boys have handled this kind of thing before. Would you like to go ahead and have our lunch or would you rather wait on J.B.?"

Michael smiled shyly. "Could we wait?" *Lunch with J.B.'s mother? Without J.B.?* "That is, if you don't mind, I'd rather wait until they come back."

"My sentiments exactly, and this will give us a chance to get acquainted."

Michael's heart sped up like a bird in a cage. She took a calming breath. "Acquainted?" she whispered. She cleared her throat and spoke in her normal voice. "Yes. We should get to know each other."

"Lets go into the living room where we can be more comfortable. Would you like a cup of coffee?" At Michael's negative headshake, she asked, "Tea?"

"No, nothing, thank you."

"Tell me about yourself, Michael." Elise sat on the couch and leaned back comfortably. Waving her hand she indicated the chair across from her. "You'll find that chair will fit you nicely." She smiled. "I usually sit in it when we're in here."

Michael, on the point of settling into the high-backed rocking chair, immediately sprang up. "Oh, I don't want to take your chair."

"But why not, my dear? I want you to be comfortable and I know you will be in that chair."

Michael looked into Elise Anderson's eyes and saw only gentleness and kindness. "Oh. Thank you." She settled into the chair and relaxing against the back, she realized it did fit her well. The seat was the right distance from the floor to be comfortable for her legs. Without conscious thought she began to rock and turned to Elise with a smile. "This chair feels perfect. Thank you."

Elise nodded. "Now, tell me a little bit about yourself."

Without realizing she did it, Michael picked at her nails, peeling nail polish. "Where should I begin? I'm an attorney."

"I know. I read all about you during the Maitland trial last year. Quite a coup, winning that one. I'm sure you are justifiably proud of the outcome of that case."

"The truth is—I'm not so sure we'd have won if Lyssa hadn't come out of the coma."

"Of course you would. It was good that she awoke when she did, but I heard all about the brilliant defense you put on."

"Really?" She paused. "Oh. From the newspaper accounts."

"No, dear. From my brainy son who, halfway through the trial, came to me and said he was beginning to think they had arrested the wrong man but there was so much evidence against Mr. Maitland they didn't have a choice." Elise smiled. "He told me he was glad you were the defense attorney."

"He did?" Michael's voice indicated surprise.

"Oh, yes. He told me you'd win the case."

"Really?" Pride shone from Michael's eyes.

"Michael, didn't you know you had every chance of winning even if Mr. Maitland's sister hadn't awakened? Mind you, I'm very glad she did. What happened to her was a nasty business."

"Yes, it was. A *very* nasty business. Linc was innocent, and I couldn't stand to think of him in prison for a crime he didn't commit." More comfortable talking about someone else, Michael felt her tension ease. "He didn't deserve all that awful publicity and speculation. His company was in jeopardy for a while but they're back on track now."

"Has he been a client for a long time?"

"Yes, but he was a friend first. Lincoln has been my best friend since we were in school together."

"Best friend?" Elise's eyebrows rose and her eyes widened.

"Yes. He's always been there for me."

Remembering what she'd always told her children—marry your best friend if you want a happy marriage—a shiver fluttered its way up Elise's back. "And have you dated him long?"

"Oh no, Linc and I don't date. We never have dated."

"I don't understand." Elise's emotions took another turn—toward hope. She'd seen J.B.'s face when he looked at Michael. He loved her. Perhaps, if there was nothing between this young woman and her 'best friend', J.B. wouldn't be hurt after all.

"Linc is married to Cari. They're crazy about each other and just had twin boys. I got a bonus in the deal as well. Cari is my friend now, too, and they've asked me to be godmother to the babies." She blushed and smiled. "They're naming one of the boys Michael and the other one Graeham. Graeham Rutherford is also Linc's friend."

"And Mr. Maitland's wife, Cari, is not jealous of your relationship with her husband?"

"Oh, my goodness, no. If you could see the way Linc looks at her you'd know. He only has eyes for Cari. She'd be a fool to miss seeing the love there."

"And do you mind seeing that love in his eyes for another woman?"

"Oh, no!" Michael finally understood the reasons for the third degree. Uncomfortable with causing Elise concern she rushed to allay her suspicions. "Absolutely not! Linc is a friend. Only a friend. There has *never* been anything else between us."

Elise couldn't hide her sigh of relief. "Forgive me. I know I sounded like an old time police officer with a rubber hose, but I know how J.B. feels about you."

"You do?" came out sounding like a squeak. Michael cleared her throat. "Has he said something to you?" A thought occurred to her. *Had J.B. told his mother about the rape?* She squelched the thought. *No. He wouldn't.* "About me?"

"I've seen his face when he looks at you. I can see the love in his eyes when he mentions your name."

"You can?" She couldn't seem to control her heart beat, her breathing, or her voice.

"Oh, yes. I've known he was in love with you from the first moment he mentioned your name. One thing you should know about my son—he is the kind of man who will never stray. I've always known that when he found someone to love, when he gave his heart, it would be for life. He won't ever knowingly hurt you or let you down in any way. At least not if he can help it."

"I know that about him already. He's a very special man."

Elise beamed. "Yes, he is. But then, as we've already established, I'm decidedly prejudiced."

"You have a right to feel very proud of the way you've raised him."

"We were able to make it through some rough times because he was the kind of man who steps in wherever he's needed."

"What do you mean?"

"While J.B. was at the end of his third year of college, Adam was injured when the tractor tipped, threw him off and rolled over on him. Among other injuries, his back was broken. We didn't know if he'd even come out of the coma—or if he'd ever walk again once he awoke. You see, his skull was fractured and he had a subdural hematoma." She shuddered at the memory. "There were other injuries that were also life threatening. We feared he wouldn't make it."

"Dear God. That must have been a frightening time for all of you."

"Yes, it was. I spent every moment at the hospital. J.B. took over here at the ranch and ran the operation as well as his father had done. He delegated the household chores between Ty, Cowboy and Champ. Benjie even had some assigned to him."

"I'd have thought, with a ranch this size, they would already have chores to do."

"Yes, they did, but they were all outdoor chores. You see, up to that time, I had the old-fashioned notion that boys were boys and should learn only what I thought of as masculine chores. I'd planned to teach Keely to cook, clean house, all the things a woman does around a home, as soon as she was a little older. This incident taught me a lesson, though it was an awful way to learn it."

"What do you mean? What lesson?"

Elise's soft smile enhanced her beauty. "Keely was only five at the time. She had, on rare occasions, helped me clean by dusting the furniture—which I can assure you had to be done again after she was in bed. She was, after all, only as adept as any five-year-old child. When the accident happened the boys had to take on responsibilities they'd never had before. They cooked, they cleaned, and they took care of Keely.

"Taking care of their baby sister turned into a task of major proportions. She didn't understand why her mommy and daddy weren't there for her when she had bad dreams. And she had a lot of those. She'd seen the ambulance come and take Adam away. And I went with him. Those wailing sirens frightened her nearly to death. Both parents were taken away by this screaming monster.

"J.B. kept everything together, growing up over night. Not that he was in the least child-like before the accident. But he was still in to pulling pranks on his brothers, and occasionally on his father or me. He was irrepressible. Fun to be around if you weren't the butt of one of his jokes, and most of the time even when you were.

"While Adam was in such terrible danger I called and talked to them every day, but I couldn't leave his side. I don't know if that makes me a better wife than I am a mother. All I know is

Adam needed me and I was terrified if I didn't stay by his side he'd be gone when I came back. The children seemed to be coping and so I stayed where I felt I needed to be."

"I can understand that. I think any woman would have done the same."

"When Adam came home he was paralyzed for a period of time. He was very lucky it wasn't permanent, but during that time I thought he'd give up. He'd always been an active man and to be confined first to a bed and then to a wheelchair nearly did him in. He went into a deep depression. I don't know what we'd have done if Lecia hadn't entered our lives. J.B. said she was 'a gift from God'."

"Lecia?" Michael was surprised by the momentary pang of jealousy and realized she didn't have a right to the feeling.

"Yes. Lecia came here as Adam's physical therapist. She saved his life, quite literally. He was losing weight, refusing to eat. Many times I would take him his tray and he'd throw it across the room."

"Oh, my."

"Yes, it shocked me, too. He'd never before behaved so abominably. I bent over backward to cater to his whims, tried not to make him angry, fixed his favorite foods—and cried buckets when he blamed me for his being alive and stuck in a wheelchair." She grabbed a tissue from the holder on the lamp table and wiped her eyes. "He told me I should have let him die." Tears rolled down her cheeks and she hurriedly wiped them away.

"I've heard of that happening in similar cases." Michael leaned slightly forward. "But how did Lecia change things?"

Elise smiled. "She refused to cater to his temper tantrums. Any time he threw a fit, she calmly handled the situation. He was never able to shake her up. He couldn't make her lose her temper and quit—which was his main goal. And no matter how hard he tried, she insisted he do the exercises."

She smiled at a memory. "He hated for me to see him during these therapy session so I wasn't allowed in the room. I used to stand outside the door and listen, not because I was being nosy, but because I wanted to be there if he did something awful to Lecia." She chuckled. "I needn't have worried. One time I heard her telling him, 'If you don't want to do the exercises that's up to you. But you might as well know, you're going to have to *kick* me out of here. Until you can do that you have to go along with every thing I'm doing because the way things are right now *you can't stop me*.'"

"That made a difference?"

"Of course it did. He began to cooperate with her, working hard instead of lying passively. He looked forward to the time he could kick her out of the house."

"He'd really do that?" Michael couldn't hide the shock in her voice or on her face.

"Adam realized she wasn't going to go away, she would stay right here until she reached her goal—seeing him on his feet. That's when he started to believe what the doctors had told us. That he would eventually recover all, or at least part, of his mobility."

"And did he kick her out of the house?"

Elise laughed. "No, he didn't."

Michael smiled. "Adam sounds exactly like J.B."

Elise grinned. "Oh, yes. It's genetic, I think. The boys *are* like their father. Well, Benjie is more like me but he still has Adam's tenacity."

"How long did J.B. run the ranch?"

"A little over two years."

"And then he went back to college?"

"No. Then he went in to the Marines."

"The Marines? I didn't know he'd been in the military."

"He served four years. When he got out he decided to finish his education. We were so proud of him." Her pride was evident on her face. "He graduated fourth in his class."

"Fourth? That is impressive. I've never doubted his intelligence—except when he is being stubborn..." She fluttered her hand through the air in a helpless gesture, embarrassed at saying something less than complimentary about J.B. to his mother... "Single-minded," she amended as her face reddened.

Elise laughed again. "Yes. He is that. As far as his college days are concerned, I think the fact he was older had more than a little to do with him doing so well. Also his military training was something the others in his class didn't have. As he once told me he had 'an edge'."

Michael sat up straighter, not even realizing she came to his defense so quickly. "But J.B. *is* a very intelligent man. I've watched how he works. He walks around talking like a country boy..."

"Which he is," Elise interjected.

Michael nodded. "True, but he uses it to his advantage. People don't take him seriously. Especially the people he brings in for questioning. They think, 'Oh, he's just a hick in this podunk town.' They answer his questions without realizing they're digging themselves into holes they can't crawl out of— and then he stands back and smiles, saying, 'gotcha'."

Elise smiled. "You've seen him working?"

Michael's hand fluttered again, "Oh, well, er..." She sighed. "I was at the police station one day when he was questioning a suspect and I, uh, I just happened to see him through the two-way mirror."

"Just happened to see him, huh?" Elise chortled when Michael blushed and covered her face with her hands. "Don't be embarrassed. The way he's been chasing you, I'd think you were odd if you didn't show a *little* interest in this man who has pursued you so relentlessly."

Trying desperately to change the subject back to J.B., Michael stated, "So he left the military, went to college, and then decided to become a cop."

Elise turned and looked out the front window, her face displaying remembered pain. "Yes. He decided to become a police officer after Keely was..." She glanced at Michael, obviously fearful of continuing.

"I know that Keely was raped," Michael whispered.

Elise was surprised. "You do?" She raised her eyebrows. "So J.B. shared that with you. That surprises me a little." She shook her head.

"Because of the shame?"

"Oh, no. It's not that he was ever ashamed of Keely. He's said from the beginning, it wasn't her fault. But he's always felt guilty because he wasn't here for her."

"He always wants to protect those he cares for, doesn't he?"

"Yes. But with Keely, it's different. They've had a special bond since Adam's accident. When I was spending so much time at the hospital with Adam, it was J.B. who soothed Keely's bad dreams away. It was J.B. who kissed her 'owies' and who held her when she cried. Even after I came home it was a long time before Keely came to me with her little hurts. She'd run to J.B."

"That must have really hurt you a lot."

"Yeah. It did. I think that's why J.B. went into the military. He wanted to give Keely and I the chance to rebuild our relationship."

"He's very insightful, isn't he?"

"Yes, he always has been. I could see it really hurt him to walk away and go to boot camp, when he felt Keely needed him. He felt guilty, too, because she cried and pleaded with him not to go away and leave her. She felt abandoned again."

"How old was she at the time?"

"She was, as she frequently told us, 'seven-and-a-half'."

"So, still a baby."

"Umm hmm. When she was raped J.B. nearly went crazy. He still feels guilty. I don't think he'll ever be free of feeling that he was somehow responsible. The boy who raped her—we'd known him all his life. He was the son of old friends. J.B. got it into his head that he should have seen this boy's tendency to violence. You see, Jared would show up here to play with Benjie during Adam's hospitalization."

"During the time J.B. was in charge of the ranch and the other children?"

"Yes. At the time J.B. was busy trying to keep things going here on the ranch. He had the care of the other kids, the house, and especially the care of Keely. I'm surprised he allowed Jared to come over. It was just one more kid for which he had to take responsibility."

"I'm not surprised he didn't quibble about one more responsibility."

"You know him very well."

"Yes. He seems to think he now has the responsibility to take care of me."

"Because of your rape, you mean?"

Michael couldn't hide the shock on her face. "He told you?" She stood and turned to the window, and with her back to Elise she whispered, "He promised he'd never tell anyone without my permission."

"He talked with me several weeks ago, Michael. He said you acted exactly like Keely and he *thought* you had been raped. He was obviously in pain when he talked to me about it because he decided last year he wanted you in his life."

"Several weeks ago?" Michael turned and faced Elise. "He said he *thought* I'd been raped?" When Elise nodded, Michael breathed a sigh of relief. "So he didn't break his word to me," she said, her voice barely audible.

"No, he'd never do that, Michael. I wasn't even sure he was right until this moment." She stood and walked to Michael. "If you ever want to talk about it, I'm here, but don't feel you must."

Michael smiled in spite of her tears. "That's what J.B. said."

"We all saw a therapist after Keely's rape. It affected the entire family and we all needed help to cope. It would have been a traumatic experience for any family. It was more difficult for us because Keely is the only girl, the baby, the darling of all her brothers—and the rapist was someone we all knew—or thought we knew. Of all the boys, I think J.B. was affected the most by it. I've begun to think he'll carry the guilt with him his entire life."

"His entire life?"

"Yes. Throughout his life, up until he left for the Marines, J.B. wiped noses, and patched up scrapes and bruises for his siblings. Many times he took responsibility for their actions, when it wasn't his fault. He wanted to protect them from everything and until we caught on, he frequently took their punishment for them."

"That's remarkable."

"Yes. It is. He has always had a penchant for rescuing wounded birds of one sort or another and he started out with his brothers and sister."

Noise erupted at the back of the house. Male voices laughing and talking. Elise stood and smiled. "It looks like the troops have returned triumphant. Let's go feed them the hero's feast they deserve—or at least think they deserve." She laughed as she walked away.

Michael started toward the kitchen following Elise. "Can I help you, Elise?"

"Sure, I'll be happy for the extra pair of hands." She walked toward the kitchen, calling to her men to wash up. She didn't see the look of sadness on Michael's face.

Michael slowed her pace as the thought intruded. *He thinks he's in love with me but am I only another 'wounded bird' needing to be rescued?*

Thirteen

Michael slowly followed Elise and stopped abruptly in the doorway. J.B. stood surrounded by other men as big—or bigger—than he. She gulped. Her gaze traveled over them trying to figure out who was who. She didn't have to wait long for introductions.

"Hey, darlin'. Have you been havin' a nice visit with Mom?" J.B. walked over and wrapped his arms around her. He ran his fingers into her hair, hooked his thumbs under her jaw and tipped her head back, claiming her lips in a brief kiss. He raised his head, looked into her eyes and mouthed the words, *I love you.*

Her face flamed at the chortles that resounded from across the room. "J.B.," she said, in a soft, but admonishing, tone. "Behave yourself."

He whispered, "Darlin', I always behave myself." He grabbed her hand and pulled her across the room. They stopped in front of the man who'd dragged J.B. away earlier. "Michael, this rascal is Cowboy. You saw him earlier but he didn't let us take time for proper introductions."

"We didn't *have* time for proper introductions if we wanted to save Mom's Herefords, big brother." He grinned down at Michael.

Michael smiled shyly and extended her hand. "I'm pleased to meet you, Cowboy." She looked into a face with a familial resemblance so strong it proclaimed him J.B.'s brother. An inch shorter and slightly heavier and more muscular, with deep blue eyes and sun bleached brown hair, Cowboy would flutter the heart of any female in his vicinity.

J.B. tugged her over in front of a younger man. "And this handsome devil is our youngest brother, Benjie. He arrived in time to help us drag Dream Weaver back to the barn."

She looked up—and up—her hand extended, into the face of a young, but masculine, version of Elise. "Benjie. I'm happy to meet the veterinarian in the family."

His grip swallowed her hand as he pulled her gently toward him. He grinned and winked at J.B. "Ah, so he's told you about me, has he?" Benjie leaned down and kissed her on the cheek.

Michael pulled back, as he seemed to surround her. She thought him a giant, at an inch taller than her father, and correctly judged him to be six and a half feet tall. His sheer size sent fear whispering over her skin. She fought it down and offered him another smile.

J.B. noticed and put his arm around her. "Back off, little brother. You go work your wiles on the rest of the female population. This one is mine."

Benjie laughed. "I don't think you need to worry, big brother. Like the song says, she 'only has eyes for you'."

Michael turned beet red and tried to turn away.

"Now see what you've done you big lug, you've embarrassed her." J.B. gave her a squeeze and leaned down to speak softly near her ear. "Pay no attention to him, darlin'. He's still a kid. Got a lot of growin' up to do." He straightened and pulled her over in front of the older man standing with the other two. "You still haven't met the most important member of this crew."

"So, you're Michael." She heard the deep rumbling voice, so like his son's, and looked up into an older version of J.B.'s face.

Her open-eyed stare displayed her shock. "Oh, my. You look and sound just like J.B.," she said in an awed voice.

Adam Anderson threw back his head as a bark of laughter erupted. Still grinning hugely, and with a twinkle in his eye, he looked down at her. "No, darlin'. J.B. looks and sounds exactly like *me*—but *I'm* the original." He chuckled as he took her hand and held it gently. "If it wasn't for the fact I have a little gray hair," he glanced over to where Elise ladled the soup into a tureen, "and a wife I adore, I'd give this young scamp a run for his money. You're absolutely beautiful, Michael."

"Well, at least we know where J.B. got his silver tongue," Michael quipped and then turned beet red, unable to believe she'd said it. She turned her face into J.B.'s shoulder inhaling the scent of his aftershave, along with sweat and something else she wasn't sure she wanted to identify.

When J.B. heard her sniffing he stepped back. "Uh, darlin', I'd better grab a shower before lunch. I wrestled that damned bull to get him away from one of Mom's cows. I'll grab a quick shower, change into clean clothes and be right back."

He loped off toward the back stairs and left her among his family. Drawing away from the overpoweringly huge men who stood grouped by the door, she eased over toward J.B.'s mother.

Elise leaned toward them and sniffed audibly. "Why don't the rest of you go get cleaned up, too? We'd certainly enjoy our lunch more if we could smell the soup and fresh baked bread instead of sweat and cow manure." Elise pointed and all three of them ducked their heads and headed for the stairs. "Five minutes or we eat without you. You and that stupid bull have held up lunch long enough." She chuckled when she heard their steps speed up as they ascended the stairs.

Michael noticed Adam walking with a slight limp as he departed the kitchen. When she saw Elise watching her she was embarrassed. "I'm sorry, I didn't mean to stare. I was only thinking, they're all such handsome men, and then I thought how lucky you were that Mr. Anderson is able to walk."

"Yes. We were lucky and we thank God for it every day. Adam still has a slight limp when he's tired. I don't intend to allow him to do anything strenuous for the rest of the day. I also noticed him limping. I'll have to use my womanly wiles on him to convince him to rest. He thinks he's as strong as an ox. I came too near to losing him to risk his health."

"Did Ty become a doctor because of his father's illness?"

Elise nodded, one eyebrow raised. "How perceptive of you. Yes, he did. And Keely decided to become a nurse because of the accident. It was her dream. Because she'd been raped, she discovered she couldn't be comfortable working with male patients. But she went into nursing anyway."

"Yes. So J.B. told me. Why did Benjie become a vet?"

"He's always had an interest in helping with doctoring the animals around here. Like his brother, he's always cared for wounded birds—or anything else that needed loving attention. We used to say that, between J.B. and Benjie, we had an over abundance of TLC for every creature on the place."

She laughed, "One time they found a rabbit burrow with babies in it. The doe was dead. Had apparently been killed by a coyote or a dog. They brought the babies home and bottle fed them with Keely's doll bottle."

Michael's eyes filled with tears at the picture drawn by Elise's words. "Did they save them?"

"Oh yes, but then we had the problem of trying to turn them back to the wild. Bottle fed rabbits don't have a clue how to care for themselves. We thought about it and realized we had no choice. We kept them until they died of old age."

A chuckle erupted as another memory surfaced. "One time a neighbor was over here and saw the rabbits. He suggested having fried rabbit. Keely heard him and tried to lift the horsewhip off the hook in the barn. She had every intention of using it on him. She was three at the time."

Michael laughed, picturing the three-year-old's wrath. Her mind skipped to the huge man who'd frightened her a little. "So, Benjie has been caring for animals all his life. The wild ones as well as the ranch animals?"

"He was doing a lot of it before he went to college and vet school. Oh, not surgery of course, but things like helping with difficult calvings and so on."

The men came trooping down the stairs, laughing, joking and shoving each other like schoolboys. Michael backed to the side of the room and watched. She'd always known she missed a great deal in life being an only child but only now realized exactly how much. She found herself longing to be part of a family like this.

No. She wanted to be part of *this* family. And it couldn't be. She must not allow J.B. to take on her problems, her fears. Not now that she knew it wasn't love he felt. She loved him too much to—she loved him. *Oh, God.*

J.B. looked for her the moment he entered the kitchen. He wondered why she stood off to the side of the room—and why she looked so sad. He walked to her, wrapped his arms around her, pulled her close and rumbled softly, "Darlin', why are you lookin' so sad? What's the matter?"

"Oh, I'm fine, really. I guess I'm tired." She looked up into his beloved face and nodded. "Yes, that's what it is. I'm just tired."

"You could take a nap after lunch, if you'd like."

"My goodness, J.B., what would your folks think of me?"

"They'd think you're tired." He kissed her cheek and nuzzled close to her ear. "They know you've had someone harassin' you. That you've been losin' sleep. So don't worry about it. If you want to take a nap you can go sleep in my bed." He paused, leaned his head back, looked at her, grinned, and did a Groucho Marx imitation with his eyebrows.

She leaned her forehead against his chest and gently whacked him on the upper arm. In spite of trying to hold it in, she burst in to laughter. "You idiot." Still chuckling, she stepped away from him and looked up to see his family watching them with loving smiles on their faces.

"It looks like J.B. just bit the dust," boomed Benjie.

"It's about time, don't you think?" murmured Elise.

Cowboy quipped, "Yeah, Ty has a head start. Big bro will never catch up."

"Leave J.B. alone. Can't you see you're embarrassin' his girl?" rumbled Adam.

Michael burrowed her face into her favorite spot, J.B.'s neck. Her face turned beet red, while at the same time she loved the feeling of being a part of this loving family.

"Hush up, the lot of you. Michael doesn't know what to make of this wacky family." J.B. stroked her back. "Come on, darlin', there's no way to beat 'em, so why don't we join 'em? Besides, the soup's gettin' cold." He walked with her to the table and held her chair.

Adam surprised her by saying grace. She'd never heard her father say grace.

The food delicious, the company superb, the sharing of the meal filled more than stomachs. Soup made from beef and vegetables grown on the ranch—prepared fresh by Elise's loving hands. Bread baked that morning—its crispy crust crackled as they broke it. Steam rose from the still warm, soft, interior as they bit into it, and nobody noticed or cared when the melted butter ran down their fingers.

The chatter and laughter continued unabated and the food disappeared. Michael didn't ever remember a more wonderful or delicious meal. Pheasant under glass served on Royal Doulton china in her parent's home would not be nearly so heavenly as the simple soup and home made bread served on Frankoma pottery here at the Anderson Ranch. Apple pie topped off the meal.

As soon as they finished, the men stood, as if on some cue, carried their dishes to the sink and each of them had some word of praise for Elise. Patting her on the back, bragging about the bread, the soup, the apple pie she'd served for desert.

Watching them, Michael marveled. Comparing their's to her father's behavior, he lost in the equation. On the rare occasions when she was summoned to the dinner table, she'd seen him get up and walk away from the table without so much as a thank you. He'd only have mentioned the food if it had *not* been to his liking.

And never having had anyone with whom to check her reality, she'd grown up believing his actions to be normal for all men.

J.B. nuzzled his face into the side of her neck and kissed her below her ear. "What are you thinkin' about? You looked really lost in thought."

"Oh, just reminiscing a little."

"You were lookin' sad again."

"Was I? I don't mean to be." She stood and pushed the chair away from the table. "I'd better help your mother with the dishes, then I think we need to head back to town."

"Any particular reason?"

She equivocated, "Don't you want to check in with Shag?"

"I can do that from here, darlin'."

"I know, but I just thought..." She gathered up the soup tureen and turned toward the sink. "I just..." She stopped and set the tureen back on the table. Looking toward the sink where Elise was busily scraping soup plates and loading the dish washer, she whispered, "Don't you think your folks might be getting tired of having me hanging around here?"

"Why on earth would you think that? Have they said anything to give you the idea they wanted you to go?"

"Oh, no, they've been wonderful, but I don't want to wear out my welcome."

Elise overheard. "I'm sorry to intrude on this private conversation. I didn't mean to overhear, but I did." She stepped up and put her hands on Michael's shoulders. "You're always welcome here. You may stay as long as you like." She smiled. "I can see why my son fell in love with you and if you two decide to marry I'll welcome you with delight. I've always wanted another daughter."

"Oh, but we're not..." She turned to J.B., a look of helplessness on her face. "Tell her, J.B., we're not..."

"Oh, but darlin', we most definitely *are*. I love you and I want to marry you. I've told you that."

"But we can't. You know we can't."

Elise put her arms around Michael and nodded her head toward the living room indicating J.B. should leave them alone. She pulled Michael toward the table and settled her into a chair. Pulling another chair out, she sat down and took Michael's hands in to her own.

"Michael, look at me. I want you to know I'm telling you the truth." When she had Michael's undivided attention, she spoke calmly and quietly. "J.B. is in love with you, Michael. I believe you love him too, but you're unsure of yourself, unable to trust your feelings, and you're afraid to commit. Am I right?"

Michael nodded. Gripping Elise's hands tightly, she whispered, "I do love him. Too much to saddle him with my problems. He needs to find someone who..." Her chin quivered and she fought to hold back the tears that threatened. "...doesn't remind him of a wounded bird."

"Oh, my dear, that wasn't said to drive you away. It was to explain to you what a gentle, caring and loving man my son is. He loves you. Truly he does and he'd be terribly hurt if you walk away from him." Elise patted the back of Michael's hand. "I do want to ask one thing of you."

"Anything. If it's within my power."

"It is within your power. Please don't hurt him, Michael. If you don't feel you can commit to him totally, then don't tell him you love him. Don't give him hope if there is none. Walk away from him now. Because, while it would break his heart to lose you now, it would kill him to have you for a little while and then have you walk away."

"I'd never hurt him. Not intentionally."

"That's all any mother could ask."

The two women joined the men in the living room for a short time. Then Cowboy got up and said, "I can't be lazy like the rest of you. I have some cattle to see to." He approached the couch where Michael and J.B. sat. "We enjoyed meetin' you, Michael. Hope you'll come back again real soon." He ambled toward the back of the house. A few moments later they heard the door shut behind him.

Benjie rose from the chair and stretched. "I have to go to the Breuster Ranch to inoculate their cattle for leptospirosis. Guess I'd better get on the road, too." Walking over to Michael he grabbed her and pulled her up for a rib-cracking hug.

"Here, now. Cut that out." J.B. came off the couch and Benjie planted the flat of his hand in the middle of his brother's chest. A shove sent J.B. backward, nearly turning over the couch.

Benjie laughed as he danced across the floor with Michael in his arms. "Settle down, bro. You know Mom won't allow scuffling in the house."

Michael didn't know how to react. She'd never been a part of a loving and playful family. She worried how J.B. would feel about her dancing with his brother. She also worried that Benjie's feelings would be hurt if she jerked away and that's what she wanted to do more than anything. She looked at Elise when J.B. bounced right back up from the sofa.

Elise rose from her chair, grabbed Adam's hand, pulled him along as she walked over and took Michael's and led them toward the back of the house. "Take it outside, boys. I don't want my living room wrecked." In the kitchen she grabbed up the coffeepot. "Coffee, anyone?"

Michael looked back toward the living room. "They're not going to hurt each other—are they?" She looked to Elise and then to Adam. "Please, don't let them hurt each other."

"Oh, they won't. Don't worry about it. It's all just horseplay. They love each other very much and they won't draw blood."

"Blood?" Michael gasped.

Adam, standing at the window looking out, began to chuckle. "Michael, come here and look outside."

She walked to the window and looked out—to see J.B. carrying his much larger brother over his shoulder. He struggled to keep him elevated and still walk toward the cattle tank. Benjie was unceremoniously tossed in—Roper boots and all. His Stetson floated for a moment until he came up out of the water shaking like a puppy dog, sending water flying every direction.

Adam burst into laughter and turned to Elise. "J.B. threw him into the tank again. That boy never learns."

"He'll have to change before he goes on his call." She grabbed a handful of towels from the stack on the dryer in the utility room and stood by the back door, waiting.

Benjie opened the door; looking chagrined, he glanced at his mother holding the stack of towels. "Another pair of Ropers soaked. Damn." With difficulty, he kicked off the wet boots, and unbuttoned his shirt.

Michael fled toward the living room.

J.B. came in the front door, his face red, and gasping for breath. "That big lug is gettin' too heavy for me. I don't know if I'll be able to do that again. Guess I'm gettin' old." He looked at Michael and grinned. "You look shocked. Don't worry, darlin', he's not hurt." He walked toward her, his hand outstretched. "This is the way we've been all our lives. It's the way we grew up. You'll get used to it."

This kind of behavior, from grown men, was totally beyond her comprehension. She didn't believe she *would* get used to it. She didn't even know if she *wanted* to get used to it. "I think we'd better go back home."

He sighed as he looked at her face. "Okay, if you're sure."

"Yes. I want to look over a couple of briefs before tomorrow."

"Are they are at home or the office?"

"They're in my briefcase."

"Oh, then they're in the car."

"Yes. I won't leave any more of my client's files out for *his* perusal."

"What concerns me is there was no indication showing where he entered the house. We found no pry-bar marks, no scratches, nothing to indicate where or how he broke in. Is it possible you left a door unlocked?"

"Are you kidding? I've been living with this nightmare for long enough now that I make sure to check and double check every night."

"But you might have gotten careless since..."

"Do I look like the kind of person who'd get careless?"

"No, that isn't what I meant. I only meant, since I'm stayin' there now, you might have depended on me to lock the door."

"I depend on only me. I wouldn't be able to sleep if I didn't check on the door myself."

"I know. And even though I saw you check the locks, I thought I'd check them myself. Just a minute ago, it occurred to me I may have turned the deadbolt the wrong way and unlocked it."

"Oh, do you think so?" Her eyes were huge as she stared up at him. "If you did, it would explain how he got in, and frankly, I think I could live with that better than believing he has a key. I've been worrying all day, thinking he has a key to my house."

"If he does, we know he doesn't have a key to mine. We'll just move over there." He pulled her against his body and hugged.

"I guess we'd better round up the folks and tell them we're leavin'." He grabbed her hand and pulled her toward the kitchen.

Michael walked a couple of steps behind J.B., dragging her heels because, in spite of the fact it had been her idea, she was reluctant to leave. She wanted to stay in this home where she'd found welcome, contentment, and an abundance of love. Going home to her house would be walking back into her nightmare. Only a fool would do that gladly.

In the kitchen his parents sat at the table chatting and drinking coffee. They looked up when J.B. and Michael entered.

"Mom, Dad, we're goin' to head back to town. Michael has some cases she has to look over before tomorrow."

Adam and Elise rose from the table and came forward, Elise going to J.B. and Adam going to Michael. Elise hugged her son and kissed him on the cheek.

Adam stopped in front of Michael and asked, "Do you think asking for a hug is out of line?"

Michael smiled shyly and, thinking of all the hugs she'd never gotten from her own father, she shook her head. He wrapped his arms around her and hugged her briefly and stepped back. It left her feeling warm all over. When Elise stepped up and, without asking, hugged her as well, Michael finally recognized the bubbly feeling in her chest. *Happiness*, an emotion with which she had been unfamiliar until now.

She stepped out of Elise's arms, a brilliant smile on her face. "I'll never be able to thank you enough for one of the most wonderful days of my life. I really enjoyed the meal. The company was delightful and the food was delicious. The best I've ever eaten."

"You don't have to praise it *that* much, darlin', it was only soup." J.B. grinned at his mother. "I have to admit though, the bread and pie were outstandin'."

"Please come back, Michael. Often. You're welcome here anytime. For a meal or overnight, for a chat or whatever you need."

"Thank you again." Michael headed for the door.

J.B. trailed behind her. At the door he turned, grabbed his jacket and Stetson from the hall tree, waved it at his parents and clapped the hat on his head and the jacket over his shoulder as they exited the house. At the car he held the door for Michael, then walked around, tossed his jacket and hat in the back seat, and climbed in on his side.

"What do you think of the ranch, darlin'?"

"It's beautiful, and so peaceful out here. I can see why your family loves it so much." She smiled. "Your whole family is so close, so loving with each other. I wish I'd had that with mine."

"I'm sorry you didn't, but you will have it now, with mine." J.B. reached across the seat, took her hand and squeezed.

"It's not the same thing, J.B." She placed her other hand on top of his, enfolding it between hers. "I don't ever expect—or want close ties with my father, but I wish I had the kind of relationship with my mother that you have with yours." She sighed. "I might as well add another wish to the list. I wish I knew where my father put my mother. I'd like to find her and get her out of wherever she is now and bring her home with me. We might have a chance to develop a closeness, without my father being around to hinder it."

J.B. glanced at Michael and saw the sadness on her face. *I'm going to find your mother, darlin' and bring her to you That's a promise I intend to keep.*

Switching on the car radio, J.B. tuned it to the local NPR station that played mostly classical music. They talked little as he drove. Without verbalizing it, they each felt they needed time to think.

While still a half hour away, J.B. dialed Shag and, after a brief conversation, they agreed to meet at Michael's house.

When they arrived, Shag's car was in the driveway and he sat on the front porch in one of the wicker chairs. He rose as they drove in and walked to the passenger side, opened the car door and assisted Michael as she exited the car.

He glanced over the top of the car and grinned. "What took you so long, pardner?"

"You been waitin' long?"

Shag chuckled. "Nah, only about ten minutes." He walked a half step behind Michael and grinned back at J.B. who stood shrugging into his jacket. "Well, are you coming in? You've held up this operation long enough."

"Hold your horses. I'll be there." J.B. grabbed his hat and loped up the steps to the door through which Michael had just gone. Shag stood holding the screen door open. Stopping in the doorway J.B. asked, "Did you bring the kit?"

"Yeah. It's in the car. I thought we'd look at the doors and windows carefully first."

"Already did that."

"Okay, I'll get the kit."

J.B. walked to where Michael was going through her briefcase. "Darlin', we're goin' to check the house for fingerprints. Could you use the desk in the bedroom so we won't disturb you?"

"And so I won't be in your way?"

"Well, yeah. There's that, too."

"Okay. No problem." She grabbed her briefcase and headed to the bedroom. Kicking off her shoes in the foyer she bent to pick them up. "I think I'll take these with me. This is my only pair of white shoes." She went through the door and shut it behind her.

Shag sprinted to his car, retrieved the kit from the trunk and was back inside in a short time. "Let's get to work."

Two hours later they'd dusted every surface the perp might have touched.

Shag stretched and groaned, rubbing his back. "J.B., you were right. The man was smart. He left nothing for us to pick up."

"Well, we knew it would be a waste of time, but we had to check it out."

"We do a lot of that in this job. Checking for fingerprints that aren't there, running down leads that don't pan out and asking questions that have to be asked over and over again."

J.B. looked at Shag with an ultra-serious expression. "Yeah, it's a thankless job, but somebody has to do it."

Shag reared his head back, an exaggerated expression of shock on his face. "You spouting cliches now, pardner?"

J.B. grinned. "Yeah, I suppose I am. That's what comes of hangin' around you so much."

Shag flipped J.B. the international sign of disrespect, and grinned when J.B. roared with laughter.

Michael heard the laughter, and stepped out. "You sound like you're working hard. Did you find anything?"

"Nah. As we suspected, he didn't leave any fingerprints." He noted she'd changed to soft denim jeans and a shirt that hugged her curves. And to him she was the most beautiful woman he'd ever seen. In a business suit, or in faded denims, it didn't matter. She was lovely.

"I suppose I can begin to think about dinner, then. It's all right to use the kitchen?" She strolled toward them.

"Sure. But you don't have to. We can either order in or go out to eat."

"What about ordering a pizza?" She turned to J.B.'s partner. "Shag, will you join us?"

J.B. glared at Shag. "Nah, he can't. He has to hit the road."

Shag's lips twitched and his eyes sparkled. "I do?"

J.B.'s eyes talked volumes, though he only growled, "Yeah. You do. I'll show you to the door."

"Not necessary. I can find my own way out. Nobody's going to accuse me of not taking a hint." Shag grinned and turned toward the hall. He grabbed his Stetson off the hall tree as he headed toward the door, a grin still lighting up his face. "See you in the morning."

J.B. sighed, and in a voice loud enough for Shag to hear as he exited, J. B. rumbled,. "I thought he'd never leave."

Shag's laughter echoed back into the house as he shut the door.

"J.B." Shock clearly visible on her face, Michael stood with her hands on her hips. "Shame on you. We should have at least fed him dinner."

"Nah, he's a big boy. He can get his own dinner."

She sighed, something she seemed to do a lot of around this exasperating, but loveable man. "I suppose, if we're going to get pizza, I should call in the order. What kind do you want?"

"Anything except anchovies."

She smiled. If she wanted to be mean she'd order a pizza with a double helping of anchovies. No... she didn't like them either. She laughed softly. The perfect joke on him and she couldn't use it. She shook her head and walked to the phone.

Much later, nestled spoon fashion on their left sides, they stretched out on the couch with Michael in front of J.B. Michael's old Mantovani recordings played on the stereo. J.B. nuzzled her neck just below her ear.

Michael arched her neck to give him easier access. She loved lying here in his arms, feeling safe and loved. His lips on her neck caused her breathing to become erratic, and amazingly she wasn't frightened. She felt warm, and her arms ached to hold him as he was holding her. She let herself drift with the sensations his nibbling lips were creating, sinking deeper and deeper into the sensual pleasure. She floated on a sea of bliss, headed toward sensory overload without a moment of fear intruding.

J.B. couldn't believe what was happening. Instead of scooting away as he'd half expected she arched her neck to give him easier access. He nibbled his way to the bend of her shoulder, and breathed in the scent of strawberries and the sweet aroma that was uniquely her own.

Returning to just below her ear he halted for an instant to gauge her reaction. Then, touching the tip of his tongue to her ear rim, he slid it down to her lobe, taking it in his mouth to suckle. She moaned softly and sent his blood roaring through his veins.

He slid his hand just below her breast and hesitated for an instant. He cupped his hand over the soft mound and, sliding his palm, gently abraded the beading nipple. Another soft moan whispered in her throat and her breathing accelerated. He felt a tightening in his loins that nearly overwhelmed him. He wanted her, more than anything he'd wanted in his life. But he had to stay in complete control of his need. She must have complete control of how far this went.

He gently turned her to face him. Kissing her softly on the lips, he pulled back and looked deeply into her eyes. "I love you, Michael. Do you believe that?"

"Yes. I know you do. And I…"

His mouth covered hers, shutting off her words. His breathing labored, he ached. He leaned his head back and murmured, "Let me love you, darlin'. I'll stop anytime you say."

Fourteen

Michael looked into his eyes. He had never let her down, had been there every time she needed him. And she knew—without a shadow of a doubt—he would always keep his word. If she told him to stop—no matter at what point—he would stop. She could trust him. That feeling—no, it was stronger than a feeling—that *knowledge* that she could trust a man—*this* man, sent any thought of fear into oblivion.

These feelings of wanting a closer relationship, and the awareness of her own sexuality, emotions *he* had awakened in her, were so new she was afraid to trust them. Fear that she would do something she'd regret—or worse, that he would regret—skittered through her mind. But she could trust J.B. He'd proven over and over again she could put her faith in him.

Her nightmare of the rape had recurred nearly every night before J.B. had firmly planted his big boots in the middle of her life. In just the past few days, since he'd been spending so much time with her, the nightmare had come only once.

She wanted to take the next step. To make love with him. She wanted to believe that, with the right partner, good images could replace the old pain. And she wanted to build those memories with J.B. He was the only one for her, the one person in this big crazy world with whom she could build a relationship. Fear that she'd let him down, disappoint him in some way, again entered her mind. Her only experience had been the rape so she didn't have a clue how to make a man happy. Would it matter to him? No, she didn't believe it would.

Uncomfortable with the long silence as she stared into his eyes, J.B. put his hand to her face. "Michael?"

"J.B., if we... uh..."

"Make love, darlin'. What I want to do is make love with you. And I want to hold you in my arms when you sleep." He kissed her softly, his warm mouth moving gently over hers. "I want to taste you everywhere." He kissed the hollow of her throat. "I want to hold you, skin to skin." He pulled her length against him as his hands caressed her back. "I want to be inside you, lovin' you." His hips moved against her. "And I want to watch you come apart in my arms." He saw her eyes widen. "You'll see. It won't be the same as what happened before," he whispered. "I want to make sure that you are happy. That's the most important part of this, sweetheart. I want to make you happy. But if anything I do makes you uncomfortable in the smallest way, you tell me and I'll stop."

When she opened her mouth to speak, he assumed she would question his statement. "Sweet darlin', you have a choice. With me, you will *always* have a choice. *That's* the difference between what happened before and what will happen now," he rumbled softly as his voice vibrated over her skin.

"I know." She looked into his eyes for a moment that seemed to last forever. "If we..." She looked at his shirt button, then shifted her gaze back to his eyes. "...if we make love, then... afterward... can you walk away?"

"What do you mean, 'walk away'? And why would I want to?"

"Just that. Walk away. No commitment, no strings."

"No, darlin'," he protested. "I won't walk away. I can't. Not ever." He said gently, "You say, 'no strings' as if we'd just met in the corner bar and this is a one night stand." He kissed her forehead. "This is not a one night stand, Michael. I won't allow you to denigrate yourself, or me, in that way. If a one night stand is all you're lookin' for, you'll have to go elsewhere to find it."

He leaned his forehead against hers, "In my heart I am already committed to you and to this relationship." He kissed her. "For me, this is forever. There are already strings." He brushed his lips across hers. "They bind my heart to yours as surely as the sun rises in the east." He kissed her eyes and his mouth drifted to her nose. "I'll still be lovin' you when I draw my last breath—and beyond that to forever."

"No." She shook her head. "You can't. You mustn't."

"Oh, my sweet love, I don't have a choice. It isn't somethin' I can decide to do or not to do. It's somethin' that already *is*."

Frustrated because she couldn't make him understand, she put her palms to his cheeks and looked deeply into his eyes. "What if what you feel isn't love?"

"I'm very sure of my feelin's for you, Michael."

"But, as soon as you've caught this nut whose harassing me, it's possible you'll see that I'm right."

"What are you worried about, darlin'?"

"I just want to be clear on this. When you no longer feel the need to protect me, if you discover that what you feel is not love, I'll understand."

J.B. glowered at her. "What do you think I feel, if not love?"

Her sad smile nearly broke his heart. "What your mother called 'rescuing the wounded bird' syndrome. And if that's what it is, then you need to know I'll understand if you walk away."

He knew she'd never been able to rely on anybody in her life—before now. He understood about her relationship with her parents, and would be surprised if she ever *completely* trusted him, or anyone. She would always have questions about the validity of relationships. Never having been loved, she needed to learn how to accept it—and feel she deserved it. When he found her mother, and he would find her, he hoped there was genuine feeling there, hoped that the lack of closeness could be laid solely at her father's feet. But he would protect her and love her and prove to her she was deserving of that love.

It would take time. And that was a commodity he was more than willing to expend for her. He would give her all the time she needed. Time to learn to accept his love, as well as give her own without fear it would be thrown back in her face.

He smiled at her. "No, darlin', you're the one who'll see. I've told you—I love you. Nothing will change that. Ever. I'm repeatin' myself, I know, but I'll go on sayin' it over and over again until you begin to believe it."

He kissed her, taking her lower lip into his mouth and laving it. He pressed nibbling kisses along her jawline to beneath her ear and worked his way back. He gloried in her response to him. So far she displayed no fear.

His tongue outlined her lips and made brief, gentle invasions, touching hers before sweeping to the inside of her upper lip. He felt her arms creep around his neck, and it sent a thrill skittering over his skin. *She hadn't pushed him away.*

As her arms pulled him closer, her lips moved under his. A thrill rippled over his skin when she responded. Tentative at first, she quickly learned from him and he reveled in her new found skill. "Oh, my love, my beautiful love. I've wanted you for such a long time." A knot of need pressed low in his belly and he drew gulps of air into his lungs.

The deep, seductive rumble of his voice enticed her closer. Michael felt the hard thrust of his erection against her belly, and marveled at being unafraid. His voice rumbled against her throat, "Are you all right, sweetheart?" and the vibrations sent her blood racing. In a torrent, it pounded and thrummed, roaring in her ears.

His hands cupped her buttocks and rocked her softness against his hardness. Her heart pounded and her breathing escalated to panting gasps.

But not from fear. Amazingly—not from fear.

J.B. felt her response and thought he would explode from the joy. He sat up pulling her across his lap. He kissed her and looked into her eyes. "Is it all right, love? Are you okay with this?" At her nod, he stood, holding her in his arms and walked toward the bedroom.

"Where are we going?" Michael breathed.

"To the bedroom. I want to take a long, sweet time lovin' you." He grinned down at her. "And I don't want to worry about fallin' off the couch at an inconvenient moment."

She laughed, burying her face in his neck. Her laughter froze as a small worry entered her mind. One of her clients, a woman who was the victim of domestic abuse, had said she dared not laugh for any reason when she and her husband made love. It made him angry. A little frisson of fear skipped down her back. Michael pulled her head back and looked into his eyes. "I'm sorry. I shouldn't laugh."

"Why not? There's nothin' wrong with laughin'. Laughter should be a part of lovin', just like it's a part of life. Laughter expresses joy, and my darlin', I want to fill your life with joy. You laugh anytime you feel like it."

He carried her into the bedroom and placed her gently on the bed. Removing her shoes, he sat beside her, and unbuttoned her blouse. As he pushed each button through the opening, he watched her face to see any sign she was uncomfortable, and then kissed the spot just bared. Within moments her blouse was open all the way down the front. He sat watching her, waiting to see if she was still willing to go forward. When she said nothing, he smiled and murmured, "You are so beautiful." He leaned over and kissed her on the mouth, his lips nibbling, and his tongue tasting her sweetness.

Michael liked the sensations J.B. awakened in her. It *was* different. Nothing he did reminded her of what happened before.

She wanted to touch him and reached with tentative fingers to unbutton the top button of his shirt. Unsure how to proceed, she watched his face, looking for a reaction.

He couldn't believe she was brave enough to be this bold—and he was thrilled beyond measure at receiving the gift of her trust. He smiled and kissed her, nibbling his way along her jawline. "I love you, darlin'."

When he raised his head she unbuttoned another button and touched his neck, her soft fingers working their way down to open another button. When his chest lay bare, she combed her fingers through the thick matte of hair she found there. The sensation of the crisp curls caressing her fingers sent a thrill of delight over her skin in places the curls did not touch.

She found the small circles of his nipples hidden in the crisp mass. Watching his face, she rubbed her fingertips across them. She loved hearing the sudden inhalation of his breath. And she delighted in seeing his eyes widen before his lids came down and his face dissolved in to an expression of ecstasy.

Believing she'd never find the courage to touch him, J.B. thrilled at the contact. As her fingers arrowed through the hair on his chest, he marveled at how much she seemed to want to give him pleasure. When her fingers again found and caressed his nipples he thought he'd sailed over the moon. His heartbeat escalated, and he dragged air in through his nose. His hands circled her wrists and he held them against his chest. Things were moving much too fast. He wanted to go slow, to gauge her reaction to every new experience, and most important of all, he needed to keep a tight rein on his own libido.

He buried his face in her neck, kissing his way down to her breast. He took her nipple into his mouth, suckling it through the lace. Within a few minutes this was no longer enough. He wanted more. Lifting her gently he unhooked her bra and removed it, dropping it to the floor... and waited to see her reaction.

She placed her hands on the sides of his face and caressed, arching slightly, inviting his return. *She enjoyed the contact.*

He took her breast back into his mouth, laving it, suckling until the areola puckered and the nipple beaded and stood at attention. Not wanting to neglect the other side, his tongue stroked until he heard her gasping for breath.

Holding his head more firmly to her, she arched to him, wanting him closer. Fire raced over her skin as his fingers drifted down to the waistband of her jeans. She moaned, her arms encircling him to bring him in to close contact. She needed. Filled with wanting she ached in that most private place. A soft moan, from the back of her throat, escaped on an outrush of breath and Michael writhed under his gentle ministrations.

She wanted to touch him everywhere. She wanted him to touch her. The feelings were so new, she had no idea how to control them. She wanted everything at once. Every touch from him was pleasure, every kiss of his lips pure joy. She wanted to feel him, as he'd said earlier, 'skin to skin' and she wanted it *now*. She frantically worked to undo the rest of his buttons and tugged to remove his shirt.

He shrugged and it slithered down his arms before she yanked it off and unceremoniously tossed it to the floor. He unsnapped her jeans and slowly slid the zipper down, while watching her face for her reaction. "Are you alright, darlin'?"

"Oh, yes." She reached to trace the outline of his mouth with her fingertip and a thrill of joy filled her when she saw the shudder that coursed over his body.

He slowly slid her jeans and bikini briefs down her legs, giving her time to protest. When she grabbed for the sheet, he halted her. "No, my love. We won't hide from each other." He kissed her ankle. "You have no reason to feel ashamed of what we're doin'." He extended her leg and kissed the back of her knee. "I want to see you. All of you. And taste you." He moved his open mouth up her thigh.

"I want you to see me." His deep, rumbling voice whispered over her skin. It was another kind of touch. Another contact with J.B. and she sighed with pleasure as his mouth and his words sent a quiver of excitement over her skin, arrowing in to the very center of her being.

He planted a kiss on her thigh and raised his head to look into her eyes. "I want you to know there is nothing to fear." He moved back up to take her mouth in a drugging kiss before quickly standing and removing his jeans. He stood beside the bed. Waiting. He didn't want to frighten her. He held his breath as she looked at his jutting erection. He watched as her eyes widened and her gaze traveled back to meet his. "Are you okay, sweetheart?"

At her nod he lay down on the bed beside her. Taking her in his arms he held her for a moment, pulling her naked body in closer contact and waiting for her response. He allowed her the time to become accustomed to the feel of him so near, their skin touching with no barriers. He looked into her eyes, whispering, "All right, my love?"

She took a deep breath and raised her head to look directly into his eyes. "Yes. All right." And it was. She gloried in the feel of him—all of him. "Oh, yes, very all right."

He kissed her belly, and worked his way to her breasts. Then beginning at her ankles, he worked his way up to her thighs, kissing every inch, fearful of neglecting any part.

"J.B." She struggled to drag air into already laboring lungs. "Please?" She was not sure for what she begged. Only that she needed something—somethng *more*.

"I want you, darlin', I want to bury myself in you. I want to be a part of you." He moaned deep in his throat and pulled her tightly against him. His hips rocked of their own volition. The friction of his erection rubbing against her belly sent hot waves of desire coursing over him, nearly sending him over the edge. He shuddered with the effort to hold on. He fought the desire to drive himself so deeply into her he'd touch her soul. He'd promised himself he'd take it slow. He had to remember—she had the right to, and still might, tell him no. "Michael?" He raised his head and gazed into her eyes.

She looked up and wrapped her arms more tightly around him, then buried her face in the curve of his neck. He thought she'd be more comfortable if he wasn't pinning her down so he pulled her over on top of him, pulling her legs on either side. Kissing her, he slowly slid into the warm moist velvet of her sheath.

She was tight. Too tight. He froze. "Sweetheart?"

There was a small amount of pain. Not like before. *Not anything like before*. She gauged, catalogued, the sensations that whispered over her body. "It's all right." And it was. "I want this. I want you." She tightened her grip around his neck. "Please, J.B. Now."

Breathing a sigh of relief he withdrew and quickly used the packet of protection he'd placed on the nightstand. Then with pure joy, in one mighty thrust he buried himself to the hilt. He'd come home at last. "I love you, Michael." He slowly withdrew and returned. Her gasp of pleasure filled him with awe. He began a slow, sweet rhythm, and was thrilled when her body answered. "Oh, my darlin', how I love you." With each thrust he repeated the words. "I love you. I love you. I love you."

Her face buried in the curve of his neck, she wrapped her arms tightly around him and breathed in the essence of J.B. Her hands kneaded and caressed his neck and shoulders as she fought to get closer. Hearing his words, feeling the friction as the pounding, driving rhythm increased, took her breath away.

The pressure built as if the pop-off valve of a steam kettle had been locked down. She feared she would explode. "J.B." She gasped, trying to drag air into starving lungs. Heat, like the flow of molten metal pouring from a caldron, coursed through her body and pooled in that most intimate part of her. Her blood roared through her veins like a river on a rampage. "Oh, please. I want... I need..."

"Yes, darlin', oh yes. Let it happen." He felt her internal spasms begin. "I want to see you, darlin'. I want to see your face." He pulled her head up and stared into her eyes. He watched them widen. The pupils dilated, shutting out all color. Her mouth opened to emit a guttural scream, "Ah-h-h-h-h, Jaaaa Beeee," just before she collapsed, quivering in the aftermath. With one last thrust he shattered, clasped her to him, and floated for long moments, lost in the glory of Michael.

He rolled on to his side, and pulled the sheet over them. A soft moan of pleasure rippled out of her partially open mouth and she sighed. He stroked her back and she was already almost asleep. He lay listening to her breathing slowly drift back to normal as she snuggled her face into the curve of his neck. He didn't think he'd ever again be able to sleep without her face in that exact spot. A while later he drifted to sleep holding her close.

When he awoke, she was planting kisses on his chest. He opened his eyes as bright sunlight filled the room, and looked up into her smiling face. His first thought was that he'd die happy if he could spend the rest of his life waking every morning exactly like this.

"Good morning, J.B." She smiled and kissed his nipple.

"Mmmm, that's a nice way to wake up. But, unless you have somethin' in mind other than gettin' out of this bed, I'd advise you to stop doin' that."

"Stop doing what?" She planted another kiss, and smiled.

"What am I sayin'?" He chuckled. "Have I lost my mind?" He groaned and pulled her tightly against him.

"No, I don't think there's a thing wrong with your mind." She chuckled. "In fact, your mind and especially your body, work just fine." She pretended to pull away as if getting ready to get out of bed.

He grabbed her and pulled her back. "I can't believe I gave you a warnin'. If I had any sense at all I'd keep my big mouth shut and just let you go on doin' what you're doin'."

She chuckled. "I think that could be arranged." She laughed and kissed him on the mouth. *This* time she shyly made love to him and his world was now perfect.

Fifteen

They had to hurry through showers and breakfast in order to get to work on time. Michael arrived at her office with only moments to spare before her first appointment.

Her morning was busier than usual, handling emergencies for a couple of her clients. At noon she ran out to file some papers at the courthouse and to meet J.B. at his office for lunch. When she arrived she waltzed through the door, looked around to see if they were observed and then dropped into his lap, throwing her arms around his neck.

"Hello, darlin'." J.B. put his arms around her and held her tight for a brief hug. But it wasn't enough.

"J.B., are you ready to go to lunch?" she murmured, before planting a kiss on his left ear.

J.B. growled, buried his mouth in the curve of her neck, and nibbled his way to her mouth. What began as a brief kiss of 'hello' soon became a conflagration of want, of need. He shifted in the chair, groaned and pulled back from her lips. He felt bereft. He pulled her head down on his shoulder for a moment while he waited for his heart to slow its rapid beat.

"Sweetheart?" When she raised her head, he put his hands on either side of her face and looked into her eyes. "I love you, Michael, and I want to spend the rest of my life with you. I want to marry you, and have babies with you, and when we are old and gray, I want to sit in side-by-side rockin' chairs and watch our grandbabies grow. I didn't plan on proposin' here at the police station, but since I spend a good part of my time here, I guess it's as good a place as any." He kissed her. "Michael, will you marry me?" His heart was in his throat, waiting for her answer.

She threw her arms around his neck, and then pulled back and began kissing him, planting little smacking kisses all over his face. "Oh, yes," she gasped in between kisses. "I'll marry you. I'll share my life with you. I'll have your babies." She buried her face in the curve of his neck and whispered, "I'll have a real family. I won't ever be alone again."

J.B. swallowed the lump in his throat and kissed her cheek. "You have my promise, Michael. You won't ever again be alone and you'll have a big family. My family." He kissed her on the nose, "They love you already," then he grinned and kissed her mouth," and my mother will put you on a pedestal the day you announce you're goin' to have her first grandbaby."

"Now let's go get something to eat. I'm hungry." He stood and let her legs slide to the floor. "And if we don't get out of here I'm going to lock that door.

"I think we'd better go to lunch." Michael felt euphoric, unable to contain her joy.

At The Whistle Stop J.B. announced to all the patrons that he and his lady were going to get married by the end of the month. The customers burst into applause, and Michael blushed, ducking into a booth.

After finishing his hamburger, J.B. grinned at her and quipped, "Darlin', you have to stop lookin' at me like that or I won't be responsible for the gossip that rages about my unseemly condition as I walk out of here."

She laughed. "J.B., can't you control your raging libido?"

"Not as well as you, darlin'. On me it shows."

Outside the restaurant, he walked her to her car and kissed her longer than he should have, but not nearly as long as he wanted to.

Rushing back into the office, she stopped at Lyndi's desk.

"Boss, everything alright?"

"Oh, yes, Lyndi. J.B. asked me to marry him and I accepted."

Lyndi ran around the desk and grabbed her friend for a hug. "Best wishes, Michael. You deserve some happiness."

"Would you call Elise Anderson, and then Cari Maitland, Lyssa Bradley and Brianna Sheffield? I want them to be in my wedding. As soon as you have Elise on the phone put the call through to me."

"Sure, boss, anything else?"

"Yes. Lyndi, will you be one of my bridesmaids?"

"You need to ask? When is the wedding?"

"J.B. told everyone at the Whistle Stop it would be before the end of the month. That's just a little more than three weeks from now. Can we do it?"

"Of course we can. I'll get started on it right away."

"Thanks, Lyndi. I don't know what I'd do without you." Michael walked into her office to try to catch up on some paperwork, sat down in her chair, and stopped dead still.

For a stunned moment, she stared at the large, square, pink envelope on her desk. How had he delivered it here? She carefully picked it up by the corner, using only her fingernails. She noted it was sealed. "Well, that's different." She grabbed a tissue and held the envelope with it. To open it she slid her letter opener in carefully and slit the mailer. Using the same procedure she'd watched J.B. use on the previous letters, she slid the contents out with the aid of the eraser on her pencil.

As she looked at the folded piece of paper, her heart rate accelerated and she struggled to regulate her breathing. She closed her eyes for a moment as she'd been taught and sought inner peace.

She flipped open the paper.

I LOVE YOU. I NEED YOU!
Be Mine! Marry Me, VALENTINE.

Michael picked up the phone and dialed. "J.B., I received another message." She listened a moment. "No, this time he left it on my desk." She paused before continuing. "No, I don't have a clue how he got it in here." She tapped the opener on the desk as she studied the note. "It's the oddest thing. It's different than the others." She replaced the paper knife in the drawer and rubbed her fingers across her forehead. "This one is a love note. He asked me to marry him and referred to me as his 'valentine'. Oh, and he sealed this one." She stood and pushed back on the chair with her legs. "Okay, see you in a few minutes." She replaced the receiver.

Lyndi stepped through the door with two cups of coffee. "I left messages for Mrs. Anderson and Cari. Lyssa was leaving for an appointment and Brianna was with a client. They'll call back. You need a break. Have a cup of coffee." She settled in one of the chairs in front of Michael's desk. "Rough day?"

"Oh, you could say that." Michael pointed to the evidence of intrusion in front of her. "My 'favorite stalker' left a note on my desk. Did you leave the office at any time today?"

"Yes, when I went to lunch, but I locked the door behind me. I always lock the door, boss."

"I know, but he still got that in here. Did anyone come into my office today when I was away from my desk?"

"Only me." Lyndi thought a minute. "No, wait a second, Winslow was in here to leave the Abernathy file but he was just in and out and he left the door open."

Michael smiled. "I don't think we have to worry about Winslow."

Lyndi's answering smile indicated affection for the young man. "No, neither do I. I can't picture him being the stalker. He seems to be afraid of every shadow."

"Oh, I don't really think he's afraid so much as shy."

"You're probably right. I guess that's what comes from living with such a strong and powerful father."

"I could tell him a thing or two about strong and powerful fathers, Lyndi."

"Maybe you should some time."

"I don't think I'm ready to share some parts of my life."

"I only wish Winslow could have the chance to grow up and make his own decisions. His father makes all of his for him."

"I know."

Lyndi shook her head at remembering an incident. "Do you know he came in here the other day with the most hideous tie on and told me his father insisted he wear it?"

"I can't imagine Clayton selecting a hideous tie."

"Well, actually it wasn't that the tie was so awful, it just looked that way with the suit he wore. When I asked him about it he told me he'd changed suits as soon as his father left the house."

"His way of controlling something in his life."

"Uh huh. I think he deliberately mismatched his attire as a form of rebellion."

Michael nodded. "I've known both of them for several years, you know."

"Did you know he talks constantly about how much he admires you?"

"No, I didn't."

"Apparently his father holds you up as an example of the expertise in law to which he wants Winslow to aspire."

"That's wrong. He shouldn't do that. It's a wonder Winslow doesn't hate me."

"He doesn't. I can hear the admiration in his voice every time he mentions your name."

"Mmm." As the conversation continued, a part of Michael's mind had been on the letter and the method of its arrival. For long moments she was lost in thought and carried on the conversation with only half her mind. "We've been so careful. Keeping our eyes open, trying to catch him." She sighed. "How in the world could this envelope have gotten on my desk?"

Lyndi watched her boss's face for several seconds as a small worry began to nag at the back of her mind. "Michael, are you worried it could be me?"

Michael's startled gaze swept to Lyndi's face. "Certainly not." She stretched her hand toward her friend. "Lyndi, you're my right hand, and my friend. I don't know what I'd do without you. I trust you completely."

"Maybe you shouldn't."

"Why on earth would you say that?"

"Because, if I was in your shoes, I'm not sure I'd trust my own mother."

Michael laughed but there was no joy in the sound. She closed her eyes and shrugged. "I did get pretty paranoid there for a while."

"You say 'for awhile'. What's changed?"

"I did."

"You changed?" She stood, blinking. "How?"

Michael smiled. "I took a martial arts course. And I met J.B. Anderson. Not in that order."

As if saying his name was a cue for his entry on stage, he burst through the door. "Are you all right, darlin'?"

Lyndi took *her* cue and exited her boss's office.

Michael smiled at him, for a brief moment forgetting why he was there. "Oh, yes. The note. This one isn't threatening. In fact, it's kind of sweet."

"Sweet?" J.B. growled. "Have you lost your mind?"

"Not lately. In fact, it's been several hours." She laughed with delight when his face turned beet red. "Gotcha," she whispered, and laughed again, enjoying his discomfiture. "It's nice to see the shoe on someone else's foot."

"Come here, darlin'. For that you owe me, big time." He pulled her into his arms and kissed her deeply, like a starving man invited to a feast.

Michael's common sense returned and she stepped back, placing her hand on his cheek. "We'd better stop now. Lyndi is just outside the door."

J.B. looked uncomfortable. "Doesn't your office door have a lock?" He reached for her again.

"Well, yes, but don't you want to take that to the lab?"

"Hmmm?" He glanced down at her desk. "Oh, yeah. The note." Fighting to regain control of his senses, he bent and looked at it closely. "Well he *is* changing his message a little, but the method is still the same. Cut and paste." He glanced at her. "Did you touch it?"

"No, only the corner with my fingernails. I used a tissue to hold it and slit the envelope, an eraser to get it out, and I unfolded it with the knife to read it."

"Good girl." He carefully slid it into an evidence bag and after grabbing her for a quick kiss, J.B. headed for the door. "I'll see you in a couple of hours. What say we run to Oklahoma City to get a steak for dinner?"

"I think I'd like that but could we go home and change first?"

"You look gorgeous just the way you are."

"You're prejudiced."

He grinned and clicked his tongue. "You bet I am."

"J.B., I'd like to shower and change. This will be our first *real* date."

"My love, it may be the first *real* date for you, but I've been dating you every time we had dinner together." He grinned and winked. "And I've enjoyed every minute of the times I've had you in my arms. Especially last night." Now it was his turn to laugh as she turned beet red. "See you later."

The afternoon seemed interminable but finally the time passed. After racing to the house to shower and change, and for Michael to apply fresh makeup, they decided on prime rib instead of steak. Stopping at a restaurant in Oklahoma City famous for their prime rib they had to stand in line. While waiting on a table they became so engrossed in each other the arrival of the *maitre d'* startled them.

They skipped the ale and ordered a glass of wine with their dinner. Lingering over dessert and coffee, they decided to take in a movie. Neither one of them could have related the plot. They never actually saw it. They couldn't take their eyes off each other as they held hands and whispered through the film.

They enjoyed a long, leisurely drive home to Michael's house, after stopping off at J.B.'s condo so he could pick up some fresh clothes and his razor.

Back at Michael's house, filled with anticipation, they began stripping their clothes off the minute they walked in the door. J.B., down to his jeans and briefs, picked up Michael and planted kisses along her jaw, on her neck and mouth. He carried her into the bedroom, flipping the light switch with his elbow. He lifted his mouth from hers, glanced toward the bed...and stopped in his tracks.

He spoke softly, "Darlin', we have a problem. Don't panic. Do exactly what I tell you."

She looked over her shoulder and gasped as she saw what was left of her bed. There was very little of the mattress still intact. It had, quite literally, been slashed to ribbons and the inner springs jutted out.

J.B. gently put her feet on the floor and led her to the wall. He checked out the closet, the bathroom and the sitting room. "Stay in here and lock the door. I'll call out as soon as I get back so you'll know it's me."

In a breathless whisper, she asked, "Where are you going?"

"I have to check out the rest of this house. He may still be here." He whispered, "Lock it, darlin'," and pulled the door closed. He waited until he heard the click of the lock engaging before he walked away from the door.

Michael ran to the telephone and dialed Shag. As soon as he answered she began to babble. "Shag, it's Michael Mainwaring and J.B. may need your help and we came home and found my mattress cut to pieces and somebody really worked it over with a knife and J.B.'s out there looking to see if anyone is still in the house and I'm scared..." She paused to breath. "What?"

"Slow down, Michael. Take a couple of deep breaths."

She blinked. "Oh. All right." She shivered and took several deep breaths. "I said—somebody cut my mattress to ribbons."

"Where is J.B.?"

"He's checking out the rest of the house. I'm so scared. He thinks the man may still be here. What if he gets hurt?"

"Are you safe?"

She nodded her head then realized he couldn't see. "I'm in the bedroom with the door locked."

"J.B. has already checked out the bedroom?"

She snapped, "Yes, of course he checked in here before he left me alone." She paced in a tight little circle. "Are you coming over here or not?" At that moment she heard J.B. at the door. "Hold on, Shag. J.B. is at the door."

"Are you sure it's him?"

"Well, of course I know it's J.B. He said it was." She started the lay the phone down.

"Don't open the door until you know for sure it's J.B."

"Shag, for heaven's sake. I can recognize J.B.'s voice. No one could fool me but his father." She listened a moment and sighed. "Okay, I'll ask him." She went to the door. "J.B., Shag said to ask you how you got the scar on your butt, and if you don't come up with the right answer I can't let you in."

"Tell that jackass the scar on my butt is *his* fault," J.B. roared.

Michael went back to the phone and picked it up, only to hear Shag laughing.

Between chortles, he told her, "Yeah, that's J.B. You'd better let him in before he kicks in the door."

When she let J.B. in he marched over and picked up the phone. "Did she call you to get help, or to hear war stories?"

Michael heard Shag's laughter from across the room.

J.B. slammed down the phone. "Darlin', I think it'd be a good idea to go to my place. That sonofabitch has a key. There's no sign of forced entry and slashin' your bed is a very vivid message."

Michael dressed, threw some clothes into a tote and was ready to go within moments."I hate it that he's driving me out of my own home. We've got to catch him, J.B. I want to catch him."

"Yeah, darlin'. So do I."

Sixteen

At J.B.'s condo he ushered Michael inside and set down her luggage. "Would you like somethin' to drink, darlin'?"

"Chamomile tea?"

He laughed, relieved she could still make jokes. "Nah. I think we've both decided we can live without chamomile tea."

"What did you have in mind?"

"There's red or white wine, coffee, tea and milk." Seeing her raised eyebrow he said, "Not warm milk. You do drink milk, don't you?"

"Occasionally. I even use it on my cereal—when I eat cereal. Right now, all I want is to go to bed."

J.B. grinned. "That sounds like a plan."

"Oh? And what plan is that?"

"You. In my bed."

"Oh, really? Did you..."

"Oh, darlin', for months I've dreamt of you in my bed, and makin' love to you all night and sleepin' with you in my arms."

She cocked an eyebrow and her lips turned up gently at the corners in a 'come hither' smile. "The night is half over, J.B. Are you going to waste any more of it talking?"

Thrilled that she had not allowed the latest incident to unsettle her, he whooped and picked her up to spin her around in a circle. "Sweetheart, I don't plan on wastin' another second." He marched toward the bedroom, pausing only long enough to switch out the light in the foyer.

"You're lucky you know this place so well. Why didn't you turn on the bedroom light before throwing us in to total darkness?"

He flipped the switch inside the bedroom door. "Better?"

"Umm hmm. Much. Now I can see you."

Eyes widening at the thought she wanted to see him, he hurried to the bed and let her legs slide down. His heart rate accelerated when she reached up and shoved his jacket off his shoulders. Fascinated by watching her unbutton his shirt, he let the jacket lay where it dropped. His breath whistled into his constricted lungs as the shirt followed the jacket to the floor.

His hands shaking, he reached behind her for her zipper. "Turn about is fair play," he rasped. Her dress slithered over her hips and pooled around her ankles. He pushed down on her half-slip, piling it on top of the dress puddled at her feet. Standing in front of him clad in a fire engine red teddy, she never looked more beautiful. "Oh, God," he groaned. "You take my breath."

His voice sent delicious vibrations of pleasure over her skin. "J.B." Michael looked up into his face as she ran her hands around his waist and over his back. She gloried in the desire she saw darkening his eyes to navy blue. His breath came fast, and as she leaned forward and kissed his throat, a moan vibrated against her lips.

J.B. groaned. "Michael. Mmmm." He inhaled sharply as she ran her tongue over the pulse point at his neck. "Ahhhh. You're killin' me. Come here, darlin'." He lifted her to the bed, sat down, kicked off his boots and shed his jeans and underwear more quickly than ever before in his life.

He rolled, taking her with him, wrapping himself around her as he took her mouth in an invasion as slow and sweet as molasses. He peeled the teddy off—inch by measured inch, nibbling his way down her body—and back again, glorying in the sensual pleasure of the scent of strawberries. He cupped her breast, caressed her nipple with his thumb and watched it bead, before his gaze locked with hers. J.B. watched her pupils dilate and listened to her moan his name and it filled him with so much joy he didn't know how he would contain it. The feel of her satiny skin drove him to explore and he wanted inside her. But he also wanted to prolong every moment, to savor it in the full appreciation of at last being this close to Michael. He took her nipple into his mouth and laved it with his tongue, delighting in her gasp of pleasure and the tightening of her arms around him.

His movements unhurried, holding on as long as possible, he made slow, sweet love to her. At last, tremors rocked her body. He held on, taking her over the top again and again, losing himself in the splendor of watching her eyes each time she came apart in his arms. At last, unable to hold on longer, he joined her as her internal convulsions sent him over the edge with her. She turned her face in to his neck, holding on as if she feared falling off the face of the earth.

Michael saw a starburst of fireworks on her closed eyelids as ripples of pleasure shook her. J.B. took her up and up, over and over again before joining her on the edge of the world.

Later, in his arms, she luxuriated in the euphoria transcending her soul. This closeness with him, becoming one with him was the most profound joy she'd ever known and like nothing before in her life. She pushed aside the fear that this wouldn't last.

Even had she wanted to, she couldn't change anything that happened only a minute ago. She had little control over what would happen five minutes from now. She could plan, and dream, but life would happen in spite of her plans and her dreams. So, she would enjoy what she had in this moment. She would worry about a future without J.B. if it happened. But for now she would cherish this time with him, store the moments in her memory so she could wrap them around her heart if she ended up alone.

She was convinced that J.B. really believed he loved her. Most of the time she believed it. But fear that she wanted and needed his love too much had colored her perception of what was real. She drifted to sleep, wallowing in a deep and abiding contentment, committing the feel of his arms around her to memory. She would remember the feel, the smell and the taste of J.B. all the days of her life.

The intrusive jangle of the telephone awoke J.B. before seven. He snatched up the receiver, hoping to catch it before it woke Michael. "Anderson."

Shag's laughter assaulted his ear. "Hey, buddy, I never heard anyone snarl in a whisper before."

"Whatcha want, Shag? And it'd better be good."

"Quit growling. I think you'll like this. We have a match on those prints from the love note to your lady."

"Oh, really?" He sat up on the side of the bed and hunched over, leaning his elbows on his knees. "Talk to me."

Michael awoke at the first sound of the telephone, fear pounding through her veins for an instant before she realized she was safe here. Safe in J.B.'s condo. The memory of last night vaulted in to her mind and she smiled. And safe in J.B.'s bed. She stretched and turned over, planning to doze again for a few minutes until J.B. got off the phone. Just on the edge of slumber J.B.'s words brought her upright, the sheet and blanket clutched to her chest.

J.B. listened to the long list of evidence and snapped, "Get a warrant for his arrest and I'll meet you at Michael's office. We're going to put that sonofabitch away for a long time and I don't care *who* his daddy is."

Michael gasped. "J.B., who...?"

J.B. turned and looked at her over his shoulder. "It's your little buddy, Winslow Rauthuell."

"No!" She backed away from him, shaking her head.

"Darlin', his fingerprints were on the love note."

"It doesn't make sense, J.B. His fingerprints weren't on anything else."

"So he got careless this time."

"J.B., I don't believe it. There has to be an explanation. Something we've overlooked."

"Get dressed, darlin', we're goin' to go pick him up."

Michael got out of bed and headed for the bathroom to shower. She was so stunned by what J.B. had told her she felt numb all over and forgot to wrap a towel around her hair. Since it was wet anyway she decided she might as well shampoo. By the time she got it shampooed, dried and put up, and her make-up applied, she'd spent over an hour in the bathroom. J.B.'s knocking on the door every few minutes, calling for her to 'hurry up' had driven her crazy. When she came out of the bathroom he stood leaning in the doorway, his Stetson in his hand and a disgruntled look on his face.

"Michael, stallin' isn't goin' to make things easier. Do you want Shag to arrest that little worm before we get there?"

"He wouldn't dare, J.B. If he does he'll answer to me."

"Why?" He shook his head, clearly perplexed. "I would have thought you'd be happy to get him stopped."

"J.B., you *know* what this maniac has done to my life. Of course I want him to be stopped. I want him put behind bars so I can live a normal life, and you know how frightened I've..."

"All right then, why are you battlin' me on this? We have him dead to rights."

"But I think you're wrong. I know Winslow. He's shy, he's under his father's thumb, but he's really a very nice young man."

"Yeah, and I'll bet all those young women thought Ted Bundy was a nice man, too."

She gasped. "J.B., for heaven's sake. Winslow Rauthuell is *not* Ted Bundy."

"Nope. He's not, because we caught him before he could go that far. But the shredding of your mattress proves to me that he was headed in that direction."

"I will not believe Winslow is the one who has been stalking me, J.B." Michael picked up her briefcase and her purse and headed for the door. "Not until I hear it from his own mouth. Let's go. We can get coffee at the office."

J.B. held the door for Michael and loped around the car. He pulled out into the street and called Shag, telling him they'd be arriving at Michael's office later than originally planned.

Michael's stomach was tied in knots, worrying about the situation, fretting about the disagreement with J.B. and concerned about how she would tell Clayton.

One minute, having listened to J.B.'s arguments, she accepted what he told her and the next minute she again firmly believed him wrong. They arrived at the office, neither of them having said a word on the trip. Michael exited the car without waiting for J.B. and headed inside the building.

J.B. hurried behind her wanting to get into her office ahead of her, still anxious about keeping her safe because experience told him cornered rats fight the hardest. "Michael, wait." Though softly spoken, it was still a command. "Let me go in first. I don't want you confrontin' that sonofabitch."

"I've been working with Winslow for over a year, and I don't believe he'd hurt me." She marched to her office door and seized the knob.

J.B. grabbed her wrist and removed her hand. He looked into her eyes. "We'll wait for Shag."

As if conjured by magic, Shag strolled down the hall. "Ready to go, partner?" He took off his Stetson and nodded at Michael. "You doing all right?"

"No, I'm not," Michael breathed. "I'm having a hard time believing it could possibly be Winslow."

J.B. growled, "Let's see what he has to say for himself."

J.B. walked through the door first, followed by Michael, as Shag brought up the rear.

Lyndi looked up from her desk and smiled... until she got a look at Michael's face. "Boss?"

Michael looked at Winslow who sat behind his desk. He looked up at her, pushed his glasses up his nose and smiled, then turned beet red.

J.B. stepped over to Winslow's desk and leaned forward, his fists planted squarely in the middle of the papers spread out there. Shag moved behind the young man who began to look more and more nervous.

"Rauthuell, you have the right to remain silent, you have the right to an attorney. If you cannot afford one, an attorney will be provided for you. If you give up these rights, anything you say, can, and will, be used against you in a court of law. Do you understand these rights as I have explained them to you?"

Winslow sat there with his mouth hanging open and his breath increasing rapidly. His gaze darted from J.B. to Michael and back again. "Uh... Uh... Michael... er... what's...?"

Lyndi stood up. "Boss, what's going on?"

She started toward them and J.B. held up his hand. "Stay there, Lyndi."

Michael stepped forward. "J.B., you're wrong. Winslow would never hurt me."

Lyndi looked shocked. "Hurt you?"

Michael looked at her law clerk, her anguish clear on her face. "You would never hurt me would you, Winslow?"

Winslow's gaze darted everywhere except to the people surrounding him. "Uhmm, no ma'am." He gulped. "I... uh... please." He started to step toward Michael, his hands outstretched. Shag grabbed him and pushed him onto the chair.

Winslow's eyes displayed his terror and he attempted to jerk away from the hands holding him.

Michael walked toward J.B., halting when he glared at her, and snarled, "Stop right there."

"But, J.B., I..."

"Stay out of his reach, darlin', we haven't cuffed him yet."

"Please, J.B., I really believe you've got the wrong man. You're embarrassing Winslow for no reason."

"Sweetheart, we've got him dead to rights. His fingerprints were on the letter he left on your desk yesterday."

"Yes, I understand that, but don't you think it's odd? They were on only that one note. If Winslow were guilty it's very strange this is the first piece of evidence on which he's left his fingerprints."

"Yeah, that bothered me too, but as I told Shag, we knew he'd screw up sometime. Nobody's perfect."

"So, you found his fingerprints on this one letter. What does that prove? He could have touched it when he put a file on my desk."

"Michael, give us a little credit. His fingerprints were on the paper which was inside the *sealed* envelope."

"Oh."

"Yes, 'oh'."

Michael raised an eyebrow. "And speaking of fingerprints—how were you able to compare those on the envelope with his? Does he have a record I don't know about?"

"Michael, you're still not givin' me credit for knowin' how to do my job. Of course our Winslow here has a little bit of a record." At Michael's gasp, he filled in the details. "He's been picked up more than once for D and D. His fingerprints were on file."

Shag filled in, "His fingerprints on the envelope and letter got us a search warrant. Guess what we found at his daddy's house?" He didn't wait for an answer. "We found the scraps of the valentines he cut up to put the letter together."

"That still only proves he sent the one letter." Michael looked at Winslow sitting cowering in the chair, his face in his hands.

J.B.'s temper now on the rise, he exploded, "Dammit, stop thinkin' like you're his lawyer, Michael. For cryin' out loud, the man was stalkin' you. How can you defend him?"

"J.B., any good attorney will ask you these questions. If you don't have the right answers, your case is blown before it ever reaches court, so let's just say I'm playing devil's advocate. Now is that all the evidence you have on him?"

"No. We found florist's bills in his room."

Even though she didn't want to believe Winslow guilty, Michael trusted J.B. too much not to take what he said seriously. "You found florist's bills?"

"Yes," J.B. growled. "Three of them."

"For roses?"

J.B. looked a little chagrinned at that question, rubbing the back of his neck as his face turned ruddy. "Well, no, that's the only thing we haven't been able to tie him to." He looked up, a determined expression on his face. "But we will. More than likely, he used a different florist for the roses. We haven't found them yet. It's just a matter of time and a little more digging. He covered his tracks pretty well on that." A puzzled expression crossed his face. "I'm still tryin' to figure out why all the other flowers were fresh and the roses were always dead."

Michael looked J.B. directly in the eye. "If he didn't buy roses..." seeing his expression, she amended, "...if you didn't find evidence that he bought roses, what flowers did he buy?"

Seventeen

"The bills we found were for mixed bouquets. Well, except for one time. That time he ordered a bouquet of lilacs."

"I received mixed bouquets here at the office, but I don't recall ever receiving lilacs."

Winslow, holding his hands prayerfully, blurted, "The lilacs were for my grandmother. I swear. It was for her birthday."

"Quiet, Rauthuell." J.B. looked back Michael. "We found the florist in Oklahoma City where he was buyin' the flowers."

Michael still hoped they were wrong. "Isn't it possible that the roses were sent by someone else?"

Shag, standing behind Winslow, shook his head. "No. This boy doesn't throw anything away. I never saw so many scraps of paper in my life. He has a receipt for everything he's ever bought—including a pack of gum he purchased two years ago. When we sift through all that, we'll find the receipts."

Winslow whimpered, "I have to show Daddy the receipts for where I spent my allowance." He became more upset at the memory. "He was angry when I bought the gum." He glared at them. "Said it was bad for my teeth." He looked and sounded disgruntled. "It was sugar free gum."

Shaking his head, Shag murmured, "Dear God in heaven."

Michael, still trying to understand, looked at J.B. "But, just because he's meticulous about keeping records of his expenditures, doesn't mean he's the stalker."

From the expression on his face, J.B.'s patience was whisper thin. "Why are you defendin' him, Michael? This man has been stalkin' you and makin' your life miserable for months."

"J.B. I've worked with Winslow for over a year and I just cannot see him doing the things of which he's been accused."

"Okay, you want more facts? You remember being paged to call a number that turned out to be a pay phone?" When she nodded her head he continued. "He has your pager number because he works in your office."

"Of course, but that doesn't prove he made that call."

"We have proof. We have a witness who saw a man fitting Winslow's description at that pay phone that night."

Michael turned to Winslow and, her voice gentle, asked, "Winslow, did you call me from a pay phone?"

At this question Winslow dissolved in tears. "M-M-Michael... uh... Ms. Mainwaring, I love you. I called one time. Only one. I just wanted to hear your voice."

"J.B., he only called one time."

"Did you expect him to confess?" J.B. growled.

Shag spoke up, "We've got a court order to run a DNA test on the saliva on the envelope. That should wrap it up real pretty for the D. A."

J.B. looked at Michael speculatively for a moment. "If you were the District Attorney, darlin', how would you look at the evidence?" He was beginning to think she would take the case and defend her own stalker.

"If I was Kopecky, I'd probably jump in the air, click my heels, and start singing, *Follow the Yellow Brick Road.* He'll leap at the chance to prosecute the son of Clayton W. Rauthuell, III. They hate each other."

"Michael, we have the valentine, the florist receipts, he admits calling you and we have the eye witness who saw him making a phone call from the booth. We can get DNA evidence linking him to the envelope." He paused, trying to decide how much more she could take. Sighing, he went on. "In addition, there's something you haven't thought about. He had access to your house keys because your purse is in the office every time you are. He could have lifted the keys, had a copy made and returned them to your purse without you ever being the wiser."

"That's guess work, J.B. You have nothing to indicate that's what he did."

He sighed, hating to give her the final damning piece of evidence. "Yeah, we do. One of the receipts we found was from a lock smith who made a copy of a house key for him."

She gasped and turned her gaze to Winslow, shock evident on her face.

"For heaven's sake, Michael, how much more proof do you need?" J.B. snapped.

Astonished by all the evidence, Michael turned to the, now blubbering, young man. "Winslow? I trusted you. Did you do what they say you did?"

"I didn't," he blubbered. "I mean, I did, but, n-n-not dead flowers. I only s-s-sent you two bouquets."

"J.B., I told you, I received two bouquets of mixed flowers here. If you remember, I thought they were from you."

Winslow sobbed, "Please ma'am, don't tell my father about this trouble."

Michael was obviously overwhelmed with the knowledge that someone she trusted had been her stalker. She shuddered and wrapped her arms around her waist, turning away from Winslow.

J.B. ignored the blubbering young man. "Darlin', the evidence is overwhelmin' enough that District Attorney Kopecky is itchin' to get his hands on this case. He said it would be a slam dunk."

"Yes, well I told you about the animosity between Clayton and Kopecky."

Shag took Winslow's arm. "Let's take him in, pardner, and we can sort all this out at the cop shop." J.B. and Shag led a now handcuffed and crying Winslow out of the office, leaving a shaken Michael and sobbing Lyndi behind.

"Lyndi, are you all right?"

"No, I'm not. I can't believe the man we've been working with all this time is the same one who has been stalking you. It makes no sense whatsoever."

Michael sighed. "I know exactly how you feel. I've been struggling with this ever since Shag called J.B. this morning and woke us up." A blush suffused her face as she realized what she'd just revealed to Lyndi. "Uh, that is..."

"Michael, J.B. has loved you for a long time. And I've watched your love for him grow day by day."

"Well, I'm not sure he loves me or just has a strong need to protect me."

"Oh, he's in love with you all right."

Michael looked at Lyndi and wanted desperately to believe what she heard, but she'd have to think about that later. Something more important had to be faced immediately. "I've got to make a phone call."

Michael walked to her desk and sat down, staring at the telephone. She reached for it and then withdrew her hand.

Standing in the doorway, Lyndi asked, "What's the matter boss?"

"I've got to call Clayton and I'm dreading it more than I would a root canal without anesthetic."

"Oh, God. I didn't think about the position this puts you in. Clayton has been your mentor."

"Lyndi, he was the father I always wished I'd had. He was wonderful to me when I worked in his office as a paralegal while I waited to take the bar exam. He helped me study for it by giving me tips on *what* to study. He pushed me relentlessly and when I was ready to throw something at him, he told me he expected me to ace the exam. He said I was capable of that and he hated to see talent wasted."

"I'm glad it's you making this call instead of me." Lyndi turned around and went back to her desk.

Michael picked up the phone and dialed the familiar number, his private line. "Clayton, I know your schedule is busy but is there any way you can come to my office in Willow Glen?" She listened a moment. "This is important enough for you to break any appointments you have." She listened another moment. "Thank you, Clayton. Please get here as quickly as possible."

She turned to the intercom and buzzed Lyndi. "Lyndi, do you have any antacid tablets?"

Thirty-five minutes later Clayton Rauthuell came through her outer office door as Michael was getting another cup of coffee she knew she shouldn't be drinking, considering the condition of her stomach.

"Okay, Michael, what's so important that I needed to drop everything and come down here?"

"Hello, Clayton. Can I get you a cup of coffee?"

"No, thanks. Just tell me what's so all fired important. Is there a problem with Winslow?" He rocked forward on the balls of his feet, as concern and the need to protect his only child were clearly displayed on his face.

"Come in, and I'll explain." She walked into her office and held the door until Clayton entered. She shut the door and indicated the chair in front of her desk. "Have a seat."

Michael wished Winslow could see his father's face right now. She knew, from observing the pair over the past few years, Clayton was not very good at letting his son know how much he loved him.

"Winslow is in trouble, Clayton, and right now he needs you more than he ever has in his life."

Clayton stiffened and sat up straighter in the chair. "What's the problem?"

"He's been arrested on the orders of..."

He leaped to his feet and shouted, "Arrested? What do you mean he's been arrested?"

"If you'll sit down, I'll explain."

As Clayton sat stiffly in the chair, Michael got up and walked around to stand in front of Clayton. Leaning her hips against the desk she began to explain about the man who had been stalking her. Clayton listened with rapt attention.

When Michael got to the part of the story relating Winslow's arrest, he again leaped to his feet. "Are you out of your mind?" He stormed over to the window and looked out, then turned around and glared at her. "You *know* Winslow would never do anything like this."

"I know that, Clayton. That's why I called you."

"If you know he couldn't have done this, then why did you swear out a complaint against him?"

She sighed. "I didn't."

He looked startled. "Then who did?"

"Kopecky."

"That sonofabitch. I'll kill him."

She shook her head and grabbed his arm as he was turning to charge out the door. "No, you won't! You'll calm down and use your head so you can help your son."

Clayton slumped into the chair he had occupied previously. "Where is he?"

"They have him at the police station here in Willow Glen. Go over there and see him. And if you don't feel comfortable representing him, then call in one of your markers. He's going to need a good attorney."

"Thanks, Michael. I don't guess Winslow was going to call me, was he?"

"No. How did you know?"

"Because *you* are the one who called me and told me about it. Not Winslow."

"Clayton, you might consider getting him some professional help, and I don't mean just an attorney."

Two hours later Michael sat slumped at her desk. This day had seemed endless. She thought dealing with Clayton Rauthuell's anger and dismay over the arrest of his son, couldn't have been any more difficult than going over Niagara Falls in a barrel. In fact, if she had a choice in the matter, next time she'd choose the barrel and Niagara Falls. He'd really gone over the edge when she'd suggested Winslow could use professional help, and barely hung on to his temper long enough to leave her office.

She didn't know what to believe. The Winslow with whom she'd worked didn't seem the type to fit the profile of a stalker. But, with all that evidence, how could she explain it away?

Perhaps Clayton would agree to a psychiatric evaluation if he thought it would help Winslow. She thought he would do anything he could to help his son.

She put her arms on her desk and her head down, wishing she could hide for the next few weeks. A knock at her office door jerked her upright and tears filled her eyes at the first thought entering her mind. Then she smiled. "It can't be J.B.," she muttered. "He never knocks."

She wiped her eyes, smoothed her hair, stood up and called, "Come in."

The door swung open and Cari Maitland came striding through, slim and trim again after the birth of the twins. "I wanted to come by and offer you my best wishes in person, and since I was in town today, I thought I'd take a chance catching you. Lyndi isn't at her desk and..." She stopped abruptly, looking intently at Michael's face. "What's the matter?" She hurried over and stretched up putting her arms around Michael.

Michael hugged her friend and then indicated the chair in front of her desk. "Sit down. It's a long story."

Nearly an hour later Michael shrugged. "And that's it in a rather large nutshell. Clayton is angry with me, but what's worse, J.B. is *really* angry with me for what he feels was my 'taking Winslow's side' in this matter. I think he's changed his mind about wanting to marry me."

"Changed his mind?" At Michael's sad little nod, Cari leaned forward in the chair, "J. B? Not likely."

"Oh, Cari, everything is such a mess. I wanted you to be my matron of honor, but I probably won't need one now."

"Of course you will. That man loves you. He's not going to allow a little thing like today's disagreement get in the way of that. Now, have you heard from Lyssa, or Brianna?"

Michael nodded her head. "I wanted them to be bridesmaids and they said they would." Tears filled her eyes. "Even if I was getting married, my mother wouldn't be there. Now there's not going to be a wedding."

"Well, of course there's going to be a wedding." Cari was totally perplexed. "Michael, why do you think there won't be a wedding?"

Michael put her head down, bursting into tears.

"Michael, what on earth..."

"I have a matron of honor, and three bridesmaids but I don't have a groom."

"Sure you do, darlin'." The deep voice was unmistakably J.B. His long strides carried him across the room in record time. He scooped up Michael out of the chair and settled into it with her in his lap. She threw her arms around his neck, buried her face in the curve of his shoulder, in her 'favorite spot', and wept. J.B. removed his Stetson and dropped it on the desk, soothing Michael with little kisses on her cheek, her ear, and the corner of her eye, while massaging her back with his big hands. "It's all right, darlin'. I'm not angry with you." He lifted her face and kissed her. "Truly. Your kindness and compassion are only a couple of the reasons why I love you."

Michael had completely forgotten her visitor and put her chin back on his shoulder, hugging him as hard as she could. "Oh, J.B."

After a few minutes J.B. looked up at the lovely blonde who stood in front of the desk with one eyebrow raised. He smiled. "Hello, Cari."

"Hello, J.B."

Michael struggled to get off J.B.'s lap. "Oh good grief. Cari, I'm sorry."

"Sit still, darlin', you're fine where you are." He pulled a pristine white handkerchief from his pocket and handed it to Michael. "Here, blow your nose."

Cari chuckled softly. "I don't suppose you need me hanging around to help, do you?" Her brown eyes twinkled and she chuckled again.

J.B. never glanced her way. His gaze, his attention, were focused on Michael. "Nope. Under control. But thanks. Tell Linc howdy for me, and shut the door on your way out, please."

Cari grinned, "You got it," and walked out of the office. The pair behind the desk didn't notice her departure.

Eighnteen

Three weeks after Winslow's arrest, Michael walked into Le Chanterelle Restaurant. Tomorrow she would marry J.B. and this afternoon her friends were throwing her a "Bachelorette Party". She couldn't believe how quickly the time had passed. Her mind was in a fog, worrying about her wedding tomorrow and trying *not* to think about Winslow's preliminary hearing next month. She shook her head and tried to remember the reason she was here.

The *maitre d'* led her toward the table and as soon as Elise spotted her, she jumped up and grabbed her in a hug. Michael couldn't prevent the pooling of moisture in her eyes as the others at the table got in line to do the same.

When they were again seated at the table, Cari picked up her glass. "Forgive me for toasting you with iced tea, Michael, but since I'm nursing the boys, I can't drink alcoholic beverages. In any case, the sentiment is the same. We are all so very happy for you, and want to wish you all the happiness you deserve." She raised her glass. "To a wonderful, bright, love-filled future with J.B."

They all lifted their glasses, making her feel "weepy" all over again.

Michael covered her face with her napkin, totally embarrassed at making a public spectacle of herself. She blotted her eyes, then looked around the table at her friends, thinking the group was complete until the *maitre d'* led a late arrival to the table.

Elise laughed and, clapping her hands, stood and grabbed the young woman, hugging her, then turning her around she said, "Keely, this is Michael. Michael, you finally get to meet your new sister. This is Keely."

"Oh, how wonderful to meet you at last." Michael grabbed Keely's hands and looked almost directly into her eyes, "This is great. *You* are tall, too."

"Uh huh. Five eleven," Keely quipped. "With five older brothers, I had to grow tall enough to defend myself."

Michael laughed. "We weren't expecting you this soon. J.B. said you couldn't get here until tomorrow."

"Some of my friends owed me so I pulled in some markers to get here earlier than first planned." Keely pulled her mother into their circle before hugging Michael and murmuring, "Welcome to the family, Michael. I've wanted a sister all my life and now I have one." She gave Michael a cheeky grin and whispered loudly, "You *will* be on my side when I battle my big brothers, won't you?"

Michael's laughter gurgled. "Absolutely."

Keely hugged Michael again and said, "Thank you for loving my brother and for taking on the entire Anderson clan as your family." Keely's dark hair swayed as she stepped back. She looked over Michael's shoulder at Elise, "Does the big lug know how lucky he is?"

"He knows." Elise laughed. "Wait until you try to talk with him, Keely. He's floating on cloud nine about half the time and you'll have to use a two by four to get his attention before he even knows you're in the house."

Michael ducked her head and flushed with embarrassment. "Thank you, Keely, but I'm the lucky one. I cannot express how wonderful it is to have brothers and a sister after spending a lifetime wishing for family." She turned to Elise, her eyes twinkling, "And he's not *that* bad, Elise. You stop badmouthing the most wonderful man in the world." The group at the table erupted in laughter.

Michael looked at her friends and thought about each of them and how they'd enriched her life.

Cari Maitland had become dear to her last year when she'd met and fallen in love with Michael's best friend, Lincoln. Cari helped Linc rescue his beloved niece, Aimee Bradley, and she stood by his side throughout the murder trial, never doubting his innocence. Cari and Linc had been married right after he was freed, and now they had adorable twin boys.

Lincoln's twin, Lyssa Bradley sat quietly fiddling with her flatware. She had no idea how lovely she looked sitting there. Her hair, as black as midnight, had a blue cast under the overhead light. She looked as if just being here was a struggle. Michael was so proud of Lyssa for making the effort. Petite and fragile looking, her large dark brown eyes were still filled with pain. Michael wondered if she would ever get over the heartache of having caused her husband's death. At the time, she'd only been protecting her daughter, three year old Aimee, but Blake's death had resulted in a murder trial for Lyssa's adored "big" brother.

Brianna Sheffield, Cari's supervisor at Child Welfare, had first been a friend of Cari's. She had become Michael's friend during Linc's trial. Bree's dark brown hair glowed in the light and she attracted glances from all the males in the room. She never noticed. Her beautiful sky blue eyes sparkled as she carried on a conversation with Elise.

Lyndi Hilliard, her charcoal gray eyes twinkling as she laughed, flipped her ash blonde hair over her shoulder. She'd been Michael's right hand since her first day practicing law. She knew she couldn't run her office without Lyndi, and Lyndi's friendship had helped Michael through some very rough times.

Her gaze fell on Elise. Just looking at her filled Michael with warmth and a feeling of having come home. J.B.'s entire family had enfolded her into their loving arms, and she'd reveled in the warmth surrounding her. But Elise had taken on all of the responsibilities of 'mother of the bride', stepping in and helping Michael plan the wedding, while not neglecting her responsibilities as mother of the groom. She enthusiastically agreed with all of Michael's choices and threw herself into making sure there would be nothing to mar the wedding day for her 'new daughter'. She had been delighted with Michael's suggestion for a color theme, saying it would be "absolutely perfect".

Elise had eagerly gone with Michael on one nightmare shopping trip after another, looking for the perfect wedding gown. And they'd found it. When Michael put it on, she felt beautiful for the first time in her life. As she looked in the mirror at the bridal boutique, she realized she was so happy with her life at the moment, that the thought of losing what she now had scared her to death. Michael couldn't have gotten through all the wedding plans without Elise's help.

As the conversation buzzed around the table she sat and listened to her friends and marveled at her good fortune. When Elise leaned over and whispered in her ear Michael jumped guiltily. "I'm sorry, what did you say?"

"Hmmm, thinking about J.B. again, I see." Elise smiled and patted Michael's hand. "I asked if you like the house?"

"Oh, Elise, have you seen it?" She didn't wait for a response. "It's beautiful. Champ and his crew did a wonderful job of restoring it to its original splendor. It's exactly the way I've always wanted to see it."

Keely leaned forward and joined their conversation. "Aren't you going to live in J.B.'s condo?"

"No. We've only been staying there until Champ got the house finished." She grinned. "I haven't been allowed in my own home until this morning."

"Haven't been allowed? By whom?" Keely sounded outraged.

Elise laughed. "Under strict orders from Champ. She's wanted to sneak over and take a peek to see what he was doing, but J.B. kept her away, keeping an eagle eye on her." She winked. "And I've helped by keeping her so busy she hasn't had time to breathe."

Cari laughed and joined the conversation. "*I'd* have figured out a way to get over there but Michael is not devious enough."

Michael leaned toward her friend, "Cari, you should see it. I couldn't take it all in, it's like it was when it was first built in 1920." She recalled her visit that morning, her gaze flying from one detail to another as she walked through the lower floor of her home. It didn't resemble, in any way, the run-down house with which she'd fallen in love on first sight. It now glowed with the warmth and beauty it was meant to display.

"The plan is to move into it after we get back from our honeymoon, but I'm so excited about the restoration that I'm thinking of saving J.B. some money and canceling the trip."

They all laughed and Keely asked, "What about J.B.'s condo?"

"He plans to sell it, in fact it goes on the market today." She smiled joyously. "We want to raise a family and the house has enough room for children."

Elise, her face glowing, leaned over and whispered, "Is that an announcement?"

"Oh, no." Michael's face turned beet red. "Uh, I'm not... no... not yet."

"How did you talk Champ into fixing up the house, Michael?" Keely asked.

"At one of the family gatherings Champ asked what I saw when I pictured the house finished the way I wanted it. We spent an entire weekend discussing it, and I was blissfully unaware of what he had in mind at the time. I assumed he was interested because he's a builder and had a love for old houses."

"Then he announced that his wedding gift would be to completely remodel and restore the house and get it ready for us to move into before the wedding. The boys even got together and moved the furniture back in. Champ said he wanted it to be perfect."

Brianna leaned forward and asked, "And is it perfect?"

Michael's excitement was evident in her voice. "Oh, yes. He put an extra crew on the job and they accomplished a miracle. I'll plan a party so all of you can come and see the house."

It had been a rough three weeks. And not something she wanted to live through ever again in her life, but she thanked God she'd had J.B. and his family. She couldn't have made it through, and stayed sane, without them.

Cari laughed. "Well, my friend, you have the rehearsal and the dinner tonight and then tomorrow you will become Mrs. Anderson. Is there anything you need done before tonight?"

"No, just make sure that your husband is on time. Tell him I don't care what emergency arises. He has to practice walking me down the aisle tonight, and he *must* be there tomorrow."

"He'll be there. You have my word. Where are you staying tonight?"

"I'll stay at the ranch, and J.B. will be at his condo." A shiver of excitement rippled over Michael. "And wonder of wonders, tomorrow at two p.m., I'll become Mrs. James Buchanan Anderson." She took a deep breath as euphoria flowed through her veins and into every capillary, spreading throughout her body in a wave of happiness. She felt as if she could float away with the joy filling her like helium. She didn't know how she could possibly be any happier than she was at this minute.

And then J.B. walked in and she knew she was wrong. She *could* be happier.

She ran across the restaurant and threw herself into his arms, laughing and kissing him. "J.B. Oh, the house is so beautiful. I love it. Have you seen it before now? Well, of course you have. Champ showed it to you. It's absolutely gorgeous. Don't you love it?"

He grinned. "So you like it, huh?"

"Oh yes. Champ didn't forget one little detail."

"Good." He laughed. "Then I won't have to kill him."

She punched him gently on the arm. "You be nice to him. The house looks like it's been set up for an appearance in *House Beautiful*. He moved the master bedroom upstairs just as I always planned, and now the rooms across the hall can be our den and a library and home office for me. It's so lovely it takes my breath away and when I think that in less than twenty-four hours I'll be your wife, I'm almost speechless."

"Speechless?" J.B.'s deep rumbling laughter rolled across the room. "I don't think 'speechless' is an apt description, darlin', but maybe babble isn't considered speech in some circles."

"Oh, J.B., I don't mean to babble, but doesn't it take *your* breath away?"

"No, darlin', but you do." He kissed her and put his arm around her waist, walking toward the table.

"Oh, I love your sister." She stopped and put her arms around his waist and gazed into his eyes. "I love being a part of your family and having a sister now," tears came to her eyes and she put her forehead against his chest, "and your mother has been so wonderful. I don't know how I would have gotten through the past weeks without her, J.B. I love her so much and am so grateful she loves me."

J.B. looked into her eyes and forgot for a moment that they were in a crowded restaurant. "I love you, darlin', more and more every day." Would she ever say the words to him? He kissed her and pulled her against him, stroking his hands down her back. Within moments he was groaning. "Ah, love, if we're goin' to the rehearsal and rehearsal dinner tonight we'd better get out of here, or I'm goin' to carry you off to our house where we can initiate that new bed *before* our trip."

They walked back to the table and J.B. kissed his mother and turned to his sister. "Keely, I'm glad you were able to get here earlier than you planned." He pulled her into his arms and held her for a moment, whispering in her ear, "What do you think of my lady?"

"I think she's beautiful, and more wonderful than you deserve."

"Yeah, she is." He turned to the guests at the table. "We'd better get out of here if we're goin' to the rehearsal. Who's goin' to drive Michael's car?"

Keely smiled. "J.B., you can be apart from her long enough to get to the church."

"Nah. Not for a second longer than I have to." At that moment his beeper sounded. He pulled it off his belt and after checking the number, pulled out his cell phone and apologized to the group before stepping aside to make his call. Within moments he stepped back to Michael, "Darlin', I'm sorry. I'm needed at the cop shop. I'll have to meet you at the church."

"It's all right. I understand." Michael watched his long, loping strides carry him out of the restaurant. She picked up her purse, and turned to the party still standing there. "Thank you." She winced. "Thank you seems so inadequate. How does one say thank you for friends and family like you?" She went to each of them and gave them a hug.

The group moved toward the front entrance and Elise stepped up to the *maitre d'* and signed the tab. On the sidewalk they each scattered to their separate cars and headed out as Michael stood and waved at each of them.

She was so happy she felt she could float off the sidewalk and almost skipped toward her car. She was free of the stalker at last. She hadn't believed it could be Winslow when J.B. and Shag first arrested him, but there had been no other incidents since he had been taken to jail. It looked as if J.B. had been right.

She looked at the beautiful blue sky, no clouds, and the weather prediction for tomorrow promised sunshine. Sighing, she slipped into the car, adjusted the mirror, started the engine and turned on the air conditioner. Looking over her right shoulder for oncoming traffic, Michael backed out into the street. Facing forward again she saw a shadow in her peripheral vision. She glanced toward her left and the shadow materialized. She froze when she saw a hand, holding a .38 aimed right at her head.

Nineteen

Michael's heart pounded as she looked up at the nose of the weapon. She couldn't focus her eyes on anything but the muzzle. As her vision locked on it, the round hole seemed to grow larger and larger with each passing moment. Her breath came in rasping gasps and her blood froze in her veins. *He's here. I have lived every day and every night anticipating this horror, dreading this moment. For months I have known he would come.* Pain arrowed through her, piercing her heart, as the next thought hit her mind with the impact of a bullet. *I won't get the chance to tell J.B. how much I love him. I can't even tell him goodbye.*

Everything seemed to be happening in slow motion. Sounds had a dull, hollow, quality as if a movie soundtrack was running at half speed. She watched as the gun tapped on the window and then a waggling motion indicated he wanted her to roll it down. A refusal to comply seemed out of the question, as she gazed at the business end of the weapon. She hit the power switch and the hum of the motor sounded, adding a surrealistic quality to the drama, as the window lowered six inches.

He waggled the gun and took a half step toward the back of the car. "Get out of there."

The snarled demand jerked her gaze to his face. "Simmons?"

He sneered. "Yeah, Simmons!"

"What are you doing?" Incredulity laced her voice as she stared wide-eyed at her father's right-hand man.

"I'm sick of this. It's gone on too long."

This is crazy. She shook her head. *That's got to be it. He's lost his mind.* "I don't understand. Sick of what?"

"I'm sick of this whole mess. Nothing's worked like I planned."

A knot of fear threatened to choke her before she remembered her training. She took slow, deep breaths, fighting for calm. *I have to keep him talking.* "What's not working?"

"Nothing went right. Nothing!" His left hand went to his temple and his fingers massaged as if he were in pain. His voice petulant, he asked, "Why didn't you do what you were supposed to do?"

Keep him calm. Keep him talking. Her right hand gripped the steering wheel. Her left arm lay along the armrest with her fingers still on the power switch to the window. Her gaze stayed unwaveringly on Simmons' face.. "What was I supposed to do?"

His eyes narrowed as he looked down at her. "You just don't get it, do you?" He leaned toward the car, hunching his shoulders and aiming the muzzle of the gun at her head.

His low, quiet laughter, and the look of madness that glittered in his eyes, sent chills up her spine. She leaned slightly toward the passenger side of the vehicle, trying to put more distance between herself and the .38. *Surely someone will come along and see him holding the gun on me.* Her gaze swiftly covered the square, looking for any sign they were observed, before swinging back to Simmons. *Keep him talking.* "No, I don't get it."

"And your old man is always talking about how bright you are," he sneered.

"*My* father?" She couldn't believe they were talking about the same man. She didn't try to control the sarcastic tone. "Yeah, right."

"Yes, your old man. Shocked, aren't you?" He waggled the gun again. "Now get out of that car. You're going with me."

She scanned the square again, looking for any sign that help was on the way. "Simmons, why are you doing this?"

"It's the plan."

"What plan?"

"*My* plan. I've worked for years for that snake and I deserve to get it all. It should be mine."

"What should be yours?" Then she knew and gasped. "The company?"

"Yeah. I've done every dirty job he's ever asked of me. He made sure his hands stayed clean. And if anyone ever caught on, I would take the fall. Not him. He thought I was too dumb to realize that."

He seemed to want to explain. And every minute she could drag this out gave her a better chance. J.B. was expecting her to meet him. If she could only stall long enough, he would come looking for her when she didn't show up. "Simmons, I think you'd better tell me all of it so I'll understand."

"You have to go home."

She'd been able to push the panic down, suppress it so she could think. The training was working. *Thank God.* "Why?"

"Because the old man needs you."

Her father *needed* her? Since when? He'd never needed her before. She asked quietly, "Is my father ill?"

"No. Like always, the old bastard is in complete control of everything..." his low, nearly silent laugh sounded again, "...except you. But you *will* go back to him."

Shock reverberated through her mind and she stared at him. "You're trying to force me to go home to my father?" She shook her head. "No! I won't!"

"Yes, you will. One way or another, you *are* going home."

'One way or another'? What had her father told Simmons to do? "You're not making any sense. I've told my father repeatedly that I would not come home, so why would he send you to get me?"

"You know he won't take 'no' for an answer if it's something he wants."

No, her father had never taken 'no' for an answer, but she intended to break his habit of always winning. "I know he always gets his own way, but I cannot believe that my father would have told you to hold me at gunpoint."

Simmons snarled, "No. But I'm just so sick and tired of trying to get you to do the logical thing." He shook his head and sighed. "He wants you home. I've tried everything I could think of to scare you into running back to the house."

"You tried to scare me?" All the pieces of the puzzle suddenly fell into place and everything now made sense. Simmons was her stalker. "Why would you even dream I'd go back there?"

"Because it's a bloody Fort Knox," he snarled. "I thought if you were scared enough you'd go running back home. For safety. With all that security, it was logical. But did you?" He waved the gun again. "Hell, no! Nothing you did made sense."

Seeing he was on the ragged edge, she spoke gently, "Simmons, my father knows I will never return to his home."

"Yeah, I know. But he told me, 'Get her here.' That's what I'm doing."

She scanned the street again and watched as cars drifted by. People came out of stores, got in their cars and drove away. No one noticed that the man standing by her car held a gun on her. "Why would you go to all this trouble?"

He laughed that low, nearly silent laugh again. "He said if I got you home he'd give me half interest in the company." He threw back his head as a bark of laughter erupted.

She closed her gaping mouth and asked, "Half the company? When?" She couldn't believe her father would give up his control of that much of the company—the company he'd built.

"Oh, I don't have it yet. When you are moved back home." He grinned slyly. "And after we're married I'll have it all."

"Married?" Her voice came out in a squeak. She cleared her throat and her gaze darted around the square again. Not a soul to come to her aid now. The street was empty. It was up to her. She mumbled under her breath, "I don't think so."

What were her options? In a split second they darted through her mind. If she stepped on the accelerator quickly enough the car would shoot forward... but she couldn't outrun a bullet. Could she duck down and make herself less of a target? Did she know—had she ever heard—if he was a good shot? What if he fired at her and his bullet hit somebody else? Not an option she could accept.

Simmons massaged his temple and began to babble, "Yeah, married. But he didn't think about that." He snickered. "He's leaving me forty-nine percent of the company and you're going to get fifty-one percent. He thinks, if you have the controlling shares, that I'll still do the dirty work." He shook his head. "And a second generation of Mainwarings would be able to keep their hands clean." He gaze suddenly focused on her. "Get out of the car."

"I'm not going with you, Simmons."

"You will." He pushed the gun toward her head through the opening at the top of the window.

Michael's left hand shot up, grabbed his wrist and pushed it sharply forward into the doorframe. A hard yank down against the edge of the window brought a yowl of pain from Simmons and he dropped the gun. Her right hand grabbed the wrist and pulled his arm across in front of her body. A flick of her finger on the power switch raised the window and trapped Simmons' arm. Michael immediately stomped on the accelerator grabbing the steering wheel with her left hand.

With all her strength focused, a death grip on his wrist held him immobile. The sudden forward acceleration of the car forced his arm to jerk down across her chest, forcing air from her lungs and pushing her back against the seat.

Michael winced as his body slammed against the back of the car, but she didn't slow down. A loud thump, as his torso hit, was followed immediately by two quick clunking noises as his heels hit the fender. A sharp popping noise sounded near her left ear and then his agonized scream rose shrilly in the evening air. Michael moaned, "Oh, please. Where are you, J. B? I need you."

Vaguely aware of squealing tires and the scent of burning rubber, she continued her careening journey down the street. Turning the corner, with one hand occupied elsewhere, proved to be difficult. She bounced the left front tire across the curb, quickly followed by the back and the hubcap went rolling down the sidewalk. The fender grazed a trashcan knocking it out into the street. The sound of Simmons' body swaying and thumping against the side of the car and scraping along the pavement sent another shudder through her.

Accelerating in the straightaway, the car swooped down to the last corner. Michael told herself, *Only a half block to go. Hang on.* The police station loomed ahead. A spin of the wheel turned the car and Michael stomped on the brakes with a shaky foot. The car clipped a parking meter, then thumped and crunched over the curb. It wobbled up onto the sidewalk and came to a bouncing stop at the foot of the steps to the building.

Unconscious, Simmons hung suspended from the window and Michael flicked the power switch to lower it and let him fall to the ground.

Looking up the steps she saw J.B. and Shag at the front door, their mouths agape. Michael put her head on the steering wheel and began to weep as J.B. charged down the steps to the car.

J.B. and Shag had come through the doors in time to hear Simmons scream followed by the squealing of tires. They looked toward the noise, at first thinking it was a hit and run. They spied Michael's car as it lurched down the street and swayed around the corner, bouncing over the curb on the way.

J.B. froze, his heart in his throat, as he saw the man flopping like a rag doll against the side of her car.

"My God. Michael?" He couldn't believe his eyes. "Is that Michael?" He watched her progress toward the police station and terror filled him, his heart pounding painfully. He had always been able to control his emotions in crisis situations but this one was different. His heart was involved. "What's goin' on?"

Shag watched, his gaze intent on her progress toward her destination. He turned to J.B. "Why is that man hanging onto the side of her car?"

At that moment Michael's car came to a shuddering halt at the foot of the steps and J.B. leaped down, taking three stairs at a time, to get to her. Shag followed and bent down to look at the man who was now slumped on the sidewalk.

J.B. yanked open the door and Michael leaped out of the car into his arms. She buried her face in the curve of his throat and cried over and over again, "I love you. I love you. Oh, I love you so much." Her grip on his neck tightened. "I thought I'd never get the chance to say the words. I don't ever again want to pass up the chance to tell you how much I love you, J.B."

He never thought the day would come when he'd hear the words from her. He felt a bubble of happiness grow and grow, enveloping his whole being. He held her close and kissed her neck. "And I love you, darlin'. Don't you ever forget that."

"I won't." She took a shuddering breath. "I won't ever doubt it again." Tears coursed down her face but when she looked up in to his eyes, he saw the love and recognized tears of joy. "I'll love you all the days of my life, J.B."

J.B. was so filled with euphoria he thought he'd burst. He kissed her and then pulled her to his side, his arm around her waist.

Shag checked Simmons' pulse and noted he was still breathing. He looked up. "Who is this man and why was he hanging on to your car?"

"He wasn't hanging on. I trapped his arm by rolling up the window. You'll find his gun in the front floorboard." She turned to J.B., "He's the one who has been stalking me."

"What?" J.B.'s shock was evident. "Darlin', what's goin' on? We arrested Rauthuell and his preliminary hearing is coming up."

"I know. It's a long story."

Shag stood up. "Maybe you'd better start at the beginning so we can file a report."

"First you need to know—this is Simmons. I don't know that I've ever heard him called anything but 'Simmons', so I don't know his first name."

J.B.'s bass voice rumbled near her ear, "Who is Simmons and why was he stalkin' you?"

"He's my father's right-hand man."

J.B.'s barked, "What?" made her jump.

"As I told you, it's a long story. I'll tell you all of it, but he probably needs a doctor. I thought I heard his arm break when I took off down the street."

"His arm's not broken," Shag rumbled. "It's a dislocated shoulder. Was that his scream we heard?"

Tears filled her eyes as she remembered that cry of pain. "Yes. I didn't mean to hurt him. I just wanted to stop him from harming me. I wish I could have gotten him here without injury."

J.B. roared, "Are you crazy? He had a gun on you! How can you feel sorry for him?"

"He's a human being, J.B., and I think he's mentally ill."

"I repeat... he had a gun. Was he going to use it?"

She nodded. "He implied he would if I gave him no choice."

"Then don't let me hear you feelin' sorry for the sonofabitch ever again."

Shag pulled his phone out of his pocket and called for an ambulance as Simmons began to stir. He put his hand on the man's uninjured shoulder and said, "Lie still, an ambulance is on the way." He looked up at J.B., "Buddy, why don't you take your lady inside and take the report of what happened here?"

J.B. grinned. "You're stickin' me with the paperwork again, huh?" It was a long-standing argument and joke between them.

Shag cocked an eyebrow and smirked. "Okay, I'll take care of the report and you can go to the hospital with the perp." He burst into laughter when he saw the look on J.B.'s face. "I didn't think so."

"You're right. I'm stayin' with my lady."

Laughing, Shag quipped, "That's what I thought you'd say. I'm good at making plans that work. I keep telling you how smart I am, but you keep forgetting."

"Nah, you just keep forgettin' that I scored higher on the exams than you."

Michael was happy to see them joking with each other but breathed a sigh of relief as she saw the ambulance coming down the street. "Now we can get him to the hospital and make sure he's okay."

J.B. glanced at her and shook his head.

The ambulance stopped and the lights continued to flash as the EMTs jumped out, dragged the stretcher from the back and ran over to the sidewalk. They checked his vital signs and then immobilized Simmons' arm before lifting him onto the wheeled litter. Shag stopped them before they loaded him into the ambulance.

"This man is under arrest." He fastened handcuffs on Simmons left wrist and then closed the other half on the sidebar of the stretcher. "I'll follow you to the hospital in my car with the key."

J.B. put Simmons' .38 into an evidence bag and with his arm around Michael's waist he led her inside the police station. He asked one of the uniformed officers to take the keys to her car and put it in the impound lot as evidence of an attempted homicide and took her into his office.

J.B. had filed the report and sat in the chair behind his desk, holding Michael on his lap. He'd forgotten where he was and what he was supposed to be doing as the kiss that started out only to comfort had gone into another realm entirely. His blood roared through his body, the heat arrowing straight to his groin.

Shag came back from the hospital, having left Simmons there under guard. He walked into J.B.'s office and stopped in his tracks, clearing his throat and backing out the door.

At the sound of the clearing throat Michael's face turned beet red and she buried it in the curve of J.B.'s throat.

He cradled her head with one hand while with the other he soothed her, his hand sliding up and down her spine. He knew who was standing in his doorway, but it was more important to him to ease Michael's embarrassment. He looked up at Shag. "Come on in, pardner."

"You don't look like you need me here right now." He grinned at J.B., then looked down at Michael, "Unless you're going to let me kiss the bride."

J.B. glowered up at his partner and growled, "Not on your life. At least, not until the weddin' tomorrow. Is Simmons handled?"

"Yeah. Under control." Shag waved his hand and walked out of the office.

J.B. pulled her close, and wanted her. More than he'd ever wanted her before. He wanted to hold her, to *know* she was safe at last. He needed to let her know how proud he was of the way she took charge of the situation today, how impressed he was with the fact she didn't lose her head. He wanted to be as close to her as one human being can ever get to another. And if her reaction to his kiss was any indication, she wanted him as well. Feeling the discomfort in the front of his jeans, he didn't think he'd dare stand up for a while.

Michael gazed in to his eyes for a moment and then smiled. "Ummm, J.B., since we aren't going to be seeing each other again until tomorrow afternoon, uh, could we spend just a *little* time at our house, er... in our bedroom?" Her cheeks turned pink when he threw his head back and laughed.

"You got it, darlin'. Right after the weddin' rehearsal."

Hours later they slipped into the house and J.B. locked the door behind them. He turned to her. "Did you get the key from Champ?"

"No, but he's not going to come over here tonight. They're expecting me at the ranch."

"Good, because I don't want to see anyone but you right now. Even though it's only been a couple of hours since we left the cop shop, it seems like I've waited forever. I love you Michael."

He didn't give her time to respond, picking her up and carrying her up the stairs. At the door of their bedroom he stopped and put her feet on the floor. He opened the door and told her to wait. Walking into the room he stripped the covers to the foot of the bed. Back at the door he picked her up and carried her across the threshold and across the room to lay her gently on the bed. He took off her shoes, her skirt and slip, then her pantyhose. Her blouse and bra quickly followed. Within moments he stripped off his own clothes and lay down beside her.

He raised up on his elbow and gazed down in to her eyes. He kissed her softly and hugged her. After one more kiss he told her everything that was in his heart.

"Michael, I have loved you for more than a year. You have been the first thought in my mind each morning and the last thought before sleep each night. I've dreamed of holding you, loving you, but the dream didn't ever come close to the reality of having you in my arms, skin to skin. Tomorrow will be the most joy filled day of my life. The day you finally are mine in the eyes of God and the world. Thank you for agreeing to tie your life to mine, for loving me and wanting to have my babies. But most of all, thank you for the gift of your trust."

His deep bass voice rumbled sending vibrations over her skin. She thrilled at the words he spoke and wanted to be a part of him, dissolve into him, become one with him, body to body and soul to soul. She put her hands on either side of his face and gazed into his eyes.

"The Spanish speaking peoples have a lovely way to say how I feel about you, J.B. *Tu es mi vida y mi alma y mi corazon.* You are my life and my soul and my heart. That's what you are, J.B. I would not have survived if you hadn't come along. Simmons would have either killed me or dragged me back to that house and I would have been held there against my will as my mother must have been for all those years. You are the light of my life and I want to spend every day, for the rest of my life, loving you."

He kissed her and it went on and on. Within seconds the flames were out of control but neither of them cared. When he finally joined their bodies her inner contractions had already begun and he joined her as they sailed first into rapture and from there to euphoric tranquility.

As he lay there he suddenly realized he had made love to her putting her beneath him and she'd never noticed. She didn't even seem to mind that he hadn't moved. The joy he felt, that she trusted him that much, nearly overwhelmed him. But, fearing he would crush her, he rolled to his side and pulled her tightly against him.

"I think we should stay in this bed for the rest of the night. I don't like the idea that you're going to be at the ranch and I'm going to be in town in my condo tonight."

"It's tradition, J.B." She laughed. "You don't want to break tradition, do you?"

"Yeah. I do. Let's just stay here and not tell anyone where we are. We can just show up at the church tomorrow in plenty of time for the weddin'."

"Oh, I don't think that's a good idea. You're not supposed to see me tomorrow until I walk down the aisle."

He kissed her nose and then put his face against hers, forehead to forehead and nose to nose. "Sweet love, can you really stand the idea of sleepin' without me tonight?"

"To be honest, I don't want to think about it. I'll be lonely without you, but I don't want to disappoint Elise either. She's expecting me."

"Ah, Mom will understand. She was young once, you know."

"You're not taking into consideration that it's considered bad luck for us to see each other tomorrow before the ceremony."

"My love, we've already had our share of bad luck" He kissed her. "So from now on it's going to be only beautiful things in our lives, like rainbows, butterflies, bird song, and hot air balloons"...he grinned... "and babies. We're goin' to work real hard at makin' babies." He laughed when her face turned red and, for a moment she ducked her face in to his neck.

"Oh, J.B." Tears filled her eyes and she rested her arms on his shoulders, her fingers locked behind his neck, ready to face whatever life threw at her. "With you beside me, I can handle anything."

"That's right, darlin'. We'll face it all. Together."

Twenty

Michael giggled. And surprised herself. She'd never before giggled in her life. Cari's startled gaze flew to her face and Michael giggled again. "I can't help it. I am so happy I feel I'm going to burst with it. It feels like this wonderful, warm, bubbly feeling of excitement balled up inside my stomach is expanding and expanding and I wonder how I can contain it."

Cari rose from her knees where she'd been putting a penny in Michael's shoe, and shook the wrinkles from the skirt of her dress. She smiled at Michael and glanced in the cheval glass behind her. Smoothing her already glossy blonde hair back to the heavy chignon at the nape of her neck, Cari smiled. "That's called 'happiness', Michael."

"I know, but the feeling is wonderful, isn't it?"

"Oh, yes. It certainly is. And you deserve a very large portion of it after what you've been through." Cari stepped back and indicated with a twirl of her finger that she wanted the bride to turn around.

Michael turned in a complete circle. "Will I do?"

"Mmm hmmm. You most definitely will 'do'. J.B. is going to come unglued when he sees you walking down the aisle. I can see it now. He's going to be grinning from ear to ear, and Champ and Shag will have to hold him at the altar."

A gurgle of laughter bubbled up and Michael covered her face with her hands, then peeking over the tops of her fingers she whispered, "Oh, I hope so. I hope he..."

"Oh, Michael, can you have *any* doubt?"

A knock at the door startled them before Michael had the chance to answer. Cari made the bride move back behind the door and out of sight before she opened it but as soon as she saw who sought entry, she swung it wide for the bridesmaids.

Lyndi Hilliard entered first. Grinning at her friend, her charcoal gray eyes sparkled. "Hey, boss. You ready for the big commitment?" She hugged Michael and stepped back for the next in line. As she passed the mirror, she glanced at her reflection and smoothed her hands over her upswept hair.

Michael winked at her secretary. "I can't believe my dreams are going to come true." She took a deep breath, closed her eyes, and smiled softly. "What if this is all just a dream and I'm going to wake up in a few minutes? Is it real?"

Lyssa Bradley followed Lyndi and laughed. "No dream, Michael." Her hair as black as midnight was worn in a chignon and, with it pulled back, her large dark brown eyes were magnified. She walked to Michael and stretched as far up as she could reach from her five foot two inch height and pulled her friend down for a hug.

"You look beautiful, Michael." Lyssa's voice, soft and husky, reminded Michael of her phone call last week. Answering the call, J.B. had said, "The beautiful lady with the bedroom voice wants to talk to you." He'd grinned and handed the phone to Michael when she'd smacked his shoulder and laughed.

"Thank you, Lyssa. I know how difficult this is for you and I'll never be able to tell you how happy I am you agreed to be a part of this most wonderful day in my life."

After hugging Lyssa, Michael turned to Brianna Sheffield who, today for the wedding, wore her dark brown hair in a French roll rather than her usual to-the-shoulder style. Her blue eyes sparkled as she walked to Michael and hugged her. "My wish for you is that from this day forward your life is filled with as much joy as I see reflected from your eyes at this moment, Michael."

"Thank you, Bree. I don't think anyone could sustain this much happiness on a daily basis, but I certainly intend to try."

Next was J.B.'s sister, Keely. She hugged Michael and murmured, "You have made my big brother a happy man, Michael. For that I will always be grateful. He deserves you in his life and from what I have seen, in the short time we've had to get acquainted, you deserve having him in yours. I wish you both all the happiness you so richly deserve." Keely's dark blonde hair was pulled back into a chignon in a similar style to the other bridal attendants.

Michael hugged her and reached for the box of tissues on the table. "Keely, you're going to make me cry and spoil my make-up. Thank you."

A knock sounded on the door and, expecting Linc, Cari swung it open. J.B. strode through with his arm around an older woman.

Cari hissed, "J.B., you're not supposed to be in here. You can't see Michael…"

"Mother?" Michael's voice had gone at least an octave higher. Shock and disbelief were displayed on her face.

J.B. grinned, still looking at the woman he'd brought into the room. "Yeah, darlin'. I found her this mornin' and pulled a few strings. Shag went and got her and brought her straight here to the…" he looked up, saw Michael in her wedding finery and gasped, "…church."

Cari grabbed his arm and ushered him unresisting to the door. She laughed at the stunned expression on his face.

Lincoln Maitland knocked on the door and then opened it immediately. His head popped through the opening and he rumbled, "Safe to come in?" He saw J.B. standing there, looking like a poleaxed steer, and didn't wait for a response but came through the door. "Anderson, what are you doing in here?" He guided the groom through the door and shut it, turned to Cari and asked, "What was he doing in here?"

"He brought Michael's mother to her wedding." Cari stood watching the two women in question with tears in her eyes. The strain between them was obvious.

Linc spoke softly, "Michael, it's time."

She glanced at him and nodded. "Give me a few minutes, Linc."

Michael turned to her mother, led her to a chair and knelt in front of her. "Are you all right, Mother?"

Miranda Mainwaring nodded her head and stretched a tentative hand toward her daughter's face but drew it back and folded her hands in her lap. "You're beautiful, Michael. So lovely." Tears gushed down her cheeks. "Your young man is very nice. He told me I could stay with you if I wanted." Shaking her head, she rushed on. "I said I didn't think that would be a good idea."

"What will you do if you don't stay with us?" A sudden thought occurred and horror shuddered through her. "I mean, you don't want to go back to that house, do you?"

Miranda shivered. "No, I won't go back there ever again. But J.B. has a solution. He said I can stay at his condo for as long as I want. He called the real estate agent and took it off the market."

Michael took her mother's hands and asked gently, "Is that what you want to do?"

"Oh, yes." She touched Michael's cheek. "I want a chance to get to know you, Michael. I was never allowed that opportunity when you were growing up. I wish I'd been a stronger person but I took the easy way and I hope you can forgive me for that."

"We'll work on it together, Mother."

Linc stepped toward them and asked, "Are you ready to go down the aisle, or should I go down there and tell that big bozo you've changed your mind?" He laughed when Michael stood up and punched him on the shoulder.

"Don't you dare, you big lug. Bozo indeed! And as for 'big', I'd say you are book-ends, wouldn't you?" She laughed and hugged him. "I'm ready. I've never been more ready for anything in my life. I'm not even nervous. But we need to get my mother seated on the bride's side of the church."

Linc escorted Miranda to the door and turned her over to one of J.B.'s friends from the police department and watched them walk toward the doors to the sanctuary.

Michael took one last look at herself in the mirror and patted her cheeks with a tissue. Moments later they filed out of the room and the bridesmaids and matron of honor got in line to walk down the aisle.

First came Lyssa in a dark shade of apple green. Right behind her was Brianna wearing brilliant sky blue. She was followed by Keely, looking beautiful in aquamarine and Lyndi was next wearing bright pink. Matron of honor, Cari, wearing violet, walked ahead of Michael.

J.B. stood at the altar with his brothers and Shag, watching Michael walk toward him and their new life together. The ivory satin gown was embroidered with seed pearls and the bell-like skirt swayed with every graceful step she took. He couldn't wait to raise the fingertip veil so he could see her beautiful face. He couldn't take his gaze from her progress and never even noticed the bridesmaids and matron of honor as they advanced toward the front of the church.

J.B. met Michael at the altar and Lincoln Maitland placed her hand on J.B.'s and took his seat as the pair turned toward the minister.

Amanda Hall, sitting on the bride's side of the church, turned to Clayton Rauthuell and whispered, "Look at that. The bridesmaids and matron of honor are in rainbow colors. Beautiful. A rainbow. The promise of hope."

The Beginning

Meet Margaret B. Lawrence

To keep herself entertained, while awaiting sleep, for most of her life Margaret told herself stories. It never occurred to her that other people might be interested in reading the tales she wove in her imagination. Then in the mid-80s a friend encouraged Margaret to write a book. After getting over the initial surprise at her friend's suggestion, she started writing her first novel. It was **To Touch The Sky**, a western historical set at the time of the Oklahoma Land Run which was published by Wings ePress in April 2002.

After completing the first draft, and while working on editing and revising, life intervened with the long illnesses and and eventual deaths of both her parents and her beloved husband. The writing had to be put aside. For more than ten years her stories waited until Margaret could begin writing again. Then in late 1993 she again began working to rewrite and revise her story.

This project was interrupted by the writing of two romantic suspense novels: **Caresse; A Loving Touch,** published in January 2002 by Wings ePress, and **Michael; A Gift Of Trust.**

She is currently working on **Brianna; A Badge Of Honor**, the third book in the romantic suspense series. She is having a difficult time trying to convince two other characters in this series that she will get to their story eventually if they will only be patient.